D0393838

Long in the Tooth

Books by David Turrill

Michilimackinac: A Tale of the Straits
A Bridge to Eden
An Apology for Autumn

David Turrill

LONG IN THE TOOTH

The Toby Press

First edition, 2006

The Toby Press LLC

POB 8531, New Milford, CT 06776-8531, USA
& POB 2455, London WIA 5WY, England

www.tobypress.com

ISBN I 59264 166 0, *hardcover*

A CIP catalogue record for this title is available from the British Library

Typeset in Garamond

Printed and bound in the United States by
Thomson-Shore Inc., Michigan

To my grandchildren, Christian, Abigail, Madelyn and Kaia; to my step-grandchildren, Jarrad, Brody and Colton, and to all of my students, both past and present, whose energy, enthusiasm, imagination and general joie de vivre, have enabled me to keep mine.

Chapter one

I've been killing time and it's been reciprocating. I put one foot before the other, perform each scheduled task, sleep and rise again—contrary to my own will. Resurrection and redemption, I know, are impossible. I won't wake some morning. Unconscious resolve can't defy a dysfunctional heart.

I used to love the Romantics. Shelley wrote that 'our sweetest songs are those that tell of saddest thought.' It was a line from his "To a Skylark". I've never watched a skylark, yet I've talked about this poem as if I had. Yesterday I did see a turkey vulture in the blue, summer sky. It said to me: "Bring out your dead!" I told it to go away. "The Dead and I are buried, there's nothing left here to digest!"—not a very romantic notion.

Almost every day now I go fishing. I leave the cabin that my father left to Satchel and me (although Satchel is not around to use it), and smoothly launch the old wooden rowboat before the sun can catch me at my mischief. I'm mindful not to forget the night crawlers, those slimy things that move in dirt and darkness without identity. I have become one of them. They are lucky enough that they will probably die today, and they have the everlasting comfort of the irrational. I imagine that they hear the clattering of the fishing rods and feel the boat surge outward. They don't ask God to save them. They don't even realize they are in need of salvation. They curl comfortably against each other in the warm humus as we move toward the middle of the lake. They offer no prayers to me.

Once anchored in the little cove by the lily pads, my favorite spot, I light a cigarette. I feel a fleeting satisfaction in flouting the fascists who insist that I must care about my health. They have put warning labels on food and passed laws to make me wear my seatbelt and keep me, the puffing leper, out of the buildings of the sinless. The nicotine is for me, not my body. The latter barely exists. It doesn't give or receive pleasure anymore. It is a thing I control like the worms and, like the worms, it is unaware of its own mortality—a kind of interesting joke I play on myself.

As the sky turns from black to gray, there is a pull on my line. The red and white bobber goes down hard. The crawler is learning something, twisted on its hook—something that I learned quite some time ago. The monsters will come for you if you bait them properly. They come out of the depths and eat you. Teaching is, or was, my profession, so I know that learning is necessary. I used to believe, like Keats, that teaching is love and love is the instigator of the imagination—the two prime ingredients in the construction of the soul. My father, the pastor, disagreed of course. He didn't understand metaphor. When he opened the Holy Book, he saw only history. Maybe he was right. Socrates wrote that love and teaching went together. Love, he thought, was manifested in the desire to educate. Love, he thought, was transferable. It's all bullshit. Religion and philosophy are nothing but our excuses for existence. We are all…a certain convocation of politic worms.

The fish is, like me, a largemouth. I can see it clearly as it leaps heavenward to find escape. It's the one that's been evading every fisherman on the lake for years. Dad called him Leviathan. I think he'd read that name in the Bible. I'm pretty sure he'd never read Hobbes.

For Dad, the Bible wasn't the great book or the good book—it was the only book. Sweeney, less Biblically oriented, referred to the fish simply as 'the Monster'.

It comes down hard on the surface of the water and slaps its tail. It knows nothing of water, as I know nothing of earth; we only live in these elements. It pulls hard and my reel whines. The crawler must be wondering if the story of Jonah is true. He must want it to be, very badly. In the shallows, among the cattails and lily pads, a heron is poking about for food. No doubt he is breakfasting on the children of the struggling bass. The world is a wicked place. We must eat each other. This epiphany is not comforting.

I don't use the net. I lift the big fella out of the water and hold him aloft by his gills, daring him to try to free himself. I'm not smiling. I know that. After Wendy died, someone sent me a fatuous e-mail about how it takes fewer muscles to smile than to frown—as if emotions should be expended according to thrift. It was the first time, I think, that I ever really hated anybody. I never trusted smilers, though I used to be one. It is, I think, the easiest expression to fake and certainly the most ambiguous. Smiles can be sardonic, condescending, embarrassed, disdainful, vacuous, perfidious, perverse, swaggering, cunning, lewd, vulgar, tractable, phony, disingenuous, efficacious, maniacal and on and on, ad infinitum. How many of those are positive? I think Sanson grinned under his black hood as noble and royal heads rolled into baskets. Even in the throes of my most intense orgasm, I am certain that the expression on my face was usually a grimace. There's a reason that smiles come easier.

I guide the stupid creature over the boat's side and let him fall, hard, to the floor. He flips around desperately in the puddled mess of water and blood. He's stunned for a moment, surprised as we all are, as Lord Papa said, by the death we owe God. His huge mouth, a third of his body, yawns open, trying to breathe when there's nothing but air. I know how he feels. For some reason he reminds me of Dad.

I place my foot on him to keep him in place and pull out the hook. The crawler is still intact, writhing on its metal rood. Does he think that now there is hope? If he does, he's foolish. I take him off the hook, lift the bass, and force the crawler down its chasmal maw. Then, because I can, I place the fish back on the floor and bring my heel down hard on his head. He shudders and lies still. There was no reason for him to die. I won't eat him. I don't like the taste of bass and I don't remember the last time I ate anyway. His death is a simple whim, something to do with the crawler maybe. I feel god-like—as I should.

I place the dead warrior back in the dark water. When I'm almost returned to my decrepit dock, I see an eagle swoop down and carry off his carcass. The bird could be an angel, but I think he's more akin to the Valkyrie, rising to feed its eaglets in some small Valhalla in the towering pines on the opposite shore.

Although it's not yet 7:00 A.M., I pour a glass of Jim Beam and settle on the wicker chair on the screened porch. I like it here. Through the weathered, web-covered screening, the world seems dim and dark and distant, though I can still see it. It's good to know where your enemies are.

The sun is rising to mock me. It's been ninety degrees or better for over a week now. This is what I used to call 'Wendy weather'. The Adirondack chaise she used to worship in still sits near the shore, strategically avoiding the shade cast by the maples and birches behind it.

The Beam from my glass produces a different kind of heat. With any luck, I'll be unconscious by noon.

Hiram Sweeney is up from Detroit as I knew he'd be, since I'd called him here a couple of weeks ago. I can hear him rummaging in the cabin next door, probably getting his gear together. He's a widower too. He's the consummate fisherman. He introduced me to Walton's Compleat Angler and McClean's (is it Mac or Mc?) *A River Runs Through It*. He would have scolded me for what I just did to the bass. Hiram and his allies, (my father among them), almost had me believing that fishing is something other than simple killing. There is nothing but fiction in the world.

He's around sixty years old, thirty years older than me. Sweeney and I share the same birthday.

4

Sweeney was my father's best friend, though they only saw one another about two months out of the year, and only here, at the lake. The two of them used to take me and my brother fishing almost every day when they were together and we were boys. They built the big cleaning table by the shore, on the property line between our two cabins. They taught us, Satchel and me, to gut and scale and filet. Butchering is an art, really. Ask God.

After Mom died, Sweeney shared his wife, Mary, with us. She made sure that we had decent meals, clean clothes and the proper lotion to put on the occasional outbreak of poison ivy. When I was eleven and Satchel was nearing the end of high school, Mary and Hi got pregnant. Hiram was into his forties then and Mary wasn't much younger. They had a girl. Her name is Moira, I think. Mary died when the girl was three or four. After that, we didn't come to the lake much anymore. The daughter must be a teenager by now. I'm sure Sweeney will fill me in when he discovers I'm here.

I came in last week on a whim. I've recently discovered that it's the best mode of transportation. I don't like to be in the house where Wendy was. Of course being here isn't much better. She once occupied this place too and the world is full of ghosts. Even that bass I just killed is haunting me. I lift my glass and hold it out toward the lake. Skoal! Jim Beam was a wise man. He knew better than Socrates or Dostoevsky or Hegel or Keats or Luther or any of them what we need. I produce a scornful smile, but only from the inside. Let my facial muscles atrophy for all I care.

My father's ghost drifts on in as I try to ignore Wendy's. In his life he was passionate about many things. Since Dad was an ordained pastor, God was chief among them of course, followed by my mother, us two boys, civil rights and baseball. Though I've prioritized them in my own mind, I'm really not sure about the order of those affections. My brother was named for the famous Negro League pitcher, Satchel Paige, which kind of lumped all that concupiscence together.

Over my mother's fierce objections, he had me christened Tinker Balune. Of course he was thinking of the famous double-play combo…Tinker to Evers to Chance, but Mom knew that every schoolyard urchin would associate the name with J.M. Barrie's fairy. She was, as usual, correct. I have often thought that if he had to name me for one of that trio, Dad would have done better to choose Chance, a more rugged name at least and one that insinuated more accurately the direction my life would take. Even Evers (though I like it less) would have been, like Satchel, a restitutive palliative to the greater issue of dad's Caucasian guilt. (The terrible experiments conducted on Evers' Boys was a favorite example in Dad's arsenal of stories of the various albatrosses that White America has hung about its red neck).

Despite this logic, I would remain Tinker Balune, and discover through first hand experience what it was like to be a tormented minority, although after a few years I ceased to give, if you'll excuse, a tinker's damn. I suppose it could have been worse. My mother would later comfort me with the disturbing revelation that Crispus Attucks Balune and Mohandas Gandhi Balune had also been in the running. As if the first names weren't bad enough, our last name, (pronounced bal-YOU-nah), was often mistaken for 'balloon'.

For a man of such liberal social views, my father was a very conservative religionist, even for the Lutheran Church, Missouri Synod. Only the Wisconsin Synod was farther right. My uncle, (Dad's brother), belonged to the Wisconsin group, and he would not set foot in any other church—not for a baptism, wedding, even a funeral. He stood outside and prayed by himself while my father, his brother, was being sent off to whichever corner of heaven was reserved for the LCMS.

Dad's congregation in Grand Rapids adored him, possibly because I don't think he ever understood the basic Lutheran premise that the next life was far more important than this one. That may be why, like Hamlet Sr., he's still hanging around.

I take another swig of Mr. Beam and close my eyes. My ghosts have no compunction about darkness or light. They come and go as they wish, so I can remember all of them, all the time, waking or sleeping makes no difference to them. They haunt at their own discretion. Wendy, especially, never rests.

'Time heals all wounds,' Wendy's sister, Kelly, told me at the funeral, but we are all Achilles and the cliché works more appropriately when reversed. My particular weakness was to love, and I have been trying, along with time, to kill it. I lost my mother, my brother, my father, my wife—all long before I should have. I blame God and Fate and myself, but I believe in none of those things anymore. They give meaning to existence and I've come to realize that there is none. Every egg produced by every female is an accident waiting to happen. It's how we're born and how we die.

"Tin? Tin Balune!"

I look up to see Hiram Sweeney's broad form fill the doorway of the screened porch.

"It really is you. Ever since you called and asked me to get things ready for ya, I been lookin' forward to this."

"Hi, Mr. Sweeney. I sure appreciate you getting the place 'summerized'."

Almost every spring while Mom and Dad were alive, my father would call and ask Hiram Sweeney to prepare the cabin for our arrival. He would drain the anti-freeze from the toilet and prime the pipes. Hi always seemed happy to do it. He was generally the first one north at the end of winter and he eagerly looked forward to our family's arrival, up until around the time his wife got pregnant anyway. After that, there was a kind of indefinable distance that grew up between the two families, one I never understood. Since my father had died, this annual ritual had become increasingly infrequent.

I address him as Mr. Sweeney now because I have already said 'Hi', which is his nickname, and it would sound ridiculous to say 'Hi, Hi.' I straighten up, put the glass aside. It's empty anyway. I want to tell him to go away, that misery does not love company. Sweeney has had his share of trouble, but it's never made me feel better to know that other people suffer too. I doubt if any prisoner in Auschwitz ever said to another, 'Cheer up, someone has it worse.' Which level of hell argues for commiseration?

I get up and pull the screen door open. He shakes my hand vigorously, so that I have to let the door go. It barks shut on its ancient spring, mounted there millennia ago by my father to keep the mosquitoes at bay because his sons could not remember to close it behind them. I wait for my mother to yell at me for letting it slam, but her ghost is unavailable at the moment.

"It's good to see you, boy," he repeats. "I gotta tell ya that I had a tough time this year gettin' the water flowin' through them blown-out pipes. It's been awhile since they been used." He is wearing that ridiculous hat with all the flies hooked on it. It's doubly ludicrous because Hi Sweeney never used anything but a hook and bobber to catch fish. He's such a fishing purist that even artificial lures are considered 'cheating'. He carries the lightest tackle box in the state of Michigan.

"Likely the water's gonna be a bit brackish at first. I'd let it run for awhile." He still has sandy hair and freckles; despite other indications of age, they make him appear boyish. It is strange, how much he looks like Satchel. He examines me with his piercing blue eyes. They're so pale that he looks blind, as if the irises are clouded over with glaucoma or something. You realize though, if you pay attention, that they take in everything.

"You finished teaching for the summer?" he says.

I just say "yeah." I don't tell him that I'm done with teaching for good. You have to feel like you know something in order to teach, plus there's that love thing that I seem to have misplaced. My personal education has extended itself far enough to make me realize that I don't know anything and feel even less.

"I just retired," he says. "Can you believe it? No more of the daily grind for me."

For Hiram Sweeney, work had been just that. He was a grinder by profession, on some assembly line at a Ford Plant in Dearborn, for forty years. I'm not sure what he ground, except it wasn't coffee or wheat or teeth, but something much less pliable.

"Sold the house and everything. I'm movin' up here permanent."

"You're gonna winter here?" I ask. This is a serious question if you plan to take on December and January and February in northern Michigan in a small cabin by yourself.

"Yeah, why not? I don't need much room. I been wantin' to do more ice fishin' anyway. God, it's good to see you, boy, especially here. You ain't been to the lake in quite a spell."

Then comes the awkward silence, a pause I'd come to know and dread. It indicates the summoning of courage to express a commiseration. "Are you...starting to get over your dad's...passing? I know how difficult all this must be for you. He was a good friend to me too."

"Yeah, well," (I glance around for Dad's ghost), "you know what it's like."

"No, I don't," he says. "Every death's different."

I wonder then if Sweeney's making reference to Dad's suicide or if he's just waxing philosophical. I decide that the old man is just trying to be kind. "I guess so."

"You've had more'n your share."

"How's your daughter?" It is a defensive question, something rhetorical, meant to shift the topic to anything else. It works. Sweeney's entire demeanor changes instantly from wrinkled empathy to grinning delight. He has the appearance of a quietly desperate man who's just been told he's won the lottery. Every line in his freckled face either disappears in the expansive, skin-stretching smile, or curves upward.

"Moira?" It's odd how people will phrase a single possible answer in the form of a question. Sweeney only has one daughter, one child for that matter, and he certainly must know her name. Perhaps he just can't believe that I would inquire so casually about the sacred. "She's great, Tin. In fact, she'll be up later this afternoon. She and her boyfriend are bringin' the U-Haul with all my stuff. I know she'll be happy to see you. She says she still remembers you, although I don't see how. She's probably only seen you a couple of times since she was a little shit."

"She's movin' here too?" I keep asking questions to avoid him asking any more. I don't want to have to talk about Satchel and everyone wants to know about Satchel.

"Moira?" He does it again. He must know that I don't mean Mary. I really want another hour or two alone with Jim Beam. His expectations of me are very, very low. "No, no, course not. She's a city girl, too rustic up here for her. That's her word—rustic."

"Where's she going to live, if you sold your house down there, I mean?" I try to intonate as if I care.

"Well in her dorm, of course. You didn't know she graduated from high school this year, Tin? Couple of weeks ago, actually. She starts classes at Michigan State in September. Hard to believe, huh?"

It is. Moira is a little girl in my memory, a bit chunky, with her mother's dark hair. I remember thinking that she looked remarkably like her mother, but there was something else in that face too, something that wasn't Sweeney either. I recall her standing by Mary's body, surrounded by a jungle of flowers not native to Michigan, the poor thing just staring at her mother with those large eyes. She was just barely tall enough to see over the cushioned edge of the casket. I knew they were taking in everything around that dystopian altar, but there were no tears. When she finally turned away, she looked at me. I'm sure she knew I'd been watching her. I think she wanted me to explain. No one could explain Mary's death, or any death for that matter.

"I would have guessed junior high," I answered.

"She's got a scholarship too," he boasted. "Finished third in her class of four hundred somethin'. Would have been first too if it weren't for a B plus in Advanced Placement Calculus."

"That must've been hard to take."

"I thought so too, but Moira didn't seem to care. She says math don't matter anyway, grades neither. I tried to tell her different, but she's got strong opinions, that one, a mind of her own." I detect both regret and admiration in his tone.

As a high school literature teacher who last used any math beyond the fourth or fifth grade to solve problems in a college class, I couldn't disagree. "I mean it must've upset her not to be Valedictorian."

"You know," Sweeney says, "she told me it didn't matter, and I really think she meant it. She's won all kinds of certificates and pins and plaques and not one of them was ever displayed in her room or anywheres else in our house. She just dumped 'em all in a drawer. I've never heard her mention them neither and when I do, she gives me this nasty look, like she don't want me to." He stops talking for a moment and looks closely at me. "Sorry to go on like this, but I can't brag about her when she's around so I thought I'd get it out of my system before she shows up."

I glance at his freckled arms. I'm always amazed at how muscled they are. Comes from years of grinding I guess, although the rest of him is very thin and wiry and seems vulnerable.

"It's okay," I lie, wanting very much for him to go away. "It's nice to hear about her."

"Hey," Sweeney says, "I'm headed out on the lake for a couple of hours. Want to come along? The bass are spawning. You can see their nests in the shallows. They oughta be bitin' like crazy. We could catch some fish and catch up at the same time. Who knows, we may run into the Monster. This might be the year. Whadya say, boy?"

I can't tell him that the Monster is dead. It's better to leave myths alone, to let legends continue. Worse, the Monster was caught easily, then thrown away. Sallust wrote that myth never happened but always is. What is my new mythology to be? "Thanks, Hi, but I'm already at my limit for today. I just got back." It's only a lie if I'm talking about fish.

He looks disappointed, but I don't care. His cloudy eyes moisten, I think. My father's ghost rattles somewhere nearby. Apathy is the only armor I have left.

I watch Sweeney lumber to the shore. Slump-shouldered, he pauses by the empty chaise, looks back in my direction, then gets into his boat. We, Sweeney and I, own the last two vessels on the lake without motors. I watch him until he has rowed beyond the point and disappeared.

It occurs to me that Wendy had never known Sweeney very well. I remember introducing her to him and he seemed, like all who met her, to be charmed, but he never mentioned her after she was gone. She and I visited Dad frequently of course but, except for a few quick excursions to the lake in the first six months after our marriage, that was pretty much exclusively at the family home in Grand Rapids. We kept away from the lake. I'm not entirely certain why. It was mostly me, I know that. Wendy suggested we come here on a number of occasions, but I would usually find a reason not to. I think, possibly, that at first I couldn't be here because of the absence of my two mothers.

Then again, the cabin became a sty. Dad's conservatism in religion had foisted the entire obligation for the godliness of cleanliness onto my mother. This patriarchal attitude also extended to the preparation of decent food. The best meal one might expect in those years after she was gone was whatever could be poured from a can or placed between two slices of stale bread. Throughout their married life he had seen Mom as his servant and, by extension, God's. Dad believed deeply in myth.

Amazingly, Mom didn't mind. She understood so much more than the rest of us. After she was gone, and I had hooked up with Wendy, visiting Dad at the cabin was a weekend of cooking and putting things right. Still, it wasn't that that kept us away. Without Mom, and then Mary Sweeney, the lake lost its grace, its beauty, and its sense of home. The same was not true of the parsonage in Grand Rapids where Dad lived three quarters of the year. That place was never a home. You must, after all, have something in order to lose it. There, so many people had always come and gone that it had seemed more an extension of the church next door. After Mom died, it got worse. The ladies of the congregation fawned on their widowed pastor, cleaning his house, providing his meals. Some of these Samaritans confused the Lutheran idea of *sola fidelis* with the more Catholic principle of good works and believed they were earning God's beneficence. Others simply muddied the waters of credence by mistaking the corporeal resurrection of long-dormant hormones with spiritual awakening. Dad cut a handsome figure.

Then again, Wendy's job kept us from the cabin too. She is, was (ironic that even tense can be cruel), the Events Coordinator at DeVos Hall, the big 2,500 seat auditorium in downtown Grand Rapids. She loved the work, booking shows like *Riverdance* and *Miss Saigon* and *Damn Yankees* as well as individual performers ranging in novelty from Jethro Tull to Diana Krall. She had collected, over the years, autographed photos from Liza Minelli, Tony Curtis, Robert Goulet and dozens of other celebrities whose framed, contented faces smiled at me every time I entered the den to work at the computer or watch TV. I never liked this iconic menage, staring at me in winsome eminence. It had something to do with a secular sense of idolatry—like giving a child someone else's name. Wendy was extremely proud of her various encounters with the Famous, but I took all the pictures down after she was murdered and burned them. They should have worshipped her.

Her job was especially frenetic in the summer months when I was free and Dad opened the cabin, but even when she could break away for a few days, we didn't go to the lake. We were too happy to want to go anywhere and, as I intimated, our house was not cluttered with tin cans and ghosts.

I pour another glass of Beam and watch the sun inch its way across the yard. I see my mother hanging wet swimming trunks on the clothesline strung between two clumps of birches, yakking gaily with Mary Sweeney. I see my father playing catch with Satchel, the slap of the baseball in their gloves echoing across the water, with Ernie Harwell's play-by-play booming from the portable radio perched like a gull on the rotting picnic table. Then I leave that childhood scene and Wendy is sitting near me, mostly naked in her yellow bikini, probably unaware of the effect her body is having on me. She worked hard to stay in shape; Wendy never let anything go. You had to take it from her. I don't think she gained an ounce in our few years of marriage. Her lovely legs, tan and wonderfully smooth, are pulled up under her. She studies the contracts she brought with her. Having no children was her idea. She didn't want any until she was through with her career. One of the straps to her bikini bra slips off her shoulder. She absently pulls it back in place. I want to touch her—another reason to be at home.

The ghosts diminish exponentially with the bottle of Beam. I drift off in a leaky boat across the dark lake. The night is starless, moonless, a void. I wait impatiently for the boat to fill with water so that I might sink into oblivion. There is comfort in the mystery of depth. My lungs fill. I think briefly of the Monster who is dead, and the one that should be. Maybe, at last, I won't come back. This is what I have come to know as rest.

Chapter two

When my eyes open, I have the discomfiting sense that something other than my faith, my desire and my soul is broken —something less metaphysical. From the rollicking horror between my ears, I conclude that it must be my skull. I didn't know it was possible for bone to throb. I close my eyes again, hoping to return to that dark place at the bottom of the lake, but it's too late. Now Jim Beam is running around inside my head with his little hammer, forcing me to surface. Being conscious these days is an expensive proposition.

I rise gingerly from the wicker chair, like an old man crippled with arthritis. Whiskey is my new god and, like the former one, only it can take away what it causes. I see the blurred bottle on the porch floor in the half-light of what is either dusk or dawn. It's empty. One depleted vessel can't comfort another. I go inside in search of a New Jerusalem. Jack Daniels is on the counter by the sink, waiting to fulfill me. I don't remember how he got there or why he replaced Mr. Beam, but it doesn't matter. In the pantheon of gods, one is as good as another I guess. My father rattles his chains again. I take a long pull, feel the whiskey burn in me. If God is internal, I guess that hell can be too. Jack takes the little hammer away from Jim and sits down to wait his turn. He won't get one. To forgive is divine, but mercy is self-imposed and an entirely human trait.

Since it's getting darker, I decide that either I am dying or it must be evening. I'm not lucky enough for the former. It must be twilight.

I'm smoothing out slowly, at least enough that I can pour my next drink into a glass. Wendy winks at me from across the room, still in her yellow bikini. I ignore her and turn on the lamp. One must disregard the unattainable. The shade has bear and moose and cartoonish pine trees, the kind you might find in a L'il Abner comic strip. Wendy disappears, but I think it has more to do with vacuity than light.

I realize I'm shaky and nauseous, but I have faith that Jack will fix things. One must have faith, my father told me, if God is to have any success at all with his interference. I find a cigarette. It tastes terrible and the end is flaming. I have lit the filter. I go to the bathroom and vomit, an action accomplished so regularly nowadays that it is done with the nonchalance of urinating. I return to the kitchen and sit down in a sweat at the big table where we all used to gather at this time of day to escape the mosquitoes and other kinds of hunger. A cup of coffee seems good to me, so I don't make any. I look around at the empty chairs and decide that I will remember that I will make a wish come true this night—when it is good and dark.

I had not come here with the intention to end my life. I'd thought that perhaps I might find a way to come to terms with all this misery in another way. But now, under the influence of ghosts and booze, it seems like the only viable solution—the remaining hope for relief. Only death can chase away death, I guess. It is time. Tinker to Evers to Chance. Dad used to say that timing is everything in comedy and baseball, so I decide to set a time. I glance at the ridiculous clock that Mom bought from some mail-order catalogue. It's a caricature of Felix the Cat. The hour and minute and second hands extend from its nose like whiskers, and the clicking pendulum is its tail. It's a little after nine.

I'll get in the boat at midnight, row out to the middle of the lake, bang a hole in the floor and wait—simple, but effective. I hear my father talking to my mother. He has recently given the eulogy for a teenager who killed himself and we are driving home. At the service, his words were comforting and diplomatic, but he tells her now that suicide is wrong. People must always strive to live, he says. Life is a gift, he says, and to throw it away is insulting to the Giver. Rage, rage, against the dying of the light, he quotes. Mom hasn't read Dylan Thomas. She goes for a simpler analogy. She reminds him that he threw away the blue tie she gave him for Christmas, the one with all the little gold crosses on it. Dad said it was as tacky as Felix the Clock. Did my action insult you? he retorts. No, she says. Sometimes people just can't wear what they're given. It was a wise thing to say. It seems to be my dilemma.

This time I light the correct end of the cigarette and take a long drag. It occurs to me that I ought to leave a note or something and actually stand up to look for a piece of paper before I realize that there is no one left to write to.

I sit down again. As I visualize my death, I realize that there will be no corpse. No one will know what happened to my body. In this country the corporeal has taken increasing precedence. I blame Hollywood, MTV and the Surgeon General, not necessarily in that order.

It's odd, but it takes much longer to be dead if they can't find the corpse—years I think—and I don't want to wait. I want an official declaration. So I rise from my chair again in search of pen and paper. I stub my toe on an empty Beam bottle. I remember there's another on the porch. Dead men all over, their spirits gone. Habeas Corpus.

The cigarette is burning my fingers. I throw it into the sink. To extinguish the butt, I turn on the water and it flows out brown and smelling strongly of iron, as Sweeney had predicted. I feel a sense of camaraderie with the faucet. Neither of us has been turned on for quite a while.

In Mom's 'junk drawer' I find a piece of paper. This is where everything is kept that doesn't have a proper place. I find an old high school photo of Satchel there. He is wearing his baseball uniform. If anywhere, that would have been where Satchel belonged. Unfortunately, Satchel didn't fit anywhere.

I shove the picture absently into my shirt pocket. There is a pen in the drawer too, but the ink is dried up, so I grab an old pencil. It was Dad's. I know this because it's a green number two, and filled with teeth marks. Pastor Balune could only write sermons with green number twos. God, at least for him, would allow his Word to be written down through no other medium. (The teeth marks, I think, are an indication that my father pondered God rather tensely.)

Romantics would say the photo is a sign; the pencil is an omen—or at least a metaphor, something to change my path. But such an assumption presumes that a Guide is necessary. If so, it follows that the Guide must be omniscient. If it is omniscient, then it must be omnipotent. If that is all true, then it must be the most heinously wicked of all beings. I've considered it all before. No need to dwell on it. Perhaps the meaning of life is simply to survive by feeding on other lives, to generate offspring, to conquer and subdue. I'm not much interested in any of those things now. All things must live—all things must die. It doesn't really matter when. I sit down and begin my note.

> To Whom It May Concern:
> Look for me in the middle of this lake, (at the bottom). There was no murder, no foul play. I made my own decision. If I had been granted any greater power, I would have chosen not to live at all. I leave this cabin, my house in Grand Rapids, and everything else I own, to my neighbor, Hiram Sweeney, and his daughter, Moira. May the ghosts be kinder to them than they were to me.
> Tin Balune
> SSN 364-75-1422

I write my social security number because it's how the world knows me. I pour another glass of Jack Daniels, leaving my brief homily on the table. I would like to talk to God now, but to do so would be to admit relevance, and I know better. I drink Him instead, my own profane communion.

I go out on the porch and sit down again in the wicker chair where I slept away the last afternoon of my life. There is a moon on the lake. Its light travels across the dark water, right to my feet. Like everything heavenly, it is deceitfully beautiful. I used to believe that the moon followed only me, but its lighted path ends at the feet of anyone on the lake who is watching it. I guess the point is that none of us should feel special about where the light ends. It's all lunacy anyway.

Do I sound drunk? I suppose I do and am. I hear a loon out there in the darkness somewhere and June bugs are pelting the screen with kamikaze fury. The world is full of the futility of life.

I nap, I drink, I smoke. I hear Felix the Clock meow the hour, another of its endearing features. It's eleven now. Almost time. I must have dozed longer than I thought.

I wonder if my students will miss me. Some might, perhaps, but those I taught last year are off to college and those coming in really don't know me that well. Perhaps the new teacher will give them less homework, in which case the mourning will be brief.

How will I make the hole in the boat? Here is a much more practical consideration. I get up and go to the little closet off the kitchen that is concealed not by a door but by a curtain suspended from a bent rod. The drape is swimming with a fish motif. I slide it aside to reveal the shelves inside, once laden with canned food and cereal boxes. On the floor is Dad's old tool chest. I flip the lid back and lying right on top is an ancient hand drill. It has the round handle on top, which you press down with one hand while the other rotates the bent elbow that turns the bit. There is a nice, long augur bit lying next to it. Perfect. If we must believe in omens, then this, surely, is the kind to trust.

Some indelicate investigator, when they pull me out, will

probably wonder why I wasted a perfectly good boat. They'll ask why I didn't just swim until I got tired and then let myself sink. Well, for one thing, I can't swim. They would probably laugh at the irony and then observe that it would have been easier for me to just jump from the boat and allow it to drift back to shore. I guess I would argue that nothing is 'perfectly good'. The ship should go down with the captain, shouldn't it? Why do I waste my remaining time with such thoughts?

I grab the drill, insert the augur bit with some difficulty since my vision is a bit fuzzy, and carry it to the table. I notice that my note is gone, then I spot it on the floor. I put it back and place a salt shaker on it for weight. I carry the drill back out onto the porch and place it on the floor next to my wicker chair. Now I'm ready. They also serve who only stand and wait—or something like that. I prefer to sit.

Jack and I commune again for awhile. Time passes—such an interesting expression. I've considered it often of late, the mobility of time. It's another fiction. I don't believe time moves any more than the hot ball of gases on which it's based. We say that the sun rises, the sun sets. Joshua was supposed to make it stand still, but I know it never moves. The moon is a lie too. It never shines really, it only reflects. Moonlight is sunlight. I gave up on history because it's surrounded by, and trapped in, time. We are all terrible liars.

Felix meows a dozen times to let me know a new day is beginning. I will never hear him again, that atrocious, dead, cartoon cat—measuring life in artificial animation. He lives, like time, by gears and myth.

I go inside, turn off the single lamp. On the porch again, I have a last drink and wish myself a happy deathday. Bottle in hand, though it is empty, I swing the porch door open and let it slam behind me, following the lunar light to the water. I'm barely conscious and weave across the lawn, but the light stays with me. From the dock, I step down into the boat. The oars, fortunately, are still in their locks. I don't think I could have managed otherwise.

I sit down as a cloud of pitiless mosquitoes gathers around

my head for a last supper. I let them feast. There is a strong, putrid smell of decay. At first I assume it is me (am I rotting already?), but then I notice the cottage cheese carton of crawlers I took with me this morning (yesterday?) and realize that the sun, mobile or not, has done its work.

I tell the old boat that we should go now. I don't think she wants to. She refuses to let go of the dock as I try to untie the moorings. I've almost persuaded her when I remember the drill. She was just reminding me. I didn't bring it. Even death requires persistence.

I have to struggle out of the boat on my knees. The world is spinning, as if to exonerate Copernicus. I wait until the dizziness fades, but like the first *homo erectus,* I fight to stand up straight. It's very dark ahead. The moon lights only what is behind me—strange how that works.

The lights are on in Sweeney's cabin. I wonder if his daughter and her boyfriend have arrived yet. No matter.

I find the screen door. I have this terrible moment where I want to sit down in the wicker chair and wait for the 'sunrise', but it passes. I find the drill on the cement floor next to the chair. I retrieve it with amazing dexterity, considering my condition. I am back out in the yard and Diana has given me light again.

Except for tripping over the Adirondack chaise and getting drenched by the tall, dewy grass, I arrive back at the dock without incident. I crawl back into the boat, drill in hand, and reach for the mooring rope.

"Going fishing?"

The voice paralyses me with fear. I cannot move. I don't know where it came from. It is a ghost or, worse, someone real. Part of the fear, of course, is guilt. I have been caught doing something wrong, or at least suspicious. Unorthodoxy is always cause for mistrust. I look up to see Wendy's long legs on the dock above me. She looks different now. She has changed from her yellow bikini into shorts and a light blouse, the bottom of which is tied by its tails about her waist. I can't see above her navel. I can't see her face. Her voice is different too, but who else would be out here at midnight?

"You don't remember me do you, Mr. Balune?" There is a girl-ish giggle I can't recall, and why does she call me 'mister'? Then she explains. "I'm Moira Sweeney, Mary's kid."

All I can think is that it's going to be much more difficult to die now. Maybe she'll go away after a little polite conversation. "No, I'm sorry, I don't. It's been a long time. I thought for a minute…well…you were pretty young when I saw you last."

"I was at your father's funeral last year with Sweeney, but I'm sure you had other things to think about. I don't think you saw me. There were so many people…"

"I don't—"

"It's okay. You going fishing?" The moon shifts from behind a cloud for a moment and I can see her nod her head in the direction of my fishing gear which is still lying in the boat from my conquest of the Monster. Her face is in shadow.

"Yeah, for bullhead. Good nightfeeders."

"Oh." She points at the forgotten drill in my hand as she slaps a mosquito. "What's that for? Getting through the ice?"

"Uh…well…promise you won't tell anyone?"

"Sure."

"It's an old good luck charm. Like all fishermen worth their salt, I'm very superstitious." I tuck the drill away under the seat.

"Oh." Though I can't read her expression, I don't think she bought it.

"Where's your boyfriend?" Redirection…another apathetic, change-the-subject question.

"How would you know about him?"

"Your father said that you and your boyfriend were driving a truck up here." This could be embarrassing, relying on my memory like this. I could have dreamt it, hallucinated the whole scene. It's dangerous to allude to anything when you see ghosts all the time. I'm not even sure that she's real.

"He couldn't make it."

"Oh, sorry." I feel a bit of relief. I'm not sure why.

"That's okay. Graham's coming up in a few days, just delayed, that's all."

"You drive the U-Haul by yourself?"

"Sure, why not?"

"I don't know. Most of those bigger ones are stick shifts and I guess a lot of...people don't know how to drive them."

"You mean females."

"I meant young people."

"Oh." She isn't convinced. "Well either way, it's a stereotype." I'm intrigued by the sound of her voice and I find myself wanting to see her face.

"Is the truck a stick or an automatic?"

She laughs. "I'll tell you if you'll tell me what that tool is really for."

"Sounds fair. Actually, I'm going to row this boat into deep water, drill a hole or two in the floor, and go down with the ship."

She is silent for a minute. She doesn't move. I want to read her face, but it's still obscured by the shadow from the birch tree branch hanging over her.

Finally, she says: "So it really is a good luck charm?"

"Yeah. Your turn." Having continually dealt with the lack of complexity in the teenage mind, I expect her to say "Huh?" Instead, she says: "Okay. The truck they gave me was a stick shift. When I found out that Graham wouldn't be able to come with me and I'd have to drive it myself, I asked for an automatic. It's not because I'm a woman though, or because I'm young. It's because it's easier to drive, period."

I feel a strange, unfamiliar change in my face. I think I'm smiling.

"Mr. Balune?" Surprisingly, she pronounces my name correctly.

"Yes?"

"Do you mind if I call you Tinker?"

"I mind if anyone calls me Tinker. Just Tin will be fine."

She moves a step closer and her face escapes the shadows. I am stunned. I thought I was finished with beauty, that it couldn't touch me anymore. Her eyes are so dark, almost cruel, and she looks at me directly, fully. "Do you think I should have tried to drive the stick?"

"What? No, not to prove something, no."

"Good." I can't really describe what she looks like. Standing there in the moonlight, she is archetypal, primitive, something above and yet below the rest of humanity. She is not so much a beauty as a beatitude. She has, at once, the indefinable allure of Marilyn Monroe and the Holy Trinity, both substance and idea. I look away by force, by sheer will. I have forgotten that I want to die.

"Listen," she says, extending a long white arm in appeal. "I know I don't have any right to ask you, but I need a favor."

"Now?" I hear myself sounding stupid.

"Oh no. You're going fishing and I know how sacred an act that is to the Balunes and the Sweeneys. No, I was thinking about tomorrow morning. Like I said, Graham couldn't make it…"

"Graham?"

"My friend."

"Oh, yeah." Who is this idiot that he would find something to distract him from this lovely girl? I have a terrible urge to step out of the boat and go with her. I want to touch her, yet I know that her real meaning to me is invisible.

"Well, Sweeney has a bad back and the truck has to be unloaded so that I can get it back to some U-Haul station in Traverse City by two tomorrow afternoon. Sweeney said he could help me unload, but I know he'll screw up his back and then I'll have to spend the summer playing nurse. He's a proud and stubborn man."

I want to say that I will. "You call your dad Sweeney?" is what comes out.

"He doesn't mind. Do you think you could help me empty the truck? Probably wouldn't take more than a couple of hours. I'll fix you breakfast. You like waffles?"

"Sure." I don't know what I've done. I'm not even sure what I've agreed to. I couldn't say no to her for some reason. God and

Woman, my father once said, require acquiescence. They're both far
superior to men.

"I just need to have help with the big stuff, some furniture and
such. It shouldn't take too long. I'd really appreciate it."

What can I say? 'I'm sorry but I won't be alive tomorrow
morning'?

"Okay. Sure."

"That'd be great. You're a lifesaver. Thanks so much. Is seven
too early?"

"That'll be fine."

"Great. See you then. I hope your good luck charm works."

She's gone before I can respond, slipping away into the shadows along the shoreline. I see her silhouette a few minutes later by
the door of the Sweeney cabin. I think she looks back at me, but I
can't be sure. Perhaps I just wish it.

I release the boat and push away from the dock. In spite of my promise, I am determined to be done with the world. The girl's absence
has made it darker than it was. The oars groan in their rusty locks.
A light breeze, caused by the motion, cools me and offers temporary
relief from the heat and the insatiable mosquitoes. I'm covered with
bites. If there is any such thing as compassion, one of the tiny blood
gluttons will have ancestors that were spawned on the west bank of
the Nile.

It is deep enough here, I think, though I'm far from the center of the lake yet. I do nothing except to shelve the oars. The coffee
can full of cement that serves as my anchor will stay where it is and
help to sink us. I feel paralyzed. Wendy and I made love in this boat,
near this very spot. It was her idea. She said she wanted to feel me
inside her and watch the stars at the same time. She wanted to see the
heavens. I remember the moon and the wonderful workings of her
mouth and her hips—such intense pleasure from a single person.

Afterward, we lay there together on the floor of the boat—
naked, entwined, drifting, holding to each other as if the world could
not hurt us.

I close my eyes to gain a better vision—the sensitivity of the blind. "Wendy." I say her name aloud as if the sound could bring her back. The word echoes both within me and without. I slide from the seat and lie down in the fetid water on the floor. The rotting worms, freed from their tomb by the water, float listlessly nearby. I am crying, I think, but I can't even be sure of that anymore.

Tinker to Evers to Chance. Tinker to Evers to Chance. Will Tinker Ever have a Chance? Does Tinker have a Chance for Ever? The whiskey is working. That's all. That's all. I cling to my ghost of Wendy. I see her face there in the shadows. The worms and I are rotting. A little girl calls my name across the dark mirror of the lake. Is it a loon? Satchel strikes me out and smirks. He is in my shirt pocket I think. How did he get there? I feel the drill pressing urgently against my back. Although I don't care, there is a life preserver on board. The Department of Natural Resources requires it. Somewhere, Wendy calls to me, but she is distant. The moonlight stops where I am. The boat and I drift off. That's all.

Chapter three

I sense the light more than I see it. I feel a gentle rocking and hear the water lap against the hull as if it would drink me. Somewhere birds are making their noise. I'm shivering. Cold, hunger and thirst assault me together, (Jack Daniels has his hammer), and I'm nauseous—all sure signs of life.

I grab the sides of the boat and pull myself into an upright position. I'm sitting in two inches of water. The worms floating next to me have turned gray and they are beginning to shred. I can see that dawn has passed me, and I smell the new day more than see it, like a vulture senses carrion. It has the same odor. My back screams in protest at its contortion, but then my head quickly consolidates all pain unto itself.

My eyes squint against the sun's harsh reflection on the water. The old boat is buoyed in a bed of reeds and cattails. They sway with us in the mild breeze. I come to consciousness with the same anticipation as an African in the hold of the Amistad. I have failed to die.

The boat has drifted all the way across the lake in the night, to the far side, the side that is not yet developed, (meaning that man hasn't torn it up yet). A small doe has come to the water's edge, twenty feet from me, for a drink. I could use one too. She glances up at me, then lowers her head again to sip. She knows, instinctively, that I am not a threat. Her ambivalence angers me for some reason. There should always be, in nature, punishment for improper respect. I think she doesn't recognize that I belong to nature. Maybe she's right, but it pisses me off anyway. I raise one oar, then let it fall to smack the water's surface. The doe bolts away into the thick trees. I can now add piddling triviality to my sins.

The number seven appears in my throbbing and muddled head. Dad used to interpret numbers. He loved them. He told us that the number four represented the corners of the earth and the number three symbolized the Trinity, so seven was symbolic of the Christ—God on earth. When I observed that the earth is round and has no corners, he laughed at me with that strange pomposity that True Believers reserve for those who would apply sense to faith. Why do I bother with all that now? Seven is also the number of deadly sins. Seven.

I lean back. My hand touches the drill. I lift it from the puddled floor. My good luck charm, I told her. Was that real? Was she real? I remember gasping when I saw her face. I think it was just my imagination, but I have come to believe in imagination. It's better than what I see with my eyes. Perception is so much greater than truth—even geography affects it. My father said that God, that great Number Seven, is everywhere, but I always liked him better in Bethlehem than on the summit of Sinai. Unfortunately, the religion with which I was raised did not allow me to pick and choose.

The wind shifts and my boat begins to drift with my thoughts, out onto the lake. I absently glance at my watch. Assuming it exists, the time is six-thirty. The numbers in the little frame on the dial tell me that it's my birthday. Then it comes to me, like the gentle urging of the summer wind. I have made a promise to someone, the girl on the dock. Did I really see Sweency's kid or was it another drunken illusion? I'm almost sure it was real, but I never planned to follow through. I planned to be dead. Seven. I told her I would meet her at seven. I was supposed to be waiting up for heaven.

Other fishermen are moving on the lake. I hear the Evinrudes as, no doubt, do the fish. I curse myself for my inability to complete a simple task, something many people have done without difficulty. I can't do it now, not in this stunning light with others around. Among my species, killing must be secret. Damning one's soul should be a private matter.

I can barely see the cove where the cabins are. The fierce reflection of the sun stings my eyes. I crawl up onto the seat—a terrible climb of twenty inches—and grip the oars. I pull against the water. I notice the drill where it lies on the floor between my feet, half-submerged. I slept on it. It was not a good luck charm, though insight might warrant a second thought about that. No, I've given up on that sort of thing. It did, however, make a strong impression on me. I feel it on my back. Perhaps I can put it to better use tonight.

The far shore is nearing as I glance over my shoulder. Viewing my life is done in much the same way, moving forward with slowness and great effort, but always facing to the rear. An occasional glance to check direction is uncomfortable with my stiff neck, and requires me to interrupt motion. I'm never sure of my destination.

The cabins grow larger. I dread seeing the Sweeneys again, particularly the girl. She is the age of most of my students, but I feel intimidated by her, probably because I lied, but perhaps because I told the truth. Now I will be forced to haul furniture all day and I'm not even sure I can walk.

I'm in the cove now. The chill is gone from the lake and I can feel the heat intensify. Droplets of sweat sting my eyes. I glance ahead, over my shoulder, searching for any sign of Sweeney or the girl. It's almost seven and I don't want to explain why I spent the whole night on the lake without catching any fish. With luck I can get to my cabin unnoticed, take a much-needed shower, drink enough to get me right, and report for hauling duty.

I run the boat right onto the beach, then laboriously moor it at the dock. My back muscles spasm as I step onto the sand. My head is pounding. What little thought is there is centered on whiskey. I'm not sure there's any left inside—either me or the cabin—and that is a very empty feeling indeed.

I cross the lawn tentatively, keeping a blurry eye on the Sweeney cabin. I fully expect the girl to come plunging forth, cheerfully demanding the fulfillment of my promise, before I have a chance to gather the various parts of myself together. I'm sorely in need of a drink, a cigarette, a shower, a toothbrush and dry clothes—in that order. If she showed up now, it would be difficult to explain my appearance. I have trouble justifying myself to me, and, at least in this regard, I am a very lenient and liberal magistrate.

I reach the porch without incident and slip inside. I hear Felix meowing the hour just inside the next doorway. I must hurry. I step into the cabin interior and there she is, standing by the kitchen table, my note in one hand and the salt shaker in the other. Felix the Clock must have muffled the sounds of my approach, because she has been surprised. We are both caught, but we know, instantly, that she can escape. Neighborly intrusion in northern Michigan is, at worst, a mere faux pas. There is no stigma attached to it at all if the intruder is concerned for the well being of the occupant, even if the primary motivation is prying.

"You *were* planning to kill yourself," she says.

It is a characteristic of the guilty, my father used to say, when accused of unrighteousness, to become self-righteous. It really is our only defense. "What're you doing in here?" I want to sound imperious, but my voice has a bit of a whine to it—very much like one of my students when caught plagiarizing a term paper—shaky and weak. I can see that she's not intimidated.

I expect her to defend her imposition. She doesn't. She just stands there, staring at me, holding the note. I look away, as much because of her striking eyes as my own embarrassment. They are dark and penetrating, a whore's eyes, unflinching and bold. She is very slim, but not angular. There is nothing skeletal about her, but she would seem too thin except for the heavy bounty of hair, lips and breasts—all of which justify their excess without detracting from the soft lines of her legs and arms. "You were going to kill yourself," she repeats, looking again at the note.

"You have an excessive imagination," I say. "I was doodling. It means nothing."

I expect her to accept what I say. A man should be able to lie under his own roof. Besides, I am older and that should count for something, as all who have the disadvantage of age continue to believe.

"You're lying." It's a simple response. Brutal. "When you said you were going to drill holes in the boat, that was the truth."

I see a pack of cigarettes on the table. I step forward, grab them, light one by turning on a gas burner on the stove. I inhale deeply. Nicotine is a wonderful drug. Like everything else in this world that gives pleasure, it kills. "It's just fiction," I say, "the beginning of an idea for a story."

"You were going to leave this place to Sweeney? You write your social security number? I'm not stupid, Tin."

The sound of my name, coming from her, is somehow intimate. I look around, avoiding those dark eyes and long, doe lashes. Jim? Jack? Where are your friends when you really need them? My father winks at me from a chair in the far corner. Belligerence is the next defense. "Okay, so what? How is this any of your business?"

"Why didn't you do it?"

"What?"

"Why are you here, now?"

For the first time, the truth seems appropriate. "I fell asleep."

"You mean you passed out. These empty bottles all over this place certainly aren't collectibles."

I'm not used to being chastised by teenagers, particularly with such flippancy, but this girl doesn't talk, act or look like she just finished high school. "All right, I was drunk. People do silly things when they drink. If you were a little older you'd know that. I passed out, now I'm here. What do you want from me?"

She is folding my note with the precision of a soldier folding a coffin flag at a military funeral. She intends to preserve it, but not for me. Strange that in my addled state I should notice the delicacy of her long fingers. I find it difficult to look at her—and to not look at her. "Let me have that," I say to her.

"No." It's a negative spoken with the authority and, (in my experience), the regularity of the divine. She finishes folding it and slips it into the pocket of her blouse. If I try to retrieve it forcefully, I will have to grab at her breast. I am tempted and she knows it. I think that's why she's smiling. I look to my father's ghost for help. As in life, he is off somewhere communing with God when I need him most. Wendy, too, is noticeably absent.

"What do you want with it?"

"I'm going to give it to Sweeney." Why doesn't she call him 'dad'? "I think he ought to know if he's going to come into a sudden inheritance." She doesn't mention herself as an heir.

She knows that Sweeney would try to stop me if he knew I wanted to kill myself. Sweeney doesn't believe in suicide any more than Dad did, albeit for different reasons. I remember the two of them arguing about it as we trolled for walleye. I must've been in my teens then. The beauty in front of me was a little girl.

I don't recall why self-destruction was the topic. I know it wasn't long after Mary Sweeney died. It was a beautiful summer day, the kind so rare in this neck of the woods. I still laugh when I read Jim Harrison's description of summer in northern Michigan as 'three weeks of bad sledding'. Anyway, the weather was perfect. Wendy was part of the future, not the past. Perhaps it was the fish. They had been hooking themselves all morning with lemming-like determination.

Whatever the stimulus, Dad, of course, cited the Holy Bible (the Good Book was never referred to, by him, as simply the Bible), as the authority *'gainst self-slaughter*. God had *fixed his canon* and there was nothing else to consider. (Pastor Balune quoted *Hamlet* often, second only to Scripture). Sweeney, on the other hand, wasn't opposed to God's Will, but was more concerned with the *reason* that suicide was a sin. God, to Sweeney, wasn't some gigantic ego in the sky who took offense at suicide because life was *His* to give and withdraw or because He was indignant and petulant over disobedience to His arbitrary rules. It was just that he knew how choosing to end one's life can harm and hurt those one leaves behind.

The conversation ended when Dad hooked a Great Northern and spent the next fifteen minutes landing it. I remember thinking then, as Dad proudly ran the stringer through its gill, that God's sacred law did not, apparently, extend to the pike.

I look back at Moira. She knows I've been away. Her eyes captivate me. They're black, I swear—not dark brown, or hazel, black. They're spectacular, bewitching. They tell me that she has been fucked many times, but also that she's still a virgin. Is that possible?

"Do what you want with it," I tell her. What does it matter anyway? People who are prepared to kill themselves shouldn't care about anything. My father always said, if you're going to do something, do it right. *He* did, after all.

She doesn't move. "You don't want it badly enough to take it away from me?"

"No." I sit down at the table, a few feet from her. The pressure of my ass on my jeans forces them to surrender what little moisture is left in them to the floor. My head is gradually coming apart. I expect that it will split open soon and spill my brains onto the table. Like my pants, I'm dehydrating.

She takes a step toward me, then another. There is something miraculous in the movement. She places her soft hand on my shoulder. It's been a long time since anyone touched me with such tenderness. I shrug it away—an automatic gesture for those who know they are not entitled to compassion.

She doesn't seem to be hurt or offended. "What are you going to do now?" she says. Her tone has softened. I'm sure Sweeney has told her all about me and she feels some empathy, but she doesn't understand the thinking of the depraved. While she is experiencing pathos, I am considering what it would be like to kiss her, as I did when Satchel first brought Wendy around. I want to say 'Go away child, you're in the presence of evil.' Instead, I say: "I don't know. If I can get a drink and a shower…"

"What?"

33

"I might feel up to hauling furniture."

"Why would you want to do that?"

"I could say in order to keep a promise, but really it's just something to get me through the day, that's all."

"And what about tonight? Will you go 'fishing' again?"

I hear my father's hardy laugh somewhere, but I don't see him. My mother is singing "Happy Birthday". She has chosen to be invisible too, as she so often was in life. I feel a fissure opening somewhere on the top of my skull. It's so real that I place my hand on my head to determine if I'm leaking. "I don't know," I hear myself say, although I have forgotten the question. "Can you find me something to drink?"

"Water?"

"No, something with more impurities."

"Oh."

The fissure is widening. I put a hand on each temple and press, trying to contain the eruption. It seems to motivate her. I hear the refrigerator door open and close and the popping sound of rupture. I sincerely hope it's a pop-top can, and not my brain.

"It's the best I could do," she says and places a foaming can of beer in front of me. I grab it eagerly and drain it in several greedy gulps. I can feel her eyes on me, but it doesn't matter. There is no shame in drugs if your condition is terminal. On the road to death, all is permissible. The controversy is about where the road begins.

The fissure begins to close. The terrible hammering subsides to a dismal pang. It's possible to think again. "Another," is all I can manage.

"No," she answers, "not until you're cleaned up. You smell wormy, like a driveway after a thunderstorm. Get up and get into the shower. I'll make you some coffee."

I do as I'm told. The water is hot, scalding me, but it feels good. I've been cold for so long in summer's heat. I hear myself, the rhythm of my mental speech. It's iambic—a poor teacher's joy, another kind of warmth.

The hot water on my head has welded the fissure. I am almost without physical pain. I rub the soap across my chest and am amazed at the protuberance of my ribs. My wedding band slides around on my finger. I've misplaced a good portion of myself somewhere.

In front of the old, flaking mirror, I really look at myself for the first time in many weeks. My features have become gaunt. *We are the hollow men,* Eliot whispers from the grave. I scrape a developing beard away to reveal sunken cheeks, an unhealthy pallor, and a terrible resemblance to my father. My dark hair, still thick, is graying at the temples. My blue eyes are bloodshot and fearful, like something hunted—or haunted. I don't like what I see there.

It feels good to run the electric toothbrush over my teeth and momentarily remove the sour taste of the Bitter Cup.

I pull on clean underwear, shorts and a tee shirt that reads *Property of Longfellow High School Aesthetic Department,* garnered from my battered suitcase. I check the pockets of my dirty clothes for things that cannot be laundered, (as trained to do by Wendy). In my shirt pocket is a lighter and a high school photo of Satchel. I can't remember how either got there. I go back to the bathroom, light the picture of my brother afire, and throw it into the toilet bowl.

I emerge into the kitchen to find the girl sitting at the table, browsing through one of my literary magazines. She glances up at me and smiles. There is concupiscence there and although I'm sure it's unintentional, it excites me.

"You look better," she says, rising from her chair. I think if I could put my arms around her I might want to live for awhile. Her black eyes are disarming. I begin to realize, as I stare at her, that a part of what makes them so provocative is the way they contrast with her skin. Her complexion is fair, pale and delicate, the kind you would normally find on someone who is blond and blue-eyed. Her skin is creamy, flawless, and the black eyes and hair are deeply accentuated by her paleness. I get the sense that she spends a great deal of time outdoors, in the sun, yet even her arms are pale. It's an exotic and erotic combination. How can she be a mere teenager? What is wrong with me? It's my nature, I think, to ruin people.

"Sit," she says as she pours a cup of coffee and hands it to me.

Again, I do as I'm told, despite, or perhaps because of, the authoritative way that she addresses me. She might just have easily have said 'kneel and bark like a dog' and I probably would have complied. The coffee tastes better than anything I've had to drink in a long while.

"Now what?" I ask as she stands by the sink, watching me sip.

"You help me unload the truck like you promised. It's almost eight and the U-Haul has to be returned by two."

"Will you give me back my note?"

"What were you burning in the bathroom?"

"What?"

"I smelled something burning, I'm sure. Then the toilet flushed."

"You're very observant."

"What was it?"

"A picture of someone."

"Who?"

"My brother."

"Satchel?"

"Yes. He's the only brother I have."

I expect her to pursue her interrogation, but she lets it go. She unconsciously touches her pocket where the condemning missive is enviably contained, cupping her breast as she does so. It amazes me that the rest of her can be so slim when those mounds are so full and protruding, pressing against her blouse in a serious effort to snap the strained button between them. I must look hungry because she says: "I'm going to fix you some breakfast at our cabin. I'll keep the note for ransom. When you're finished helping me, you can have it back. Fair?"

"Do I have a choice?"

"You always have a choice."

"Spoken like a true naïf."

She laughs—a wonderful, scoffing, delightful laugh. "Because I'm young, you see me as an ingénue," she says. "It seems to me that kind of bias is the greater naiveté."

What child talks like this? She takes my hand and pulls me to my feet. The soft warmth of her is wonderful. It is the physical connection of imagination. We're outside before I have a chance to protest. As she pulls me across the sparse, sandy grass between our two cabins, she doesn't know that I'm studying her. Her black hair glistens in the morning sun. It extends far below her shoulders. She flips it backward with the familiarity of a jeweler handling precious stones. The curves of her body remind me of Shakespeare's body of work—so much existing on a narrow frame of reference. She seems oblivious of her own beauty. There is something terribly *relaxed* about her, even when she moves with this kind of authority. Most women, let alone girls, would be terrified of a drunken, disheveled man who has just tried to kill himself, yet she pulls me along as if I were one of her school chums.

When we enter the Sweeney cottage, I am overwhelmed with the scent of pine. The walls are lined with it. I haven't been in here for quite a while, but I remember it being much the same. Mary loved apples, and they're everywhere. The clock over the sink, the cookie jar on the counter, the dish towels, the hot pads, the cupboard knobs, the curtains, the wooden knife holder, the magnet collection on the white refrigerator, the toaster cover, the cutting board—all are shaped like, or decorated with, apples. That hasn't changed. Nor has the great fieldstone fireplace in the living room with Hi's trophy walleye mounted just above the mantle. Part of the dorsal fin is still missing, from when Satch took the trophy off the wall and I tried to grab it from him. It fell on the hearth. Mary saw it happen, but Hi didn't. We put it back and Hi has never said a word about it. I was always trying to steal things from Satchel.

"Tin!" Sweeney says, emerging from the back hallway. "So Moira roped you into hauling my stuff, huh? Listen, don't let her intimidate you." (This coming from a man who is, experience would tell me, completely cowed by his daughter). "If you don't want to do this, don't. She can be pushy and I'm not as helpless as she'd like to think." He winks at me, but avoids looking at Moira, who we both know is frowning at him.

"It's all right," I assure him. "I volunteered." Despite what my father taught me, lying isn't always wrong. Sometimes, it's even closer to what's real.

"You look good this morning, Tin," he says. "It's amazing what a night's rest can do for you." Without as much as a glance in her direction, I know Moira's frown has changed.

"I had to wake him up," she says. She shrugs when I look at her, the black eyes flashing impishly. I enjoy our conspiratorial bond.

"I don't wonder," Sweeney says. "Looked to me, when I saw you yesterday, that you'd had a few, Tin." By way of atoning for this observation he adds: "Happy birthday by the way."

"Yeah. Same to you."

"It's your birthday too?" Moira asks me. "You were born on the same day as Sweeney?"

"Give or take a couple of years."

She has moved into the apple kitchen and is pulling a waffle iron from a drawer. It makes a loud bang when she puts it down on the counter. "Well, birthday boys, waffles?" It's a rhetorical question. I can see that eggs, pancakes and especially nothing, are not options.

"Sounds great."

"I can do that," Sweeney says. "You kids go ahead and start unloading." Kids? I feel somehow that I'm older than Sweeney. I am eons beyond Moira. Why does it seem odd to me to say her name? For some reason it doesn't feel right to think that she even has one.

The truck isn't all that big. We pull up the rear door and yank out the ramp. It feels good to sweat from honest labor. My head is clearing. I can feel the venom dripping from my pores. My eyes seem to focus better and I don't see any ghosts. It's pleasurable to watch Moira walk and bend and lift. By the time Sweeney calls us to eat, we're half finished.

I am ravenously hungry. Sweeney stares at me as I wolf down my food. I don't care. It's such a good feeling just to *want* again. Can a simple shower, work, food, erase the past? Something has happened to me, I know—it's not enough to engender enthusiasm, but something has removed, for a few moments, the pall of death.

The conversation is small, carefully limited, to avoid any mention of my parents or Wendy or Satchel or even Mary Sweeney—any of the dead or missing.

Moira shovels her waffles, leaving her plate swimming in maple syrup. Sweeney speaks of her boyfriend who, I discover, is named Graham Van Houten. Moira is forced to talk about him, but her description is not fervent. She seems, in fact, almost apathetic about him. I'm convinced that he's more an inconvenience than a passion.

She says she will stay with Sweeney, here at the lake, for a week. She seems to study my reaction. Graham is coming later, perhaps on Monday. My response to this revelation also appears to be scrutinized. I'm trying to remain interested while I ponder what day it is. I know the date.

"Why didn't your friend come with you?" It's none of my business, of course, but I find myself genuinely curious.

Moira spoons up the remaining syrup and drinks it, like soup. Her face is down so that I'm unable to read it. Sweeney sips his coffee noisily.

"We argued," she finally says. "I told him not to come." She glances at her father who is frowning. "He volunteered to help his friend paint his yacht this weekend when he'd already told me he'd help me move Sweeney's things. I don't like broken promises. Besides, he's a child. He offered to pay for a moving van. He thinks money is the answer to everything."

"You met him in school?"

"On the beach at Grand Haven actually," she says.

Sweeney cuts in. "His father is one of the richest men in Michigan—old money, from lumber and iron freighting. Graham just finished his business degree at Yale." From the way he talks about him, I can see that Moira's father has more affection for Graham Van Houten than Moira does.

"He has no soul," Moira says bluntly, as if this sums up the man. "We should get back to work." She rises imperiously, indicating that my interrogation is finished. She can see that I'm reluctant to give it up. She withdraws my note from her breast pocket, unfolds it, opens her lovely mouth as if to begin reading.

"Yes," I say, "we really *should* finish up."

"What's that?" Sweeney asks, pointing at the paper.

"Grocery list," Moira answers, and smiles at me as I hurry to my feet and follow her outside.

By noon the truck is empty. As we slide the ramp back into its crib and pull the door shut, I comment on how the accumulated possessions of a lifetime can so easily be shifted.

"I took half the stuff," Moira says, "mostly Mom's junk. Sweeney didn't want it around."

We stand by the back of the truck, both of us sweating. The heat is intense. Her saturated blouse sticks to her, outlining her shape, emphasizing her chest. She knows I'm staring at her. She smiles.

"Men are such helpless creatures," she says.

"What?"

"Even when they want to die, they're driven to perpetuate the species."

I can feel the color burn in my face. It's a terrible thing to be reduced to such simplicity.

"Now you'll be angry," she says.

I was going to shout at her. I hold my tongue.

"Now you won't be because I said you would."

I'm beginning to see why Graham opted for an afternoon of beer and inanity.

"What about my pay?"

"Your pay? Oh." She reaches into her pocket, slowly extracts the suicide note, and hands it to me. Her sweat has made it flaccid.

"What are you going to do with it?"

"Burn it." I put my lighter to it, but it's too wet. It won't catch.

"See, you're meant to save it," she says. "You can look at it five years from now and laugh."

I fold it neatly and slip it into the cellophane of my cigarette package.

"You're going to lose it if you put it there." .

"I can always write a new one."

"You can, but you won't."

"You think so?"

"I do."

"What makes you so sure?"

"Because you've met me now. You have something interesting to keep you occupied." Her dark eyes are flashing with a kind of challenging flirtation that I find difficult to believe.

As I turn from their brightness, she says: "I wish you would stay." .

I stop, turn back. "Why? My work here is done."

"But mine isn't."

"What does *that* mean?"

I expect much more than what she says. "I have to take the truck back. I wish you'd go with me. It's a nice drive along the coast. It'll only take a couple of hours and we'll be back well before sunset, in case you want to go 'fishing' again. I could use the company and I promise not to rag on you too much."

What else do I have to do on this, my thirtieth birthday? This is what I say to myself, but the reason I assent goes much deeper. "I need to shower and grab another beer."

She smiles broadly and the dark eyes glow. "Meet you back here in half an hour."

"Okay."

The second shower feels better than the first. I skip the beer. By one o'clock we're on the road. We must have a vehicle for the return trip, so we each have to travel alone on the first leg. I ask to drive the truck. She says she'll follow in Sweeney's Lumina. It isn't until we're fifteen miles down M-31 that it registers. The truck is a stick shift.

Chapter four

From Loon Lake to Traverse City, (the closest drop-off point for
U-Haul trucks), is forty miles. The terrible heat of the afternoon is
kept at bay by the air-conditioned cab. The view of Lake Michigan
along the two-lane is quite extraordinary. It's very different from the
inland lakes. It's blue and green, like the ocean, and white sails dot
the great expanse of it, along with magnificent freighters whose decks
could serve as football fields.

Moira is right behind me in Sweeney's old Lumina. I find
myself studying the side mirror to make sure I don't lose her. I have
lost too much already. It's not comforting to be sober. I smoke con-
tinuously. Self-abuse is something one does not give up easily.

I'm not entirely alone. Dad is here. He chatters away in the
seat next to me, cleverly alluding to my recent failure without ever
actually condemning me for making the attempt. How could he?
Still he has that talent, developed in the pulpit, of making insinuation more damning than sin. I can't blame him. His sorrow must be
greater than Adam's. *Both* of his sons are murderers.

I don't know where the rest of the ghosts are; probably bouncing around in the back of the truck. They never stay at home. I sincerely regret that I didn't drink that beer.

Within a long half-hour, we enter the outskirts of Traverse City, coming down a steep slope that curves into the central environs of this tourist town. The traffic is teeming and we move too slowly for living things. Along the lake are hundreds of motels and resort cottages and restaurants and gift shops. The sandy beaches are swarming with vacationers, as are the streets and sidewalks.

I pull up to a traffic light and watch them cross in front of me. They all seem happy—young couples with kids; still younger pairs, preparing to have them without a thought as to why they should, nuzzling each other in the eons-old foolish mating ritual that they always think is original to them; old couples, respected for this same accomplishment of propagating the species—prolonging, grown hoary and wrinkled and nostalgic and serene together. They too, will be ghosts in their turn, but they blithely stroll along through time as if it is only the street they are crossing. Just a few feet away, I have the means to destroy them, but I let the truck idle.

Moira has to honk at me to get me moving again. I hear my mother singing "Happy Birthday" somewhere in the back of the truck.

At last I spot the U-Haul sign about two blocks ahead. It declares what we all must do, unless we have great luck or lots of money. I believe I've had an inadequate allotment of both. Why do I think about such things?

"You cannot serve both God and Money," my father declared to my mother as he deposited a new bike or a pair of jeans in the collection plate. I didn't learn from it what he wanted me to learn. It only taught me that God was more covetous than I was. Further living has confirmed that impression. Either that, or Dad was protecting his own soul at the family's expense. People in Lutheran congregations believe that their ministers should live on nothing while they go about the business of accumulation. As far as their clergymen are concerned, *The servant is worthy of his hire* and *Judge not lest ye be judged* are the only two passages from Scripture that were, in the main, ignored by most of them.

I pull into the U-Haul lot and watch Moira drive to the front entrance to take care of the paperwork. I climb out of the cool cab into the oppressive heat. The public beach is just across the street. The water looks inviting—in a different way than it did last night.

It's a bizarre place to have a truck rental business. All the trucks and trailers seem incongruous, firmly ensconced as they are around the seasonal motels and gift shops. It must be difficult for the employees of this place to see the beach that is a part of their normal lives desecrated by these tourists. All these vacationers in their bright Hawaiian shirts and orange swimsuits enjoy themselves as the truck people go about their daily rite of survival in their drab uniforms, just east of Eden.

I find a spot of shade under a gnarled old maple at the edge of the concrete lot and lean against it to smoke a cigarette. I wonder how the tree has managed to survive. My head aches, but not as badly as I thought it would. I think about what I will do when I'm alone again and it frightens me. I'm amazed when my stomach growls, as if it has a voice in that decision.

I hear Moira laugh as she emerges from the building, a young man in a tan shirt and dark brown pants immediately behind her. He is studying her from the waist down, smiling in appreciation—following her with lolling tongue, like a young buck positioning himself to mount. He should be cautious. He might, like many bucks in Michigan, get mounted himself—in an entirely different way of course.

"Tin," she says as they approach. "This is Mike. He's going to check the truck, then we can go. Mike was nice enough to give us credit, even though we didn't fill the tank with gas. Cool, huh?"

Mike extends a dirty hand. I shake it. "Are you her dad, Tim?" Mike speaks in innocent sincerity, but I want to punch him anyway. He can't be twenty yet.

Moira laughs again. "No," she says, "he's my paramour."

Mike looks at her stupidly, like a dazed bull. "Huh?"

"My lover."

"Oh."

I look at her and she winks, provocatively. I feel my cheeks burn. Mike is obviously embarrassed. "Sorry dude," he says to me as he opens the back of the U-Haul for his inspection. His demeanor has suddenly taken on a much more professional air. He begins checking things off on a form attached to the clipboard. Moira seems to be enjoying the discomfiture her beauty and boldness has caused both of us. I feel like a toy, a child's plaything. It's not something I enjoy.

Moira wanders off as Mike closes the sliding door and moves around to the cab. When he's finished, he hands me a half-pack of Basics. "You must've left these, Tim," he says.

"It's Tin, like the metal."

"Oh."

He tears off a copy of the inspection form. "Everything's cool," he says. "You're all set." I want to tell him to turn his hat around. Only catchers wear their hats with the bill in the back.

Moira is by the Lumina, waiting for me. His eyes are on her. "You're really lucky, man," he says as he crawls into the cab and starts the truck. He has no clue. The roar of the engine prevents any real response.

As I approach her, Moira throws me the keys. "You drive," she says, the impish smile still partially visible. She has enjoyed her machinations.

We pull back onto the main drag in silence, except for the hum from the air conditioner that is wheezing asthmatically. The traffic is crawling.

"Why did you say that?"

She looks at me with wide eyes that have their analogue somewhere in the soul's code. "Say what?"

"That I was your boyfriend."

"I didn't. I said you were my lover." She waves one lithesome arm as if she were brushing away my concerns like an unwelcome fly. "Did it make you uncomfortable?"

"Yes, you know it did."

"Why?"

"I'm too old to be…compatible."

"In what way?"

"What do you mean 'in what way'?"

"Cultural incompatibility, intellectual incompatibility, physical incompatibility…"

"All of the above."

"That's rather biased of you."

"I know my limitations."

"And you think you know mine."

"Yes."

"Look, I didn't say I *wanted* you for a lover, I was just having a little fun."

"Good."

"Okay."

"Okay."

We sit in silence for a few minutes. The air conditioner is fighting a losing battle with the oven-like heat. Moira's long legs glisten with moisture.

"How old *are* you?" she says.

"Thirty."

"As of today."

"Yes."

"No way."

"What?"

"You look older than *that*."

"Thanks."

"It wasn't meant as an insult. I think you're lying anyway."

"Why would I lie?"

"To impress me."

"And why would I want to do that?"

"Because you're attracted to me."

"I'm not into pedophilia."

"Very cute. Let me see your wallet."

"What? Why?"

"I want to know if you're telling the truth."

I hand it over, anxious to prove myself, although why I should suddenly care about vindication is beyond me. She unfolds it, extracts my license."

"You *are* thirty," she says.

"Yes." I savor my triumph.

"Why didn't you tell me earlier that today was your birthday?"

"I really didn't have much of a chance before Sweeney spilled the beans."

She puts the license back and hands the wallet to me. "Why do you hate your life so much?"

The question hangs in the fetid air between us. It drifts and settles in the trenches of my misery like poison gas. I want to tell her that I don't hate my life, nor do I necessarily crave death, I just can't tell the difference anymore and death seems like it might be less taxing.

We are finally clear of the inner-city traffic and the road opens wider. We are heading straight uphill. I fumble for a cigarette from the pack that Mike rescued for me. There is a white piece of paper tucked in the cellophane. I can't remember what it's there for.

"Are you going to tell me?"

"No."

"Your wife was a beautiful woman. I remember her. It was terrible the way she died."

At the summit of the hill is an overlook, a brief exit from the two-lane that affords a panoramic view of the lake for shutterbugs. It's deserted. I slow down and pull off, killing the engine. I get out of the Lumina and slam the door.

She is right behind me.

"Wait," she shouts, "wait a minute will you? What're you doing?"

"You take the car and go home. I'll find my own way."

"Look, I'm sorry," she says. I feel her hand on my shoulder. I step away. "I didn't mean to upset you."

I turn to look at her. Seeing her face diminishes my anger considerably. It's the only time since I first saw her last night that she seems unsure of herself. "What *did* you mean to do?"

"I don't know. Maybe find a way to keep you alive."

"And you figured that chatting about Wendy's murder might cheer me up?"

"They say that if you confront—"

"And who the hell are *they?*"

"My psych book says—"

"Lovely. The little girl has taken a course in high school psychology and now she's prepared to straighten me out."

Her sympathetic expression disappears, replaced by glowering anger. Her dark eyes have become malevolent. I expected as much, even hoped for it, but I'm not prepared for what happens next. She slaps me, hard, across the left side of my face. It's a vicious, stinging, roundhouse blow that makes me totter backwards a couple of steps and shuts out the sound in my left ear.

"I'm *not* a little girl, you self-righteous bastard!" she shouts. "I'm not stupid either! Go ahead and kill yourself. I'm going home." She marches to the car, starts it, and pulls away, spraying gravel in her wake. Just that suddenly, I'm alone.

I feel a tickling sensation running down the edge of my jaw. I assume it's sweat. I brush it with my hand and it comes away red. My ear is bleeding.

I sit down on the guardrail that's meant to prevent little kids from falling over the ledge a short distance away, a cliff that plummets a hundred feet or more to the rocky shoreline below. The rail isn't much of an impediment to serious attempts at self-destruction. I think this must be the only place on the Lake Michigan shoreline that isn't flat and sandy. It is precipitous fate to have wandered onto such a precipice.

I light a cigarette and squint against the dazzling blue of the lake. It would be a simple thing to just take a few steps and jump, but my mind is different now. I don't know why. I listen carefully for voices, but I can't hear any. I'm thinking maybe the ghosts must've stayed in the truck, or it's my damaged ear.

I'm missing Moira. She was right, I *am* attracted to her, but where would it lead? She's just a kid. Sweeney would hate me. Besides, she's gone. I've ruined it and I would have ruined her, as I've ruined everyone. How could I explain that to her?

I don't feel like killing myself anymore, at least not in this place. Is it fear? I never did like heights, never could watch *Vertigo* all the way through. Still, I think it has more to do with this child than anything else. It felt good for someone to do *me* violence for a change.

I decide to hitchhike back to the cabin, pick up a fifth of Jim or Jack at the Lakeside Grocery and Bait on the way, and drink myself into the next decision. There's always the rowboat.

After several vehicles have passed me by, mostly mini-vans filled with kids or ATV's hauling campers, I begin to think it might be wiser to walk back into Traverse City and rent a car. It can't be more than a couple of miles. I cross the road to the opposite shoulder and begin moving in the direction my life has generally taken—downhill. The heat is terrible. My stomach is rumbling and my ear aches. I wish I had something to drink. My tongue feels like dried leather.

In spite of my physical discomfort, the girl dominates my thoughts. I am, I notice, for the first time in quite awhile, living in the present—even thinking ahead. The ghosts are still absent although, since Moira is gone, I suspect they'll return soon. I wonder what Sweeney will say when his daughter arrives back at Loon Lake without me. I wonder what she will tell him—probably the truth.

I picture her face clearly. She is exceptionally beautiful. No doubt she's used to the attentions of males, maybe women too. Her eyes are so expressive, so perfectly placed. Her mouth is equally fascinating. It is full and wide, almost excessive. Ah, the mouth, the locus of life. Through it travel breath and food and speech. When lovers first couple, it is there. Their lips touch, they open to receive each other's tongues—the thrilling desire to consume one another. I think about what it would be like to put my mouth on hers, to *stop up the passage to remorse,* to make its purposes my own. I fancy her mouth as even more than that; *os uteri,* the mouth as vulva. What a sweet thing it would be to have her kneel before me…such are the thoughts of a pastor's son.

I will leave the lake when I get back—or become a part of it. I will leave her to Graham or Spam or whatever his name is. Is it possible to hate someone you've never met?

I want to see her once more before I go though, just to tell her that she gave me another day and something else to think about besides death and the dead. I want to let her know that I'm not angry with her. I think she cares about me and I think that that was at the heart of her vexation. Why she should be concerned about my life is beyond me. She doesn't know me at all.

I stretch my memory to find a picture of her before this day. I do manage to form the image of a chubby little girl, toddling beside the Sweeney cabin. She must have been what, three or so when her mother died? But there is another snapshot somewhere in that foggy album of my brain. It is the portrait of a precocious, thinned out, nine or ten-year-old, asking Wendy embarrassing questions on her first visit to the lake, including which brother she belonged to. Wendy had smiled and answered 'Satchel.' Moira, I remember, had responded with 'good'. I wonder why.

A car pulls onto the shoulder behind me. With an enormous sense of relief, I turn to face my deliverer. It is Moira. I can see through the sun-reflecting windshield that she is still angry. We just stare at each other for a few minutes. It's clear that she has no intention of getting out. I know that if I turn away and walk on, she won't follow. The sun vanishes behind a cloud for a moment and I can see that there is hope in her face too.

I take a few steps forward. She slides across the seat to the passenger side. It's as far as she will go. I move to the door. It's locked. She hits the release button and I get in.

We sit there in silence for some time, listening to the parking lights click on and off and the gasping of the air conditioner. I feel her dark eyes on me.

"I'm hungry," she says. "Would you like to get something to eat?"

"Where?"

"There's an inn back up the road about five miles. I turned around in their parking lot."

"Can I get a drink?"

"I think so, yes."

"Okay."

I make a quick U-turn. Some idiot half a mile away honks at me as if I had endangered him somehow. People don't want you to break the law, even if it makes sense to. She gets out her cell phone. "I'm going to call Sweeney, let him know we'll be a bit later."

"Hey Sweeney," she says. "Tin and I are going to stop and get something to eat. Just didn't want you to worry. What? It's called the Stoppe Inn I think, just south of Traverse City. I don't know, Sweeney, what difference does it make? I'm a big girl. Tin's been a perfect gentleman." She glances at me with those dark eyes and winks. "It's on the main drag. You okay? You sound a little tired. I don't know, coupla hours probably. Okay? Don't worry. I got a birthday present for you when we get back. Okay. See ya." She flips the phone shut and puts it back in her purse.

"I didn't think you'd come back." I say.

"No?"

"No."

"Neither did I."

The inn is a beautiful old place. It's Cape Codish—white clapboard exterior with green shutters that match the weathered shingles. Gull guano spots the roof like measles, but somehow adds to the charm. The place is called The Stoppe Inn—terrible name, we agree, for such quaintness. In the East, it would bear a more romantic moniker, like The Cliffton Arms or Queensbury Heights or Knoll Cottage. America, particularly the Midwest, has honored utilitarianism for so long that it's forgotten romance. That's why Hemingway is so venerated here.

A waiter conducts us through the dark, air-conditioned main dining room, which is empty, to a large veranda outside, where people dressed like us can be kept away from the formal diners who will be arriving soon. Class does exist here after all.

I order a Scotch on the rocks, Moira a diet coke.

"You don't want something stronger?" I ask her this after the waiter leaves.

"I wouldn't mind," she answers, "but the state of Michigan frowns on it."

She's too young to drink legally. I'd forgotten. "Sorry." What am I doing?

"It's okay." She takes her napkin and dips it in her glass of water. "Here," she says, offering it to me. "You have some dirt or something on the side of your face."

"Left or right?"

"Left."

I use it. When I'm through, there's a reddish tint on the napkin.

"It's blood," she says. "You're bleeding."

I'd forgotten that too.

"Did you cut yourself?" She looks alarmed.

"I'm okay, probably a mosquito bite or something."

She rises resolutely from her chair and strides around to my side of the glass table. She puts her hands on my head as if she were examining a cantaloupe and tilts it to get a better look. "My God," she says, "it's coming from your ear. Your ear is full of blood. Is that where I hit you? God, Tin, I'm so sorry. I didn't think I'd hit you that hard."

"I'm okay, please quit fussing and sit down."

She takes the napkin from me and begins daubing. She leans over. I feel her breath on my ear and the back of my neck. I'm hoping she doesn't notice the goose bumps and other things she's raising. At last she returns to her side of the table and sits. She examines the bloody napkin. "I really hurt you."

"I'm fine."

"Your hearing's damaged."

"Nonsense."

"I just whispered in your ear and you didn't hear me."

"How do you know I didn't?"

"Because you didn't react."

"Why should I?"

"I told you I wanted you to kiss me."

"No you didn't."

"You'll never know, will you?" The dark eyes bore into me. She can tell, I think, that I'm looking at her mouth and imagining. "I want you to get that checked. I feel terrible, but you really pissed me off."

"I have that affect on people."

She smiles. The waiter wordlessly sets our drinks in front of us, along with menus, then shuffles away.

"I had it coming," I tell her.

"Yes, you did." That wonderful mouth broadens again and I can't help smiling too. "But I didn't want to hurt you."

"Yes, you did."

She laughs. It's beautiful. It's not like Wendy's laugh though, and I find that strangely disturbing. I glance around, but there's no one else there. "What would Graham think of all this?"

"Of what?"

"Of you saying that you were my lover and whispering such things in my ear."

"Graham is Sweeney's attempt to interfere in my life. He's not my choice. Besides, there's no harm done when you turn a deaf ear."

"Maybe. You'll never know will you?"

She grins and sucks on an ice cube. "Touché." I'm utterly enthralled.

"Where is your brother now?" She says it nonchalantly, as if she were asking directions to the restroom. She's going to keep probing. I have to decide if I'm willing to pay this price for her company or leave. "I don't know."

"He hasn't tried to contact you?"

"No."

"Not even when your father died?"

"No."

"The police, they don't have any leads?"

"No. Listen, why do you insist on talking about my family?" I try to keep my voice even though I'm shivering with something like rage. Except for her voluptuous mouth and midnight eyes and the hope that her flirtations mean more than simple vanity, the leaky boat on Loon Lake is beginning to have its attractions again.

"You were going to kill yourself last night," she says, "and I don't want you to die. I think you need to face it."

"Face what?"

"All of it. You tell me."

"I have faced it."

"Then it shouldn't be so hard to tell me about it. I want to know."

"Why?"

She hesitates. The waiter is coming back. We both order something, though we haven't really studied the menu. When you're just trying to stay alive, you become less selective. A starving man doesn't consider the consequences of cholesterol or the whimsical aroma of his wine. At last the waiter goes away, rather offended, I think, by our apathy.

"I want to know," she whispers, "because...well, I'm attracted to you."

I want very much to tell her I feel the same way, but I can't. I know how naive teenaged infatuation can be—and how transient. "You're very young. What? Eighteen?"

"Implying that I don't know what I'm doing?"

"That's right."

"You're drinking yourself senseless and contemplating suicide and I don't know what *I'm* doing?"

I don't respond. How can I?"

"Listen," she says. "Let me find out if I know what I'm doing. Tell me why you want to die."

I think about it. I haven't ever made a list. "Maybe it's just because there are more options."

"What?"

"There are more ways to die than to live."

She gives me a look that makes me want to protect my undamaged ear. I decide to concede. Concession has always been my strong suit anyway and sometimes you get so sick you just have to vomit, as unpleasant as it is.

"All right, I'll tell you why I'm a bit depressed. My mother, father, brother and wife are all gone because of me. When I was ten, my mother wanted me to go to town with her for groceries. We were up here, at the cabin. Dad and Satchel, as always, were playing catch. She was tired, she said, and needed some company. I was her darling boy. Satchel was Dad's. I never liked the arrangement. I think that's why I told her 'no'. Besides, I was busy trying to capture minnows for bait. She fell asleep and drove head-on into another car. She was cut in half by the engine as it came through the dashboard. A woman and her two little kids, the ones in the other car, died too. A decade later, I stole my brother's girlfriend and married her. Satchel was one of the most promising pitchers in major league history. He gave it up and wasted away, until he decided to get back at me by murdering my wife. My father, the pastor who always preached about the sanctity of life, killed himself over it all. I think I might be feeling a bit guilty, what do you think, Doc? That direct enough for you?"

I expect her to lash out at me, but she says nothing for a few minutes. The shadows of late afternoon and the breeze off the lake are beginning to have their affect on the searing heat. Somewhere in the distance, a freighter bellows. The maitre'd is seating another couple nearby. A solitary gull lands on the handrail of the veranda, apparently searching for scraps. The pitiful mendicant has made a poor landing. He's perched immediately adjacent to a sign that cautions the Stoppe Inn patrons not to feed him. My mother would have fed him anyway.

"I call him Sweeney for a reason you know."

Moira's voice draws me back.

"What?"

"Sweeney. He's not my father."

"What're you talking about?"

"You asked me earlier why I call him Sweeney. I'm telling you. It's because he's not my father." Her dark eyes moisten, but she maintains her poise. It's the first time I've seen her vulnerable.

"You're adopted then?"

She smiles, broadening her lovely mouth into a representation of sad irony. It's difficult for her, what she's telling me. She's giving me something. I'm not sure I want her to continue. Her black eyes refuse to let mine go.

"No, Mary Sweeney carried me for nine months. She was my mother."

Mary had blue eyes. So does Sweeney.

The waiter returns with our food. More people stop in. There are some in the interior dining area now, dressed in suits and long dresses. Piano music can be heard as waiters open and close the door that leads inside. Moira has ordered some kind of fish that's lying, decapitated, on a board. It's steaming and sprinkled with sliced almonds. She pokes at it with her fork as if to determine if it's really dead. My prime rib swims in its own blood as if it were just torn from some living thing. Rare means rare at the Stoppe Inn. The waiter has brought the entrée with our salads—a gastronomic faux pas in Grand Rapids. When he's gone, I ask the inevitable: "Who *is* your father then?"

"I don't know." She stares hard at me. I can see she will demand some return on her investment. "My mother never had the chance to tell me anything. Five years or so after she died, I think I was seven or eight, Sweeney told me that he wasn't my biological father. He said it was okay to call him papa anyway, perhaps because he'd come to terms with my mother's betrayal. I don't know. He continued to be 'papa' to me until several years later, when I was a teenager."

"He could've waited until you were older to tell you that, or never told you at all. It would seem to have been the kinder thing to do."

"Sweeney never let compassion interfere with directness."

"That's probably why he and my father were such good friends. Who is your *real* father then?"

"I told you, I don't know."

"Hiram never told you?"

"He doesn't know either."

"You believe that?"

"Yes."

"You ever wonder about it?"

"All the time."

She keeps prodding the fish as I am prodding her. It's all torn apart. I don't think she's tasted it yet. Her salad is gone, but I don't remember her taking a single bite. I'm surprised to see that my prime rib is nothing more than a couple of scraps of fat. I wonder if that gull is shiftier than I originally suspected or if I'm just completely captivated by Moira Sweeney. The sun is gold over the lake, turning the sky hundreds of shades of orange and red. I think that sunsets must have a great deal to do with property value on the coast of west Michigan.

Something else occurs to me. Moira has answered all my questions with uncomfortable honesty. She's revealed something intensely personal. She's opened herself to me as surely as if she was lying on my bed with her legs spread. Love can be unrequited, but never trust. Reciprocity is required.

Mary Sweeney! That kind and loving second mother to me, my own mother's close friend—guilty of a secret affair, an illicit love. I wouldn't have thought that shy, sweet lady capable of such intrigue. Hiram Sweeney, the cuckolded husband, the gentle grinder, Dad's fishing buddy. He remained devoted to Mary and no one could be more paternal. I remember the pride with which he told me about Moira's high school honors (was that only yesterday?). I think Pastor Balune's God is something like Sweeney—sexless, at once omnipotent and impotent, sadly gazing down at all the bastards he's cared for who recognize his existence, even his authority, but cannot rightly call him 'Dad'.

Moira is studying me. The waiter returns. I order another scotch. She orders some gooey dessert with cinnamon ice cream. After he clears away the dishes, she asks me for a cigarette. I give her one.

She lights it, inhales deeply once, and then puts it out. She places her elbows on the table, leans forward, opens that incredible mouth and says softly: "Now, tell me about Satchel."

Chapter five

He was my father's great hope. It was in him that he placed his faith, at least as far as baseball went. Even as a Little Leaguer, Satchel showed enormous promise. Dad worked with both of us, of course, from the time we could walk. I say 'worked' because with our father, baseball was much too important to ever be 'played'. The game was second only to God; at least I think God was first. Our training was viewed not as a game, but as preparation for a career. It was work for me. For Satchel, it was natural.

"I was the second son in birth order and in baseball expectation. As we grew older, there was never any doubt among the three of us as to who was the best hitter, the best pitcher, the best fielder, the best at every aspect of Doubleday's invention. No, I take that back. I knew baseball's *history* better than Satchel, better even than Dad. I could tell you Don Drysdale's ERA for any given year, Al Kaline's career stats, the scores of every one of Denny McClain's thirty-one wins. I was a walking baseball almanac and I had the best card collection in the state of Michigan.

"But Satchel was, as I said, the Natural. Like his namesake, he chose pitching, primarily, I think, because pitchers were more important than any of the other eight players on the field. A coach will always say that all positions are crucial, but nobody focuses their attention on the rightfielder. It's the duel that everyone comes to watch, the great test of will between pitcher and batter that's the heart of the game—and batters are only center stage for three strikes.

"Anyway, that's about all any batter ever saw from Satch when he first started playing organized ball. In Little League, there wasn't a kid his age that could even foul off one of his fastballs. In his debut, a seven-inning game, he threw sixty-three strikes and no balls. That first year in organized ball, he pitched eight no-hitters and three perfect games in an eight-game season. The remarkable thing was that he had phenomenal control, even at age nine, probably a result of all those games of catch with Dad, the distance between them carefully measured out to match mound to home plate. He could place the ball precisely in the catcher's mitt. If he threw the occasional ball instead of a strike, it was usually either the catcher's inability to handle his speed or the batter's older brother was the umpire. This I know from my father, since I was too young to remember it myself.

"In high school, his fastball was timed by a gun for the first time—eighty-seven miles an hour. He was a varsity starter as a freshman and he didn't lose a game in four years. How does one compete against that? We were six years apart in age, but talent separated us by light years. I became a starter, finally, in my senior year and we won the league championship when I bloop-singled in the winning run. Dad wasn't there to see it. He was following Satch's career.

"My brother went directly to the minors, Triple A Ball, out of high school. There, he was throwing in the nineties and had developed a nasty slider and deceptive curve ball, still with his incredible control. It was there that he lost his first game ever—on a two-hitter, 1-0, but losses were few and far between. He was probably the best southpaw prospect in the country."

"Southpaw?"

"Lefthander. Satch is a lefty."

"Oh."

"I quit playing after high school because I was never going anywhere with it. I decided, instead, to be a teacher. I remember being terribly disappointed when Dad said he thought that that was a good idea.

"Satchel met Wendy in Chicago. She was in a bar with some friends where Satchel and his buddies were celebrating his shutout over the Peoria Chiefs of the Midwest League. His teammates had convinced him to come with them to Chicago to eat and drink at Joey Buona's, one of the most popular nightspots in downtown Chicago. Wendy didn't know anything about baseball and was unimpressed by his growing reputation. She thought, she told me later, that he looked unhappy.

"They went out that night and Satchel, whose experience with women was limited to a prom date with a girl named (believe it or not) Merry Krismas, fell helplessly in love. Everyone fell in love with Wendy of course, but Satch surrendered his life to her.

"A few days later, while tossing the ball around in warm-ups, something snapped in Satch's shoulder. The doctors said it was tendonitis and he would get over it quickly, but Satch wasn't the same after that. His fastball became average, his control faltered. He began losing—regularly.

"He saw Wendy every couple of weeks, as much as he could, until he was sold to the West Michigan Whitecaps in Grand Rapids. Before he came back to Michigan, he bought her a diamond. She refused it. His ensuing depression contributed to the diminishment of his talent.

"Dad quit going to Satch's games. He couldn't take it. He said it was like being accustomed to seeing Marlon Brando in films like *On the Waterfront* and *The Godfather,* then watching him play Superman's father.

"Satch struggled like that for five years. He kept trying to get his stuff back, to get Wendy back. Neither came.

"I tried to help my brother. We worked all through the late fall and winter trying to get his arm back in shape, along with his psyche. The fastball was gone, but we kept working on his curveball and he even developed a knuckler. It all began to work. He became enthusiastic again.

"In the third game of the Whitecap's season, he came out of the bullpen to record three shutout innings and a save against Battle Creek. A week later, he got his first start in over two years and shut out the Lansing Lugnuts on a four-hitter. The following season, after another winter of therapy on the arm and long workouts with me at the high school gym, Satch returned to Triple-A ball. He was back on the mound and Dad was back in the stands.

"In the summer of 1996, Satch was in Chicago when he got the news that he'd been waiting for all his life. He'd finally been called up to the majors. I think he was twenty-six, maybe twenty-seven by then—getting old for a ballplayer. He also ran into Wendy, who was still unattached. She agreed to date him again. Everything was going right. In July, the weekend before he was to report to the Tigers in Detroit, he once again asked Wendy to accept the ring that he had never returned. She said yes, and the two of them made the fatal visit to our cabin on Loon Lake.

"Although Satch had spoken of her many times, I wasn't prepared for Wendy. My brother often exaggerated, but his praise of her beauty was nothing short of understatement. How does one hyperbolize perfection?

"There was an immediate attraction between Wendy and me, despite the fact that she was three years older than me. We both struggled to suppress and conceal this mutual affinity. There was little doubt that we would fail at both. I prayed to God just as fervently as the lowliest Hebrew slave in Egypt to be released from my bondage, but the Almighty knows insincerity when He hears it, I think. I knew that, when it came to it, I would relinquish peace, honor and family for this woman, just as surely as Adam, Samson and Solomon had for theirs.

"Circumstance might still have rescued us, but God or Fate or the Devil or whoever controls such things made a phone call to Satch, ordering him to report to the Tigers a week early. One of their starters had taken a line drive right between the eyes and would be out of action for a long time with a bad concussion. Satch might start a game as early as the next day or two. Dad was feverishly excited and agreed to drive him to Detroit, arranging for the associate pastor to give the next morning's sermon. I suggested that I do the driving but Wendy had to be back in Chicago early Monday morning and either someone would have to take her or she'd have to catch a bus. My brother begged me to stay at the cabin that Saturday night with Wendy and drive her home the next day, opening me to my betrayal.

"Satch and Dad left that afternoon and by evening, Wendy and I had connected in every imaginable way that word can be interpreted. I don't know how it happened, I don't even remember much about what we said to one another. I don't know who made the first move. It was the happiest night of my life.

"On Sunday, we talked throughout the day about what had happened to us. Wendy had no better understanding of it than I did. I asked her when we should leave for Chicago. Her response was to call in at her office and request a couple of vacation days. I knew then that what had occurred between us was not entirely spontaneous. 'I don't know what's going to happen,' she said, 'I just want to be alone with you, here, for as long as I can.'

"We went swimming in the lake and hiked the back trails in the wilder area across the water. We ate well and often. She lay in the sun in her yellow bikini in the Adirondack chaise while I read Shelley and Keats to her from the shadows of the nearby birch. We talked incessantly, trying to find out as much about each other as our little time together would allow."

"How long was it before you slept together?" I had almost, in the drumming of my narrative, forgotten that Moira was there.

"What kind of question is that?"

"Crass and uncalled for."

"Then why ask it?"

"Because I want to know."

"About three or four hours after Dad and Satch left."

"Some people would call Wendy a slut."

"You?"

"No."

"Why?"

"Because you can't help who you love or how long it takes to develop." She brushes a dark strand of hair away from her eyes. "Besides, I can understand why she would want you."

"Well, for all that, there were tears and guilt and confusion when it was over."

"But you did it again."

"Yes. I had about as much control over myself as a thirteen-year-old alone in the bathroom with a copy of *Playboy.*"

"How long were you together that time?"

"We had Sunday and Monday. On Tuesday morning we got in my car and drove to Detroit." Suddenly, one of those missing photos found its way back into that soggy album I call my brain. "My God."

"What?"

"Wendy waved to you. I just remembered. Where did that come from? You were what, ten?"

"What year?"

"Let's see…1996."

"Nine."

"God you're young."

"Cut the personal comments and tell me."

"You had asked her which of us she was with and she had told you 'Satch'. That was on the first day Wendy was there, before Satch and Dad left for Detroit. This second time you were just outside your cabin, sitting on the wood pile as we were preparing to leave for Detroit. You didn't say anything and you waved to us as we were leaving, but you had this impish smile on your face that was, at the same time, a kind of pout. Wendy commented on it. She said it was as if you knew that Satchel wasn't the favored one anymore. Do you remember?"

She shakes her head back and forth, negatively.

"Well, I don't see why you should. The significance of the

moment was all on my side of the driveway. Anyway, we drove straight to the downtown hotel in Detroit near the Renaissance Center where Satchel had told us he would be staying when he called to check on Wendy on Sunday and wish her a safe trip back to Chicago. I'd scouted the newspapers and I knew the Tigers had a home game that evening, under the lights. Since it was early afternoon yet, it seemed reasonable to assume that Satch would be at the hotel. He was.

"He was surprised, especially to see both of us. He'd been trying, he said, to reach Wendy at her apartment in Chicago and at her office. Her employer had told him that she'd called to ask for vacation time. He assumed that we'd come to watch him play. He was scheduled to make his first major-league start that night. When he looked at Wendy, his face radiated a pride and satisfaction that I had never seen on him before, even with all his accomplishments in baseball. It made me want to crawl under a rock somewhere and die."

Moira's eyes were full of such intense sympathy, that it frightened me to think that I was telling her about something that really happened. "How did you break it to him?"

"I didn't. Wendy gave him a sisterly kiss. I remember, that puzzled him. Then she sat down with him on the edge of the bed and began to tell him. She tried to be gentle, diplomatic, sympathetic, but I could see the rage boiling in him. Something went dead in his eyes, and something else came alive. It was a more frightening and horrific change than Stevenson's gentle doctor could ever imagine. It was, I think, the hasty evolution of a different kind of monster."

"What did he say to you?"

"To me? Nothing. I remember, though, that his eyes were fastened on me throughout her crushing explanation. There was a reptilian cold in them that grew with each word. It terrified me. He listened without moving. There was no rage, no throwing of furniture, no tears. There was just that frigid stare. He didn't even glance at Wendy as she described her love for me and mine for her. He was coiled and tense, like a cobra that refuses to move from the path of an elephant. On his face was the knowledge that life was ending for the three of us and that death—without the simple justifications of food, or power, or even mating rights—would be the only victor.

"When Wendy finally stopped talking, his silence became insufferable. She tried to embrace him. He stood up to escape it and went to the window."

"He didn't say anything to you, even then?"

"He only asked me if it was true, but he knew it was. He could see my shame. I only said 'yes'. With his back to us, at the window, he said good-bye—just that, nothing else. I lost my brother that quickly.

"We left the room, Wendy in tears. We went back to the cabin at Loon Lake. We drowned our guilt in lovemaking. Dad called. Satchel had disappeared. He'd simply vanished. Apparently he'd said nothing to Dad about our visit, although Dad was staying in the same hotel in the room right next to Satch's. My poor father was at the ballpark trying to calm Tiger management. He asked me if I had any idea why Satch would just take off. I told him. I don't remember all that he said. Pastors can be verbose, and my father was no exception, particularly when it came to sin. I remember the word 'Judas' was used a number of times.

"In the morning, I drove Wendy back to Chicago and stayed with her there until she could quit her job and pack her things. We were there about a month. I met her sister, Kelly, and her parents. Wendy agreed to move to my place in Grand Rapids and we planned to be married. Satch was gone and he would stay gone. It was all over the radio."

"He never contacted you again?"

"Not me, no. Our father would see him one more time. Almost a year after Satchel had disappeared, Dad got a phone call from the Los Angeles Police Department. Satch had been arrested at Dodger Stadium when he'd crawled out of the stands over the dugout and onto the field in an attempt to 'take the mound' from the Dodger pitcher. He was looped on cocaine. They'd found my mother's ten-year-old obituary from the Grand Rapids Press in his wallet and managed to track my father down through the Lutheran Church Worker's website, since he was mentioned in the clipping as a Lutheran pastor. Dad flew to LA and bailed Satch out of jail. It was his grandest error as a father. He got his prodigal cleaned up, bought him new clothes and a meal, and begged him to come home. When Satch asked about Wendy, Dad told him we'd gotten married. Satch responded by upending the table in the restaurant where they were eating, spilling food and dishes all over the floor. Then he disappeared into the streets again. Dad cried when he told us. Wendy and I, wallowing in our guilt, tried to comfort him."

Moira continues to stare at me with those black eyes. There were no tears. "Did you ever think," she says, "that it might have been your brother's fault? That he might be responsible for his own actions?"

"In any tragedy," I tell her, resorting to my professorial persona, "the protagonist is helped to his ruin by outside forces. Macbeth had the witches and Lady Macbeth. Othello had Iago. Hamlet had the Ghost. But there was, in each case, that fatal weakness of character that was the ultimate cause of ruin. There was something in Satch that caused him to destroy himself—I tried to argue that for Wendy and for Dad. I wanted to believe it, but in truth I knew that I would have acted the same had it been me who'd lost her. Satch would test that supposition, of course."

Moira looks away. The waiter comes. She asks for another Diet Coke. I order a double scotch. "What happened after that?" she says.

"We went on trying to live. Wendy got hired as the events coordinator in Grand Rapids and we settled down to our jobs and culpable happiness. Dad continued his preaching and ministering. We heard nothing of Satch for over a year, which led us to believe that he had cleaned himself up to avoid any further entanglements with the law—he was wanted for jumping bail, among other things. Either that, or he was dead.

"Dad changed. The death of our mother had diminished him, but the loss of his athletically brilliant son made him virtually disappear. After that initial phone conversation, he never issued another

word of recrimination against Wendy or me, but his naturally ebul-
lient and optimistic personality melted away. This strong, irksomely
confident man became unsure of himself and his God. Publicly, he
continued his ministerial duties. Privately, he began to question
everything he'd spent his life avowing. It was a terrible thing to watch
him come apart.

"Wendy and I spent three years of our life together and thousands of dollars trying to locate my brother. I began to believe that
his reclamation might be our only hope for Dad's, but Satchel had
vanished utterly. Even now, I don't know how he's been able to
conceal himself so successfully. He kept moving. I know that. Our
private investigator, a guy named Connor, had followed him from
California to Taos, New Mexico then Fort Worth, Texas; Biloxi, Mis-
sissippi; Mobile, Alabama; Memphis, then Chicago. But according
to Connor, Satch was always a week or two ahead of him. We heard
nothing about him for over a year again.

"I should have recognized that he was working his way east and
north—to me, but many of the reports were never adequately veri-
fied and were often months apart. Time and distance, the desire to
be free of guilt, and the hope that Satch was through hating us, kept
us from ever considering what would actually happen."

"You don't have to go on if you don't want to," Moira says. I
think she can read something that I'm not aware I'm writing.

"It happened in October of 2001. Wendy was alone that night.
She had a concert to oversee at DeVos Hall and I had gone to the
lake with Dad to close up the cabin for the winter. She was supposed
to join us the following morning.

"Of course the whole country was occupied with the terror-
ist attacks of nine-eleven and the featured name in the media was
Osama Bin Laden. None of that, or our own guilt, or my father's
obvious decline, kept Wendy and me from our happiness. Joy is a
terribly selfish thing. In the five years since I'd met her, Wendy had
managed to erase my conscience—not through any selfish manipu-
lation you understand, but simply because I couldn't worry about
what price I had to pay to have her. Her mere presence erased my

ignominy. I did continue to feel guilty over Satch, but there was no real remorse. I wasn't seeking absolution or even forgiveness when I talked to God about what I'd done. I wouldn't have given Wendy up for anything, even paradise. I was willing to suffer my soul's damnation to keep her, and both God and I knew it. What does one pray for then? Understanding? Sympathy? Exception? Exemption? If God is Missouri Synod Lutheran, I knew I didn't have a prayer.

"I didn't enjoy going to church. Wendy and I went mostly to be there for Dad and on the outside chance that God might be less parochial than I'd been taught."

Moira laughs. It's good to hear. I'm rambling, trying to avoid what I have to say.

"I'm not sure which Scriptural directives Wendy and I had broken anyway. As far as I could tell, there were no clear commandments about stealing a brother's fiancée. But there's all kinds of stuff about coveting and betrayal and falsehood and fornication and being a brother's keeper that a case for damning Tinker Balune could easily be made.

"I still couldn't help thinking though, that the condemnation of unrepentant sinners might just be overcome by the same kind of pure love that Wendy and I had for one another. In spite of what I said earlier, at this point I think I would have forgiven her anything—certainly disobedience, probably even betrayal. That's where the Old Testament God—and Satchel's—love differed from mine. Theirs were divinely jealous, possessive and concerned with self. Mine was haplessly human."

Moira sighs and mixes the ice in her glass with a little red straw. I can't tell what she's thinking, but I must be hallucinating because the look on her face seems to be something akin to admiration. It's beginning to get dark. The waiter comes and lights a candle at our table.

"When Wendy didn't show up at the lake on Saturday, I called our house in Grand Rapids. I got the cheerful message she'd recorded after we'd installed the new phone. 'Hi, this is the Balunes, Wendy and Tin. We're not available. Leave a message at the beep.' She had wanted to say that we couldn't come to the phone because we were probably fooling around in the bedroom, but it wouldn't have been appropriate for her clients or my students to hear, though considerably more honest.

"I tried her cell phone. Because of her occupation, she was never separated from it. No response. I waited a couple of hours, tried again. By this time it was late afternoon. In all the time we'd been together, Wendy had never failed to communicate with me, especially if she was going to be late. I began to worry.

"At about four, I decided to take a shower. Dad promised to man the phone. When I returned to the kitchen, he was just hanging it up. I was sure it'd been Wendy and I felt a short-lived sense of relief—until I saw my father's face. He'd gone dead pale. He told me that Myra Jenkins had called."

"Who's she?" Moira says. She's leaning across the table as if she wants to better hear what I'm saying. I have lowered my voice to a whisper.

"She was one of the ladies from my father's church in Grand Rapids."

"Why did she call?"

"Her son worked at the Burger King on Plainfield Avenue, near my house. He was a real baseball addict, maybe even as much as we were. The kid worked the Drive-Thru window. He told his mother he'd waited on Satchel Balune the day before. He'd said that Satchel had long hair and a beard, but he knew it was Satchel. He'd have recognized him if Satchel had been dressed in women's clothes. He used to idolize him, always pestering Satchel for his autograph at church and such things."

Moira is silent and begins drawing back as if to avoid what comes next.

"My father just stood there, dumbstruck, the phone still in his hand. My mother's clock, the one that looks like Felix the Cat, meowed. I think that's when I knew that Wendy was dead. It was time to go home."

"God!" Moira says.

"Dad and I got to the house just before dark. As we hurried through the front entrance, Dad tapped me on the shoulder and pointed to a family portrait, which hung on the vestibule wall. It was taken when Satch and I were kids, just before Mom died, just the four of us. Satchel's grinning face had been obliterated with a black, permanent marker.

"I remember calling out for Wendy and the daunting dread as I mumbled a prayer—a dying reliance on the God of my naïve youth. Neither answered.

"Dad tried to hold me there in the vestibule, fearing, perhaps, the death of our mutual faith should we venture on. I broke away. I ran to the living room. Lamps had been smashed. The large mirror over the sofa was shattered. It was as if he didn't want to be seen, or to see himself. The coffee table had been splintered, chairs had been upended. It was a scene of terrible rage, festering for years, finally released—the random destruction of lunacy. I remember the awful terror, the anxious horrific apprehension of my last moments of hope.

"I cried out for her again and again. I was surprised at the sound of my voice. All semblance of masculinity was gone. I was a bleating little lamb, desperate for mercy, unwilling to sacrifice my happiness at any altar. God had never had a more groveling sycophant.

"My baleful whining ended in the kitchen where Wendy lay in the center of the floor. She'd been dead, they told me later, for almost a day. That lurid, ghastly image of her, sprawled on the tile floor, whose color she'd chosen after an entire afternoon of deliberation, would be forever seared into my consciousness. It would, many times, be saturated with alcohol, occasionally blurred, but never gone."

"Oh, Tin I'm so—"

"Don't say anything. I'm telling you. Let me get through it."

"You don't have to—"

"Dad called 911 while I tried to bring her back, but everything I'd learned about CPR didn't apply to an established corpse. I prayed then. No one had ever been more fervent. If God could raise Lazarus, could raise Himself, I reasoned, then surely He could bring Wendy back. I'd been taught all my life that Jesus saves, but there, then, in that single macabre moment, He either couldn't help or He wouldn't, making Him too limited or too cruel or too selective or too concerned with His rules to be a father, divine or otherwise. Most human fathers would have taken pity on anyone in such a dismal, pathetic state. Had they the power, they would have changed what happened. I would have done it for a total stranger. How can a person believe in a God less compassionate than himself?

"And Wendy had died in the cruelest way. The coroner determined that she had been bludgeoned to death, but he never explained what was evident to me in my kitchen. Every major bone in Wendy's body, from the neck down, had been fractured or broken. Satchel had methodically crushed the humerus, radial and ulna bones of each arm. Both hips were splintered. The clavicle and sternum, ribs, femora, tibia—all shattered. But the skull, encasing the brain, protector of pain and misery, went untouched."

Moira is shaking her head. Her eyes are full of tears. Baron Masoch and the Marquis de Sade dance on my tongue. "His purpose, obviously, was for her to suffer. I wonder now, in my most lurid depravity, how long it took Wendy to die. I imagine my brother, his sanity gone, leering in wild-eyed fascination at her anguish, and giggling like some hideous demon each time another blow forced a scream or a plea for mercy from her lips. Sometimes…often, I wonder if she died cursing my name."

Moira reaches for my hand. I pull it back. "You wanted to hear this. Let me finish.

"We knew it was Satchel of course. His fingerprints were found, and he'd never been to my house before. The bloody murder weapon, left conspicuously on the tile floor by Wendy's body, was a special handcrafted ash baseball bat, my name burned into the wood, a gift to me from him for my seventeenth birthday. He'd made no effort to conceal his identity. He *wanted* me to know who had taken away my happiness, as I had taken his.

"Hate kept me alive. I spent all of my free time and extra money trying to hunt down Satchel. In the summer months I wandered around the country, following this lead then the next, that Connor

0

or the police or the FBI had uncovered, but Satchel had evaporated like the mist on Loon Lake at mid-morning. Two years ago, I gave up the search for him. My hate went away and, when it did, there was nothing left to fill the void. I tried to numb myself with whiskey and, at first, it worked. But that dulling, alcoholic haze became harder and harder to obtain as the ghosts kept coming back.

"Dad tried valiantly to counsel me, but I refused to listen to any more sermons about God, especially since they were given with such little conviction. Dad's dreams of Balune baseball immortality were gone, perhaps with any other hope of eternity. His wife was dead, his family in ruins. His God was silent. I took no part in comforting him. One drowning man can't save another. He lasted three years after Wendy's murder before he sealed off his garage, sat in his car, and let the carbon monoxide relieve him of the hypocrisy of his life.

"So here I am, on my thirtieth birthday, confiding my intimate history to a girl practically half my age and wondering why I'm still alive. My mother and father are dead because I ignored them. My wife is dead because I loved her. My brother is a fugitive killer for both of those reasons. You ask why I want to die? There you go. Death is just easier."

Chapter six

She is silent for a few minutes. The waiter comes and asks us if we're ready for our check. With the crowd increasing, he's anxious for our table. I order another whiskey to placate him and my other demons.

"I'm so sorry, Tin," she says as she watches me drink. "All of this must have been devastating for you."

There is so much empathy in that lovely young face that I almost feel a sense of guilt for evoking it. She reaches across the small table and places her hand over mine. There is something wonderfully soothing about that simple gesture. I think that perhaps it's the first time I've felt anything resembling comfort, since Wendy died, that I couldn't pour down my throat. "I've tried to deal with it, but..." I silence myself to avoid coming apart.

"You loved her very much."

There is something in the eyes, the expression, the way she cocks her head—something recognizable. Is it Wendy? "I did, yes."

There is a poignant silence between us for a few minutes. Her hand remains on mine, though it must be uncomfortable for her to stretch like that. Her bosom rests on the edge of the table. The setting sun strikes her silky, black hair. I want to touch it. I believe that now, in her vulnerable compassion, I *could* touch her. I could coax her.

She sits back, withdrawing her hand, perhaps sensing my unconscionable attraction.

"You knew my mother," she says, reminding me that I am not the only tragic figure in the world.

"Yes."

"What was she like?"

"You don't remember her?"

"I was three when she died."

I try to retrieve an image of Mary Sweeney. It's there, instantly.

"She was very kind, shy, beautiful. I remember that she spoke with a funny accent."

"Irish."

"Yes, it must have been, though I didn't recognize it at the time." Mary had been born in Ireland. Her brother still lives there, if I'm not mistaken. "I think I was about ten or so when my own mother died. Satch, of course, was sixteen. She practically adopted us. She doted on you, I remember that. She called you Baby Girl, all the time. 'We'll have lunch in a few minutes boys,' she used to say, 'but first I have to feed my Baby Girl.'"

Moira smiles, but her eyes are filled with tears. I realize that my own suffering has taken priority over everyone else's. I also begin to see that my memories of Mary Sweeney are not painful. I think, perhaps, it's because she was the only one I loved whose death I had no part in.

The waiter brings our check. It's clear that he's no longer waiting on us, but *for* us. He stands there while I get out my Mastercard; there's none of the customary pretense of doing something else while he waits. I tip him lavishly. He gives me a curt "thank you." I don't think he's impressed.

It feels good to stand up. How long have we been here? Probably two hours at least. A rather disgruntled-looking man in an ascot and his far-too-young companion take our table. The shouldering crowd offsets the air-conditioning in the main dining room. Every table is occupied and the lovely piano music produced by a young man in a tuxedo, who is almost hidden behind a baby grand, is nullified. Moira and I are studied as we run the gauntlet to the front entrance. It may be because we are so underdressed. More likely it is just admiration for her.

"Tin!"

Though I hear my name, I'm hoping it's a mistake, that there's someone named Tim around. It's happened to me before. Moira hears it too. She stops in front of me, arresting our progress.

"Tin Balune! I'll be a sonofabitch!" There's a large hand on my shoulder and it turns me around. I recognize the big, beefy face as I find myself confronted by a giant. "It's me, you bastard," he says, "Buck Wolfram! We worked together on my first boat, remember? Summer of '92 I think. Jesus Tin, it's been a long time. How the hell are ya?"

"Good, good," I lie as he grabs my hand and nearly destroys it with his meaty grip. Along with the rest of me, my memory is jolted into recognition. "You still live in this area, Buck?"

"Mackinaw City, yeah. Still boatin' the tourists too, 'cept I got three boats now. Goin' to a boat show in Chicago tomorrow to get another'n. Givin' old man Shepherd and his line a run for his money. Doin' thirty percent of the Island traffic now. My wife and me come down to Traverse City ever coupla weeks to do some shoppin', then we eat here. Great food, but a little stuffy for my tastes. I hate this fuckin' tie." He pulls at it as if he were being choked. So much of it is necessary to just get around his massive neck that it ends barely below his chest. It's very apparent that he's unaccustomed to wearing it.

A small woman, only half his size, appears next to him. She's very petite, blonde, attractive. She's not the wife I remember him having. She's dressed in a sequined black gown that barely conceals her largest assets, most of which are spilling out over the top. She's wearing expensive jewelry, gold necklaces and bracelets, along with a diamond pendant and ring which are very noticeable against her tanned skin. It's clear that she was once a knockout, but too much sun and too much make-up give her a painted, leathery look. She smiles pleasantly, although she's observing my shorts and T-shirt with displeasure.

"Listen, Tin, I want ya to meet Sabina." The woman extends her hand and I give it a gentle shake. "We been married almost a year now. Met her on my boat the summer before last when she was goin' to stay at the Grand." He wraps a huge arm around her and she almost disappears. "She's my third wife. First two couldn't wait long enough for me to get rich." Buck bellows loudly at his own crassness while Sabina smiles reservedly. "She's the best of the bunch though, by God." He squeezes her and I fear for her safety. "She's a keeper."

Behind me, I hear Moira clear her throat. Buck is looking at her, obviously enthralled. "This is Moira Sweeney," I say, "a friend of the family. I helped her return a truck to Traverse City today and we thought we'd get a bite to eat on the way back to Loon Lake. Moira, this is Buck Wolfram. He gave me a job working on his boat, one of those big ones that ferry vacationers back and forth between Mackinaw City and Mackinac Island. Buck had just started his company. What's it called?"

"Strait Shot Lines."

"Yeah. Buck was maybe, what, thirty then?"

"Twenty-four, boy. Don't make it any worse'n it is."

That would make him somewhere near forty now, and he doesn't look any different—well, meatier maybe. "I was a junior in high school."

"Too young to know enough to keep it in yer pants, that's for damn sure. Pleased to meetcha, Moorah." He takes her hand and kisses it gallantly, as if he were in the Romanov court. "She's a beaut, Tin."

"I'm right here," Moira says softly.

"What?"

"You don't need to refer to me in the third person, Mr. Wolfram, when I'm standing in front of you, although I appreciate the compliment."

Buck looks at me as one might look at the parent of a misbehaving child. Then he calmly turns back to her, bows low, and says: "Please forgive me, Moorah my dear, my enthusiasm sometimes gets the better of me."

"No problem, Buck," she says.

"Listen," he says, turning back to me, "why don't you two join us for dinner?"

"We've already eaten, Buck," I tell him.

"A drink then? We can catch up on old times."

"We're really not dressed appropriately."

Sabina looks relieved.

"Then we'll go someplace else."

"As much as I'd like to, Buck, we have to get back. It's Moira's father's birthday. Maybe some other time." This last excuse is, apparently, acceptable.

He fishes around in his coat and extracts a small card. "Here," he says, shoving it into my hand, "this has my phone number and e-mail address. Strait Shot Lines, that's us. Next time you're in the Mackinaw area you look me up, okay?"

I put the card in my pocket. "Sure. Absolutely."

"Take care then, you sonofabitch. It's good to see ya. Say hi to your old man for me, alright?" It's a strange thing for him to say, since my father is dead and he'd never met him. He hugs me and I feel myself slightly lifted off the floor, in spite of the fact that I'm over six feet myself.

"Pleasure, sister." He kisses Moira lightly on her cheek after he sets me down. She responds warmly.

Sabina smiles politely and pulls him back toward their table.

It's night in the crowded parking lot. We have difficulty finding the car, although it should be easily recognizable among the sports cars and mini-vans and RVs.

Once we find it, we sit quietly in the Lumina for a few minutes without moving. I expect her to ask me why we're not leaving. She doesn't. There's a pleasant tension between us, preferable to any comfort I've experienced lately.

"Buck is interesting," she finally says.

"Look I'm sorry about that. I worked with him one summer when I was a kid."

"When you were my age, you mean?"

"When I was younger, yes."

"He seems very attached to you."

"He's a better guy than he seems. He'd do anything for you. He's just not very polished."

"A little rough around the edges."

"Yes."

"His wife couldn't take her eyes off you."

"Bullshit. She could hardly wait to get away from us."

She smiles. There's something impish in it. "He didn't know Wendy?"

"I was seventeen when I worked for him. I did it for a summer to earn money for college. He was doing it for a career. I didn't know Wendy yet. He hadn't met anybody connected with me. He knew who my brother was, that's all. Satchel was always in the newspapers."

"Why do you think they haven't found Satchel yet?" The subject is allowed now, she knows that.

"We Balunes are evasive by nature."

My allusion to our previous conversation on the veranda is not lost on her. "Really."

"I don't know. He might be dead."

"You think so?"

"No."

"Why?"

"I don't think he's finished with me."

I expect her to ask me what that means, but she doesn't. She pushes her sandaled feet against the floor, raises her arms over her head, and stretches languorously. The arching of her back is sensuous. She notices that I notice, but she merely smiles and says nothing.

"Sweeney told me you have a scholarship to MSU."

"That's right."

"In what field?"

"Guess."

"Biology."

"No."

"Music."

"No."

"Certainly not math."

"No. Literature."

"What?"

"It surprises you?"

"Frankly, yes, although I don't know why it should."

Probably in order to avoid burying myself any further, I start the car. The air conditioner begins its incessant whining. Tall pines line the blacktop on either side of the road, hiding the lake and what's left of the diminishing light. I feel like we're in a tunnel. A family of raccoons crosses ahead of us and I brake to allow them to make it. I don't know why I'm merciful now; perhaps my dark heart has regained some degree of sanctity.

I light a cigarette and notice that I'm down to three or four. People who do not plan their lives around their addictions cannot understand what that means.

"You wrote a book," Moira says from the darkness nearby.

"A long time ago."

"It's good. I read it."

"You're one of the three."

"But you were so young to be a published novelist. Still in college, right? That's an exceptional accomplishment. Have you tried to do any more?"

"No. Your major is American Lit.?"

"Brit. Lit. I love the Victorians, especially Dickens and the Brontës. Tennyson too."

"I took you for a Modernist. Stein, Eliot, Pound, Hemingway, Williams."

"Hemingway was a frightened man. So was Gertrude Stein."

I can't help but laugh. I drop my cigarette on the floor and then burn myself trying to pick it up. "Hemingway gave the world a new voice."

"Not one I care to read."

"Why?"

"It's...it's circumcised."

I'm forced to laugh again. "Circumcised? What in hell do you mean by that?"

She paused for a moment, then said: "Unnecessarily clipped." This is no child. I almost choke in suppressed amusement.

"Who's *your* favorite?" she asks.

"You've probably never heard of him."

"Of course not. How could a naif such as myself know anything about writing?"

"I didn't mean anything by that."

She raises her eyebrows above those black eyes.

"It's Jim Harrison."

"*Farmer* was quite good," she says. "*Dalva* was better. *Sundog* has great archetypes and water metaphors, but his best is, in my humble opinion, *The Woman Lit by Fireflies*. It's the most accurate portrayal of a desperate woman ever written by a man. He used to spend a lot of time near here. He grew up in Lower Michigan, attended MSU. He has one eye and chain smokes. I love his stuff. I met him once at a little bookstore in Sutton's Bay. He signed three of my books."

I'm enormously impressed, but I try not to show it. It doesn't matter, she knows anyway. "Why literature?"

"I want to be a writer?"

"Why?"

"Without stories, we're all dead."

"It's not a very practical profession."

"That's what I like about it."

"Unless you're enormously talented, it's difficult to make a living."

"I *am* enormously talented."

"Is that so?"

"Yes."

"Humble too."

"It's only the truth. Besides, humility is probably the *least* practical of virtues—if it is one at all. I certainly don't see it as virtue. Why did *you* start to write?"

"I don't know for sure. Perhaps...an act of faith."

"In what? God?"

"In humanity, I think. It lets you know that you're standing shoulder to shoulder with everyone else. C.S. Lewis said, 'We read to know that we are not alone.' Maybe I wrote for the same purpose. I used to believe that good writing came from something divine in us. The human race hasn't only produced beauty in words, but it guards and honors and perpetuates it."

"So it becomes sacred."

I'm sorely tempted to embrace her. I think she would respond. Only the fact that I'm driving keeps me from further idiocy. "Yes, I used to believe that."

"Literature gives you hope then?"

"Hope. Well, hope is an ideal, it's not real. Idealization seems to be essential to people and we generally find it in our imaginations. I have become increasingly unimaginative."

She turns toward me. I see her fold one beautiful leg beneath the other. She's not wearing her seat belt. I want very much to just lay one hand on that skin.

"What do you do when you're depressed? Besides drinking I mean."

"I don't know. I sleep, I guess. I read a lot."

"Why do you read?"

"Escape, maybe."

"Into beauty."

"Yes, probably."

"You should read more."

"Why?"

She laughs. "To keep you out of boats."

"Why?"

"Because I want you to stay alive."

"Listen, if I hadn't passed out last night I wouldn't be here now. You would have unloaded the truck yourself and Sweeney would be sitting next to you now. You'd still be at MSU in the fall, majoring in literature. What difference would it make?"

She's twisting her hands. "How's your ear?"

"Don't change the subject."

"You want me to tell you that I care about you?"

"I want you to tell me why you want me to live. Is it general compassion, like dodging raccoons in the road? A philosophical aversion to suicide? Ethics? What?"

"I think I would like to...get to know you." She says this coolly, quietly, looking straight ahead into opposing headlights that reveal a similarly calm expression on her face. The beauty of her—and the words—make my heart race. I have difficulty concentrating on my driving.

"Why would you want to do that?"

"I'm attracted to you. I can't explain it, really. You're handsome, intelligent—"

"Sounds like a bad case of sympathy, pity even," I say, but secretly I'm thrilled.

"If you believe that people spend time evaluating potential... relationships as if they were purchasing a new computer, you're wrong. That's not what happened with Wendy, is it?"

We sit in silence for a long time after that. I smoke another cigarette. Down to two. It's very dark now, no moon and, even with the phone call, Sweeney must be concerned. We're long overdue. I want very much to touch her. I'm sure she would allow it, even welcome it. I should jump at the chance. We're on Loon Lake Road now, just a few miles from the cabin. I could pull off. The road is deserted. I could embrace her, taste that mouth, fondle those young breasts, maybe even feel those long legs around my hips...it's possible. I come to my senses. It wouldn't work. She's half my age. I would ruin another family.

She knows it's our last chance to be alone. She puts her hand on my leg. She's looking at me. I can feel her dark eyes. I place my hand over hers and hold it. I just hold on. It's enough for now. She sighs.

I pull onto the gravel drive behind Sweeney's cabin where the U-Haul was parked this morning. A mercury light illuminates the exterior. Sweeney was one of the first on the lake to get one installed. Dad never did.

"Something's not right," Moira says. Her voice is jittery, nervy—totally unlike her normal equanimity. She is keenly studying the exterior cabin wall. She has removed her hand.

"What is it?"

"There're no lights on, inside."

"Maybe Sweeney went to bed early."

"He'd leave a light on, for when I get in. He always does. Besides, I told him we'd celebrate his birthday when we got back. He's a night owl anyway. Something's wrong."

When I glance over at my own place, I know she's right. I left at midday. Now, every light in the place is on. Ghosts?

Chapter seven

Moira hurries inside Sweeney's place as soon as I stop the car. There is no response to her probing calls. Nothing seems disturbed or out of place in the shadowy interior as far as I can tell. Moira flicks on the kitchen light. An apple orchard appears. In the dim light from the Mercury, nothing is out of place except for a few half-unpacked boxes that Sweeney had obviously been rummaging through. The sparse tackle box and fishing pole are in their usual corner next to the knotty pine door that leads out to the lake. The empty aluminum tray of a Swanson's TV dinner is on the apple-kitchen counter. I go into Moira's bedroom as she checks Sweeney's. I have to turn on the light. On her dresser is a copy of Wilkie's *The Woman in White*. Next to it is some sort of animal skull, bleached white by sun or weather. I have never seen anything like it. As I pick it up to examine it more closely, she enters the room. She reports that in Sweeney's room, everything is neat and tidy. The bed is still made.

"What the hell is this?" I ask her, holding up the grotesque object.

"Beaver skull."

I look at it again. "It can't be, Moira. I've seen beaver skulls before. They don't have this kind of bone structure."

She sighs. In her anxiety to find out where her father is, I can see that she really doesn't want to take the time to enlighten me, but she humors me anyway. "I found it a couple of years ago at that beaver pond in the state forest across the lake. A beaver's incisors never stop growing. They wear them down by constantly gnawing on wood and by grinding the uppers against the lowers, even when they sleep. This animal had somehow lost its upper teeth, so that it had no way to control the growth of the lower ones. They grew up over its snout, across its face and curved downward, penetrating the top of its head. Eventually the pressure of the growth fractured its skull and must've ruptured the brain cavity. You can see the split."

As I look at the skull again, I can see she is right. The unfortunate creature must have died an agonizing death.

"The skull was so unusual, I decided to keep it."

I put the thing back on her dresser and feel something akin to gratitude.

"Where the hell is he?" Moira looks at me with a façade of composure. Her voice is edgy, tense, on the cusp of panic.

Like most people trying to calm a friend, I offer an unlikely solution. "He's probably at my place. That's why the lights are all on."

She shakes her head. Her midnight hair shimmers under the open bulb above her. A large moth flutters around her head in no apparent pattern—just staying close to the light. Wendy would have been startled. Moira seems not to notice. Outside, the loons are fluting their haunting cries. There is something insane about the noise they make. "Sweeney wouldn't go into your place uninvited."

"Unlike his daughter?"

"Sweeney and I aren't really related, remember?"

"He could've been worried about the time it was taking us to get back and gone over to my cabin to see if we were there."

"Then there would've been lights on here too and, like I said,

I don't think he'd go in without permission. Sweeney's just too conscious of convention."

I recall him waiting for me to open the screen door yesterday before he'd step onto my porch. "Well someone was over there," I say. "I'm fairly certain I didn't turn on the lights. We left in the middle of the afternoon, didn't we?"

"I turned your kitchen light on when I went over there this morning—when I read the note. What was it? Seven or so?" I can feel my face crimson. "Did you turn it off when we left? I didn't."

"I don't think so, but there are other lights on now too."

"You took a shower, changed your clothes. You could have left other lights on."

It doesn't sound right. I don't remember turning any lights on and even so, I've been trained since infancy to save electricity. A pastor's family must be frugal. Even when I was drunk I turned off lights. I'm basically a creature of darkness anyway, always been more comfortable there.

"I'm going over there to check it out," I say. "You stay here." I open the screen door.

Moira grabs my arm. "Tin, wait."

I like the sound of my name coming from her. It seems to reduce the gap in our ages with its familiarity. Her touch is meant to restrain, but it titillates instead. "What?"

"There's another possibility."

"What?"

"Satchel."

The name takes away all comfort and shifts my arousal to a different gear. I want to say it's impossible, but I know better. The authorities have long since given up any serious searching for my brother. I stopped calling to bug them about it what, a year or two ago? I had called off the private detective too. It's been a cold case for a long time—for them and for me. Satch is smart, determined. He would lay low, bide his time. It's my birthday, an appropriate date for vengeance. It could be. It could. If so, Sweeney might be laid out on my kitchen floor, soaking in his own blood. A good fisherman always uses the appropriate bait. I can see that Moira is thinking the same thing. Her fear reveals a vulnerability I haven't seen yet. I am desperately thirsty.

"I don't think it's likely," I tell her, knowing that very little of what has happened to me in the last seven or eight years was. When the improbable happens to you consistently, it does, itself, become probable, doesn't it?

I continue out the door. She's right behind me. "I told you to wait here."

"With all due respect, Mr. Teacher Sir, fuck you."

I think she must have been fun to have in class.

We step outside into the darkness. Her hair and eyes blend with the black night, giving the rest of her pale head a skull-like appearance. Immediately, a horde of ravenous insects flock to us and begin to feed. It reminds me of the time I went to visit Wendy's grave and was, in my terrible grief, stung by a bee. There is very little pity in the natural world.

Moira grasps my hand and we move stealthily across the yard, looking at the lit-up windows for passing shadows.

She pulls at my shirt. "Maybe we should just call the police," she whispers.

"And tell them what? That we're a little nervous because the lights are on in my cabin? That your fath…that Sweeney's been missing for what, ten minutes or so?"

"That a known murderer, a wanted man, might be here."

"Or he might be in Bogota, Colombia." Images of Wendy's battered body flash across the dreary landscape of my mind and I know she could be right. "Listen, you go and get in the car. If I'm not back in five minutes, drive down to the bait shop and call 911."

"I'm not going anywhere," she says. She produces her cell phone from under her blouse, apparently once fastened to the waistband of her shorts. "I can call from here. I'm not leaving you alone. If it is Satchel, he didn't come for me and your instincts for survival aren't at their best right now."

It's pointless to argue. I know she won't back off. We can't call the cops—they don't prevent crime anyway, they just punish it—sometimes. We have to find Sweeney. There's no other option but to continue, though I am faint with apprehension and sweating like a stuck pig, as my father used to say.

We approach the cabin from the lakeside, by the screened porch. There's no evidence of anything awry here. There's no movement inside—no sound, except for the insects and the occasional cry of a loon. If anyone is in there, they're hidden, waiting.

The screen door makes a noise like a wounded animal. As I pull it open, we both become rigid at the eerie sound. Moira squeezes my hand with the unconscious strength of terror. Felix the Clock meows, setting us both further on edge. We cross the porch and step through the open doorway into the kitchen.

Chapter eight

I see no one inside, but I think someone has been here, might still be here. There's a note. At first I think it's mine, but I pull out the cigarette package and the one I wrote is still encased in its cellophane. I'm certain now that it wasn't there when we left this morning. This new one is conspicuous because it's lying on the table, directly in front of the chair where Satchel used to sit for family dinners. Like mine was, it's weighted with the salt shaker. Each of us had our place. Apparently, we still do. Moira doesn't see it. "Sweeney?" she calls out. I hold back to stay with her, fearful that the intruder hasn't left, ignoring the paper for the moment. We move together, searching each room. Nothing.

"I don't get it," Moira says. "Where could he be? It doesn't look like anybody's been here."

"Look," I say, and gesture toward the table. She sees it then. A little gasp escapes her. We move in unison again, as if our safety depends upon proximity. African herbivores and big city dwellers prove this wrong every hour. We lean against the table and read it together.

> *Happy Birthday!*
> *Have I made an impression?*
> *I got him.*
> *Twenty-four hours is what you have.*
> *If you don't find him he will die.*
> *St. Clair and Ontario, just off Michigan.*
> *When pigs fly. 432.*
> *Quite an exhibition.*
> *Get the point?*
> *Leave Moira. No police.*
> *I want you to save him. I really do.*
> *Okay, one more.*
> *Everyone knows it's windy.*
> > *Bye.*
> > *Satch.*

I run to the door leading to the driveway at the side of the cabin. I rush out, hoping to see a car pulling away, a license plate number. He's gone though, probably been gone for quite awhile. *Twenty-four hours.* How much time is left?

"Oh God," I hear Moira inside. She's collapsed into a chair and she's staring at my brother's note. As I return, she looks up at me with eyes that are even darker than I remember and I can see accusation there, whether she intends it or not. "Your brother has Sweeney," she says.

"It looks like it, yes."

"God."

"I'll find him," I promise her, though I have no idea how to start or even if it's possible. I saw what he did to Wendy.

I can see that she's concerned, but she doesn't cry, she doesn't come apart. "We have to start with this," she says, holding the note in her hand, but then suddenly her eyes widen, her lips gather in a circle

96

of panic and she's out of the chair and rushing to the light switch on the kitchen wall. *"Behind you,"* she whispers frantically.

"What?"

"Headlights. A car just pulled in the drive. He's come back!"

She flicks off the kitchen light and disappears into the bath-room. The light goes out there and I see her moving again, toward my bedroom. I hear an engine die. There's something about the way the door is slammed—a nonchalance. Footsteps on the gravel. We're in darkness now. I search the shadows desperately for a weapon. There's nothing. Across the table from me, Moira, back in the kitchen, slides out a drawer and I see the flash of a blade caught in the intrusive light from the Mercury. She has thought all this out and accomplished it in the time it took me simply to crouch.

The footsteps hesitate at the door. Whoever it is has seen the lights go out. He knows someone's inside. Moira creeps stealthily toward the door. *"Stay back."* she whispers to me.

A silhouette appears behind the screen. I strain my eyes to see if it's Satchel, but I can't tell. It seems too big, but…

The door begins to open. I can't see Moira anymore. She's somewhere near the intruder.

"Moira? Sweeney? You guys over here?"

The overhead light blinks on, nearly blinding me. I see Moira by the door, knife poised above her head. Slowly she lowers it as the stranger steps inside.

"Mr. Balune?"

I've been spotted and I feel ridiculous, crouching behind the kitchen chair.

"It is Balune, isn't it?"

The man steps inside. He's very tall, with a shock of blond hair that hangs low over his forehead. He's dressed Ivy League. Tan pants, white polo shirt, a pastel sweater tied around his neck. Expensive watch, gold chain, diamond ring. He's very tan and has spent much of his time outdoors, probably on tennis courts or golf courses or in swimming pools. He reeks of mammon, as my father would say. He's not Satchel—that's all I care about. The door slams behind him.

"Yes," I say, straightening up. "Tin Balune."

"The writer?"

"Teacher, mostly."

"You wrote *How to Lose Your Soul?*"

I nod.

"That was a good book. It was required reading for Contemporary American Literature when I was at Yale. Everything all right? You look a bit startled."

"Yeah," I blurt, "just thought you might be someone else. You are?"

"Oh, sorry." He steps forward, extending his hand. "Graham. Graham Van Houten. I was just looking for Moira Sweeney, your neighbor. Have you seen her by any chance?"

I shake his hand and point to the area behind him where Moira is still standing with the knife. His hand is very smooth and it escapes mine as quickly as possible, as though I were carrying some kind of contagion. He turns away from me.

"Hey, sweetie," he says. He sees the knife, even though she tries to hide it behind her. He looks back at me, then back to her. "What's going on?"

"Jesus, Graham," she says, "you scared the piss out of me."

A marked response of distaste manifests itself on his plain face. I think it might have something to do with the way she expressed herself, but I'm not sure. "Sorry, but you gave me a bit of a start as well. You just get back?"

"Back?" she says. "What do you mean?"

"Well, Sweeney said you and Mr. Balune here went to Traverse City to return the truck and you were long overdue." Graham looks at me suspiciously, then probably decides that I'm not really much of a threat. "He was worried, so I went looking for you. What's with all the cloak and dagger stuff?"

Moira moves toward him and despite his obvious advantage in size, he backs away. She grabs his sweater and pulls his head down into her face. "You saw Sweeney? Today?"

"Yeah. Listen Moira, what the heck is—"

"How long ago?"

He glances at his watch, which is more jewelry than time-piece.

"I'm not sure. It was still light."

Moira releases him and walks past him to me. "Did you hear that? He can't have that much of a start. If we call the police—"

"He'll kill Sweeney."

"You're sure of that?"

"Listen, a known murderer kidnaps Sweeney and tells us not to call the police. The assumption is that he has a hostage for a reason. He wants me to come to him—alone. If we send the cops instead, what's to stop him from…well, you get the idea."

"What on earth are you people talking about?" Graham says. I dislike his voice already. It's too high, too cautious and too smooth, like his hands. I remember Richard Dreyfus's line from *Jaws* about 'working class hero crap' and recall that my own hands are pretty smooth. My resentment, like Robert Shaw's, is probably economic.

"Sweeney's been abducted," Moira says. Her voice is level, but I can see distress in her eyes.

Graham looks befuddled. He reminds me of a dog I once had that got caught in a drainpipe. "Abducted? By who?"

Not very impressive for an Ivy Leaguer. I want very much to say *by whom*. I've been teaching too long. "My brother."

Graham looks in my direction and gives me a mendacious smile. "Your *brother* kidnapped Hiram Sweeney? Why on earth would he do that?"

I want to say to him "Because Sweeney wasn't on Mars." That's the second time he's used that 'on earth' expression. Why can't he just say "what the fuck is going on" like a regular guy? I'm pretty sure he wouldn't say 'tit' if he had a mouthful.

"I stole his wife away from him and he wants to get back at me."

"I don't think that's right," he says softly.

"No, not very ethical at all," I reply. Moira gives me a wicked glance.

99

"No, you misunderstand me, Mr. Balune." He gives me the empathetic look of someone who's making an effort to tolerate those less fortunate than himself. "I meant that I don't think your brother kidnapped Hiram Sweeney."

"Oh? Why's that?"

"Well, I saw Mr. Sweeney this evening, as I said. After he explained where you and Moira were, and how late you were, I told him I was going to go out and look for you. He seemed nervous, and very grateful for the suggestion. I left right away, but I was only a mile down the road when I remembered I was going in the wrong direction. It's easy to get turned around when you're unaccustomed to a place. I came back and passed the cabin going the other way. That's when I saw Sweeney walking across the yard to your place, here. There was no one else with him, and he seemed to be taking his time. All the lights were on in your cabin. I thought at first that maybe he was just going to check to see if you guys had gone to the Balune cabin first, but then I noticed that the car still wasn't back, so I kept going. The thing that strikes me now is that Mr. Sweeney looked, well, a bit more relaxed. I think he might have even been whistling. Anyway, he was obviously alone and under no duress." He looked at his watch again. "That was forty-five minutes ago."

"You just said, Graham, that you weren't sure how long it'd been since you left Sweeney. Now you're saying it was forty-five minutes?" Moira is clearly irritated.

He looks at the floor. I see his face redden slightly, then he takes a deep breath and continues. "Exactly. I remember looking at my watch. It was eight forty-five, now it's nine thirty."

Moira shakes her head and sighs. I would learn that whenever Graham used the word 'exactly', he didn't have a fucking clue.

"Even so," I say, "forty-five minutes is enough time to force someone into a car and drive off."

"Don't think it's likely."

"Then how do you account for this?" Moira says, shoving the note at Graham.

"Well, of course," he says after reading it, "I didn't know about this."

"Then maybe you shouldn't offer an opinion until you know what's going on," she says. Her tone is harsh, even ruthless. The bull is completed cowed.

"Did Sweeney tell you that we were stopping to eat at a restaurant before we came back?"

Graham looks genuinely surprised—and disturbed. "No." He buries his face in the note. "It still doesn't say *who* he has," Graham says in self-defense.

"If we're not going to call the police," Moira says, ignoring him and turning those dark eyes on me, "then we have to do this ourselves."

"Don't be ridiculous," Graham says.

Moira ignores him, snatching the note from his hand. "That means we have to figure out what this means. He's telling us how to find him."

"Why not just come right out and say it? Why the code?"

"I don't know. Maybe to buy time to get a head start on us, maybe to make it more stressful for us, maybe out of sheer vindictiveness. It doesn't matter. We have to solve it if we're going to rescue Sweeney, or even find out where he is."

She sits down at the kitchen table and I grab the chair next to her. We lean into the note. She's forgotten about Graham who, I notice, continues to stand in the middle of the room looking abandoned.

"St. Clair," Moira mumbles.

"St. Clair could be the name of a saint or a place or maybe a body of water," Graham says. "My parents live in Grosse Pointe, right on the shores of Lake St. Clair."

"Pretty exclusive neighborhood," I say.

He shrugs as if it means nothing, but I can see from the smugness on his face and the stiff formality of posture, that it means everything to him.

"Lake St. Clair connects two of the Great Lakes," Moira says, "but they're Erie and Huron, not Ontario or Michigan."

"That's true," I say, "but the Canadian *province* of Ontario is on the eastern side of Lake St. Clair and the *state* of Michigan is on the western."

"That has to be at least part of it then." Moira stands up and gets a glass of rusty-colored water from the pump at the sink. She looks at it with the same expression she's been bestowing on Graham. She turns to me. "Did you know they sell bottled water now?"

"I don't drink water."

"Right."

"Listen," Graham says, "am I in the way?"

Moira dumps the water in the sink and returns to the table. "I'm sorry, Graham. If you can help in any way, please feel free. I know how fond Sweeney is of you and you of him." She puts just enough emphasis on Sweeney's name to indicate that it is not her wish for him to be here.

"Have a seat," I say, motioning. He grabs a chair, across from us, obviously missing Moira's insinuation.

"None of the rest of this makes sense at all," Moira says as she peruses the note and watches Graham sit down,

"There's something else that bothers me," I tell her.

"What?"

"Unless Satch's handwriting has changed considerably, I don't think he wrote this."

She leans into me to examine the note more closely. "How so?"

"He's a southpaw." She looks inquisitively at me, then she remembers. "When he writes, his letters always lean toward the left. These are tending to the right. Now maybe he's intentionally trying to disguise his handwriting, but why would he do that and then sign the note?"

"You said a known *murderer?*" Graham says as he pulls the sweater from his neck and lays it on the table. Moira ignores him.

"He could have forced Sweeney to write it. It looks a lot like Sweeney's writing," she says.

"That's the only explanation I can come up with, but why didn't he have the note all set when he got here? He's obviously planned this whole thing very carefully. You don't manage to evade the police and the FBI and a damned good private detective for almost a decade without being careful."

"Maybe he was injured," Graham says. We both look up at him. "You know, maybe your brother hurt his hand or something."

"It's possible," Moira admits.

"Okay, well regardless of the handwriting thing," I say, "what about all the rest of this stuff? He clearly doesn't mean for us to look for him in the middle of Lake St. Clair."

"When pigs fly?" Moira says. "And what about that number? 432."

"An address? Apartment number, maybe?" Graham offers.

"The numbers are in descending order," she says. "4, then 3, then 2."

"So?"

"I don't know, just an observation. Numbers aren't my strong suit, remember? It just seems to me that if they were an actual address or something that the chances that they'd be in descending order in this kind of cryptic message would be slim."

I shrug. "Makes sense." I look up at Graham. His attention isn't on the note. He's watching our every move and his focus on us leads me to believe that he is aware of how relaxed Moira is in her proximity to me. I think he also notices that, despite the circumstances, I'm enjoying it.

"As far as the 'pigs fly' thing, that's generally a euphemism for 'never'," Moira says. "Any other thoughts?" She notices Graham's disapproving look, but she doesn't move.

I reach in my pocket for a cigarette. I have one left. I light it. Graham coughs, though the smoke hasn't really had a chance to do him any damage yet. No doubt he's letting me know he doesn't approve. I put the empty package on the table, next to the ashtray. "Not about the pigs flying, no."

"Listen, Moira," he says, "this is too much for amateurs to deal with. My father knows some pretty important people in law enforcement. I'm sure he could call in a few favors and—"

"No!" Her tone is emphatic. "I don't want Sweeney to get hurt. We've got to figure this out ourselves. We know, at least, that Satchel has taken Sweeney to some place around Detroit. It makes sense that Satchel would go there, it's where you told him about Wendy and you. It seems appropriate to me that he'd want to get revenge at the place where he was hurt so badly. What was the number of the hotel room where you and Wendy met him? Could it have been 432?"

"I don't think so. Seems to me that it was more like twenty floors up. I remember that elevator ride. There could be a room 432 though. It's possible that that's where he wants us to be."

"If we're pretty sure he's in the Detroit area, wouldn't it make sense to get on the road and try to decode the rest of this on the way? It's at least three hours to Detroit. It would save time. I need to be *doing* something."

"What about the instructions to 'leave Moira'?" Graham says. "Won't you going along endanger Sweeney too?"

"He may be right," I say.

"He won't know. When we figure out exactly where to meet him, I stay in the car or you drop me at a hotel or something. I can't just sit here and wait. I won't do it. Besides," she says, looking over at Graham, "I can't let Tin deal with this by himself. Sweeney's my problem, not his. I can't just sit by and let Tin be murdered to save Sweeney. There's got to be a way to get them both back here safely."

"Then I'll go too," Graham says. "I was once recruited by the CIA. I'm pretty good at this stuff."

"You never told me that," Moira says.

"Sure. When I was at Yale, they came to the campus and asked for me, did a background check, the whole nine yards. I was going to go down to Quantico and start training, but my mother talked me out of it. She thought it would be too dangerous."

Moira sighs. "I thought Quantico is where they trained agents for the FBI."

Graham quickly looks down at the floor again, then back up. "Well, it is, of course. The FBI wanted me too, because of my experience in the ROTC. I just got them confused for a second."

It's quite obvious to us both that this man has been wading knee-deep in bullshit most of his life.

"Thanks for offering, Graham, but I'd feel terrible if anything happened to you. Tin and I are directly involved, but this isn't your problem. I think you should just drive home and we'll call you if anything develops. You're right there in the Detroit area, and you'll be close enough that we can reach you if we need help."

"You said your brother was a murderer, Mr. Balune," Graham says. "What'd you mean by that? He's killed before?"

Moira sighs and rolls her eyes.

"After my wife left him for me, he beat her to death with a baseball bat."

Graham looks appalled. "That must have been awful for you. They never caught him?"

"No."

"Listen, Graham," Moira says. "We just don't have time to bring you up to date on everything. We have to get going. Every minute counts."

"Sure," he says. "I'm going in the same direction though. You'll take 131 to 96 won't you, Mr. Balune? Moira and I can follow you in my car and we'll work on figuring out this thing."

"Whatever Moira thinks is best, is okay with me," I say—though I'm not sure, until she looks at me and speaks, that what I said is true.

"I'm going with Tin," Moira says. "You can follow us if you want."

"I see," Graham says. He glowers at me, but when I don't turn away from his anger, he does.

Moira stands up, clearly anxious to be gone.

"I think I have the windy business figured out," Graham says.

"What?" Moira sits again, fidgeting.

"The windy thing. Lake St. Clair is one of the best sailing lakes around Michigan. It's windy, but it's protected from the storms you see on the Great Lakes. Sailboats are out there all the time. I grew up looking at the white sails from our living room. I've sailed quite a bit in Dad's yacht. This weekend they're having the annual Detroit River to St. Clair River Run. I just helped a friend paint his boat." He looks guiltily at Moira and quickly looks away. "Your brother must be making some sort of reference to the St. Clair Yacht Race in his note, Mr. Balune."

"It's a song," I say.

"What?" Moira and Graham speak in unison.

"It's a song, by The Association. You're both a little young to remember it, although so am I, I guess. It came out in the late sixties. It's called 'Windy'. *Who's peeking out from under a stairway, Calling a name that's lighter than air, Who's bending down to give me a rainbow, Everyone knows it's Windy.*'"

"That's got to be it," Moira says. Her voice is raised in excitement. "Do you know the whole song?"

"I think so, yeah. Satchel loved The Association. He played their songs over and over, especially that one, but he knew all their stuff—'Cherish', 'Never My Love', everything."

"That *is* it, then. Definitely. C'mon, Tin, we've got to get going." She yanks me out of my chair.

"Let me get my keys." It takes me a few minutes to find them in a dresser drawer where I must have placed them when I was in one of my less-lucid moments. When I get back, Graham is standing next to Moira with a meaty hand on each of her arms. There is anger reddening his tanned features, matching the crimson on her upper arm where he's gripped her. Moira doesn't look the least bit intimidated.

"Is everything okay?" They both turn their heads toward me and he releases her. It's an inane thing to say. Nothing is okay —nothing is ever okay. We're human—we pretend we don't live in the same world where everything is dangerous, where everything is hunting everything else. Despite what my colleagues often tell our students, there *is* such a thing as a dumb question.

"Graham was just leaving," Moira says, rubbing her upper arm.

"Yes," he says, turning and grabbing his sweater from the table. "Will you call me when you get to Detroit, Moira?"

"Yes," she says.

"Good luck then, to you *both*." He shuts the door hard behind him, leading me to believe that his parting exclamation was less than genuine.

"You were a little hard on him, don't you think?" I say.

"He's a liar and an idiot. He would've put us all in greater danger than we already are. Now let's get going." She stops at the door. "Do you have any money?"

"A hundred bucks or so in cash, maybe. I have credit cards too. Then there's always the ATM."

"Okay."

"You sure you want to go?"

"Are you?"

"I'd rather do almost anything else."

"Like take a boat ride?"

"No. That's not one of them."

"Good. I feel the same way. Let's go."

The working air conditioner in my Jeep Cherokee is a welcome respite from the obnoxious heat. I find myself beginning to dry out for the first time since I got up. We should have used the Jeep to go to Traverse City, but Moira insisted that I shouldn't have to put any miles on my car for her benefit. I hadn't argued, knowing what a disaster area my Jeep is. There are bottles everywhere, along with burger wrappers and french fry cartons. The ashtray is overflowing with cigarette butts. To my amazement, Moira says nothing about it.

There is no sign of Graham as we pull out of the driveway.

On our way around the southern curve of the lake, I see that the Grocery and Bait Shop is still open. There's a crowd of people with their little kids around the ice cream window and a solitary woman is at the public telephone a few feet away. "I'm going to stop and get some smokes," I tell Moira. "It'll make our drive a little less tense." She nods, engrossed in the note that Satchel left.

I feel like I'm stepping into a furnace as I exit the car. It almost takes my breath away. The moisture immediately returns to my skin and I discover that I'm very thirsty. Inside, there are fans blowing down all three crowded aisles of the place. Nettie Hines, one of the fattest women I've ever known is, as always, behind the counter. She runs the Grocery and Bait Shop year-round, manning the place with her daughter, (or womanning it, as she would be more apt to say), from seven in the morning to ten at night, seven days a week. I don't know how someone of her bulk can continue to breathe in this heat. Her shirt, which is large enough to house a couple of campers, is badly stained with sweat and grease. She's sitting on her stool by the cash register taking the money of two locals I recognize as Milton and Jasper Wykowski—brothers who operate a mechanic's shop down the road. It appears that their chief comfort this evening is going to be a couple of twelve-packs of Budweiser. Nettie waves to me over their heads as I stroll down the bare floorboards of the center aisle to the coolers in back where I grab a six pack of the Wykowski vintage. Nettie greets me with a big smile as I approach the counter.

"Looks like Juna is pretty busy tonight," I say as the Wykowski brothers grab their loot and head out the door with a brief double nod in my direction. Juna is Nettie's daughter, who takes care of scooping the ice cream.

"It's crazy, Tin," Nettie says. "Been goin' like a house afire since late mornin'. Poor gal ain't goin' speak to me after today. Her arm must be 'bout to fall off." I don't believe her. Juna has arms with bigger biceps than most linebackers in the NFL.

She watches me place the six-pack on the beat-up counter. "No hard stuff tonight?" I am Nettie's best liquor customer.

"No, think I'll give it a rest tonight. Listen, can you get me a couple of packs of Basics too, Net?"

"Ultra-Lite One Hundreds, right?"

"Right."

She swivels on her stool and deftly retrieves them from the rack immediately behind her. "You smoke them others already?"

"What?"

"Hi Sweeney was in here a while ago and bought a pack. I knew he don't smoke so I asked him who they was for. He told me he was pickin' 'em up for you. Didn't he give 'em to ya?"

I feel the blood draining from my face. My heart begins to race frantically. "No," I mumble, "he didn't."

"You okay, Tin?" Nettie rises from her stool and leans across the counter. "You need to eat more, boy. You been losin' too much weight. You're skinny as a wild turkey."

"Listen Nettie, how long ago was Sweeney in here?"

I think the desperation on my face must frighten her a little—and nothing much frightens Nettie. She shot a guy once who was trying to rob her. It happened when I was a kid. I remember my parents, and everyone else around Loon Lake, talking about it.

"Not more'n an hour ago, probly."

"Was anyone else with him?"

"Nope."

"You're sure?"

"I'm gettin' older," she says, "but I ain't senile yet. Wasn't nobody else in the store." Nettie would have recognized Satchel in an instant anyway. She's known us both all our lives.

"Did he seem nervous or worried at all?"

"Sweeney? Naw, he was his usual friendly self. Joked with me 'bout becomin' a local. He's retirin' ya know. Guess his daughter's goin' ta college this fall."

That can't be right, I keep thinking to myself. She must've made a mistake. That can't be right.

"Want me ta put this on your tab? It's fourteen eighty-nine."

"Yeah, that'd be great Net. Catch you next time."

She puts the beer and cigarettes in a paper bag and slides it across the counter to me. I suddenly realize there's another customer waiting behind me. "Did Sweeney say where he was going?"

Nettie laughs. "You know Hiram, he don't go anywheres. I didn't ask, but as far as I know, he was just headed home."

"Right."

"Is everything okay?"

Dumb question, dumb question, dumb question.

"Sure."

Dumb answer, dumb answer, dumb answer.

"Have a good one, Tin."

"You too."

"I will now. It's closin' time."

Outside, the moths around the single bare bulb above the door flutter around my head, simulating the activity within. The woman at the phone yells *"Fuck you, asshole!"* It's loud enough to make me jump as she slams the receiver into its cradle. I hustle to the jeep, trying to imagine what Moira will say when I tell her about this—possibly the exact three words I just heard.

Chapter nine

A re you sure that's what she said?" Moira is looking at me with such an expression of remonstrance that I feel like a child reporting to its mother. Incredibly, I am simultaneously imagining what her breasts must feel like. Romantic love, like so many other things, is firmly tied to the imagination. I have already opened a can of beer. It's half-gone.

"We can go back in and talk to Nettie again if you like. I don't blame you for not believing me, I'm not sure I believe it myself."

"Is it possible that Sweeney could have come down here before Satchel showed up?"

"In that amount of time?" Her voice, like the sneer of an upper lip, rises. "I highly doubt it. Graham said that Sweeney was alone when he saw him, just before nine. If that's true, then Sweeney would have to have been with Satchel when he came here, wouldn't he? God, it's only a couple of minutes after ten now."

"Unless Graham had his times mixed up."

"Even so, we had Sweeney's *car*. He'd have had no way to get here, then back to the cabin by himself."

"He could have walked."

"Three miles and back? Six miles total? No way, not enough time. Besides, if he wasn't buying the cigarettes for you, who was he buying them for? Satchel had to be with him."

"Then he had to be waiting in the car, because according to Nettie, Sweeney was by himself in the store. And if that's true, why didn't Sweeney say something to Nettie, have her call the cops? And there's something else. Satchel doesn't smoke either. At least he didn't when I knew him. Of course he didn't take drugs either."

"It doesn't make any sense."

"No."

The lights go out inside the store. Juna slides the outside window to the ice cream parlor shut as the last of the customers wander away. Nettie flips the 'Open' sign in the front door to read 'Closed' and within a couple of minutes she and Juna emerge.

"Nettie!" Moira is suddenly outside the car and hurrying over to the two women as they approach their rusted pick-up truck parked under the single Mercury light. Nettie embraces Moira, as does Juna. The latter is just a smaller version of her mother, very large, but diminutive by comparison, like a baby blue whale. I realize then that Moira knows them as well as I do, maybe better. After all, she's spent much of her life on Loon Lake too. They chatter amicably for a few minutes, then Nettie's face sags into a serious frown. They hug again. Nettie kisses Moira on her forehead, then Moira is on her way back to the Jeep.

"What? You didn't think I was telling you everything?" I say as she crawls back into the front seat and buckles up.

"Not at all."

"What then?"

"You're a man, and men aren't thorough."

"Really?"

"Really."

"You found out something I didn't?"

"Yes."

"What."

"You didn't talk to Juna."

"Juna wouldn't have been in the store when Sweeney came in. She's always dipping ice cream."

"That's right. Which means that she could see *outside* while Nettie couldn't. She saw Sweeney get out of a car, a blue Ford Taurus actually, that someone else was driving, although she couldn't tell who. She did notice that he was tall, by the way he hunched behind the wheel. Also, you didn't ask what kind of cigarettes Sweeney bought. They were Marlboro regulars and Nettie told me she thought that was strange since Sweeney told her they were for you and she knows that you smoke Basics."

I'm staring at her and she knows it. Though her head is down and she's trying hard to be nonchalant, that beautiful mouth is formed into a wry smile. "I would suggest that we get moving," she says.

I swallow the rest of my beer to wash down the pride that immediately preceded it. I throw the can in the back with the other bottles and start the engine. Within an hour, we're on 131, the main north/south artery in western Michigan.

"The additional information still doesn't tell us why Sweeney didn't alert someone while he was at Nettie's place," I say. "It doesn't make any sense. He was alone. He could have had Nettie call the cops or even just stayed inside until Satchel had to come in to get him. Nettie and Juna would have recognized Satch in a minute."

"He would have put their lives in danger," Moira responds.

"Then why didn't he just leave a note or something—he could've done that."

"Maybe Satchel told him that he already had us and he was taking him to us."

"Could be, I suppose."

"Maybe he had another hostage, someone we don't know about."

"Who?"

"I don't know, but it's possible—anything's possible."

"Ever try to strike a match on a wet bar of soap?"

"All right, almost anything, smartass."

She's studying the note, leaning forward to make full use of the map light next to the visor. As she does, she begins humming. "Is that the song?" she says. "I've heard it before. I think Sweeney has the CD."

"Yup. That's it."

"I always thought they were singing about some girl named Wendy." She looks intently at me, searching for my reaction to the name.

"Satch thought so too, right up to the time that he met Wendy and she straightened him out. It didn't matter, he told me, he still substituted her name for Windy."

"Do you know all the words?"

"I'm not sure."

"You should. It's your generation isn't it?"

"Do you know all the words to all the songs from your generation? Besides, I wasn't even born when that song came out. I'm not as long in the tooth as your beaver friend."

"No?"

"No."

She giggles as she rummages in the glove compartment for a pen and some paper which, I'm surprised to discover, are in there. "Go ahead," she says.

"What?"

"Give me the words you know."

I've been trying to remember ever since I first saw the note, and I think I have a pretty good idea of the lyrics. "Okay, here goes:

Who's peeking out from under a stairway,
Calling a name that's lighter than air.
Who's bending down to give me a rainbow,
Everyone knows it's Windy.

Who's tripping down the streets of a city,

> *Smiling at everybody she sees.*
> *Who's reaching out to capture a moment,*
> *Everyone knows it's Windy."*

I take out a cigarette and light it.

"What about the part that goes ta ta-ta-ta ta ta taaaa?"

Like the rest of her, her voice is charming, youthful, exotic. "Just give me a minute.

> *And Windy has stormy eyes,*
> *That flash at the sound of lies.*
> *And Windy has wings to fly,*
> *Above the clouds, above the clouds.*

"I remember the last line because I always thought it was nonsense syllables—ba ba-ba ba. Satch and I bet on it. He took five bucks from me on that one."

"That would be another reason for him to know that you'd remember it. Is that the whole thing?"

"I think the last stanza is just a repeat of the second."

She's writing furiously. When she's finished, she holds it at arm's length, as if examining a fine painting. "Okay. Now, what the hell does it mean?"

"It's a song that Satch associated with Wendy. I can see why."

"What do you mean?"

"Giving rainbows, smiling at everybody, capturing a moment, stormy eyes, hater of lies...it's her, was her, in a lot of ways." I can feel tears forming in my eyes and I detest myself for them. Moira places a comforting hand on my knee and I wish it would creep higher. This is why I don't trust who I am. Perhaps sensing this, she withdraws it.

"I think there might be more to it than that."

"Like what?"

"I know your last name is pronounced bal-you-nah, right? Anyone ever mispronounce it?"

"As if my first name weren't bad enough, every teacher I ever had, when they took attendance for the first time, would call out 'Tinker Balloon.' I got into a lot of fights over that—so did Satch."

"Calling a name that's lighter than air," she says, without looking at me. She continues to study her scribbling.

Maybe she's right about men.

Maybe not.

Chapter ten

After an hour and a half on the road, we're nearing Grand Rapids. This is home territory for me of course. The house where Wendy and I lived, and where she died, isn't more than five miles from this spot.

Moira sees the exit warning sign for 96 East to Detroit and she points it out to me. "Better get in the other lane," she says.

"I don't think so."

"I'm telling you, Tin, the exit for Detroit is just ahead. I know you know your way around here, but I just saw the sign."

"We're not going to Detroit."

"What?"

"Satch wants us in Chicago."

"What? What in the hell are you talking about?"

It's my turn to be smug. "Like I told you, Satch and Wendy met there, at a place called Joey Buona's. A few years later, Wendy and I were in Chicago to visit her family when she suggested that *we* go there. I really had some misgivings about it, but she insisted.

She said she wanted a different memory of the place—something with me in it." Moira must be sensing the difficulty I'm having with the recollection, because her whole demeanor oozes sympathy. "Joey Buona's is only a block off Michigan," I continue. "Little hole-in-the-wall, but great food. I had a superb *cavatappi alfredo* and a really garlicky gnocchi. They were generous with the booze too. It helped assuage my guilt over my brother."

Moira fidgets in her seat. As we pass the exit to Detroit, she's clearly agitated. "Look," she says, "I don't want to seem insensitive, but what—"

"Joey Buona's is *just off Michigan*. I remember that the other streets in that area are named for the Great Lakes too, like Ontario. There's also a St. Clair Street."

"You're sure?"

"Yes."

We travel in silence for a few miles as we zip past the skyline of downtown Grand Rapids. Moira is squinting at the note again. Her black hair is hanging down, erasing her face. "You could be wrong, it could still be Detroit."

"There's an atlas in the back seat somewhere. Can you grab it?"

She unbuckles her seatbelt and gets on her knees, facing the rear. I imagine myself sitting under her. "I don't see it. How can you find anything in this mess? Wait, never mind, here it is." She turns around again and sits down, atlas in hand. "Just off Michigan could mean just off *Lake* Michigan too," she says as she settles back, "that would describe the whole damn city."

"Find the state of Illinois first. On the next page there should be a map of the city."

She's leaning over the atlas intently. She brushes her hair back behind one ear to keep it out of her vision. "Yeah, here's Illinois. Chicago and vicinity are on the next page over. Now what?"

"There should be a list of all the street names off to the side somewhere, along with a letter and number that will help you to pinpoint it on the map. Look for Ontario Street." I can see her moving one slim finger down the list. "Bingo," she says.

"Now look for St. Clair."

After a long minute she says: "Yup, one of those too."

It's a fearsome thing to be right when you don't want to be.

"In fact," she says, "they intersect."

"Where?"

"Downtown Chicago. Looks like a couple of blocks off Michigan Avenue."

"What's there?"

"I don't know. We need to get a different map, like a tourist map—one that has the hotels and businesses on it. Could Joey Buona's be there? Maybe 432 is the address for the restaurant. Maybe that's where he wants us to meet him."

"I don't think so. Joey's is only a block off Michigan. I remember because Wendy and I parked on Michigan Avenue and we only had to walk a block, go around the corner, and it was right there. I don't think Satch would want to conduct this business in such a public place anyway."

"Ontario, Erie, Huron and Superior all run east/west and cross Michigan."

"Superior. That's it. Joey's was on Superior Street, so it can't be Joey's. There's got to be something significant, though, at the intersection of Ontario and St. Clair. These other clues have to do with that."

"And you know what they mean?" Moira says, "like these underlined words here? Impression and point?"

"No, I haven't figured those out yet."

"Then how do you know that it's supposed to be Chicago? I don't think that we can eliminate Detroit yet. And, by the way, if you knew this all along, why did you send Graham off to Detroit?"

I laughed. *"Me? You* sent him, darlin'. I just went along."

"But you knew, then, that we weren't going to Detroit. I didn't. Why would you let him go?"

"You like Virginia Woolf?"

"What? Why?"

"Virginia Woolf once wrote: 'The older one grows, the more

one likes indecency.' I guess that's as good a reason as any. I didn't want him along."

"Why not?" she asks.

I look over at her. She has a wry smirk on her face that tells me her question is moot. "For the same reason that you didn't."

"Okay, but he may still be headed in the right direction."

"No," I say with absolute certainty, "we're supposed to go to Chicago."

"How can you be so sure?"

"Moira," I say, placing my hand on her knee, "everyone knows it's windy."

Chapter eleven

I hate Gary, Indiana. I don't think there's an uglier city in all of America, maybe the world. Of course I'm not really giving it a chance. As with everything, it's subject to my imagination and the real meaning of a person or a place is invisible. We live an image.

The problem with Gary is that, before I ever saw it, I had it firmly established in my mind as the town of *The Music Man*. Shirley Jones steps out of the library and wanders through quiet, gaslit streets to her ornate house with the broad porch, where folks in dresses and suits wander by in their straw hats and whisper "good evening". It's the place where little Ronnie Howard struggles with his stuttering problem while the townsfolk gather round the latticed gazebo in the square to hear Robert Preston sermonize about the evils of the pool hall and the mayor's wife valiantly attempts to preserve the arts of antiquity with her feathered followers as she roots out the perfidy of Balzac. It is a small, rural town, full of small, rural thinkers. It is a naïve and false and charming place where the primary punishment for rebellion is to be the object of gossip.

When I saw the real city, I was amazed at how large and dirty and industrial it is. It's full of old run-down buildings and factories and slums; a grimy, modern urban center where the people who wait to grab the elevated railway for home look out of place in that morass of concrete and steel and machines. Though it is night now, I have been through here on a summer day when the blue, crystalline sky can suddenly disappear under a canopy of gray pollution pouring from factory chimneys. In Gary, it's always twilight. I can understand why Stephen King had his crazy pyromaniac, the Trashcan Man, set the place ablaze.

It's close to 2:30 A.M. and Moira is sleeping, Satch's note clutched in her right hand. I'm forcing myself to stay awake with coffee and cigarettes. We've tried to decipher the rest of the note—to no avail. Impression? Point? 432? When pigs fly? These have to be the clues that pinpoint Satchel's location, but they've been beyond us thus far. I listen to her easy breathing; glance when I can at the gently rising and falling chest that never falls very far.

I know that I'm probably on my way to dying and it seems ludicrous for a man to feel regret about it when just last night he was prepared to kill himself—but I do. All the death and dying had depressed me to the point that death seemed a welcome relief. It became the kind, old carriage driver of Emily Dickinson's poem, taking me home to my 'swelling of the ground'. But now, after meeting Moira, I'm not so sure I'm ready to take that ride. I'm not sure what I feel, in fact, unless it's confusion. I do wish she would wake up. I miss her company. Her head is leaning against the window and I wish that she was leaning this way. I want to touch her, to feel her warmth against me, to feel *alive,* like I have all day. *I want to get to know you,* she'd said.

She'd been flirting with me all day. How can this girl, this *child,* be interested in me? Maybe it's just sympathy for the wreckage that I've become. Maybe it's curiosity. She isn't the first girl her age to have taken a shine to me. I even had one of my senior students tell me she wanted to stay in town and give up college so that she could be nearer to me, help me to get over the death of my wife.

Adolescent silliness? Maternal instinct? Hormonal overdrive? Humanitarian zeal? I had no trouble recognizing the impossibility of those situations. Why is this girl so different? I don't have the answer, but I know when she looks at me in a certain way, when she issues those flirtatious intimations, it thrills me. It isn't just physical either. She's smart, aware, clever, mature—way beyond her years. High school must've been terribly difficult for her.

A car honks loudly at me as it passes me on the left. I've been drifting, and have allowed the Jeep to do the same. I take another drink of coffee and try to focus on the road. It's time to get out and walk around for a few minutes. I glance at the gas gauge. It's less than a quarter full. I'm thinking that I haven't seen an open station for quite awhile when one looms up at the end of the next exit ramp. Its towering, lighted sign prints 'Citgo' on the polluted canvas of the Indiana night.

As I pull in under the yellow glow of the neon lights, Moira stirs and sits up.

"I'm sorry, Tin," she mumbles. "I guess I just passed out. How long have I been sleeping?"

"Not long. Less than an hour."

"Where are we?"

"Just west of Gary."

"Indiana?"

"Yes, on the 90 toll road."

"How far to the Windy City?" She winks at me and my heart leaps. She's hiding her anxiety about her...about Sweeney, very well.

"Half hour, forty-five minutes."

She pulls on the handle and opens the door. It takes her a few seconds to realize that she's still belted in before she releases the buckle. She stretches, then shakes herself, like a long distance runner might in order to loosen up before a race. I try to concentrate on pumping gas.

"It's kind of chilly out here," she says, rubbing her arms. "I'm going inside. I'll wait for you there."

"Hey, look for one of those tourist maps we talked about. We may be close enough to Chicago to find one now—and grab me another coffee will you?"

"Cream? Sugar?"

"Black."

I watch her saunter away and my imagination gets obnoxious again. I feel desperately alone when she's gone. I curse the pump for being so slow. When the trigger finally clicks off, I almost run inside. The florescent lights are blinding. It's silly how so many of us believe that light keeps bad things out. After all, I'm in here, aren't I?

She's standing by the checkout counter, studying a map. The man behind the counter, a skinny, middle-aged guy with a greasy ponytail is eyeing her appreciatively. I get this sudden impulse to punch him. I suppress it and smile instead, as he looks my way in reaction to the little bell that rings when the door opens. He smiles back and returns his attention to Moira. "Man," I say, trying to draw his attention, "it's gettin' cold out there." I look around.

"Heat's finally movin' out," the checkout guy says. "Cold front comin' down from Canada with rain ahead of it. Supposed to be a high of seventy today—and thunderstorms." He sighs and reluctantly turns in my direction. "Help you find anything?"

Cold front? Seventy degrees? Toto, I don't think we're in Michigan anymore. "Coffee?"

"Right behind ya."

He turns back to Moira, as do I. She seems oblivious to us both. I pour the coffee, which bears a striking resemblance to tar, snap on a lid, and return to the counter. "Did you find one?" I shout at Moira.

"H-m-m-m? Oh, yeah." She heads toward us. "Sorry, I forgot about the coffee." She slaps the map down on the glass counter next to the steaming styrofoam cup.

"We had thirty-five in gas too."

He looks at me and back at her. "You guys together?"

"That's right." I stare at him, daring him to say something. He doesn't. He gives me back my credit card. His smile suggests that he is giving me credit for more than our purchases. I sign the slip and head for the door.

"What was that all about?" she says as we reach the Jeep.

"What do you mean?"

"You looked like you could have killed that guy."

"Bullshit."

"I saw what I saw," she says, and she's right. I feel as Satchel must have felt.

"I didn't like the way he was looking at you."

She smiles as she buckles her seatbelt. I start the engine and place my cup of tar in the holder.

"Why don't you just kiss me and get it over with?" she says.

That fantasy, that complex image in my heart, lifts me from myself. I grab the nape of her neck and pull her toward me. With the aggression of my approach, I expect resistance, fear, a terrible regret from her. Instead, her mouth melts into mine. I feel the loving investigation of her tongue, the wild breath of her nostrils, that wonderful sense of total *agreement* that I believed would never come to me again, and I marvel that this beautiful girl could want me. When I let the back of her head go, she doesn't move away but stays close, her black eyes fierce with longing. I want to say I love her, instead I blurt out, "What is this?"

She kisses me again, lightly this time, familiarly. "Mutual attraction," she answers.

"You can't be attracted to me."

"Why not?"

"Because I'm almost twice your age. Because I've been taught for many years that if there's any regret after something like this, it's always the older person who should have known better."

"That why you let Graham go to Detroit? So you wouldn't have to deal with temptation? I think you knew what you were doing. I know what I'm doing."

"You think I arranged this little tryst?"

Her gentle smile is erased. "Is that what you call it? A tryst?"

"What is it?"

"Nothing right now. Drive."

My considerable talent for ruining things has manifested itself yet again. I pull out of the Citgo station and back onto the toll road. Moira unfolds the map we bought and studies it. She says nothing, but I know she's upset. I see her wipe something from her face. She's trying to hide it. I can't see her very well in the darkness, but there are little spots of dampness on the map. "Sweeney's going to be okay," I say.

"Yeah."

"Look, I'm really sorry about what I said. It wasn't my intention to demean it. I guess it's just hard for me to believe that someone as young and beautiful and intelligent as you could be interested in getting tangled up with an alcoholic, suicidal sonofabitch like me. I've ruined everyone around me. I don't want that to happen to you."

"It's not your choice, Tin."

"What isn't?"

"Whether I care for you or not. The only thing you have control over is whether you want to care back."

"It would be very easy to love you."

"Then don't make it difficult."

She places her hand on my knee and I take it.

"I'm not worried about Sweeney. I'm worried about you. Satchel wants *you*."

"It'll be okay," I tell her, but I don't believe it myself. We're all liars after all—the only difference between us is the intent. "See anything on that map?"

She pulls her hand out from under mine in order to straighten it out. "It shows the hotels and the tourist attractions—the Art Institute, the Field Museum, Shedd Aquarium, Soldier Field; shopping—Nieman-Marcus, Saks, Ralph Lauren—and restaurants."

"Look."

She glances up to see a billboard advertising the Seurat exhibit at the Chicago Art Institute. "Maybe we can stop in and see that after all this is over with," she says. "I love the impressionists, especially Monet and Van Gogh."

"Not Seurat?"

"I can appreciate what it takes for him to create those canvases from a series of dots. What's that technique called?"

"Pointillism."

"Yeah. *A Sunday on Le Grande Jatte* is brilliant and it's so large—it must have taken him half a lifetime to paint—but, for some reason, it's just not as pleasing to the eye as *Crows in a Cornfield,* or Renoir's *Two Sisters,* you know what I mean?"

The expression of epiphany on my face must have startled her. "Tin? What is it?"

"Impressionists. Pointillism."

Comprehension slowly spreads across her face as she turns to me and the yellow lights of the Dan Ryan Expressway illuminate her features. "Point. Impression. The words that your brother underlined in the note!" She turns back to the map. "So we're supposed to find him there, at the Art Institute?"

"I don't think so, no."

"Why?"

"Too public. Did you find what's at the intersection of St. Clair and Ontario yet?"

"So it's just another reference to Chicago?" I see her slim finger moving over the map as if it were written in braille.

"I think so, yes. What's there?"

"Three hotels. The Red Roof Inn, The Courtyard Marriot and the Wyndham."

"What's on the fourth corner?"

"Doesn't say."

She grabs the note and grimaces at it. "When pigs fly and the number, 432, are the only clues left if we've got everything else right."

"Pigs," she reiterates. "Hog, sow, boar, slob, cop, pork, silk purse..."

"What're you doing?"

"Word association. Just trying to think of any word that has to do with pigs. Bacon, ham, Porky, Babe..."

"Wait a minute. Ham. You said ham."

"Yeah. So?"

"The Wyndham Hotel. Wind. Ham."

Her mouth, eyes—her whole face opens. "Pigs fly!" she says. "You think that could be it?"

"It's on the corner of St. Clair and Ontario, just off Michigan Avenue. 432 could be a room number. Unless you can come up with something better, it's all we've got."

The skyline of Chicago looms in the distance. Like my mind, the black night behind it is alive with electricity.

Chapter twelve

Three-thirty on a Tuesday morning is the ideal time to drive in Chicago, at least as far as traffic is concerned. Lake Shore Drive is virtually deserted. Skyscrapers, dominated by the Sears Tower, rise in the starless sky to our left. Lake Michigan, hidden by darkness, opens in a vast, liquid veldt to our right. Only a solitary freighter floating in the distance, and sporadic streaks of lightning, reveal the enormity of the black waters. Not until this moment have I felt so acutely the glaring contrast between the imaginative world of nature and the concrete world of man.

Satchel is waiting here somewhere, only a few blocks away. Moira has kept my mind away from death, but now I begin to sense that the approaching dawn will be my last. The light may be a long time in coming. Rain sweeps in out of the darkness and assaults the car with heavy drops. Thunder accompanies the deluge. In a few minutes, I'm forced to slow to a crawl and, though the windshield wipers are operating at their fullest capacity, I can barely see. I feel like we're *in* Lake Michigan instead of next to it.

Through the watery blur, I spot the Ohio street exit. Although it's not the street we want, it will allow me to get out of the open and in among the tall buildings where nature's wrath won't be quite as effective. A gust of wind rocks the car as I turn west and I struggle to get it under control.

"According to the map," Moira says, "Ontario is the next street up."

"Okay. Well, St. Clair Street should be right ahead somewhere. It runs north and south, right?"

"Right."

"We'll just go north a block when we get there and we should be at the Wyndham."

"Pull over," she says. "We need to talk about how we're going to handle this. Maybe the rain will let up in a few minutes too."

I glide to the curb, relieved to be momentarily rid of the tension of driving by braille. I turn off the windshield wipers and let nature have its way.

"What're we going to do when we get to the hotel?" she says.

"I thought I'd go to the main desk and ask them if anyone named Balune has reserved a room."

"They're going to say no. You know that. No fugitive in his right mind would register under his own name."

"Probably not, but I'm not so sure my brother, or anyone in my family for that matter, operates within the boundaries of the exalted state of 'right mind'. Besides, what else can I do?"

"He might have registered under Sweeney's name."

"Could be, or he might not have registered at all."

"We could ask—"

"*We* are not going to do anything. You're staying with the car."

"Is that an order?"

"No. It's the safest thing for Sweeney, but you do what you want."

"Thank you." A few seconds later she adds: "I'll stay with the car, but I want you to promise me something."

"What?"

"If you find out they're in there, you'll come and get me."

"To what purpose?"

"I think I value your life a little more than you do. Just promise, or I go in with you now."

"Okay."

A little tune suddenly emanates from somewhere on her side of the jeep. I recognize it as "The Cell Block Tango" from the musical, *Chicago*. "Appropriate," I say as she extracts her cell phone and opens it.

"Oh-oh," she says, reading the caller identification. "It's Graham."

"Oops."

"Hello?" Pause. "We're in Chicago." Pause. I can hear his voice. He sounds like a very angry insect. "Because we figured out the code in that note, that's why." Pause. More buzzing. "They were street names and the 'pigs fly' thing is a hotel, the Wyndham. We're only a couple of blocks away now." Pause. Buzz. "His age really isn't an issue, Graham. You act more like a father than he does." She looks at me and shrugs. Buzz, buzz, buzz. "I don't think that'd be a good idea. I'll call you when we know something."

She closes the phone and puts it away in the secret place it came from.

The monsoon is calming down. Outside, some kids are dancing down the street. They're drenched, and happy about it. They look like they have as much liquid inside them as out. I don't think any of the bunch are over twenty-one. What are they doing here, crawling around at this time of night? They shouldn't be happy.

"Graham's angry?"

"He is."

"Why?"

"He's jealous." She gives me a wanton smile and I feel the familiar longing that has been with me ever since I saw her standing in my cabin, reading my suicide note. "Do you think he has reason to be?"

"I…I know that I want very much to touch you, to kiss you again."

We watch the kids stumble by, oblivious to our presence. They disappear inside a parking ramp. "That's a *good* thing," she says.

"What did you tell Graham wouldn't be a good idea?"

"For him to come down here."

"Let's go see what we can find out."

"Okay."

When I pull in front of the hotel, a valet comes to the car and opens Moira's door. His brown hair is turning prematurely gray at the temples. Even so, he looks about my age. He's a big, beefy fellow with a broad smile and he's dressed in some kind of blue uniform with a 'W' on his billed hat, which he tips as he extends his hand to assist Moira out of the car. "Good morning folks," he says, "welcome to the Wyndham. Would you like to pop the back sir, and we'll get your luggage?"

"I'm waiting here," Moira tells him. "My husband will only be a moment. He's just checking on rooms." She turns and winks at me. How can she not be twenty-five?

The valet's white teeth disappear with his smile. "You folks don't have a reservation?"

"Not yet, no."

"You won't be able to park here, then," he says. "We have to keep this area clear for our guests."

"At four in the morning?"

"Twenty-four seven," he replies without hesitation. "It's management policy, sir."

"It's okay, Tin," Moira says, shifting across the leather seat and forcing me out the door with her hip. "I'll drive around the block while you check it out for us, okay? I'll meet you back here in a couple of minutes."

Reluctantly, I comply. "I won't be long, darling," I tell her and turn back into the car to kiss her. She smiles and utters a throaty giggle as she reciprocates. "That was a cheap move," she says.

"One must take advantage of one's opportunities."

I watch her pull slowly onto St. Clair Street as I stand next to the valet. "It's our honeymoon," I say to him.

"Congratulations, sir," he responds, with the condescending tone of the rich. Like many people who work for the elite, he has mistaken his servitude for inclusion among them, entitling him to practice the ancient art of exclusion—snobbery by association, I guess.

I hurry through the revolving door. The check-in desk is nowhere in sight and it takes me a few minutes to discover that it's on the second floor, just up the marble stairs. There are two people behind the high counter, one male, one female, both dressed in blue and looking very tired. As I approach them, however, they both put on their best Wyndham smiles and greet me. "Good morning, sir," the man says. He's a little African-American guy with large eyes and an intelligent face. He reminds me a bit of the photos I've seen of James Baldwin. The woman, also African-American, is strikingly beautiful and several inches taller than her companion.

"Hi," I say, trying to appear nonchalant. My heart is beating violently and for some reason I expect my brother to appear at any moment and clobber me right there in the lobby with a baseball bat. "My name is Tin Balune and I—"

"Yes," the woman says, expertly plucking some paper work from the desk in front of her, "your room is all set sir. We've been waiting for you to arrive."

"My...my...room?"

"Yes sir. You're in the corner suite, one of our best. You *did* request a smoking room didn't you sir? If not, we can change—"

"What? Oh, no, no that's fine."

"Here's your keycard then sir," she says, smiling sweetly at me. "Your agent took care of the bill personally."

"He did?"

"*She* did, yes sir...several days ago as I recall."

"She?" I'm sure my confusion, which is considerable, is very apparent. Satchel has a woman with him too? Who in hell could she be? It has to be Satchel, who else would even know that I would be coming here? I take the keycard that the beauty is extending to me.

"Is everything satisfactory sir?"

"What? Yes, yes fine, thank you. You say my agent was here a few days ago?"

"Yes sir," she glances down at the paperwork, "about a week or more, actually. I took the reservation myself." The woman gives me a flattering, flirtatious smile. James Baldwin has turned his back on us and is occupied with other matters. "Will you be staying alone, sir?"

"No. My, uh, my wife will be joining me shortly." I'm pleased to see that this revelation bothers the beauty. "Did my agent say that she was staying here at the Wyndham as well?"

The woman's puzzled expression suddenly changes. A knowing grin creeps across her perfect face. "It seemed to me, sir, that she already had accommodations. I thought, perhaps, she might be staying with you. She's a very beautiful woman, sir, if you don't mind my saying so. Efficient, too." I want very much to ask for a more detailed description of this 'agent', but that would make me seem more bizarre than I already do. Best to let this woman think that I'm in some kind of matrimonial difficulty.

"Thank you."

"Certainly, sir. Let us know if we can be of any further service. The concierge desk is just down the hall here and he can assist you with information about the hotel or provide you with maps to the city. We hope you enjoy your stay at the Wyndham." Her tongue is literally pushing against her cheek when she says this.

"One last question. How long is my stay?"

"Sir?"

"How long did Miss…did my agent book the room for?"

"Two nights, sir. Tonight, what's left of it, and tomorrow night. Checkout is 11:00 A.M. on Thursday morning."

"Thanks again."

As I turn away from the desk and head for the stairs, my head is spinning. Why did Satchel arrange for a room for me? Is he here somewhere? Where's Sweeney? Can I save him? Who is this woman? Can I keep Moira out of harm's way? What the hell is going on?

Clearly, my brother is, as always, way ahead of me. What do we do now? I feel as though I'm being played, and I don't like the feeling.

I glance down at the keycard as I spin through the revolving door back out into the damp night. It has the room number on it.

432.

Chapter thirteen

Moira pulls up in the Cherokee just as I emerge from the lobby. The valet is standing nearby, keeping a sharp eye out. I open the passenger door and lean in as the Guardian of Management Rules approaches from behind. "Sir, please, I told you that you can't—"

"Our room is ready, darling, come along." She is surprised, but unbuckles her seatbelt and gets out. I turn to the valet and place a ten-dollar bill in his hand as I show him the paperwork identifying us as guests. His meaty smile returns and he bows slightly. "Thank you sir," he says. I can see that despite the money, he's a bit chagrined, as if I've gotten away with something. "Any luggage, sir?"

"No."

He raises one eyebrow. He's got me pegged. "Very good, sir."

"Keys are in the ignition," I say.

"Your retrieval number is on this ticket, sir," he says, handing it to me. "Whenever you need your vehicle, just phone the concierge and give him the number. It takes about twenty minutes."

"Anytime? Twenty-four seven?"

"Yes, sir." His face is redder now, if that's possible. I wonder what he will think when he gets inside and sees all the beer cans and whiskey bottles and burger wrappers. I couldn't possibly make a worse impression.

"Good." I grab Moira by the arm and lead her inside.

"What the hell is going on?" she says, as I pull her toward the elevator.

"We have a room. Someone, a woman, came in here several days ago posing as my literary agent and reserved a room for me."

"There's a woman with them?"

"It's room 432. Anyway, who else would even know I'd be coming here?"

"Who's the woman? Are you sure she's *not* your agent?"

"My agent is Walt Kupke. He lives in New York and he certainly wouldn't be booking rooms for me. He has better things to do with his time. I have no clue as to who this woman is. I guess we have to assume that Satchel has an accomplice."

The elevator's rising contributes to my queasiness. I swallow hard.

"You think Satchel's in that room?"

"That'd be my guess."

"With Sweeney and this woman?"

"I don't know. The woman could be holding Sweeney somewhere else."

"What're you going to do?"

"I don't know yet. I'm thinking."

The elevator stops and the panel of numbers shows a lighted four. The doors slide open and both of us step back defensively as a man in a Hawaiian print shirt and tan shorts, his back to us, slowly turns around. He has the hapless, shit-eating grin of the inebriated on his pale face, one I've often seen in the mirror. It's not Satchel. The guy is at least sixty and looks as though he's cleaned out the cash bar in his room. "Goo moanin'," he says, tipping a hat that isn't there. He's wearing a nametag on his shirt. Apparently he's in Chicago for some kind of convention. It says Mastheader's Corp. on the tag above a handwritten name that appears to read 'Earl Schmidt'. He staggers past us into the elevator car as we step out. I don't think he knows that he'll be going up. I don't think he cares, really. Just as the doors start to close on him, he leans over and vomits onto the floor.

"Nice," Moira says.

"I feel a bit like that myself," I say.

"Don't you dare."

We stand there for a few minutes, uncertain as to what to do next. If Satchel is holding Sweeney in the room, and he has a weapon, we're screwed. Moira is with me, contrary to his specific instructions. The only hope I have is that he will let Moira take Sweeney back to the car and allow them to leave, satisfied that he has me. I'm very much aware of what my fate will be when that happens. On the other hand, he could kill us all or Sweeney could be held elsewhere.

"I think you should go back down and stay with the car. If I can work the exchange, I'll send Sweeney down, then you two get out of here."

"And leave you here to die? Not happening."

Room 432 is just around the corner from the elevator, at the end of a small, well-lit corridor. "All right," I say, as I move toward it. "Do this for me will you? I'm going to unlock the door and push it open. If you see anyone inside, I want you to run. Will you do that at least?"

"Let's play it by ear."

"Damn it, Moira!"

"Damn it yourself, Tin."

There's no hope for it. I can't tell her what to do. She doesn't understand that it's not an authority issue. I simply can't bear the responsibility of another death. I keep thinking that if she dies, I'm going to make damn certain that I do too.

I slide the card down the slot in the door. The little green light goes on. I turn the handle and push the door inward. There are no lights on, but I can see the Chicago skyline through the huge window that seems to occupy one whole wall. I flick the switch. Lights on either side of the king-sized bed go on. I don't see anyone, but there's another door further on, presumably leading to a bathroom. He could be in there. I try to control my shaking hand. I wait for his voice, or a crushing blow from someplace I'm not aware of.

Suddenly, Moira rushes past me. "Nobody's here," she says, "and I'm dying to go to the bathroom."

I manage to grab her arm just as she swings the door open. "Stop!"

She turns on the light. "Let me go, Tin," she says. "See? No one in here. You think your brother, Sweeney and this mystery woman are all crammed in here waiting to jump us? I'll be right out. You look around and see if he left any more instructions. I really, really have to pee."

She's right. My nerves begin to settle, like a man facing a firing squad who's been offered a cigarette. I know that I've gained a few precious minutes, but I'm only delaying the inevitable. I go so far as to get down on my knees and look tentatively under the bed. There's nowhere else to hide. I hurry to the door, shut it, bolt it. What's next? I look around the room. Nothing's out of order. I examine the desk by the window. There's a room-service menu, some tourist magazines extolling the wonders of Chicago, a blank pad of paper with the Wyndham monogram on it, a pen, a TV guide, a telephone, an empty ice bucket and glasses on a tray. On the table by the bed is an alarm clock. I open the mahogany doors to the entertainment center and discover a television, coffee maker, and a mini-bar underneath. Nothing seems out of place.

Moira emerges from the bathroom, looking considerably relieved, although for different reasons, I suspect, than mine. "Find anything?" she says.

"Nothing."

"What now?"

"We wait, I guess. We did what we were supposed to do. We figured it out and got here within the time constraints. Maybe he didn't think we'd get here so quickly. Maybe he'll call us, or send this mystery woman. I don't know. This has got to be the place, though. We got it right, I'm sure of that."

"We should have packed some clothes. All I have is what I'm wearing."

"Me too. Maybe we'll have a chance to buy some things when the stores open."

"We're going to need some sleep too." We're both aware of the fact that there is a single king-sized bed, but neither of us says anything about it.

"Amen."

"I'm going to take a shower. Why don't you lie down on the bed and see if you can grab a catnap? I'll wake you in a little while."

"You sure?"

"Positive."

She disappears into the bathroom again and I hear the water from the shower begin. I've been awake all night and, having slept on the floor of a leaky boat the night before, weariness is setting in. I lie down on the bed. My muscles, tense for so long, melt into the mattress. My eyes, though only half-open, sense the dim light of approaching dawn outside. Then she opens the door to the bathroom and just stands there. Even though she's silhouetted in the frame, with the light behind her, I can tell that she's naked. She walks slowly toward me. Her hair is wet, matted to her head and shoulders. "Wendy," I whisper, but she doesn't respond. Her body isn't right somehow. One arm hangs at a terrible angle. Her leg is forced in. The flesh on her hips sags like that of an old woman whose bones are unable to support the flesh any longer. She is wet, but not with water—something thicker, syrupy. It drips off of her in gooey strings. I can see her face now. It is beautiful, kind, loving. She holds out twisted limbs to me, arms that shouldn't work they are so skewed and grotesque. She places a knee on the bed and leans forward so that her face is above mine. Liquid drips on the sheets. As she crawls toward me, she leaves large swathes of scarlet. She wants so much to be held and I try to hold her, but she's sticky and slippery. It doesn't matter. Her lovely, undamaged face is above mine. Her mouth is on mine. She whispers "Tin." Her mouth tastes of salt. I wipe it away with my hand. There's blood all over us. She touches my face with fingers that are broken and splay in every direction. I hear Satchel's voice from somewhere in the shadows. "She wants you, brother dear. She wants you to fuck her. Go ahead, I don't mind. I think you should make her happy—if you can find the hole." There is a wicked giggle, a demonic laugh. I open my mouth to scream, but Wendy's face covers it. Her blood fills my mouth. I'm gagging, choking.

"Tin?" There's a hand on my foot. "Tin!"

I realize that my eyes have been closed only when I force them open. Wendy is gone. Moira is standing at the foot of the bed, shaking my foot. She has a towel wrapped around her torso. "Are you all right? God, you were screaming like a banshee! I thought Satchel had broken in here and...." I realize she has tears in her eyes, making them darker. I didn't think that was possible.

"I'm sorry. I'm okay. Bad dream, I guess." She's gripping the towel with her right hand, near her left armpit. She erases a solitary tear with the palm of her left hand.

I should say something, get up to comfort her, but I'm paralyzed. The sight of her has frozen me, like a prophet's vision. I simply stare. I know my mouth is gaping like a drooling dog, but I'm incapable of shutting it. I'm trembling. Every muscle in my body has either gone AWOL or is in a state of rebellion. Is it the remnants of terror? The effects of alcohol deprivation? Lack of sleep? I know it's none of those before I even wonder about it.

She is staring at me too. Our eyes are locked. She lets go of the towel. I want desperately to look at her body, but I can't escape her eyes. She pushes her long, wet, black tresses back over her shoulders, baring her neck and upper chest, then she kneels on the end of the bed.

"Moira," I say, finally calling my ridiculous mouth to obedience, "we can't."

Her black eyes are still fiercely connected to mine. "Yes," she whispers, as she crawls toward me and pushes me prone. "We can."

My hand touches the naked skin over her ribs and I feel such warmth, such pleasure, that it makes me shiver. Her flesh reacts in the same way. "You're eighteen, for God's sake."

Her long fingers run gently across my forehead. She leans closer to me. I feel her breath, sweet with the scent of mint, caress my cheek. "You want to, don't you?"

I want to lie to her, but I can't. "Yes."

My hand, with a will of its own, cups her breast. It feels like my fingers were made for the sole purpose of resting there. "M-m-m-m," she groans. I feel her nipple swell between my fingers. "I love you, Tin," she whispers to me. "Do you hear what I'm saying?

"Yes."

"What you are holding is not the breast of a child and what I told you just now doesn't require a response. This is my decision. I want you to make love to me."

Her mouth covers mine and I pull her body hard against me, as if to invite her, to force her, to come inside me. Instead, in a very short time, the opposite takes place.

Chapter fourteen

I wake first. I hear traffic in the street below. I prop myself up on one elbow and look at Moira. I am appalled at how incredibly beautiful she is. Her head lies in a pool of black silk, her hair contrasting wonderfully with her creamy skin. She is supine, on her back, the sheet barely covering her pubis. Her upper body is nude. I wonder at the lovely slope that rises from the valley of her flat stomach to the rising foothills of her ribs to the tender mountains of her chest. I kiss the summits, higher than Edmund Hillary ever felt, I'm certain. I feel her hand on the back of my head. Her eyes come open.

"Are you molesting me while I sleep?" she says.

With Hillary still in mind I answer: "Just exploring."

She raises my head so that we're face-to-face. "What are you thinking, Tin?"

"That I'm very lucky for an aging pedophile."

"I'm serious."

I consider honestly. "All right, I'll be honest. I'm thinking about being afraid. You, my dear, have brought fear back into my life."

Her lower lip juts in a charming pout. "What does that mean?"

"It means that I care very much for you and I'm afraid of losing something again."

She kisses me hard. "You care for me?"

"Yes."

"Even though I'm a teenager?"

"You're eighteen going on forty-five."

"Was the...did you.... You know what I mean. Was it good? It was my first time."

"I know."

"Were you surprised?"

"No, more like flattered. Did I hurt you?"

"Only for a coupla seconds. It was wonderful after that."

"I couldn't stop."

"I didn't want you to."

Then it just came from me. I don't remember considering it at all. "Moira, I really believe I might be falling in love with you. I don't know how that happened in such a short time. You're different than anyone I've ever met, even Wendy."

"Then this isn't just a tryst?"

"No."

"What about Wendy? Is this about her?"

"No, it's not about replacing her either. It's not gratitude for helping me to care about life again. I don't think it's this whole situation with Sweeney and Satch. Although making love to you was wonderful, it's not physical either. I just—"

She puts her hand on my groin. She grips me. "Oh my," she says, "somebody's a little excited." She nuzzles her face next to my ear and licks it. "You know," she says in a husky whisper, "I'd think I'd like to know what it's like to have this thing in my mouth. What do you think?"

I am, of course, beyond thought.

When I awake the second time she's gone. At first, I think she may just be using the bathroom, but then my awakening consciousness begins to offer more grotesque scenarios. The world is, after all, the world. I throw aside the sheet that's covering me and lunge into the bathroom, hoping desperately to find her. She isn't there. I return to the main room in a full-blown panic. Across the street, someone in a fourth floor room of the Courtyard Marriot is looking at me. It's a woman. She's very attractive, blonde, fairly young I think, but it's hard to tell from this distance. I realize I'm buck-naked. She waves at me to let me know she's seen me and I slowly begin to comprehend how observable we have been. Satch has a female ally. Could this woman be her? I close the drapes, shutting out the early afternoon sunlight and prying eyes. Where could Moira have gone? My nutcase brother is wandering around somewhere in this city. Did she find out something while I was sleeping and decide to pursue it on her own? Did Satchel lure her out? God, oh God, not again.

There's a knock at the door. I freeze. Moira wouldn't knock unless she forgot to take the key. I go to the closet and slip on a hotel bathrobe that's hanging there. I also remove one of the wooden hangers, for lack of a better weapon, then I approach the door. There is another soft knock. Moira would have been yelling at me by now. It can't be her.

"Who is it?" It's the only thing I can think of to say. I have to find out who it is before I open the door.

A young, male voice answers. "Room service, sir."

It isn't Sweeney's voice. I don't think it's Satchel. It's not a woman. Did Moira order something for us? She could have, but then why would she leave? Where the hell is she?

I slowly twist the door handle, raising the coathanger in the process. I pull the door slightly ajar and peek out. There's a young man standing there beside a wheeled cart that's covered in a white cloth. The aroma of bacon coming from somewhere underneath it resurrects another appetite. "Oh, wonderful!" says a voice from behind him and I look up to see Moira prancing down the hallway toward us, wearing a hotel bathrobe, a canister full of ice in her hand. My sense of relief is enormous, but it quickly turns to self-righteous anger. She squeezes between us into the room. "C'mon in," she says to the steward as she brushes by. "I'm starved."

I have no recourse but to open the door and try to demonstrate that all is as it should be. When the young man, who has far too great an appreciation for Moira's beauty, finally leaves, I turn to her. "What in hell is wrong with you?" I say. She's already munching on her omelet and gulping orange juice.

"Whaddya mean?" she says, chewing blissfully.

"You could have been killed, Moira! God, Satchel could have been waiting outside. What the hell were you thinking?"

"All that exercise this morning gave me an appetite." She winks at me lewdly. "I was hungry. You were sleeping. I ordered some breakfast and walked thirty feet down the hallway to get some ice. I turned around and came right back. Didn't seem too risky to me."

I grab her head in my hands and force her to look at me. Her questioning look, the innocence of it, assuages my ire. She has a bit of egg hanging from her lower lip. "I'm not your property," she says.

"You're wrong, darling. You are exactly that. You've made me care about you, so you have to be careful of yourself. You're *obligated* to keep safe. You wouldn't let me be reckless with my life; I won't let you be reckless with yours. We belong to each other. If you don't believe that, then this is a tryst and we should end it right now."

She raises one hand and places it over mine. She lifts my hand from her face and kisses my palm. "You're right. I'm sorry."

"Okay."

"Have something to eat. I ordered you bacon and eggs and hash browns. That okay?"

I sit down next to her on the bed. I kiss her. "What kind of eggs?"

"Over easy. It seemed appropriate."

I smile and attack my toast.

"Why is it so dark in here?" she says, looking around. "You've closed the drapes."

"I felt a little too exposed. Some woman was looking at me from a room across the street."

"Can't say as I blame her." She's eaten half of her omelet and is now playing with the rest of it. "I don't want you to think about our ages anymore. Can you do that?"

"Why?"

"Well, partly because I think it makes you more protective than you should be and partly because age difference is inconsequential, an artificial thing. What we did this morning is just a natural connection between two adults who are attracted to one another—an act of nature."

"Like the beaver that died, that skull you have in your room?"

"I suppose so. What made you think of that?"

"Nature didn't do *him* any favors."

"Look at it this way," she says, scooping another mouthful of her breakfast. "Supposing that poor thing didn't lose those upper incisors. He would have gone on to gnaw his way through his life, live a few more years—if he wasn't killed by predation or disease—and die. Which death is the natural one?"

"Are you saying that all death is 'natural'?"

"I don't know, exactly, but that beaver may have created a pond, provided a place for other things to live, fathered some kits, or at the very least it gave its body as food for scavengers, left an interesting skull for me to find—all meaningful things."

"So the beaver and I just acted according to our natures? This somehow justifies what we do, who we are?"

"I guess we all just go on until we're finished, regardless of the pain."

"So we're the same, Mr. Beaver and I?"

"Probably not to Mrs. Beaver, and certainly not to me." She kisses me. "Finish your breakfast, we've got other things to think about. What time is it?"

"Almost eleven."

"We're supposed to be checking out."

"Not until tomorrow, Thursday."

"Satchel took the room for two nights?"

"This mystery woman did, yes."

"Then he's probably going to contact us today, somehow."

"That'd be my guess. He'll give us instructions on where to meet him, and we make the exchange."

Moira gets up and goes to the window, opens the drapes. Sunlight floods the room. "There's not going to be any exchange."

"What?"

"I'm not giving you up, Tin."

"Don't be ridiculous. There's nothing else we can do. He'll kill your father, Moira. He's a murderer."

"I told you, Sweeney is *not* my father and if Satchel is a murderer, that means he'll kill *you*. I won't let that happen. There's got to be another way."

"There isn't."

"You don't know that. This woman, for instance, she might work to our advantage if we can figure out who the hell she is. Maybe she doesn't know what Satchel is up to. He could have paid her to come here and pretend to be your agent. He's been running from the law for years, I doubt if he'd have any serious love interest. Why don't you get a shower and we'll get out of here."

"Where are we going to go?"

"We'll talk to the clerk at the front desk, the one who talked to her. We can at least get a description, maybe a name, I don't know. Then we're going shopping. You're going to buy me some new clothes."

"We should wait here for him to contact us."

"There's no way I'm sitting around here all day. He'll get ahold of us. It's the only way he can get what he wants."

I shake my head while swallowing a last bit of bacon.

"What?"

"Either you're underestimating Satchel or you're not overly concerned for Sweeney's safety. My brother means what he says."

She comes back to me, sits on the bed, turns my face to hers. "Four years ago, shortly after we heard about Wendy's murder, Sweeney tried to...well, to put the make on me. I kicked him in the balls and told him if he ever tried that again I'd call the police. He's *not* my father, okay? I care about him, maybe more from pity than love. I don't want to see any harm come to him, but you are so much more important to me, Tin. Satchel has a lot less leverage than he thinks. Now, will you go take your shower please? There are limits to your charm."

I'm shaken with disbelief. Sweeney? Kind, old, neighborly Sweeney? My father's sandy-haired fishing partner? Mary's gentle and long-suffering husband? *That* Sweeney? A child molester? It can't be. "Wait a minute," I say, "you don't just drop a bomb like that on me and expect me to go about my business. Why didn't you tell me this before? Whatever possessed him? God, it must have been terrible for you to live with him."

"Fortunately," she says, "I was blessed with a high IQ and a personality that's far more aggressive than his."

"How could he do such a thing? It defies belief."

"It's probably partially my fault. I was used to walking around half-naked in front of him. I hadn't paid much attention to the effect it might have. Mom was gone. I didn't have her to tell me what to do. I just bounced through the living room in my bra and panties one night, kissed him goodnight on the cheek, and went to bed. Half an hour later, he was sitting on the edge of my mattress rubbing my stomach. When I woke up, he tried to kiss me. Like I said, I kicked him, hard, and he went down on his knees. He cried, he tried to explain how much he missed my mother and how lonely he was. I told him if he ever entered my bedroom again, I'd have him in jail. He never bothered me after that. He kept his distance and I became very conscious of my wardrobe. We've never spoken of it. He became 'Sweeney' to me that night. That's it."

"But he's so proud of you, he talks about you as if you *were* his daughter. He bragged to me about all your accomplishments in high school. I just can't believe he'd do something like that."

"Well, he did and I have no intention of trading you for him." She grazes my face with the back of her hand, gently studying me. "He's my past Tin. I don't want to see him hurt, but Satchel isn't going to have you, I love you too much. So we'll play this out and see what happens. I'll do what I have to do to save him, but not at the cost of giving you up."

"How did Mary...how did your mother die?"

"Why?"

"I just want to know."

"She drowned. I don't remember much about it. I was only three at the time. She died at the lake."

I want to hear more, but I can see that she doesn't want to talk about it.

"Sweeney never got over my mother's death. I think he was lonely and I wasn't careful. That's the way I see it. Now, I'm certainly not going to wear the same clothes again today, so take your shower or I'm going out by myself."

We try to get in touch with the beautiful clerk who checked me in and got a look at Satchel's woman-friend, my 'agent', but we are told she doesn't come in again until nine at night.

Within an hour, we are walking down Michigan Avenue, and Moira puts my charge cards to good use. It is rainy and cool, but I've never felt quite so exhilarated. I've forgotten about Satchel and Sweeney and the mystery woman. There are no threats. There are no ghosts. There is only Moira in the world and because of that, I love the world again.

Chapter fifteen

I t's mid-afternoon by the time we return to the hotel. I feel
somewhat like a pack mule, weighted down as I am by the packages.
We've been to Nordstrom's, Bloomingdale's, Saks and, (my personal
favorite, but her idea), Victoria's Secret. She has promised to model
everything for me. I have picked up some things too, but it wasn't
an easy task for a guy who trusts J.C. Penney to keep him abreast of
fashion. The doorman at the Wyndham greets me cheerfully as Moira
brushes by him and he, gratefully, relieves me of much of my burden.
At the door of 432, I tip him lavishly and he gives me a look equally
balanced between envy and commiseration. He sees me, no doubt,
as her Sugar Daddy who is paying significantly for his pleasures.

Inside, the room has been put in order again. There are no notes
or written messages. Moira checks the voice mail. Nothing. While
she rushes to the bathroom with armfuls of packages, I break into the
cash bar. I fix myself a whiskey and water, sans ice, and settle into the
leather chair next to the window. The housekeeping staff has opened

the drapes again and I glance over to the Marriot to see if the ogler is still at her window, but it looks as though her room is dark.

I'm very tired from all the walking and other 'exercise', but not at all sleepy. Surprisingly, the whiskey doesn't appeal to me and I set it aside. I pull a cigarette out of a pack that is almost spent, and light it with the new Zippo that Moira insisted I buy in a tobacco shop. It's just a regular Zippo, much like my old one, except that it has a bulls-eye insignia on it with a miniature heart in the center. She said I had to buy it. That way, every time I light a smoke, I'd have to think about her and what I'm risking. I keep remembering her eager face as she raced through the stores this afternoon. Never has spending money given me such pleasure.

Then she's standing there, by the bathroom door, wearing a plunging bra, thong, garter belt, silk stockings and heels—all of them the ebony color of her eyes and hair. She not only looks like she bought these things at Victoria's Secret, she looks like she just stepped from the pages of their catalogue. She is as far from eighteen as one can get without being old, but it isn't the marvelous maturity of her body that accomplishes it. Rather, it's her demeanor, the way she cocks her hip, the way she glides in those three inch heels—completely unlike the bent-ankled staggering I have seen in so many girls her age at senior proms. She is full of confidence and surety and I really believe she's having fun. She isn't doing this for me, but for her. "Whaddya think?" she says as she sashays a few feet toward me, turns twice to let me examine every inch of her, then stands and cocks that hip again.

"How much do you think an old man's heart can take?"

She laughs, but I really do fear for my health. She walks toward me, stands directly in front of me. She leans over with a slender hand gripping each arm of my chair. The aroma of her perfume is overwhelming. Her long, black hair hangs in my face. "I'll leave you alone," she whispers, "if you can help me get these things off without getting a massive hard-on."

"Too late."

She smiles, widening that sensuous mouth. "Then you must submit to fate."

"What?"

"That's what my name means you know. Fate."

"How entirely appropriate."

She sits on my knees and wraps those lovely arms around my neck, smothering me with a wet and lingering kiss. "Fuck me, Tin," she orders, with the authoritative voice of a spoiled child.

Mine is not to reason why.

When it's over, I lie gasping with her on the bed. As my awareness of the world slowly returns, I glance out of the open window. The woman is back, looking this way with the concentrated expression of a geneticist at her scope. She's smiling. She waves again. I feel somewhat like I did when our teacher caught Charlie Matterby and me in the boy's bathroom examining a rubber Charlie had stolen from his older brother.

"Moira," I whisper without moving. "I want you to look out the window and right across to the Marriot, the hotel across the street. There's a woman at a window there, watching us. This is the second time I've noticed her there. Can you see her?"

Moira takes a deep breath and raises her head to peek over my shoulder. "Yes," she says, giggling, "I do see her. Has she been there the whole time? Is she looking at us? Maybe she's just looking at the skyline or something. It's a beautiful view."

"She waved at me."

"What?"

"As soon as I look at her, she waves. This is the second time."

"Really?" Now she gets up on one elbow and stares more intently. "She's a pretty woman, from what I can see, young too. I bet she's in her mid-twenties. H-m-m-m she just closed the curtain. Apparently her curiosity is centered on you, my love. I wonder if she might be the woman who posed as your agent. Maybe her interest in us is more than prurient."

"That's what I was thinking. But it's almost as if she *wants* us to notice her. Would a conspirator wave at us? It doesn't seem like she'd be that…well, *friendly.*"

"I'm going to get dressed," she says. "Be back in a minute." She slides off the edge of the bed and walks about three steps before she stops dead in her tracks and assumes the frozen posture of stone statuary. "Tin."

"What is it?" I sit bolt upright, throw my aching legs onto the carpet and stand. "What?"

She points in the direction of the door to our room. There's a piece of paper on the floor. It looks as though it was shoved under the door. She moves gracefully to it, picks it up, and bolts the door, in one fluid motion.

"It's in Sweeney's handwriting again," she says as she unfolds it and reads.

"What does it say?" Never have I been so disconcerted by a simple piece of stationery. It brings the world of the past into this sacred place, where hedonism has been the only philosophy. Sweeney and Satchel and even Wendy have skittered in under the door, like clever rodents. Like Adam before God, I'm suddenly aware that we are both naked.

Moira hands it to me and pulls a sheet off the bed to cover herself, apparently feeling equally exposed. I can't help but notice how rosy her face is around her mouth where my whiskers have abraded her delicate skin, and the other red marks on her body where I have tugged or pulled or pinched or rubbed. Collectively, it is the appearance of despoliation, defiling, rough eagerness. Somehow, the look of it gives me pleasure. It is, I think, an archetypal joy, born of millions of years of lust—the driven desire to reproduce, to continue. It isn't her image, it's my imagination. It gives me courage. I read the note.

Navy Pier 8:00 P.M.
You shouldn't have brought her.

That's it, no specifics. It tells us very little—except that we're being watched. I open the door to see who the messenger might have been. The hallway is empty, as I knew it would be. I back up to the edge of the bed and sit down next to Moira, pulling part of a blanket over my exposed mid-section. "What do you think?" she says. She has a sheet wrapped around her like a long evening gown and her upper legs are folded against her chest. Her head rests on her knees. It's a position that youth thinks nothing of and one that's no longer possible for me without an aching back.

"Navy Pier is a big place. You ever been there?"

"No."

"It's like a big boardwalk or carnival, right on the Lake Michigan shoreline. Lots of boats and docks and little shops and rides for kids and places to eat—that type of thing. It's extensive. I don't know how he expects to hook up with us without giving us a designated spot to meet him. It's also very public, hundreds, maybe thousands of people, all the time, especially on warm, summer nights. I don't get it."

"How does he know I'm with you?"

"Maybe the lady in the window across the street? Maybe he's tailing us himself. I don't know."

"Tin?"

"Yeah?"

"Do you feel any guilt—about what we've done I mean?"

"Because you're so young?"

"No, because you were raised in the home of a minister. From my observations—and I'm looking at this from a very secular background—Judeo-Christian culture pretty much teaches that every natural impulse is sinful unless cleaned up by some ceremony or ritual, like a wedding for instance. You can't help but be influenced by that."

What kind of an observation is that for someone her age? "I ought to be on the road to hell, I guess, for what I've been up to, but I feel just the opposite. There's more of God in the warmth and texture of your skin than in all the rules I ever read. And if you're wondering whether I intend to marry you or not—I do, assuming that you want to saddle yourself with an older man and my brother doesn't find a way to accomplish what he wants."

She turns my face to hers, forcefully. "What did you say?"

I want to kid with her, say something clever or silly, but her expression won't allow it. "I said that I want to marry you."

"Then this *is* real to you. I'm not just a convenience, a diversion."

"No."

"Tin, I—"

"What is it?"

"My mother is dead. My stepfather tried to molest me. I don't know who my real father is. Some people would say I'm searching for a parental figure, but my heart tells me that my life is inexorably tied to yours. We're *supposed* to be together. You know what I mean?"

"Some kind of teleological destiny?"

"I don't know that word."

"Well I'll be damned."

"What?"

"Something the kid doesn't know."

"Don't be a smart ass. What does it mean?"

"Teleology? The belief that events are pulled by a purpose toward a definite end."

"Yeah, something like that. I'd simplify it by just saying that I've adored you ever since I was a kid. I've wanted you for a long time." She kisses me. "You don't have to marry me, you know. Just stay with me, always."

"You don't seem to understand, Moira, *I* want to marry *you*. It's an entirely selfish thing. It has to do with *my* happiness, not yours. Besides, I want all those young assholes on MSU's campus that'll be constantly staring at you to see a ring on your finger, to know that you're not available. Call it the insecurity of the aged. Those 'ceremonies and rituals' were invented for old guys with broken teeth, you know."

She laughs. She's quickly on her knees and hugging me, almost to the point of strangulation. The sheet slips from her and my hands enjoy the smooth, soft skin of her back. She kisses my cheek, my nose, my mouth, her tongue slips between my lips. She laughs again as she withdraws, watching me trying to catch my breath. "I'm not going to MSU," she whispers. "I'll go to school somewhere in Grand Rapids, maybe Grand Valley State. I'll live with you. That way," she giggles, "you'll always have this," she places my hand on her exposed breast, "whenever you decide to go fishing with a drill."

"That'll never happen again."

"No? Why?"

"Because it's a lousy way to try and catch fish."

She gives me a tolerant smile. "Promise?"

"Cross my heart."

"Oh Tin, I love you."

"I love you too." I say it without thinking, but I mean it. "Now, I think we'd better concentrate on solving our current dilemma before we make any plans for the future, don't you?"

She nods her head and reluctantly gathers the sheet around her again. "I'll get dressed." She glides off the side of the bed, and hesitates at the bathroom door. "The note said eight?"

"Yes."

"What is it now?"

"Five."

"We have some time then," she says, wickedly dropping the sheet.

"Time for thinking about how to handle this. Get thee into the bathroom, Satan."

"You're just exhausted. I've worn you out."

"Out of the mouths of babes—"

"Shut up."

"Get dressed or I'm going to rape you, then I'll be too tired to fight the bad guys."

She blows me a kiss and shuts the door. I release a heavy sigh. I glance at the room across the street—no one there. The curtain's still closed. I count the stories. It's on the fourth floor, facing Ontario Street. I find the single bag on the floor that contains my own purchases and begin removing tags and labels and laying the clothes out on the bed.

What a distance I've come in forty-eight hours. I'm in love with this wonderful creature who actually loves me. "Forgive me, Wendy," I whisper. I feel, rather than hear, her answer. Be happy, Tin. Be happy.

Somewhere very distant, but audible, is another voice. "I'm still here."

Chapter sixteen

I finish dressing. I'm staring at the closed curtain in the window across the street when there's a knock at the door. This time I'm more curious than tense. I know, logically, that my visitor can't be Satchel. He's arranged our confrontation to his own benefit, at his own time, tonight at Navy Pier. It could be this mysterious woman, I suppose, but I doubt it. She has to be allied with him somehow and why would she reveal herself now, when all is arranged? More likely, as before, it's someone from the hotel staff—a housekeeper perhaps, or a porter with some further message. I stride to the door and open it with the confidence of ignorance.

He's there, a cartoon version of me. His face is the same, except for the freckles—so inconsistent with maturity. His carroty hair is cropped short around the neck and ears, but the bangs hang in his eyes, as they always did except when he wore his baseball cap. Redheads are supposed to have blue or green eyes, but Satch's were always very dark. He still looks younger than me. He's smaller, thinner, drawn tight from tension and the wariness of the hunted, but there's no mistaking that face. It's the one I've seen many times in the worst of my nightmares.

I'm taken so unawares that I do nothing but stand there and stare at him. He says: "Tin, I didn't kill Wendy. We need to start with that."

I'm trembling with fear, hate, anger. I don't know what to do with my useless limbs. I want to kill him, but my hands are frozen— one to the door, the other to my side. This isn't what I expected. I thought he would sneak up on me, attack me, with all the virulence of Cain. I want to hate him, to tear him apart, but even now there's something in me that wants to embrace him, to tell him that I've missed him, that I love him. I really don't know what to do. My senses have been carrying images to my mind all my life. Those images are transformed by perception, joined with insight, then transformed into imagination. This is how I, all of us really, see the world, see those around us, learn to love—and hate. Long ago, my imagination locked Satchel into his role as murderer, the person to blame for Wendy. Evidence was part of that, but unimportant. It is the Blame that matters, the necessity to condemn. Something, someone, must be held accountable.

Without thought, I strike out with my fist, landing a crushing blow on my brother's jaw. He does nothing to deflect the roundhouse. He simply accepts it and staggers backward before falling to the floor of the hallway. I stand there over him, staring at him, surprised at the ease with which the loathsome monster has fallen. I take a step forward and he raises his hand to ward off further assault. A scarlet stream of blood is running from the corner of his mouth. "You had to do that, Tin, I understand. Now I want you to listen to me. I didn't kill Wendy."

Words come to me without thought. "Bullshit, Satch, you were there. Your fingerprints were all over the place. You killed her with the baseball bat you gave me. You were spotted in town at a fast food place that night, by one of Dad's parishioners. It was you, Satch. Now you've come for me. Fine. Let's end it." I step forward and he struggles to his feet, staggering. I want to punch him again, break his jaw if I haven't already and watch his mouth sag in dumb shock.

"I *was* there, yes. I was, Tin. But I didn't kill her. She was dead when I got there. I swear to God, you've got to believe me."

The greatest of all lies. Even so, I want to hug him and put it all behind us. I want to tell him how sorry I am that I ruined his life and Wendy's life and the lives of our parents. I also want to kill him and erase the final obstacle to my recovered happiness.

"Fuck you."

"I was as devastated as you, brother, when I found her."

"Yeah? Why'd you come back to our house? Why were you even there?"

"I came to see Dad, but he wasn't at the rectory. I decided to come to your place. My intention was to try to heal the rift between us. I found her like that."

"Bullshit. Why'd you run then? Why didn't you call the police? Why didn't you call *me*? You had to know that Dad and I were at the cabin. Where else would we be? What about all the time since? You couldn't pick up a phone? You're full of shit."

He looks surprised when I say that, confused. He wipes the blood from his jaw and steps forward. I raise my fist again and he stops. "I was wanted, Tin, on a drug charge. I'm a lot of things, but I'm not stupid. A fugitive with a history of addiction, found in a house with his murdered sister-in-law, who used to be his fiancée until his brother took her away. Motive, murder weapon with my prints—case closed. I ran, Tin. I panicked and I ran and, honestly, part of me wanted you to find her, to suffer as I was suffering, but I didn't kill her. I'm guilty of cruelty, but not murder. I didn't kill her."

"You expect me to believe that some stranger beat her to death in that way? You saw her. She was systematically tortured. Any other intruder might have killed her, but not like that. It was a vendetta, Satch. Someone who hated her, or me, or both of us, killed her. She wasn't raped, nothing was stolen. Motive, Satch, who else would have that kind of motive?"

"Tin?" It is the sweet voice of the feminine, interjecting into this hateful confrontation of testosterone. I can tell by Satchel's pale smile that he too believes the voice came from Wendy, though we both understand how impossible that is. No ghosts here. I can sense Moira's presence behind me, though I do not turn around. Satch can see her and I want to kill him just for looking. "Who is it?" she says.

Satch steps forward, but stops when I put my hand on his chest. "Stay back," I say, both to him and her. He opens his arms and spreads them wide in a gesture of surrender. "It's Satchel," I say, and I hear her gasp.

"Where's Sweeney?" she says.

His face is inches from mine and I'm befuddled by the confused expression I find there. "Sweeney?" he says. "You're Moira? Are you talking about your father, Hiram?"

"Yes. Where is he?"

"I don't know. I was supposed to meet him here yesterday, but he never showed." I turn slightly to look at Moira and see that she has stopped gathering the Victoria's Secret lingerie that she left sprawled across the bed and floor and that she's staring at my brother.

"What the hell are you talking about?" I say.

He looks back at me. His demeanor is calm, composed. I lower my arm. "I came here because Hiram asked me to, and because I've had enough of running and hiding."

"He *asked* you to? How could he do that?"

"He called me, several days ago, asked me to come here, to Chicago, on your birthday. He said new evidence had been found about Wendy's murder, proving that I didn't do it. He wanted me to meet with you both so he could tell us, at the same time, what the evidence was, so that we could...reconcile, I think was the word he used."

"Bullshit!" I say. "How would he even know where you were?"

"I don't know. I asked him. He wouldn't say...no, he said he *couldn't* say."

"And where was this? You're on the run and he calls you? What, you have a cell phone?

"I was in Montana, have been for quite awhile."

"Of course you were. Sweeney just looked you up in the phone book, huh?" He doesn't respond. "How did you know what hotel we'd be staying at?"

"Hiram told me, although he didn't say that his daughter would be with you. Even gave me the room number."

"Come in, Satchel," Moira says.

As I turn my head to protest, he's by me and inside. I follow him, but leave the door open. Moira grabs a white towel from the bathroom and hands it to him. He smiles appreciatively as he wipes the drying blood from his jaw. "You pack a punch, brother," he says as he sits on the end of the bed.

Moira goes to the table by the window and snatches a piece of paper from her purse. She hands it to Satchel. "This was left on the kitchen table in Tin's cabin. It's how we figured out that we were supposed to come here."

He reads it quickly. "I didn't write this," he says. "It's not even my handwriting."

Moira looks at me. We both knew that Sweeney had written the note and assumed that Satchel had forced him to do so.

"You're full of shit," I say. "Why would Sweeney tell you to come to Chicago anyway? Why not just come to Loon Lake? We were all there."

Satchel tenderly rubs his swelling jaw. "I asked him the same thing. He told me that everyone in the area knew who I was and he didn't want to risk anyone identifying me. He said that until he took this new evidence to the police, I was still a wanted man and that it would be safer to meet in Chicago."

"So you just came, no questions asked."

"No, not at all. I was very concerned that it was some kind of trap, a way to draw me in, and I told him so."

"What did he say?" Moira asks.

"He gave me my address. He told me the exact location of where I was at the time. He said that if he wanted me captured, he could just call the FBI and give them my location. It made sense."

"But how would he know where you were?" Moira repeated.

"I told you. I don't know." My brother points at the mini-bar by the television. "I don't know about you guys, but I could use one of those little bottles."

Moira moves to the door of our room, shuts it, and surprises me by saying "Me too."

The world I lived in up until yesterday was full of horror, but at least I understood it. Now, I am completely confused, and Jim Beam, as Satchel suggests, seems like the only reasonable recourse.

Chapter seventeen

I mix the drinks and hand one to Moira. She sips it slowly. Satch swallows his in a couple of gulps, as do I. He grimaces, either from the intensity of the drink or the injury he sustained or as a reaction to my hateful staring. His jaw is swelling noticeably. The silence in the room is unnerving. I fix myself another drink, ignoring Satch, and sit down in a chair by the window. Moira leans against the desk behind me, perhaps consciously keeping distance between herself and the intruder. He seems not to notice.

"Who else?" I say finally.

"What?"

"Who else would have killed Wendy if you didn't do it?"

"I don't know."

"Well, hell, that proves it then. I'm sorry I ever doubted you."

"I can't tell you what I don't know, Tin."

"You know Dad is dead?"

"Yes."

"And you never contacted me, even then."

Again, he looks surprised. "I couldn't. Besides, I didn't find out until months later."

"Do you know how he died?"

"No."

"He killed himself."

It pleases me to see him wince, to see the deep sorrow and regret my revelation causes him. Tears form in his black eyes. "Why would he do that, Tin? He hated the whole idea of suicide."

"Why? Why the hell do you think? His daughter-in-law is brutally murdered. The pride of his life, his precious baseball protégé, is the murderer and a drug addict to boot. Eventually he just gave up. He closed off his garage, fired up his old Chrysler and inhaled deeply. I'm sure his last thoughts were of you, if that's any comfort."

"Tin!"

Satch's hands cover his face now. He sobs. Moira looks at me as if she doesn't know me. Perhaps she doesn't. I'm beginning to regret falling asleep in that boat. It's so much easier not to have hope. God certainly has a sense of humor. He gets you to care, then fucks you over yet another time.

"C'mon Satch, you can cut the act. It's working for Moira, but not for me. Murderers don't cry, not real tears anyway."

He looks up, and wipes the drops away. "You look so much like your mother," he says to Moira.

She ignores the remark. "If you want us to believe you, Satchel," she says, "you're going to have to answer a lot of questions and we don't have much time."

"Give me another drink and I'll tell you whatever you want to know."

Moira nudges me and I go to the mini-bar. I fix myself another while I'm there. Moira is still nursing hers. I give Satch's to him. I'm sure he notices how I avoid touching him, like handing something to a leper. As he takes it, I see that he doesn't grip it with his left hand, his pitching hand, but seems to have to support it with his right, although Satchel uses his left hand for everything.

"All right," Moira says, "you say you came back to Michigan

on the day Wendy was killed to try and patch things up between you and Tin."

"Yes."

"Where were you before then? You left Detroit, wound up in Los Angeles, according to Tin, where you were arrested and your father flew out there to bail you out. You overturned a table at a restaurant and ran away. Was that the last time you saw your father?"

"Yes."

"Why did you run away?"

"I didn't know what I was doing. I'd lost Wendy. My baseball career was over. Everything I'd worked for since I was a teenager was done. I saw the pain in my father's face and I wanted to turn it all around, but he told me that Tin and Wendy were getting married. It was too much to take. I just exploded and got out of there. I needed a fix. You have to understand. I'd been going through withdrawal in jail. I was nervous, edgy, at the absolute breaking point."

"So then you started traveling cross country, back to Michigan."

"After I scored a few hits, yes." His dark eyes turn to me. "You would know where I was at that time brother, wouldn't you?"

Moira looks at me for explanation. She can see, apparently, that I have none.

"Wendy and I spent a lot of time and money trying to find you," I tell him. "We hired a private investigator, a guy named Connor. He kept on your tail, but you were always a day or a week or a month ahead of him."

Satchel laughs, as if he knows something I don't, but I don't know why. "At first, I was just wandering. I'd pick up some work here and there, stay for a few weeks or months, then head out again. Someplace in Alabama, I stole a car. It was a stupid thing to do, but I was tired of buses and hitchhiking. At a state fair in Mobile, I found the same model and make of the car I'd taken and switched the license plates. At an auto supply place, I bought some paint and I hand-brushed the car in a cornfield outside of town. Then, I headed north. I think I went to Tennessee, then up here, to Chicago. I stayed around here for a week or so, then I decided to head home and see Dad. You know the rest."

"Bullshit," I say.

"Somewhere along the way I found myself again."

Moira pinches my arm. "And you found Wendy. Tell us what happened that night."

Satchel swallows his drink and sighs deeply. He lights a cigarette and winces again as he inhales. I don't ever remember him smoking. His left hand goes unconsciously to his swelling jaw.

"When did you start smoking?"

"Long time ago."

I look at Moira. "Marlboro regulars," she says, remembering what Hattie had told us.

Satch looks at his cigarette and shrugs. "I went to Dad's first, as I said. No one was there. I found your address, Tin, in a phone book in a public booth. I hung around for awhile, just trying to decide if I had the strength to go through with what I knew would be a difficult confrontation. Finally, I went to your house. I rang the doorbell a couple of times and there was no answer. The door was unlocked so I went in, hoping that you were out in the back yard or something. It was dark in the living room. The only light in the house was coming from the kitchen, so I headed in that direction. I stubbed my toe on the baseball bat. When I picked it up, it was wet and sticky. I didn't know it was blood until I got completely under the light. When I saw Wendy, I dropped it, I think. I went to her, held her, tried to coax her back, but she was gone. I knelt there, next to her, for a long time. I cried. I loved her, Tin. I really loved...." He breaks off here and begins to sob again. I feel pity rising in me like a sickening nausea. I force it down with a hard swallow. He's a better actor than I remember.

"What about your picture?"

"What?"

"We kept that picture of Mom and Dad and us two kids in the foyer of our house, you know, the one that Mom insisted we have taken and almost made us late for one of your games. Your face on it was obliterated with a magic marker. It had to have been done by the intruder. You telling me you didn't do that?"

"That's right. I didn't even know it was there." He's looking at Moira again. If I had an ice pick, I would cure that. He turns toward me, suddenly, and I hope that he can read my mind. His expression tells me that he can, at least, read my face. "Besides," he says, "why would I ex out my own face? Why not yours? If I came to hurt you, to get vengeance, why wouldn't I deface *your* photo?"

"We thought—Dad and I and the police that is—that it was some kind of manifestation of self-loathing over what you'd done."

"I've never hated myself, Tin. I haven't done anything to hate myself for, other than to be a cuckold and drug myself silly. I've never even contemplated suicide."

I'm convinced that he can read me. I feel my cheeks flush. I feel Moira's eyes on me. I'm thinking of the drill and our father and the dark depths of Loon Lake.

"I think he's right there, Tin," Moira says. When I flash her a look of anger, she adds: "The picture, I mean, it doesn't make a lot of sense."

"Okay," I try to direct the irritation in my voice. Moira places a delicate hand on my shoulder and squeezes, as if to reassure me that she's still on my side. "If what you say is true, if you didn't kill Wendy, if your conscience is so clean, then why all this secrecy for so many years?"

"C'mon brother," he says, "that was your wish, not mine."

Something comes away in me, like a ripped muscle or broken bone, only it's deeper, not physical, not so easily healed. I throw my glass against the wall. I shrug off Moira's hand and walk to the bar again. "What the hell are you talking about?"

"Take it easy, man," Satch says.

My hands are shaking as I try to pour another shot. I give up and drink straight from the little bottle. I cannot seem to anesthetize myself. "Fuck you, Satch. Don't tell me what to do or I'll put your teeth through the backside of your fuckin' head."

"Tin—"

"No, Moira. Leave it alone."

She looks wounded, and I feel like a complete ass, but she doesn't say anything further.

I try to regain some measure of self-control. "What'd you mean when you said it was my wish?"

"Don't deny it now," my brother says, "if we want to get all the truth out here, let's get it out. Connor was never a day or week behind me, he was always near. He knew where I was every step of the way. You just admitted you hired Connor to track me down. Well he did. I sensed that someone was near, all the time. I even saw him a couple of times, but I thought he was an FBI agent or a cop. I didn't know then who he was. In spite of the fact that I knew I was being tailed, I had to go back to Michigan, talk to you and Wendy, get this all straightened out. After I found her like that, I panicked and ran. A few weeks later, in Kentucky, in that motel where I was staying, Connor confronted me, told me who he was and who he was working for. That's when he gave me your message. I knew then that there could be no reconciliation. It was a hard order to follow, I wanted very much to explain things to you and Dad, but my life was beginning to come together and I didn't want to hurt either of you anymore and I certainly didn't want you to carry through on your threat. So I stayed away."

My head's throbbing. The web of cable that holds my mind together is beginning to come apart, like snapping wires on a falling suspension bridge. "Connor? Connor saw you? He talked to you?"

Satchel's scoffing laugh rings true. "Talked? Yeah we talked all right—the first time in a cheap, roadside motel outside of some place called Corbin, a couple of weeks after Wendy was killed. He broke in while I was sleeping, put a gun to my head, and told me never to contact you or Dad again."

"You're full of shit, Satchel."

"It's the truth, Tin, and you know it. He said I was wanted for Wendy's murder, which I already knew of course, and he'd let me go if I'd just disappear and stay that way. He said that's the way you wanted it. You didn't want me dead, or in prison, for Dad's sake—just gone. I told him I couldn't do that, that I couldn't have you and Dad believing that I killed Wendy. I was on my way to Florida and I was going to try to hide for a while until I figured out how to approach you guys. Connor pulled my hand around toward him, held the gun to my palm and shot." Satchel pushes his left hand toward me and I see the terrible thick, white scar. "I knew then that the sonofabitch was serious, that he wasn't threatening idly. Like I said, I'm not the suicidal type. I did what I was told."

"I can't believe this," I say, looking at Moira, whose expression of incredulity must look very much like mine.

"I saw him several times after that," Satchel says. "Once in Georgia, Albany I think, and twice in Florida. Each time I was threatened. Connor let me know that I was being watched and followed. On a couple of occasions though, in Florida, he warned me that the FBI were close, even helped me to avoid them."

"Satchel, I never told him to keep you away or to help you get away. He was paid, handsomely I might add, to bring you in. Why would he do that?"

Satchel shrugged in the way that a man accustomed to living surrealistically might shrug. "I don't know, brother. Maybe he wanted to *continue* being paid handsomely. I thought it was because you wanted me to suffer."

"How did you happen to hire this guy, this Connor whoever-he-is?" Moira says to me.

"Sometime after Satch was released from jail, after that escapade in Los Angeles, Wendy and I and Dad and Hiram were sitting around on the front porch of our cabin, discussing how the police and the FBI hadn't been able to find him. Sweeney said he knew of this top-notch private investigator in Chicago—"

"Sweeney?" Moira says. "Why would Sweeney even *know* a private investigator, let alone know if he was quality or not—especially here, in Chicago?"

"He said something about a friend of his, used to be a cop in Detroit, knew this guy, Connor."

Satchel lights another cigarette. It looks so strange in his hand.

"Seems to me," he says to Moira, "that your father's name keeps popping up in all of this."

"And you don't know why."

"No."

"You haven't had any contact with Sweeney since Wendy's death?"

"Except for the phone call a few days ago? No."

Moira shakes her head, as if such an action could chase away the incomprehensible. "Are you saying that Sweeney arranged all of this? That he kidnapped *himself?*"

"No," Satchel said, calmly. "I'm not making any inferences at all. I'm just trying to get at the truth."

"This is a waste of time," I say.

Moira looks at me with those penetrating dark eyes. "Why?"

"Because Satch is lying through his teeth."

"Then he has to be behind all this, and if that's true, why is he here, now, when he supposedly arranged to meet us at Navy Pier tonight?"

"What?" Satch butts his cigarette out in one of those tiny glass ashtrays on the nightstand at the edge of the bed that non-smokers think are sufficient for addicts. Imagination is such a faulty thing, but outside of direct experience, it's all we've got.

Moira hands him the second note. He shakes his gray-red head. "I don't know anything about this," he says.

"Of course you don't," is my sardonic response, but I'm unconvincing and the other two people in the room know it.

"Let's play supposition," Moira says.

"What?"

"Let's just suppose that your brother is telling the truth. What does that mean? Who wrote the notes, then? Who killed Wendy? Why was this Connor guy helping Satchel to get away rather than bringing him in? Are there answers?"

"You said the notes are in Hiram's handwriting?" Satchel says.

"Yes."

"He recommended Connor?"

"Yes."

"He knew you'd be in Chicago at this hotel?"

"If what you tell us is true, yes."

"But he wasn't there when you came back to the cabins yesterday?"

"No, but Graham said he was there somewhere around an hour before we got back."

Moira looks at me. She understands the insinuations and Satch sees that too. Perhaps because of that, he doesn't pursue that line of interrogation.

"Who's this Graham guy?"

"Moira's boyfriend."

"*Former* boyfriend," she emphasizes and smiles at me. I can tell that Satchel notices. "He wanted to come along, but I said no. He's Sweeney's choice for me, not mine." Again she glances my way.

Satchel can't resist. "Seems to me your father is involved in a lot of things here," he says. The swelling on his face is getting so bad that it's difficult to understand him. "Do you have any ice?"

Moira grabs the bucket from the desk by the window and heads for the door. "I'll be right back." She's gone before I can object.

"Never mind Sweeney," I say when Moira's left. "Where have you been all this time? You can't have been constantly on the run. You disappeared. Where did you go?"

"Montana."

"What?"

"About a year after I...found Wendy, I left Florida and was heading back to California, thinking that I'd have a better chance to get lost out there. My car had broken down outside of some town in South Dakota, Watertown, I think it was, and I'd been hitchhiking for weeks. I'm not even sure how I got into Montana. I was broke and damned near starving to death. In fact, I'd passed out on the side of a dirt road. When I woke up I was in the back of a pick-up truck. Joolie Bullkiller and his family were standing around the truck staring at me. Joolie is full-blooded Oglala Sioux. According to him, he's descended from Crazy Horse. It sounds like a girl's name, but it's spelled J-O-O-L-I-E. I think it means something like 'Jumper' in one of the Native American languages. Joolie's wife, Santee Child, (most of the family and the ranch hands call her Santy), gave me food and a place to sleep. When I got so I could work again, Joolie gave me a job. Been there ever since. At first, I just cleaned the stalls, mended fences, that sort of thing. I slept in the bunkhouse. Eventually I learned to ride horses, do corral work, hunt down strays. Last year, Joolie made me foreman."

Satchel is smiling as much as the burgeoning swelling on his jaw allows. "They gave me a home, Tin. I love those people."

Moira returns. She dumps some of the ice in a towel and hands it to Satchel. "Thanks," he says. Moira sounds her age when she responds with: "No problem."

"If I called this Joolie Bullkiller to verify all this, he'd vouch for what you've said?"

"As long as you tell him you're inquiring about Joe Reed."

"What?"

"That's the name they know me by, mainly. I gave them my real one a few days ago, but I don't know if they'd remember. In fact, I been called 'Joe' for so long that when I hear you say 'Satchel' it seems to me like you're talking to someone else. You are, I guess." He seems to wander for a minute or two. His eyes have a distant dreaminess about them. Even though the towel hides most of his face, I can tell he's smiling at whatever it is he's seeing. Then he leaves his imagination and comes back. "The BK Ranch, Joolie's place, is really remote. Nearest town is a place called Castle Rock, northwest of the Little Bighorn and due north from a big Cheyenne Reservation. I think it was sometime in the spring of 2002 when I came down Interstate 94, then highway 39, then some county road. I knew I should stay put at BK when I'd been there six months and there was no sign of Connor. I was sure I'd lost him. I was happy, Tin—eating well, working outdoors in the fresh air, mountains in the distance—simple things. I was accepted without question, appreciated for who I was. I began to forget about you and Wendy and hate and lost opportunities. I met...someone too. Joolie and Santy's daughter. Her name is Moon. She was just a kid when I first met her, not twenty yet. I know I sound like a dirty old man, but I love her and she loves me. We're going to get married when I get all this cleared up. She's part of the reason I took Hiram up on his offer and came back. I can't be hunted anymore. I can't start a new life with her until I've gotten rid of all this baggage."

He looks me straight in the eye. I don't see any deception in his face. Who could make this up? I notice for the first time that Satchel is wearing those pointed-toe, high-heeled cowboy boots I used to see in the movies—something he never wore in his life. I also see, my imagination now stimulated by his story, that his skin in tanned and weathered, like leather, although not enough to assimilate his freckles.

I look to Moira. Her expression is empathetic. She must be thinking that the propensity for being dirty old men is a dominant trait in the Balune gene pool.

"You say that you haven't seen Connor for how long?"

"Not since I left Florida, probably two years now, maybe three."

That would be about the time that I last talked to Connor and told him I didn't want him to continue the search for my brother.

"Why didn't you contact us then, when you knew you were free of him?"

"I was afraid that you'd turn me in, that I'd lose everything I'd gained. I wanted to stay lost, Tin, or rather I guess I wanted to stay found. Like I said, Moon's changed me. We want to be together and I can't start off our life with a lie. I really love her. I told her everything. Joolie loaned me his pick-up and here I am. You and I get it all straight now, or I go to jail and fight it out in the courts, either way I'm not going back until it's set right. It's up to you. The phone's right there," he says, pointing to the table by the bed. "Three easy numbers, nine, one, one."

I walk to it and lift the receiver. He doesn't bat an eye.

There's a long silence. Satchel shifts the ice pack a little and tries to smoke. Moira is attempting to dry out her long hair with a towel and looking at me with an expression of entreaty.

I put it down and retreat to the mini-bar, looking for some guidance that I know, by experience, isn't there. Finally, Moira breaks the impasse by asking Satchel to tell her what she missed while she was out getting the ice. He tells her about Moon Bullkiller, (such an impossible name for one's lover), and he is entirely convincing. My brother has to be the best bullshitter that ever lived—that, or there's no deceit.

She comes to me, takes my hand. Those dark eyes capture me. "I believe him," she says, "and it's not because I'm eighteen and it's not because I'm a hopelessly romantic woman. Bizarre as it is, it rings of truth, Tin."

"You've forgotten," I tell her, "that Sweeney's been kidnapped, that Juna Hines saw someone else in Sweeney's car, that Wendy *was* murdered, that whoever is involved in all that has been sending us notes. Who could that be? Who else would know that yesterday was my birthday? Who would know that I was with you and would instruct me to leave you behind? Who would know that we're here, sent here by that note?"

"What kind of car are you driving?" she says to Satch.

"I told Tin," he says, "Joolie's pick-up. It's a Dodge."

"Not a blue Ford Taurus?"

He glances at her, curious. "No, why?"

"Never owned one, drove one?"

"No."

She shrugs and smiles. She kisses me on my cheek. "Why don't the three of us go out to Navy Pier and find out who's waiting for us?"

"Four," Satchel mumbles through the towel.

"What?"

"Moon's downstairs, circling the block in Joolie's truck."

"I take it, then", I say, "that you've met the Guardian of Management Rules."

"What?"

"The valet."

Satchel brings the towel down from his jaw. The ice is working.

The angry bruises and swelling are fading. He gives me his eternally comfortable smile. "Right."

In spite of myself, I smile back. It's a beginning. God knows, it's a beginning.

Chapter eighteen

Ly the time we're ready to leave, it's after six. Downstairs, in the street, Satchel spots the pick-up just pulling away from the hotel entrance. Moon will have to circle the block again. The valet has a look of triumphant smugness on his face that he directs toward me. I think he's thrilled to discover that the pick-up is connected to me and that four of us will have to ride in its cab unless we're willing to put ourselves at his mercy and have the Jeep brought around. In which case, of course, we'd have no place to park the truck. The only solutions are to get the Jeep and drive two vehicles, or leave Satchel and Moon at the Wyndham and borrow the truck, options that I share with Moira and Satchel.

"I think I can remember how to get to Navy Pier," Satchel says, "if you can meet us at the main entrance to the park. I want to go along."

I grab Satchel's arm as he steps into the street to look for Moon's return. "If this is some kind of ruse to get back at me, you better make sure that I don't survive it. You understand me?"

I see the sorrow in his black eyes as he unconsciously pushes away the red bangs. "If I'm lying, Tin, you'll know soon enough. If I'm not, I want you to take me to Wendy's grave—me and Moon, you and Moira, so we can all make our peace. Okay?"

"Okay."

"Dad's too."

"Yes."

I wander over to the valet to give him our number and order the Jeep. In a few minutes, the pick-up appears around the corner and, shortly after, glides to the curb in front of us. Satchel opens the door. Inside, I can see the woman who must be Moon Bullkiller. She's very dark, with high cheekbones and long, silky-black hair. She's quite beautiful. She's wearing jeans and cowboy boots, and a tucked blouse that does little to hide her generous chest. She's sporting big, gold, hoop earrings, the kind you associate with gypsies. She's wearing virtually no make-up outside of a little lipstick. Her face looks younger than Moira's. Her pleasant smile immediately changes to concern when she sees my brother's bruised and swollen jaw. "Joe!" she says, "what happened?"

"An accident," 'Joe' says. "Slide over, I'm gonna drive."

He moves round the truck to the driver's side while Moon examines me with suspicion. Once behind the wheel he says: "Moonie, this is my brother, Tin, and that lady right behind him is his…friend, Moira Sweeney." Although I don't turn around to look, I can tell that Moira is looking over my shoulder, probably gesturing some kind of amiable greeting, from the look on Moon's face. The girl's expression is much colder when she nods at me. Two things are immediately apparent about her: she's full-blooded Native American and she's very devoted to Satchel.

Satchel pats her slim leg when he's settled. She smiles and covers his hand with her own. "Where're we going?" she says.

"A place called Navy Pier. It's down by the lake."

"Fine, anywhere I can see the sky again. I don't know how people can live in places like this. It's like being in a gigantic tomb. Even the *trees* are surrounded by concrete!"

"Not like Montana, huh?" I say. Satchel looks my way. He knows I'm testing.

"Not in any way," she answers, without hesitation. "Out there we live *near* the mountains, not *inside* them." I hear Moira laugh.

"I'm sorry folks," a familiar voice says behind me. "You'll have to move along. This area is reserved for hotel guests."

I turn around to face The Guardian. "I *am* a hotel guest."

"Yes sir," he retorts, pointing a finger in Satch's direction, "but *they* aren't and there's a limo waiting right behind them."

I look back at Satch. He shrugs and smiles at me. "Can't fight the law. See you in a few minutes." Then he's gone.

Moira pulls me back to the curb and out of the way of the approaching vehicle as the valet gives our number to a subordinate and moves to open the door of the limousine. For the first time since Satchel arrived, I take a good look at her. She's wearing a new pair of hip-hugger shorts and one of those abbreviated shirts that are designed to expose the mid-section—the kind that slants open from just below the chest on one side of her torso to her opposite hip. I have sent more than one fashion-conscious co-ed to the assistant principal's office for a dress code violation when more modestly clothed. I think again how fortunate I am.

"Well," she says, "*that* was certainly unexpected."

I notice that my hands are shaking slightly as I attempt to light a cigarette. Part of the reason is her astonishing beauty, but I don't tell her that. "I spent so much of my life idolizing my older brother, then hating him. It's hard to think straight right now."

"I think he's telling us the truth, Tin."

"It seems that way," I admit, "but then how do you explain all those things I talked about upstairs? Who was Sweeney with when he stopped at Nettie's place on the lake to buy cigarettes?—and they *were* Marlboros, just the kind Satch is smoking. Did you notice that? Juna Hines saw someone else in the car. It was a blue Taurus. Who was it? Who murdered Wendy? Who would have reason to? Any way I look at it, nothing makes sense."

"Is there anything else I missed, when I went to get the ice for Satchel?" she says.

I tell her about how Satchel said he'd wound up at Joolie Bullkiller's ranch. "The girl seems nice," she says. "Helluva name though."

"I wish the damn Jeep would get here."

She looks at her watch. "It'll probably take another fifteen minutes."

Then it occurs to me. I begin to walk, with enough purpose to make Moira follow close behind. We're about half way up the block on Ontario Street when I stop and look up, counting the floors of the hotel across the street by the windows. I look at the Wyndham in back of me and try gauging where the window to room 432 would be on our side, then turn back, calculating. The woman is there. She's looking directly at us. I point at her. Moira says: "I see her too." The woman waves. She's wearing a red dress that clings to her, as if it were painted on. I point again, shrug my shoulders and give her a questioning expression as if to ask her who the hell she is. I think she shrugs and smiles.

"Are you watching?" I say to Moira. "Can you see what she's doing?"

"She wants us to notice her, that's for sure. She's pretty hot too, as the boys at good old LHS would say. She's got platinum blonde hair, probably dyed. Almost no one's hair is that color naturally. She's got a movie star body as far as I can see, and she's wearing a lot of make-up. It could be, you know, that she's just some hotel guest who's voyeuristic and has a little too much appreciation for my man."

"She's got to be connected somehow. There's something familiar…" I step off the curb. "I'm going over there."

"Wait a minute," Moira shouts, grabbing my shirt. She prevents me from stepping right into the path of an oncoming taxi, whose driver honks and gestures to me, out of his open window, with the great American Finger of Dissatisfaction.

I look up. The mystery woman has disappeared. "We don't have time to chase her right now," Moira says, still grasping my shirt.

"And if we're going to live happily ever after, as I'd like, you better start paying a little more attention to your safety." As usual, her logic matches her beauty.

We walk back to the entrance to the Wyndham, where I wait for the Guardian to say something about where we should stand. I'd like to take my mounting aggression out on him. Fortunately, he's busy talking with other hotel staff and ignores us.

"How does she fit into all this?" I say. "She has to be the one who pretended to be my agent. Who's she connected with? Who's she working for?"

Moira shrugs. "Right now, I'm just concerned that we get to Navy Pier by eight and find whoever forced Sweeney to write those… ah here's the Jeep."

Navy Pier isn't more than a few miles from the Wyndham, but the traffic is crawling and more than once we have to sit unmoving, impatiently trapped in a chasm of concrete and steel. Far down this man-made canyon, we can just see the blue waters of Lake Michigan.

"Do you believe your brother?" Moira says, as we barely move forward. The accelerator hasn't been used for a block or more.

"I'm not sure I believe any of this. I don't want to believe him. If he's telling the truth then I don't have a clue as to who's to blame for Wendy's death—or Dad's. And what about Sweeney? He has to be a part of this bullshit if he knew we were coming to Chicago and staying at a particular hotel in a particular room. What reason would he have, though, to get involved in this? He didn't know Wendy all that well. I think he only met her a few times. He knew that Wendy left Satch for me, but we never talked about it. Wendy liked him and he seemed to like her."

Suddenly, the muffled strains of "Cell Block Tango" permeate the Jeep. Moira reaches into the pocket of her shorts and extracts her cell phone. "Damn it," she says as she checks the number to see who the caller is. "It's Graham."

"You better talk to him, see what he wants. Maybe he's discovered something that will help us out."

"I guess," she sighs reluctantly, "but in my experience the only person Graham ever thought much about helping was himself." She hits the 'send' button and moves her long, black hair away from her ear with a toss of her head. "Hi." Pause. "We're still down here in Chicago of course." Pause. "What?!" Pause. She shifts in her seat, gives me a worried glance and rolls her eyes. "Graham, what're you thinking? I told you there wasn't anything you could do." Pause. "Don't be an ass." Pause. "As a matter of fact I do, yes." Pause. "I really don't think…." Pause. "As far as we know, he's still okay." Pause. "Navy Pier." Pause. "Whoever's doing this told us to." Pause. "No! You stay where you are. Graham? I'm warning you…"

She lowers the phone and flips it closed. I find it incredible that in the midst of all this confusion and probable danger I find myself admiring her legs again. "That big, dumb, pompous—"

"What's going on?"

"He's here. Graham's *here*. Can you believe it?"

"In Chicago?"

"Yup. He just missed us at the hotel. He's a couple of blocks behind us right now."

"You can't be serious."

"'Fraid so. I'm really sorry Tin, I don't know what's possessing him."

"I do."

"What do you mean?"

"I wouldn't give you up that easily either."

She smiles and pats my knee. "What do we do about him?"

"Nothing, I guess. He knows we're going to Navy Pier. It's a big place with a lot of people. He'll have to fend for himself. We need to concentrate on finding Sweeney and figuring out if my brother's a killer or not. We'll deal with the jealous boyfriend when we have to. Okay?"

"Okay. If it's any comfort, I doubt if he'll find us. He thinks he knows where everything is, but its just bravado. He gets lost going to the gas station. He used to drive me crazy on the expressway when he'd get in the right hand lane ten miles before he had to turn off and stick himself in slow-moving traffic because he was worried about missing his exit." She squeezes my leg. She says, "I love you," without looking at me.

"I sure as hell hope so."

Ahead of us, the traffic finally begins to thin as the cars merge onto Lakeshore Drive. The open waters of Lake Michigan lie just beyond. I see hundreds of sails gliding across its glassy surface and as many boats without canvas. Behind us, the city is getting dark but out here, in the open, away from the monolithic buildings, there's at least two or three hours of daylight left. I glance at my watch. Ten minutes to seven.

We pull into the entrance drive and follow the circular road that leads to the front gate. We pass Gateway Park with its running arch and sculpted children at play. "Those are statues," Moira says. "I thought they were real kids at first."

My immediate priority is to find some place to leave the Jeep. We cruise by the taxi stand at the main entrance. A huge sign has recently been hoisted above it and tied off to two stone pillars. There are people everywhere. All across the park in front there are boats of every imaginable size, hoisted on trailers to allow prospective buyers to examine them. Salesmen dressed in deck shoes and white pants and captain's hats man the tables, distributing free brochures describing their products and moving among the crowds like lions in a herd of wildebeests, searching for the likeliest prey. "Are there usually this many boats?" Moira observes. I point to the big sign between the two pillars. It reads: *Welcome to Navy Pier's Sixth Annual Boat Dealer's Show* in large, black letters. "Ah," she says.

"Where the hell do we park?" I feel my frustration growing. Too many unanswered questions, too many wild emotions, too much to be wary of. I want to stay alive, and I'm not sure this is the best place to be to accomplish that ambition. I have no idea what awaits us here—or who. My brother is somewhere among these herds of humans. So is Sweeney, probably, and the author of our guiding notes. Behind us, the irate boyfriend is after me. It's all better than that leaky boat on Loon Lake, but I'm afraid it might produce the same result.

I pull into the parking lot, but the attendant tells me that the place is full. He says that I can find a spot in one of the perimeter lots and take the trolley in. We cruise for ten minutes before spotting a lot on East Ohio Street. I pull in, pay the guy, then we have to wait for the trolley to show up.

"Everything'll be alright," Moira says. "No matter what happens, we'll be together."

Tears form in my eyes and she sees them as clearly as I can see their cause in my mind. "Tin, darling, what is it?"

"You said you believe in destiny, the teleology of existence."

"Yes."

"When Wendy and I went to Detroit, the night we told Satchel how we'd betrayed him, she said virtually the same thing to me." I light a cigarette in an attempt to control my emotion. "I'm not sure I could stand it if anything happened to you."

She smiles at me. "Listen, I *know* that I'm supposed to be with you and my destiny is different than Wendy's. I'm sure of it." She gives me a long, lingering kiss that has no taste of farewell in it. I appeal to my imagination and I'm comforted. I see the trolley pull up in the rearview mirror. It's already half-full and, like me, filling fast. In a brief moment, we're clanging merrily toward our destiny with bright-shirted vacationers and I'm wondering if I'll make the return trip.

Chapter nineteen

Within a few minutes we step down from the trolley into the soft light of a Chicago summer evening. We're at the main entrance. The lowering sun creeps across the long pier, extends itself into the water, and turns the white sails on the lake to crimson.

I've been here before, once, with Wendy. We came to Chicago to visit her family and her sister. Kelly insisted that we double-date with her and her boyfriend and come out to Navy Pier for an evening. She was a striking brunette who, Wendy once observed, went through boyfriends like Tampax—pretty much on a monthly schedule. Wendy later added, somewhat ungenerously, that her sister used men in much the same way—for absorption and disposal. I liked Kelly and thought Wendy was a bit harsh, but then I didn't really know Kelly that well.

At that time, Kelly was a lovely woman in her early twenties. It was obvious that she liked food almost as much as she liked men. She wasn't fat, by any means, but fully rounded. Kelly was flirtatious and flaky and Wendy would often upbraid her for her concupiscence,

but the sisters were devoted to one another. When Wendy was murdered, Kelly took it harder than anyone except me. Wendy was Kelly's
only sibling. Although she'd called me several times and we'd talked
very briefly, I hadn't seen her since the funeral. Being here makes me
think of her again and prompts the thought that I should give her a
call while I'm in Chicago.

I remember being impressed by Navy Pier as much then as I
am now. As wide as a football field and ten times as long, it juts into
Lake Michigan like a floating carnival. At the western end, closest to
land, is the Headhouse that contains Chicago's Children's Museum.
It's a brick and terracotta building with two prominent towers, each
of which houses a two million-liter water tank for the fire sprin-
kler system. At the other end of the pier is the auditorium, which
is called, simply, the Hall. It encloses the Grand Ballroom with its
hundred foot, half-domed ceiling. In between the two structures
are a 400 seat IMAX Theater, a 32,000 square foot indoor botanical
park called the Crystal Gardens, the 1,500 seat Skyline Stage (used
as an ice rink in winter), the Smith Museum of Stained Glass Windows, the Chicago Shakespeare Theater and 40,000 square feet of
restaurants and retail shops. Also part of the pier is the 150 foot high
Ferris Wheel, an old-fashioned musical carousel, a swing ride and an
18-hole miniature golf course. There're always crowds of people, especially in good weather. I notice as we pass the parked cars that most
of the plates are from outside of Illinois. The boat show, of course,
has certainly increased the mob. There are vessels of every description on the water and jammed into the many moorings along the
shore and the pier. People are almost shoulder to shoulder. This is a
good place to get lost in.

As we approach the entrance, I spot Satchel and his young
paramour. They look so out of place in their jeans and wide belts,
western shirts, cowboy boots and weathered features—rubes in the big
city. Cowboys used to be common in this town when they brought
their herds from the Great Plains to the slaughterhouses, but no
more. Sandburg's 'city of the big shoulders' has moved away from
its blue-collar origins. It's become a town of theater, art, fashion, and

merchandising. The Bears at Soldier Field still cling to its rough past, but even they are learning that modernity is much more finesse than muscle. Satchel is leaning against a pillar just under the boat fair sign, glancing around nervously.

"There they are," Moira says.

"I see them."

"Your brother looks edgy."

"He's been running and hiding for a long time. I don't imagine he's used to crowds."

"The fact that he's exposing himself like this might be another reason to believe him, Tin. He never even flinched when you reached for the phone."

"Or he might think they've given up on finding him. I don't think anyone's been seriously pursuing him for quite awhile." As we draw nearer and they spot us, Satch's demeanor changes. He sees something I don't, something behind me. I don't have time to turn all the way around before I feel a hand on my shoulder. "Jesus, Joseph and Mary," the booming voice exclaims. "Tin Balune! What the hell are *you* doin' down here?"

The strength of the bellow and the hand that's twisting me around immediately identify my captor. "Buck?" I try to sound good-natured, but the coincidence of seeing this old acquaintance in two different states in the course of forty-eight hours, and the strained circumstances, arouse my suspicions.

"I'll be a sonofabitch! Here's a real jawjammer, ain't it, seein' you in Chicago when I just saw you in TC? I'm down here for the boat show. I told ya I was lookin' for another vessel. Remember? Ain't no better place to find it. Ever damn dealer in the world is here! So, that's my reason, what's yours? You returnin' another truck?" He laughs heartily and winks at me.

I can't, of course, tell him the truth. It would take too long and I'm not sure he's leveling with me. "Moira and I sort of hit it off," I say, winking back. "We're just vacationing a little."

"*Moorah!*" he shouts and envelops her. I notice then that his wife, the leathery blonde, is standing right behind him. She doesn't appear to be enjoying the reunion as much as he is, especially while he's groping Moira.

I extend my hand to her and she takes it. "Sabina, isn't it?"

"Yeah. Hi." She nods at Moira. Moira nods back.

"I'll be damned," Buck says, still holding me with one gorilla arm and Moira in the other. "Ain't this sumpin? I mean I come down here ever year, but to find *you* down here after runnin' into ya at that restaurant, I mean hell, what're the chances?"

I look over my shoulder and see that Satch and Moon have disappeared. A quick glance at my watch tells me it's exactly one hour before we have to rendezvous with Sweeney's captor. I can see that Moira is considering our difficulties as well.

"When did you get here?" I ask, for lack of anything better to say.

"This mornin'" he bellows, finally releasing us. "We rented a car and left Mackinaw City around 5:00. I tell ya," he grins, "it's hell tryin' ta get Sabina outta bed. 'Specially when I'm in it!" He roars at his own wit.

"You rented a car?" Moira says.

"Yeah. I was plannin' on buyin' another ferry, like I told ya at the restaurant—and I did! We're goin' take her back by way 'a Lake Michigan tomorrow. She's a beaut, Tin. Don't know what I'm goin' name 'er yet. Sabina probly." He glances lovingly at his wife. "They dropped 'er in the water this afternoon. They could've hauled her up to Mackinaw, but I'm savin' myself a grand and a half by runnin' 'er up there myself—by water. You gotta come see 'er. She's moored over on the north side of the pier. Hey! Let's us take 'er for a spin, huh? You guys gotta see how she moves, smooth as silk for a three-hunnerd seater."

What do I tell him? Sorry, old friend, but I have to meet my wife's murderer in less than an hour? Moira rescues me.

"Boy, Buck, that sounds like a lot of fun, but I can't. I get seasick just sitting in the bathtub."

"No shit? Listen, these big ferries ain't like being on a sailboat or pleasure-cruiser ya know. Ya don't even know yer on the water." He looks pleadingly at me. I shrug.

"Really," Moira says, "it's a motion thing. I threw up three times coming down here in the car. I have to take Dramamine to go fishing in a rowboat. It's terrible. Tin can go though. I wouldn't want to spoil his fun."

She smiles at my astonishment and raises her eyebrows. If I didn't love her so much, I'd throttle her.

"Don't be ridiculous sweetheart," I respond, "I couldn't leave you here, all alone. Tell you what, Buck, why don't we all grab a bite to eat and catch up on old times. We've got to meet someone later, but I think we can squeeze out some time for a burger. What do you think?"

He beams. "That'd be great! My stomach was startin' ta rumble anyhow. Who ya meetin' anyway?"

"Kelly," I say without hesitation, only because she was the last person in my thoughts.

"Who?"

"My former sister-in-law," I say. "She lives here in Chicago. We called her from the hotel where we're staying and she arranged to meet us out here. Haven't seen her since...well, since her sister, my wife Wendy, was killed."

Buck lowers his head, staring at his gunbolt shoes. "That was a shitty thing ta happen ta anyone, Tin. I read about it."

"How did she die?" Sabina says, finally looking interested.

"I'm sure it's sumpin that Tin don't wanna talk about, babe."

"It's all right, Buck." I look at Sabina who is actually leaning forward in anticipation.

"She was murdered," I say, "beaten to death with a baseball bat."

"How terrible," she says. "Did they ever find the guy?" In spite of her declaration, she doesn't appear to be that surprised.

I can tell by Buck's expression that he knows about Satchel. He waits for me to explain. I simply say: "No."

"Listen," Buck says, rescuing me, "I know a great little place—"

"Oh, not the Buppa Gump Shrimp Company again," Sabina moans. "We eat there all the time."

"Naw." He shrugs his massive shoulders. "What can I say? I love shrimp. Naw, I was thinkin' of Luigi's. It's about halfway down the pier on the south side. They got ever kind of food ya want. Great Italian stuff. They got this forty-foot long exhibition kitchen where you can watch everthing they make. Got an outside café too. My treat."

"Now you're talking," Sabina says.

Moira looks at me. "Tin," she says, "why don't we meet the Wolframs at the restaurant in, say, ten minutes. I want to go back to that shop where they sell all the Russian stuff and pick up that Ukranian painted Easter egg for my mom. You know how crazy she is about anything Russian." She glances at Buck. He looks at her suspiciously, as if he knew she was lying. She sees it too and adds; "My grandfather was born in Kiev. It'll only take a minute."

"Hell," Buck roars, the frown on his massive face quickly evaporating, "we'll go with you!"

"I think it's going to take a while to get a table at this time in the evening. If you and Sabina wouldn't mind going on ahead to get a reservation, then we wouldn't be late meeting Kelly. We'd really appreciate it."

"We can do that," Sabina says, sensing our eagerness. "We can get a drink in the bar while we wait. We'll see you in a few minutes." She grabs Buck's arm and pulls him off into the crowd like a cat leading an elephant.

"Good thinking," I say to Moira after they've been swallowed up by the crowd, which in Buck's case at least, requires quite a few people. "What happened to Satch and Moon? Can you see them anywhere?"

"No."

"One question about your little ruse. How am I supposed to know your mother loves anything Russian when we just got together?"

"You told him before, when we met the first time, that I was a friend of the family, remember?"

"Oh, yeah. Okay, what now?"

"We've got to find your brother and explain what's going on. He may think we've betrayed him. He might think Buck is a cop or something."

"Even if he does, he said he wanted to settle this now. If he's telling the truth, the cops shouldn't scare him away. Where the hell is he?" I can see over the heads of most of the people in the crowd. I look again toward the pillar where he was leaning a few minutes ago. Nothing.

"What do we do about Buck?" she says. "Are we going to meet him or do we just forget about him?" She glances at her watch. "We've got about forty-five minutes."

"I don't know. I've never done this before. Maybe we should just go meet Buck and Sabina and let the people who wrote the note find us. I think whoever got us to come here is probably very much aware of our presence. All indications are that they've been watching us pretty closely at the hotel. They're probably watching us now."

"Maybe," she says, looking anxiously around, "but they might think Buck is a cop or something, I don't know. Even if they don't, they won't contact us with other people around, will they?"

"Let's take a walk up the pier, toward Luigi's. We're not going to accomplish anything just standing here. We'll never be able to find anyone in this crowd anyway, they'll have to find us."

She nods her head and we start to shoulder our way toward the south side of the pier. We finally break out of the milling crowd a short distance from the entrance. Here, at least, we can walk relatively uninhibited. There are still masses of people, but they're flowing in a more orderly east/west pattern and stopping to browse in various shops and kiosks, allowing for occasional spacing. The effect is less suffocating.

My brain is muddled with a thousand questions, mixed into a gray soup of apprehension. Not the least of these are: who is responsible for Wendy's death and Sweeney's kidnapping? I sense that this night I will have an answer and the irony is that I'm not certain I want to know. What's happened to my brother? Who is this woman in the window who's been watching us? Will we get out of here unharmed? It's all beyond my capacity for understanding. I look at Moira, take her hand. She interrupts her scrutiny of the crowd to turn and smile at me, which generates yet another question. How can this girl, this woman, be attracted to me? It's the greatest of all these mysteries.

"How far is this restaurant?" she says.

I want to tell her it doesn't matter to me. I have her hand and I will walk to the ends of the earth with her, straight into the jaws of hell if necessary. I can see, in those black eyes, that it doesn't need to be said. We'll just walk on, together, toward whatever fate brings us.

"Not far, I think. Another fifty yards or so maybe."

When I turn my head away from her, I am conscious of a figure at my elbow, strolling quietly beside me. Apparently destiny waits for more than two of us.

Chapter twenty

I t's Moon. When I look down at her, her face is grave and she doesn't turn her head to talk to me. "Joe...I mean Satchel, wants you to come with me." She almost whispers.

At first, Moira doesn't notice her, concealed as she is by my size. When she does, she stops walking. Moon stops as well, but I can see that she's uncomfortable, standing here, in the middle of the boardwalk as the crowds flow around us. She's wearing jeans and a colorful blouse that's tucked in and held by a thick, leather belt with turquoise beads and a silver buckle. Her waist looks so small that I think I could put a hand on each hip and my fingers would touch. Her straight, silky-black hair falls to her shoulders and is kept from interfering with her vision by the strategic placement of simple bobby pins and the big, hooped earrings. I think if she were not wearing heeled cowboy boots she would be less than five feet tall. The only indications that she is not a twelve-year-old are her substantial breasts and her face—both of which argue for adult experience. The high cheekbones of her race enhance her striking beauty.

"Where is he?" I ask.

"I'll show you," she says, and scurries off in the direction from which we'd come. Looking at her from the back, struggling through that crowd, it seems to me as if someone should be holding her hand.

"What'd she say?" Moira asks.

"She's taking us to Satch." I grab Moira's hand and attempt to stay with Moon who, by now, is several yards ahead of us. Her diminutive stature allows her quicker movement through the onslaught of tourists. There are hundreds of gulls screaming overhead, each trying to maneuver a landing among thousands of human legs to get at spilled popcorn and peanuts and other assorted morsels that litter the pier. A big, beefy fellow in a Hawaiian print shirt is standing in the middle of the mob, swearing like a madman, as his mousy-looking wife tries to remove gull guano from his front with toilet tissue and his teenage kids laugh hysterically at his expense. Moon skirts around them and slips into the pavilion, out of the open air, where the crowds are even denser. I can see her shiny hair work its way just below the surface of the flowing stream of humanity and into a store. A sign above the place reads *TransPIERency*. As I pull Moira through the entrance behind me, I can see Satch, now rejoined with Moon, standing in front of a counter. Above him is a sign that reads *Official Stained Glass Store of Navy Pier*. Everywhere there is glass; glass window panels, glass keychains, glass night-lights, glass candleholders and various other glass items, along with a hundred or more browsers. Satch is talking with a clerk who's showing him an oval portrait of Babe Ruth, constructed of glass, of course. He looks disturbed. I can see he's trying to be polite to the clerk who is giving him some kind of sales pitch. As Moira and I approach, he breaks off the conversation with the salesperson—abruptly, from the offended look of her, and comes to meet us.

I open my mouth to ask him why he didn't just come with Moon to find us, but he beats me to the punch. "I saw Connor," he says. I don't react, probably because the name is one I've almost forgotten. "Connor, your hired thug. He's here. What the hell are you trying to do, Tin?"

"What? What would *he* be doing here?"

"That's what I'd like to know, brother. I sure as hell didn't invite him."

"You sure it was him?"

"Most people have a tendency to remember someone who shot them." He holds up his scarred hand. It's no longer capable of making a fist, or I'm pretty sure he would have punched me with it. "You're saying you don't know anything about it."

"No."

"Bullshit."

"I'm telling you, Satch, I haven't talked to the guy since I fired him, years ago. He said he hadn't been able to find you. I told you all that. He's gotta be working for someone else. It's the truth. I swear." How ironic, I'm protesting my innocence to the man who is supposed to have murdered my wife. It's a measure, I guess, of my growing belief in his. "Where did you see him?"

"Here, in this shop. Moon and I wandered in, looking for you, and there he was."

"He didn't say anything to you, tell you what he wants?"

"No, I don't think he even knew we were here. And while we're at it, who's the big dude with the blonde?"

I had momentarily forgotten about Buck and Sabina. "A guy I used to work for on the ferries at Mackinaw City. You remember me working there, don't you?"

I can see he's trying. He has, after all, spent the last few years trying to forget everything about his past.

"He was just starting his own line. I worked on his first boat. He's down here with his wife for the boat show."

"This guy just happens to run into you here?"

"I know it sounds bogus," Moira says, "but it's the truth. We're supposed to meet them for dinner in a few minutes at Luigi's. We couldn't get away."

When Satch looks at her, his face softens a bit. I glance at Moon. I can see that she wants to believe us. Why is it, in America, that we don't have faith in women to run things?

"What does this Connor guy look like?" Moira says. The question is obviously directed to me.

"I don't know. I've talked to him a lot over the phone, but I've never seen him."

My brother just stares at me for a minute. His blue eyes seem like two lasers to me, cutting into my recent contentment and excising it like a tooth rotted from too much sweetness. "You mean you've never even met this asshole?" Satch says. "You paid him money and had him go after me and you didn't even know him?"

I feel my cheeks flushing red. "Sweeney knew him, I told you. Sweeney recommended him and I was too washed out to care."

"What's his last name?" Moira asks, trying to stave off the growing tension.

"Connor is his last name. His first name is Cian."

"Key-un?"

"Yeah. I think it's spelled C-I-A-N."

"That's bizarre."

"It's unusual, Irish I think. The guy had an Irish accent anyway."

"No, I mean I have an uncle whose name is almost like that."

"A brother of Sweeney's?" I ask.

"No, I told you, Sweeney's not my father. I'm talking about my mother's brother, Keenan O'Connor. Sweeney used to joke about how he was Irish, like that actor, you know 007—minus the looks."

"Sean Connery? He's Scottish," I say.

Moira laughs. "I know. Sweeney thinks everyone is Irish."

Satch, I can see, has become very interested in this conversation. "What's your uncle look like?" he says.

"I don't remember much about him, to tell the truth," Moira says. "I only met him two or three times in my life. He came to visit us in Detroit. He flew over from Ireland, stayed about a week I think, then went back. I do recall thinking that he looked a lot like Sweeney—more than he looked like my mom, anyway. He had the same sandy-colored hair and fair skin—and he was tall, unusually tall. But I was a kid, like I said. Everyone looked tall to me. Oh, yeah, and I remember he had really bad teeth. They were crooked and the front two protruded—buck teeth, you know?"

"Wouldn't we have seen him at your mom's funeral?" I say. "I remember Dad took us to it, some huge Catholic church. This O'Connor would have been there, right?"

She shakes her head. "No. He couldn't get there in time, couldn't catch a flight from Ireland. He showed up a couple days later at Sweeney's house in Detroit, stayed for about a week, and left. That's what Sweeney told me, anyway. I was only about three or four years old."

"How do you remember what he looks like then?" Satchel says.

"I saw him again, when he came to Detroit another time—maybe ten years later. I must've been in junior high then, twelve or thirteen. I think he had moved to the States. Anyway, that was the last time I saw him."

Satch looks at me. "Cian Connor is about six-eight," he says, "with reddish hair and buck teeth."

I glance at Moira. I can see that her belief in Satch's innocence is growing alongside a suspicion of her own family. She looks confused and helpless and I want to kiss her.

Satch pulls at my arm to regain my attention. "He has an accent too. Irish. It can't be coincidence that he's here. He was looking for someone and I don't think it was me."

"Where'd he go?"

"He left about three or four minutes before you guys showed up."

"Did you try to say anything to him, get his attention?"

"Yeah, right. I'm going to walk up to the guy who shot me and threatened to kill me and ask him how's it hangin'? C'mon, Tin. I turned my back to him and struck up a conversation with that clerk over there and sent Moon to find you. When I worked up the courage to turn around and see what he was doing, he was just looking at the glass stuff. He kept glancing outside the shop. He seemed to me to be nervous, tense, and I don't think he was in here because he's a glass collector."

"Why don't you believe he was after you?"

"Because he would have seen me then, noticed me, even with my back turned. Sweeney was right when he told you the guy is good. He managed to track me down when I went to a lot of trouble not to be found. I think his mind was on a different target."

"What target?"

"I don't know. Maybe you, or Moira, or both. Maybe *he* kidnapped Sweeney and Sweeney got away."

"Why would he kidnap his own brother-in-law? It doesn't make sense."

"*Somebody* was kidnapped," Moon observes. Moira and I both look at her. "Isn't that what the note says?"

I look at my brother and he shrugs. "I filled her in on the drive over here. Moonie can be trusted. She's got a lot at stake here too."

"Well we can't just stand here," Moira says. "What are we gonna do?"

I glance at my watch. It's ten to eight. "I think all four of us should go to Luigi's and hook up with Buck and his wife. We'll be out in the open, easy to find. Whoever wrote the instructions for us to come here will probably spot us, then we'll have to go from there. If anything happens, at least we'll have another ally."

Moira shakes her head. "We can't take your brother and Moon with us. Buck knows Satch is wanted for Wendy's murder."

"Buck's never met Satch," I tell her. "I'll introduce him as someone else—the alias he's been going by—what is it?"

"Joe Reed."

"Yeah, Joe Reed."

"We don't have another option as far as I can tell," Satchel says, "what else can we do?" He directs his question to Moira.

"I guess so," she responds, although the tone of her voice is pure apprehension. Moon pats Moira's arm with her small hand. The two women smile at one another. A bond is developing there. I look at Satch. He sees it too. How did these lovely women get mixed up with us?

As we emerge on to the dock again, I glance in the direction of the city. The sun is beginning to set behind the gigantic buildings of downtown Chicago. The sky is a conglomeration of brilliant colors—reds, oranges, pinks, purples, blues. The skyscrapers stand like sacred monoliths, black and ominous against the brilliant sunset, and I picture myself as a hairy, half-evolved human with a bone in my hand. I don't know why.

We turn in the opposite direction, toward the fiery water that's alive with light and shadow and moving vessels. As we swim against the human river it seems to thin, as tourists with younger children head for the exits, to rescue themselves and their offspring from the oncoming night. There's something primordial about it, and I wish we could do the same.

We're all silent as we hurry along. Moon is almost running as she tries to keep up with Satchel who, as always, leads. Moira and I trail only slightly. I can see a canopy ahead, extending out almost to the thoroughfare, with several tables and chairs beneath it, around which are seated a number of tourists who're happily obeying, probably without understanding, Epicurus' grand injunction. It's eight o'clock.

Buck and Sabina are sitting at a table under the canopy outside, with, conveniently, four other chairs. Buck's quick eyes have spotted us long before we approach. He stands up, drink in hand, and waves at us. His beefy grin is spread ear-to-ear. "Tin! Tin!" he shouts as if we have not seen him. Satchel slows to a halt and I take the lead.

"Jesus, Tin," Buck says as our group approaches the table, "we thought you'd stood us up. Where the hell ya been? Was it crowded at the Russian store?"

It's only then that I realize that we haven't been to the 'Russian store' and that I must come up with a different alibi. "Sorry Buck," I say, as I pull out a chair for Moira to sit in and then follow suit. Satchel and Moon stand by the other empty chairs. "You're not going to believe it, but I ran into another old friend from Michigan, just after you left us. We got to talkin' and...well, we lost track of time." I point to Satchel. "This is Joe Reed and his girlfriend, uh—"

"Moon," Moon says.

"Moon? Like the planet?"

"The moon isn't a planet, Buck," Sabina corrects. She doesn't look pleased to have additional company, but she takes Moon's hand as Moon extends it to her. "Sabina," she says.

"Nice to meet you," Moon says.

"Moon. I'll be damned," says Buck.

"And you're Buck?" Moon says. "Like the deer?"

"It's a nickname," he says, apparently unaware of the reprisive nature of Moon's comment. "I was s'posed to be named after my old man, but when he lit out, while my ma was still pregnant with me, she couldn't stand the idea of it. She jes started callin' me Buck. Ain't got nuthin' ta do with deer." He shakes Satch's hand. "Sit down, Joe. Hell, the more the merrier." His words are jovial, but oddly, the tone is apprehensive—very unlike the big man.

Moira smiles at me. I smile back. Moon is beaming and even Satch is amused.

As we all settle into the captain-style wooden chairs, the waiter appears and takes our orders for drinks. Moira and Moon both settle for Diet Cokes, which does not go unnoticed by the head of our table. "You boys is kinda robbin' the cradle ain'tcha?" he guffaws.

"They're more easily impressed," I say. "Not everyone has the money and the charm to win a mature, sophisticated woman like Sabina." Buck's wife smiles, and even though I wink at Moira, (who winks back), Sabina is now squarely in my corner. She clears her throat and nods toward an envelope resting on Buck's placemat.

"Oh yeah," Buck says. "The waiter brought this to us a few minutes ago. At first I thought it was *from* you, tellin' us ya couldn't make it, but then I noticed it's got yer name on it. Seems like ya know everone in Chicago, Tin."

He extends the envelope across the table toward me. I glance at Moira, then Satch. When I open it, I can clearly see that the note inside is written in the same handwriting as the others. It reads:

Tinker Balune
My patience is wearing thin. I will be at the Fourth Church

on Michigan at midnight with Sweeney. An appropriate place
for redemption.
    Satch.

Chapter twenty-one

Moira sees the tears in my eyes, I guess, because she grabs my arm and says: "Tin, what is it?" I can't explain to her, in this place, in front of Buck and Sabina, that I have proof of my brother's innocence. This note is Satchel's final vindication, and all the wasted years of hatred and desire for vengeance come flooding over me. I see my poor father, asleep forever, in a sacrilegious cloud of carbon monoxide, and I mourn my own culpability.

I hand the note to Moira, swallow my drink in one gulp, and excuse myself to go to the restroom. There, hunkering over a sink, I bawl like a baby, my cold control completely gone. The booze, the mood-tempering nicotine, even my recently discovered happiness with Moira—nothing can hold back the guilt of lost parents, lost opportunities, lost years, lost faith. Only the last, I know, has any chance of reclamation.

I recover sufficiently to realize that I may not be alone and that such sounds as I've been making would be embarrassing should someone be occupying one of the two stalls behind me. I test the doors on both and they swing open without resistance. Empty. I have returned to the sink to wash my face when Satchel enters the restroom. He looks at me, studies me, actually, with concern. His bruised lower face, the result of my most recent treachery against him, forces itself into a smile. "You all right Tin?" he says. I am all wrong, of course—have been for many years. I stole his woman, believed the worst of him, cost him his baseball career, made him a hunted man, almost got him killed, failed to save his desperate father and when he came to try to straighten it all out, punched him in the face. Yet, here he stands, smiling at me, not a trace of vindictiveness in that pleasant, still-youthful face. I'm suddenly overwhelmed with love for my brother. He's shocked when I hug him and cling to him, my head on his shoulder, soaking his western-style shirt with my tears. I feel his hand on my back, cautiously caressing me in the uncertain and tentative fashion of men unaccustomed to comforting men.

"It's okay, Tin," he says. "What is it, man? C'mon brother, it's gonna be okay."

Still holding him tightly, I raise my tear-stained face to look at his. My guilt makes it difficult, but I force myself. I owe him directness from this point on, both in demeanor and behavior. "You didn't kill her."

"No."

"So I destroyed your life…for nothing."

"You didn't destroy—"

"Yeah, Satch. Yeah I did. I took Wendy away from you, then blamed you for her murder."

"Wendy made her own decisions, Tin. She left me for you. It was what *she* wanted. Her murder wasn't your fault either. The way things appeared, if the situation had been reversed, I would have blamed you too. It looked like it should have been me. The police thought so."

"Then Dad—"

"I loved Dad, you know that. You know what he meant to me. But I also know what I meant to him. He focused too much on me and too little on you. He wanted me to be a great baseball player and

I still could have done that, even after Wendy died, but I just wanted to be a son and I couldn't be. When he came to LA to talk to me, only part of it was about Wendy. He was concerned about baseball, about how I was squandering a promising career. I rejected him because of that. Because of that, I ran away. I left him to deal with the misery of disappointment. I could have tried to do then, what I'm doing now. Instead, I was so full of self-pity that I ran. I turned to drugs. I threw away my own opportunities. I should have trusted more in you and Dad and who I was. Dad should have trusted more in what he'd always preached as truth. I've had a lot of time to think about it all, Tin, and I know this for certain, it was more than one person's fault." His eyes probe me. They do not turn away. They have never turned away. "What did the note say?"

"It's not important what it said," I tell him. "It was signed 'Satch'. You couldn't have written it. It's someone else trying to put the blame on you. It...it's pretty solid proof, combined with everything else, that you're not behind any of this. It was too much, Satch. It all came flooding down on me. I had to get out of there." I keep my eyes on his. "Forgive me, brother." The words are so simple and so complicated. He kisses my cheek.

At that moment another man enters the restroom. He looks at us, embracing by the door. He's a little, fat, bald guy. His face wrinkles up in wincing disgust. "Oh shit," he exclaims, "why can't you people show a little propriety when you're out among normal folks? I don't make out with my wife in public."

"Maybe you should," Satch says without a moment's hesitation. "When I walked past your table out there, she was studying my belt line pretty eagerly."

I can't help a muffled laugh. The top of the little man's bald head turns red. He looks up at us both with complete disdain, shakes his head, and leaves, without relieving himself.

"It's good to see you laugh, brother," Satch says as he lets go of me and lights a cigarette. I follow suit. The bulls-eye and the heart send their message.

"You can forgive me?"

"I think we can forgive each other. I want a clean slate, Tin. I really just want my life to continue the way it is. I want to stay with Moon on the Bullkiller ranch, have some kids, get up every day and watch the sun rise over the mountains. That's all. I don't want to have to hide anymore. I'm willing to do whatever it takes to accomplish that. Looks to me like you've got someone special in Moira too."

"I love her very much, like I loved—"

"Wendy, right. Me too." He takes another drag on his cigarette and flips it into the toilet. "We have to figure out why Wendy died and who did it, then we go to the authorities and get it straightened out. It's the only way. Agreed?"

"Agreed. So what's the first step?"

"You have to fill me in on everything. I want to see this latest note you got, and the others too, and what about your friend out there? You gonna tell him what's going on or get rid of him? I think you have to do one or the other."

"That would mean me telling Buck who you really are."

He shrugs his lean shoulders. "Whatever's necessary. You trust him?"

"He's a blowhard and a little short on sophistication, but I think he'd go along with whatever we asked. He's a decent guy."

"Let's go then."

I notice as we struggle through the crowded dining room that Mrs. Little Bald Fat Guy really does leer at Satchel appreciatively. He gives her a wink and a pleasant smile in return, as her husband turns scarlet. When I look back, I can see they are beginning to argue. It has always given me a bit of wicked pleasure to see pomposity distressed.

Moira and Moon both seem enormously relieved as we return to the table and take our chairs. "Everthin' okay?" Buck says.

"Gettin' better all the time," Satchel responds, smiling widely at Moon.

Moira looks hopefully at me. A quick wink of my eye is enough to assuage her anxiety.

"We gonna order?" Buck bellows. "I'm starved."

"We might as well," Moira says. "We've got to figure out where to go at midnight anyway."

It's funny how the mind remembers small things. I order the porcini mushroom-crusted New York Strip Steak, cannellini beans with escarole and roasted garlic relish. Moira gets the Ahi Tuna Tartare, pickled cucumbers with orange ginger-infused soy sauce and wasabi caviar. Moon opts for the goat cheese ravioli with fennel marmellata. Buck requests their finest cheeseburger and a bottle of 1994 Moet and Chandon Dom Perignon. I ask him if he notices that the price is $250.00 a bottle. He laughs boisterously. "Ya only live once," he shouts. "Don't worry, the chow's on me." Satchel orders linguini alfredo; Sabina, some kind of onion soup and a salad.

The meal is worth lingering over and we do, we must. There's a lot to be explained. We're well into our repast when I'm finally finished telling the whole thing to Buck. Oddly, he doesn't appear to be all that surprised, although he scrutinizes Satch with a very discerning eye. "So you can see what we're trying to deal with here," I tell him. "I think it'd be best if you and your wife just ducked out of this and headed home. There's likely going to be trouble and it's not your problem."

I am surprised both by Buck's silence and the fact that it's Sabina who speaks out. "Not on your life," she says.

Buck looks at her with astonishment, a string of linguini (Satchel's leftovers), firmly attached to his greasy chin. Moira and I are flabbergasted as well. "What the hell ya talkin' 'bout, babe?" Buck says. "I thought sure as shit you'd wanna get outta here."

"No offense, darlin'," she says, "but being a housewife isn't the most exciting thing I've ever done." She takes another long swill of the Dom Perignon. She's getting her money's worth. "Outside of you bangin' my ass three or four times a week, there isn't much fun in it. Catching a murderer sounds like a good time to me."

Buck shrugs and stares questioningly at his wife. "Guess she knows what she wants," he says to me, although for the first time I detect a note of hesitancy in his voice. I get the impression that his eagerness for adventure does not match his wife's. I am, frankly, a bit shocked by this apparent role-reversal. Buck and Sabina seemed to have switched personalities while Satch and I were gone.

"Absolutely."

"What do we do first?" Moon says.

"We've got another puzzle to solve," Moira answers, waving the note. "We've got to figure out where we're supposed to meet whoever wrote this note."

Satch nods. "Anybody got any ideas?"

The waiter returns to clear our plates. Buck orders another bottle of Dom Perignon at Sabina's insistence. As the waiter turns to leave, Buck says: "Hold on a minute there, partner. We're supposed to meet a friend later on and we can't remember exactly where he said, something about the fourth church on Michigan."

The young man considers for a moment, tilting his head and staring off into the distance. "Yeah," he answers casually, "so what's your problem?"

"Well, he must've been talkin' about Michigan Avenue. How many churches are there on that street? Which one would he be describin' d'ya think?"

"Well," the waiter says, "I would think he means Fourth Presbyterian Church. It's on Michigan Avenue right across from Hancock Building. Been there since the First World War, I think. It's considered a historic site. Everyone calls it Fourth Church here in Chicago."

"Too easy," I say when the waiter leaves.

"An appropriate place for redemption," Moira says.

"That's gotta be it," Buck says. He, at least, seems totally convinced.

"That's where I'll go then."

"Where *we'll* go," Moira corrects.

"She's right, Tin," Satch says. "You're dealing with a killer. I think maybe we ought to call the police and let them straighten it out."

"I'm not too sure that's a good idea," Buck offers.

"You're right," Moira says. "What about Sweeney's safety?"

Satch glances at me. I can see we're thinking the same thing. I'm the one who'll have to say it. "I think Sweeney's part of this whole set-up."

"It looks that way, I know," Moira says, "but I just can't believe he'd do—"

"You think her *father* is involved in this?" Buck asks.

"Satch says it was Sweeney who told him where we'd be, right down to the hotel and the room number, days before the note appeared on my kitchen table," I tell Moira. "How would he know where we'd be unless he was in on it? And another thing—the note. It was in Sweeney's handwriting. If someone had forced him to write the note, how would he know what it meant? Sweeney's the one who recommended Cian Connor to me and now Satchel sees Connor down here, in that gift shop? His name is an awful lot like Keenan O'Connor, your mother's brother, and he fits the description that Satch gave us to a tee."

"All of what you said is based on what Satch has told us," Moira says, looking apologetically at Moon. "I'm sorry, but we have to consider everything. Satch told us he talked to Sweeney and Sweeney told him where we would be. Satch was the only one to see this Connor guy."

"Yes."

"We're assuming your brother is telling us the truth. I want very much to believe Satchel, but he could have fabricated all this. He could have instructed Sweeney's abductor on what to write. How do we know that what he's saying is the truth?"

"It has to be, Moira. You know Satch didn't write this latest note. He was with us."

"When it was delivered, yes. What about the song too, the one by the Association that was used as the code for that first note? I'm just trying to see every angle. It was Satchel's song right? About Wendy. Don't get me wrong, I'm not Sweeney's greatest fan, but he did provide for me most of my life and he didn't really ever do me any harm. Most significantly, whoever's leading us on now would have to be Wendy's killer and what possible reason would Sweeney have had to do that? I don't believe Satchel did it either, but we have to consider every possibility, don't we?"

I look at Satch. He shrugs. "I don't have an answer for that."

"Moira, you told me that Sweeney owned an Association CD with that song on it."

"Okay, it's possible that Sweeney knew the song. But he didn't have good reasons for using it, like Satchel. I'm sorry, Satchel," Moira says, "but I have to understand all this. How do we know that you didn't write this latest note," she waves it in front of her, "then slip it to the waiter before we hooked up with them again?"

"That's an interesting possibility," Satch says, "but then how would I know what restaurant to take it to? How would I know you were even meeting these folks for dinner before you told me in the glass shop? How would I get Sweeney to write it?"

Moira shakes her head. She looks lost.

"Hey!" I motion to the waiter who's a couple of tables away.

He hustles over to us, fully aware of the enormity of twenty percent of the price of two bottles of Dom Perignon.

"Listen," I say to him. "Did you give this note to this gentleman?"

"Yes sir."

"The man that gave you the note, what'd he look like?"

"Oh, well, it wasn't a gentleman at all, sir. It was a lady."

"A woman?"

"Yes sir. A very attractive lady, if I might be allowed the observation—probably in her early thirties or so."

"Blonde?" Moira asks.

"Yes ma'am."

Moira glances at me, knowingly.

"Where'd she go?" Buck asks.

"Sir?"

"Did she leave right away?"

"Yes sir."

"You watched her leave?"

"Yes sir."

"Why?"

"Why did I watch her leave?"

"Yeah."

"Pardon my boldness, sir, but I think every man in the restaurant probably watched her leave. She was wearing a tight, red dress, very short. She was pretty hot."

Buck laughs heartily. "That ain't bold boy, that's jest normal. Did ya see her leave *with* anyone? Did ya see her meet anybody?"

"No sir."

"Okay, thanks kid."

"Wait," Satchel says. "This woman told you who to give the note to?"

"Yes sir."

He looks over at Buck. "How would this woman or the writer of the note know who you are, Mr. Wolfram?"

Buck seems, just for a second, to be a bit disconcerted. "Damned if I know. Mebbe he saw us talkin' to yer brother."

"How would he know you were going to meet him here for dinner?"

Buck looks at Sabina. Her cheeks are flushed, and she quickly looks away. He looks back at Satch. He shrugs, in what seems to be nonchalance. "No idea."

Satch turns back to the waiter, who now seems very impatient to be gone. "You see anyone unusual in here in the last hour?"

"Unusual, sir?"

"A man. A very tall man, with bad teeth, sandy-colored hair?"

"No sir. I don't think so."

After the waiter leaves, we all sit looking at one another. Satch is the first to break the silence. "Any idea who this woman is?" I look over at Moira. Neither of us has said anything yet about the woman in the window of the hotel across from us. So we tell the group.

"And you think this woman who delivered the note here is the same one who was masquerading as your agent? The same one who was watching you from the room across the street?" Satchel says, after Moira and I are finished filling them in.

"The description fits," Moira says.

"But you never got a close look at her?"

"No."

"This uncle of yours," Satch says, "does he have a wife, or daughter, a girlfriend maybe?"

"No. From what I understand, he never married. He was the bachelor uncle. I can remember Sweeney telling me not to ask any questions about women in Uncle Keenan's life when he came to visit. I guess, as a kid, I wasn't known for my tact." She takes a sip of Dom Perignon. No one has asked her for I.D. "My uncle and mother were orphaned. Their parents were killed, caught in a crossfire between IRA insurgents and the British authorities, Sweeney told me. I guess they had an awful time of it as kids, living in abandoned buildings and eating garbage, at least until the authorities put them in an orphanage. Sweeney said my mother told him that she owed her life to her brother, many times over."

A wonderful, cool breeze comes in off the lake. It's almost dark now. The sun has set behind the Chicago skyline and lights twinkle on in the boats anchored in the harbor.

"What time is it?" Moon asks.

Sabina glances at the expensive gold watch on her tanned wrist. "Just after ten."

"So," I say to the group. "What do we do now?"

"I think what we do next is going to have to be based on some assumptions," Satch says.

"What assumptions?" Moira asks.

"If you still think I'm a part of this plot, conspiracy, whatever you want to call it, then Moon and I go someplace of Tin's choosing and wait for you there until this is all over. If you believe what I've told you, then we go along and try to help. We'll do whatever makes you guys," (he looks specifically at Moira), "feel comfortable."

Moira lowers her head and stares at the white tablecloth. The breeze plays with her long hair, partially obscuring her face so that I can't read her expression. The candles at these outdoor tables flicker in their glass jars, but don't go out. I touch Moira's hand. I know that she's thinking that trust in my brother means an acceptance of betrayal elsewhere.

"I say Satch and Moon are in." My brother gives me a warm smile.

Moira looks up at me, brushes her hair aside. "I'm with Tin."

We both look across the table at my brother and his Diana. There are tears in his eyes.

"Good, me too," says Buck, "if I'm allowed a vote. Well, what the hell do we do first?"

"You sure you want to get involved?" I say. "This could get pretty hairy."

Buck swallows a glass of Dom Perignon without taking a breath, then he unbuttons the top of his ridiculous Hawaiian shirt and pulls at both collars, exposing a mass of thick hair that looks as artificial as that of Mike Myer's groovy spy. "Can't get any hairier than this," he roars.

For the first time, I see Sabina smile. "Like makin' love to a bear," she says, "and there's nothin' more dangerous."

When the general gaiety dies down, Buck's question still hangs over us.

"We've got a couple of hours," Moira says. "I'd like to go to the hotel across the street from the Wyndham and find out who that woman is. If we can track her down, maybe we can get some information from her that would help us figure this out before we have to rendezvous with the…note writer at this church. She could at least tell us who arranged for her to set up the hotel room for us, and she might know a whole lot more."

"I think that's a good idea," Satch says. "In the meantime, if it's okay, Moon and I can drive over to this church, park in their lot, and just see if anyone shows up—maybe just keep an eye out 'til you guys get there."

"Makes sense," I say. Moira nods.

"We'll go to the church too," Sabina says.

"I don't know if—"

"Look," Sabina says, cutting me off. "I don't intend to sit

around here and wait for you guys to figure this out. It sounds like too much fun. Besides, I got this...." She pulls out her cell phone and looks at Satch and Moon. "You got one of these?" They both shake their heads. "How about you guys?" Moira pulls hers from her purse. "Then that's the only way we can keep in touch—and I think we'll need to, don't you?"

"You could loan it to Satch and Moon," I suggest.

"No way. My phone stays with me. Take it or leave it."

"Ain't she a bitch?" Buck observes, but there is little humor in his tone.

"All right," I say.

We exchange cell phone numbers, Buck pays the bill and we step out into the Chicago night, the six of us—all wondering what will happen. I think we could all say, at that moment, that we'd never felt quite so alive.

Chapter twenty-two

We split up in the parking lot, Buck and Sabina driving away in their rented, ostentatious, white Cadillac, following Satch and Moon in Joolie Bullkiller's battered truck, since Satch knows his way around the Windy City better than the Wolframs. After they're gone, and we're alone, standing by the Jeep, I kiss Moira. I've been waiting all evening to touch her again, to taste that wonderful mouth. It seems that in spite of all the possibilities of danger and the extreme emotional trauma of the day, I have not lost my lust for her. As we drive back to the Wyndham, I am considering, incredibly, how I might be able to convince her to let me make love to her one more time before we have to face all this. It is love, really, not lewdness and I want to know that it can happen again before I have to die. To have the blood hot is life-affirming, and carries with it a feeling of invulnerability that contributes to that elusive and tenuous sense of courage that has so recently become a part of me. Moira has brought emotion, perhaps even faith, back into my life, and the sense that Christ's passion must mean much more than His suffering and death.

First things first. We meet the Guardian and he relieves us of the Jeep, then we cross Ontario Street to the hotel on the other side. We're about to enter via the revolving door when Moira tugs at my shirtsleeve. "Wait a minute," she says. "How are we going to go about this?"

"What do you mean?"

"Well, we can't just walk up to the room and knock. For one thing, we don't know what room she's in."

"Judging from the windows, it's the second from the end, facing Ontario Street. I counted."

"What if there's a suite or something along that row that has more than one window? Then you wouldn't have the right one. We don't even know for sure what floor it is."

"It's the fourth, same as ours."

"You know as well as I do that some hotels, like the Wyndham for example, count from the bottom floor up. But some call the bottom floor the Lobby and the second floor is actually labeled as the first."

"It doesn't matter what they call it. We just go to the fourth level and we'll be directly across from our floor at the Wyndham."

"You don't think we should try the front desk and see if they can help us?"

"What're we going to say? That we're looking for a knockout blonde who's been watching us from one of their hotel rooms? That she might be involved in kidnapping and murder and we need to talk to her?"

Moira is not pleased with the sarcasm in my voice. "Of course not, but we could make up some story—maybe that she's a relative and we have to get hold of her because of a family emergency."

"Don't you think they're going to be a bit suspicious of our motives when we can't give them the name of this relative?"

"Okay. Your way is best I guess. I just wanted to think it through, consider every angle. No point in going off half-cocked."

"I can assure you, my love, that that is a condition I am never subject to in your presence."

I elicit a laugh, which somehow makes me feel better about myself.

The lobby is virtually deserted except for a couple of sleepy-looking desk attendants who pay us no attention as we hurry to the elevators.

We emerge into a narrow vestibule from which two hallways extend on either side. I confess that I have gotten turned around and I'm not sure if the corridor on our right or the one on our left faces the Wyndham. For no particular reason we move cautiously down the one on the right. A young man, probably in his twenties, emerges from a stairwell at the far end of the hall and heads toward us. He's dressed in a sweatsuit and has a towel around his neck. Apparently, he's just returned from a late-night workout in the hotel's fitness center. He's a handsome guy and obviously is noticing that Moira is eyeing him appreciably. When we are within ten feet of him, he stops and pulls a keycard from his pocket, sliding it through the slot in one of the doors. As he enters his room, Moira rushes toward him.

"Excuse me," she says in her most sweetly appealing and artificial voice. He stops. The irritable expression on his rugged features changes immediately when he sees her. He smiles broadly, revealing flawless white teeth. "Yes?"

"I'm sorry to trouble you," she says, standing too near to him now, "but I wonder if you could answer a question for me?"

His eyes are intent on perusing her exposed mid-section and I have this perverse desire to cure his 'wandering eyeitis', as I call this affliction, with an ice pick. Fortunately, I don't have one.

"Of course," he says, without shifting his attention in the least.

"We seem to be lost," she says. "We live here in Chicago and we have some friends staying here, at this hotel. They asked us to come over and visit, but we forgot what room number they gave us. We know it's on the fourth floor and faces the hotel across the street. Does your room face the Wyndham?" She smiles appealingly. Why the change from provocatively?

"Yes, yes it does."

"Oh thank you so much, you've been a big help."

She turns back toward me, winking. I think she's somewhat surprised at what must be a terrible scowl on my face.

"Listen," says Mr. Hollywood, "you and your…uh…friend are welcome to come in for a drink if you'd like. If you have a phone number, I'd be happy to let you use—"

"Oh no, really, thank you very much for the offer though. He's my husband. The thing is, we've still got to see our friends and we really can't stay out too late. He needs his rest, you see. Maybe some other time."

"Oh," is all the lascivious bastard can manage. "Sorry," he says to me and I offer him a smile that is only slightly dissimilar to giving him the finger as he shuts the door to his room.

"I need my rest?"

"You don't think that was droll?"

"More like sardonic."

"Oh c'mon, I found out what we needed to know, didn't I? Quit being so sensitive." She's almost to the end of the corridor before I can think of a response.

When I catch up to her, she's standing in front of the door to the room that should be occupied by our Peeping Thomasina—second from the end. "What do we do now?" she whispers. "Knock?"

"Well, it'd be a bit impractical to break it down. Besides, at my age I might hurt myself."

She rolls those beautiful eyes. "Will you get over it?" She makes a fist and taps lightly on the door. We both step away and I stiffen in anticipation of trying to keep the door ajar when it's opened. Nothing.

Moira knocks a second time. There's no sound coming from inside. She puts her ear to the door and knocks a third time. "Maybe, if she was the one who gave Buck the note at Navy Pier, she's not back yet."

"Or she's just not answering. She would have had more time to get back here than we did."

"We have to get in there."

"If she's not inside, what's the point?"

"We could go through her stuff, at least find out who she is."

"There's no way to get in. We'll have to forget it for now, maybe try later."

Moira whirls round suddenly and begins to walk away. "You stay here," she says, "make sure she doesn't leave. I'll be back in a couple of minutes."

"Hold on," I shout in a sort of stage whisper at her retreating figure. "Where the hell are you going?"

She turns slightly, placing her finger to her lips. "Hush. Don't let her leave. I'll be right back." In the space of a few seconds, she's disappeared around the corner to where the elevators are. I am slowly learning that Moira cannot be contained.

I feel totally exposed and abandoned. I realize that this is the first time I've been without her since we left Traverse City to head back to Loon Lake, an event that seems years distant. My mouth is terribly dry and I desperately want a drink. It occurs to me that in her absence it wouldn't take long for me to fall back into my old ways. I try to think of other things. I tentatively press my ear to the door and listen carefully. I hear nothing. Perhaps our Mata Hari is asleep. I knock again, more loudly this time, to see if I can rouse her, then listen once more—still nothing but silence. I knock louder—no response, no hint of movement inside. I turn around and lean against the door. I long for a cigarette, look at my watch. It's almost eleven.

Then...a sound.

It comes from the other side, the interior of the room. I don't know how to describe it exactly. It's as if something were brushing against the door, just a whisper of motion, a shadow of sound, but unmistakable. I feel it on my back as much as I hear it. Someone is in there, listening for me.

I must be as quiet as thought. Some improbable intuition tells me patience will bring her out. I have to convince her that I'm gone. I take two pantherine steps away, stand, then with slow and deliberate stealth, turn to face the door. I've made no sound—no squeaking of floorboards, no wisp of shoe on carpet, no breath. I am composed, shut up, pulled inside myself. At eleven on a week-night, all is silence.

I focus on the handle. It must move first, if the door is to move at all. I stand frozen for several minutes, although it seems much longer. Another almost indecipherable sound from inside. I imagine that this is how vampires move—like a slight breeze against a rotted tapestry, feet above the floor. I am tempted to draw closer. I resist the urge and keep focused on the door handle.

It moves. It's like the slow rotation of the moon, unrecognizable to those who must corroborate sight with time and change, but I see it. I *feel* it. Nothing else in the world is in motion but the doorknob and my accelerating heart. It continues to rotate with terrible caution, twisting steadily, almost imperceptibly, but it *is* moving. This is no illusion, no temporary delusion created by fear or desire. When it's finished with its orbit, I tell myself, then I will rush forward and lay my weight against the door, forcing it ajar. This woman will have to reveal her identity and we will have some answers.

It stops! I must act. I step forward and press my open hand against the door, expecting the minimal resistance possible from a petite woman. The door opens, but only a few inches, before a pow-erful counterforce arrests momentum and holds the door firmly in place. I throw my full weight against the door, but it doesn't budge. I'm aware of two things in my struggle. The first is that my opponent is much more formidable than I'd anticipated, and the second is that this has to be the right room, or its occupant would be protesting with vehement screams or shouts of distress at my intrusion. I force my left hand around the edge of the door—a terrible error. Who-ever is inside sees my fingers and immediately releases their pressure, but only for a split second. It's long enough for me to lose my foot-ing and release my own inward tension. Then, while my resistance is gone, whoever is inside slams the door on my hapless fingers with decidedly unfeminine force. There's a sickening thud. My rising gorge sticks in my constricted throat. I try to pull away. The pain is excruciating. I want to scream, but all I can manage are sharp gasps of vulgarity. To my left, my peripheral vision, tear-clouded as it is, detects movement. It's Moira, running toward me, waving something in her hand. I can't see. The corridor shrinks into a black box, with me in it whirling around in fetid, sweaty air. My damaged hand is suddenly released and I feel, rather than see, that the door to the air-conditioned room in front of me has opened. I catch a glimpse of a gigantic figure before me. At eye level, I can see a blurry pen in a shirt pocket. I have no thoughts of protecting myself. Every nerve is focused on the pain in my hand. Everything I have learned in life tells me that whoever is standing there, on the other side of my blurred vision, should be feeling great sympathy. They should rue their rash action, be overwhelmed with regret, come to my aid. Instead, a fist slams into my jaw and the whirling box takes me down, down. It becomes a leaky boat. Water spumes from its floor, round and round into dark spirals, eddying underneath the surface, sinking, sinking. I hear my mother or Mary Sweeney or Wendy or Moira call my name. I inhale deeply. My lungs fill with liquid and I lie down to answer the call of sweet oblivion.

Chapter twenty-three

Sometimes, when pain overwhelms, nothingness can mean everything and you don't want to leave it, especially when even awareness of decision is gone. There is, literally, nothing to be done. When else, in all good consciousness, can we say that? But the Imp, robed as Choice, wakes me. Do I rise back to the surface, or do I stay down here in the dark water? He uses someone else's voice to call me back to the very human, inhumane torment of awareness. It's a sweet voice, a voice I love. I have to go back. Thus does the Lord of Pain use us for our own affliction.

"Wendy?" I say as my disobedient brain breaks the surface. In my return to the living, I hurt my new lover. She is bent over me. She kisses my forehead.

"It's me, darling," she says. "Moira." I have the sweet, coppery taste of blood in my mouth. My jaw aches. My hand is dead. I think I left it down in the boat somewhere.

"Where is she?"

"Who? Wendy?"

"The woman. Is she still in her room? She hit me, slammed the door on my hand."

"It was a man, Tin. I think it was my uncle. He was very tall, had reddish-blond hair. I didn't see his face though, so I can't be sure. Are you all right? You're bleeding."

I sit up for no reason other than to not look quite so ridiculous. When I place my hand on the floor to assist me, it comes alive. As Moira examines it, I realize that it's as bad as it feels. "Oh my god," she says. "We've got to get you to a hospital."

"I'm okay."

"Bullshit. I'd bet that at least a couple of your fingers are fractured. You need a doctor."

"Help me up."

She does. I'm light-headed for a minute, then the full agony of consciousness kicks in. I lift my arm instinctively to keep the blood out of my hand. The more I can numb it, the better.

"Where is he now?"

"He went down the same stairwell that the other guy came out of, you know, the guy with the towel. I thought about chasing him, but I couldn't leave you here, on the floor."

"Did he see you?"

"I don't know."

For the first time I get a clear look at my left hand. The fingers are already badly swollen, except for the pinkie that, due to its size, probably escaped the brunt of the trauma, and my thumb, which was on the outside of the door. The three middle fingers are close to doubling their normal size and turning from red to purple. The index finger is cut and bleeding. I won't be playing the piano anytime soon.

"What was he doing in her room?"

"I don't know." I take a degree of comfort in the fact that my jaw seems to be working, although it's sore and the taste of blood tells me that I might be avoiding salty foods for a while. We glance at the door simultaneously. "It's closed."

"We should go in," Moira says. "Can you make it?"

I test the door handle with my right hand. "It's still locked."

She deftly produces a card key and slides it through the accommodating slot. The little green light goes on and she pushes the door open. "How did you—"

"I assured the nice man at the desk downstairs that the lady occupying this room is a close friend and that I wanted to surprise her on her birthday. You'd be surprised what a pleasant smile can accomplish."

"I don't think it was your smile that did it," I say, looking once again at her revealing outfit. She giggles. Obviously this guy didn't take his hotel training as seriously as the Guardian does.

"Let's go in."

"Your hand—"

"It'll have to wait." My stoicism is fake. I want very much to be tended to.

We move forward cautiously. It's dark in the room. The fact that no lights are on bothers me. If Cian Connor or Keenan O'Connor or whatever the hell his name is was in this room just to chat with our mystery woman, wouldn't a lamp still be on? He wouldn't have had time to turn it off when we came calling. Why would they speak in the dark? The curtains are open, and lights from the Wyndham are outlining the room in gray shadow. "Look," Moira says, pointing to the window.

"What?"

"That has to be our room over there. The lights are on. Did we leave a light on when we left this afternoon? I didn't turn any on, did you?"

"I don't think so, no, but I'm not sure."

I flick the light switch by the door.

"Oh god, Tin."

The switch controls two lamps on either side of the bed. The comforter and blanket have been pulled back. She's lying on the white sheets, on her stomach, her face turned away from us. Her platinum hair is resting in a red pool that circles her head like a halo. The scarlet puddle obviously originates from a terrible wound in the back of her skull. The color is identical to that of her skin-tight dress. It doesn't take a forensic expert to see that she's been shot in the head, execution-style. This is no accident, nor the random work of an amateur intruder. She was forced to lie down, the gun was placed against her head, and someone who's used to killing terminated her life. It's apparent to me that the bloodstained pillow next to her, its stuffing protruding, was used to muffle the sound of the gun or, perhaps, to prevent the murderer from getting splattered.

I approach the bed, and reluctantly touch her wrist to check for a pulse. Her skin is cold. The veins underneath are silent.

Behind me, Moira whispers "I'm calling 911." Her voice is shaking. She picks up the phone on the table next to the bed.

"It won't do any good. She's gone."

"Are you sure?"

"Yes."

"Tin, sometimes they can bring them back. I've heard of people being saved when everyone thought they were dead. We've got to try."

I take the phone from her with my good hand. "She'd dead, Moira. She's dead, okay?"

Tears form in her black eyes. "How could anyone…it's awful, Tin." I can see that she's trying very hard to collect herself. "We *have* to call someone. We can't just leave her here. We should call the police."

"Just give me a minute, will you? I need to think this out." I place the phone back on the hook and kneel on the bed. The woman's body turns slightly toward me, reacting to the depression in the mattress that my knee has caused. It's an unsettling moment because it seems as if she moves on her own. I notice that there is a dark border along the side of her face next to her hairline. It isn't blood. I slowly come to the realization that she's wearing a wig. The platinum hair isn't real. The wig is hiding much darker hair underneath. I brush the bloody wig aside. Below, some kind of nylon skullcap is stretched over her head. The hole caused by the bullet has loosened it. When I draw it away as well, long, dark folds of ebony hair spill out onto the sheets. I reach across her prostrate form as well as I can with my undamaged hand, grab a cold arm, and turn the stiff body over. "Dear Jesus," is all I can manage as the shocked and open-eyed visage stares blankly in the direction of God. I recognize this face, now that I see it close.

"You know her?" Moira says. "Who is she?"

"I just can't believe it. This can't be happening."

Moira pulls at my shirt. "Who is she, Tin?"

"Kelly. It's Kelly."

"Kelly? Kelly who?"

"My sister-in-law, Kelly. Wendy's sister."

"Are you sure?"

"Yes."

I take Kelly's cold hand as if I can somehow comfort her now. Its cool, unnatural rigidity makes me let it go. I close the open eyes. Eyes that can't see should not *be* seen—ask Ray Charles.

Her mouth, growing pale even with the heavy lipstick, gapes open as if to speak to us, perhaps to accuse us. I don't know. The question constantly circling above the pain in my head is why? Why were you here, Kelly? What part have you been playing? What did they tell you to get you to do this? Why did they kill you? Why do I think in terms of 'they'? Why? Why? Why?

I remember her as a vivacious kid, yakking away, flitting from boyfriend to boyfriend and still managing to appear innocent. But she looks old now, hard, covered in her heavy make-up. The life has gone from her and it was her primary attribute. I am flooded with guilt and somehow certain that whatever role she played in this horrific plot, it was the part of the ingenue.

"I'm so sorry, Tin," Moira says, finally breaking the silence. "Why would she be mixed up in all of this?"

"I don't know. She didn't have anything against me, I'm sure of that. When we'd come to Chicago to visit Wendy's family, we always hung out with Kelly and one of her innumerable boyfriends. She and I kidded all the time. If anything, I was fonder of Kelly than Wendy was. We didn't speak much after Wendy died, but she'd call every few months and I'd keep her informed about the investigation. She didn't blame me for Wendy's murder and she always appeared to have great empathy with my misery. Someone must have got her involved in this under false pretenses, probably because she lived in Chicago. She must've figured out what they were up to and it cost her her life."

"Tin," Moira says, her hand on my shoulder as I stand up, "this isn't your fault."

"No? If I had never lived, Wendy and her sister would still be alive."

"If you had never lived, and these things had never happened, we wouldn't be together, would we?" She kisses me on my cheek. Her smile temporarily rescues me from my guilt, but I wonder at the same time how long it will be before *she* becomes another ghost to haunt my sanity. A barbaric anger rises in me, a horrific hatred of Cian Connor or whoever the sandy-haired ogre is who has accomplished these ugly atrocities. The grisly *why* of it keeps pounding in my tortured mind like a gigantic bell that will not be silenced. A primitive hate begins to replace my sense of guilt, my sense of almost everything.

"Why would your uncle want to kill Kelly?"

"I don't know."

"You've got to have some clue. You must know something. You've got a *murderer* in your fucking family and you don't know it? Goddamn it, Moira, there's got to be a *reason!*"

I expect her to cry. She doesn't. "Listen," she says, her voice soft and even. "I told you I haven't seen my uncle for quite a while, at least five or six years, and even then that was just for a few days. I'm not even sure it was him. I didn't get a good look at him. For the last few years you've been thinking that you had a murderer in your family. Did you have an explanation? Don't put this shit on me, Tin, I don't care how upset you are." Her dark eyes are drilling into mine, fearless and sure.

"Okay."

"Okay. What do we do now? Call the police? We can't deal with this."

"What're we going to tell them? That we just happened to find my sister-in-law's corpse in a hotel room? That we were led to Chicago from Michigan by some lunatic posing as my wanted brother who's kidnapped your stepfather? That my brother, who's accused of my wife's murder, is waiting for us to show up at a church where we're supposed to rendezvous with the real murderer? I can tell you that it's going to take us all night just to tell them what's happened and by then, Sweeney or Satch or all of them will be dead. This guy isn't playing games, Moira, and he's a fruitcake. By the time we convince the authorities that they have to check out the Fourth Presbyterian Church, it's going to be way after midnight. We're going to be the prime suspects in Kelly's murder until they're convinced that someone else is responsible and by then, if that ever happens, the guy who smashed up my hand is going to be long gone."

"You need medical attention."

"I'm alright. I think we should go back downstairs, go over to the Wyndham and get the car brought around. While we're waiting for it, we can go up to room 432 and check it out, see if anyone's been in there. The lights are still on. We can use some sheets or something from our room to wrap this hand. Then we head for the church on Michigan Avenue. We'll call the police and tell them about Kelly from the car. At least then we're not just leaving her here. We'll call Sabina's phone, see what's happening with Buck and Satch, let them know what we've found. Then...I don't know, we'll have to play it by ear."

"The police will know we've been here, you understand that. Our fingerprints are here; you...you've touched her body, and look at the carpet."

I do as she says and notice a small circle of blood on the beige rug where I'm standing. As I'm watching, another drop falls from my damaged hand directly into the center of the little pool. "Your blood is on the door too. Not to mention the fact that the guy with the towel saw us in the hallway and the desk clerk downstairs can identify...oh my God!"

"What?" She is looking out of the window. "What is it?"

"Someone just closed the shades to our room!"

"What?"

"The blinds are closed. They were open before. Look."

She's right. I can still see that the lights are on across the way, but that's it. Someone's in our room.

"Who would be in there?"

"Well, I doubt if it's maid service after eleven at night. Did you see them do it?"

"No, I just looked up and they were closed."

"It can't be the guy who did this. He wouldn't have had enough time to get over there would he?"

"I don't know. I wouldn't think so. Who else could it be though?"

Moira's dark eyes are glistening in the dim light. I'm amazed at how long her black eyelashes are. They're almost fairy-like, surreal. I feel a mixture of arousal and adoration—something profane and entirely holy. I want to worship her and ravage her. I want to gently comfort her, to kiss those wide eyes. I want to lay down with her on the bloodstained bed and make love to her, even with the corpse of my sister-in-law lying there. A magical predation rises in my loins and I understand, for a moment, the passionate ties between love and hate, tenderness and brutality, goodness and evil.

The pain in my hand is excruciating now. The world is full of death and sorrow and hurt, but there is that sense of beauty, that comprehension of oneness, those brief moments of coupling that atone for it all. That, perhaps, is the most macabre characteristic of all human life—because it makes us want to continue. We don't drive, we are driven. "Let's get out of here," I say and I grab her hand with my good one. She has no protest except a request to cover Kelly's body, which we attend to without comment.

In a few moments, we are in the dark streets below, crossing to the Wyndham. I give the Guardian my number and he sends one of his innumerable minions around the corner into the secret place where the machines are kept. "Twenty minutes," are his only words.

We fly through the revolving doors, heading for the elevator.

When we reach the fourth floor, it's very noisy. Music is blaring from somewhere down the hall and doors are opening and closing. Apparently some group has taken over a number of rooms and they're enjoying themselves at the expense of the rest of the hotel guests. When we get to our room, one thing is immediately apparent—the door has been forced open. The little electronic box that flashes green when the plastic key is inserted has been jimmied off the door—and not very delicately either. Whoever it was used a crowbar and he wasn't too concerned about whether we knew we'd had a visitor. The most unsettling thought is that he might still be in there.

I place my good hand on the door handle.

"Wait," Moira says. "We can't just walk in there. If it *is* the same guy, he'll have a gun and he'll use it, you know that. Even if it isn't, and the intruder is unarmed, you're not in any kind of shape to protect either one of us." Her reasoning, of course, is impeccable. What she hasn't taken into consideration is the depth of my hatred and my willingness to risk almost everything in order to avenge Wendy and Kelly. I can only see myself dead or in prison when all this is finished, and the former seems preferable. I have no intention of living anywhere in this world without Moira.

I push the door inward and step inside. There, in the middle of the room, is Graham Van Houten. We have forgotten all about the poor cuckold, but he has not forgotten about us, apparently. In his hands, he's holding the lingerie that Moira was wearing earlier. He looks at me with an expression of anger, tempered with fear, then his wide eyes move to Moira, who has stepped in behind me.

"Graham!" she shouts. "What the hell are you doing here? You scared us half to death!"

"What am I doing here? I've been following you around for the four hours, not to mention driving all the way down here from Detroit. I wandered all over Navy Pier looking for you. What on earth have you been doing, Moira?"

It's not until he extends his long arms to encompass the room that we look around and see that the place is torn apart. Drawers are pulled out and lying on the floor, the sheets and blankets are torn off the bed. Our packages and the clothes we purchased are strewn in every direction.

"I know you're upset, Graham," she replies, "but that's no reason to pillage like a simple-minded barbarian. You've even broken the lock off the damned door."

"I haven't touched anything," he whines in that voice that's far too high for his appearance. He sounds like a grizzly bear mimicking Mickey Mouse. "I found the place just like it is. The door was already open. When I realized you guys weren't here, I called the police. They should be here any minute."

"You what!?"

"I called the cops. You didn't do this to your own room did you?"

"Oh shit." Moira expresses it for us both.

"What?"

"God, Graham, why couldn't you just wait for us to contact you? You don't know what you've done."

"Maybe not," he says holding the lingerie up for her to see, "but I know what you've done."

Moira, as usual, ignores him. "We've got to get out of here, now," she says to me. She grabs a pillowcase off the floor. "Bandages," she says. "Let's go."

"Right."

Before the startled Graham can raise any objections we're out the door. He's hustling to catch up with us as the elevator door closes, leaving him stranded in the hall. As the elevator falls and my stomach rises, I hear the "Cell Block Tango" playing muffled strains from somewhere on Moira's person.

She extracts her cell phone. "This is Moira," she says, "go ahead."

She listens intently for a few seconds. "Okay," she responds to whoever is on the other end. "We're on our way."

She folds the phone and puts it away. "That was Buck's wife. They're at Fourth Presbyterian and there's another car there—a Ford Taurus."

The elevator lands and the door slides open. At the front desk are three uniformed policemen.

Chapter twenty-four

We can only pray that the Jeep is outside and ready to go—*if* we can manage to get to it. Fortunately the policemen have their backs to us and the attendant at the desk is absorbed with their questions.

"What should we do?" Moira whispers.

"Move across the lobby to the revolving doors as fast as you can. Stay on the other side of me. You're more easily recognizable than I am. Keep your head down and don't look at them."

"How do you figure that they'd notice me before you?"

"They're all men. Now go!"

As we hustle across the marble floor, I'm expecting someone to yell "stop." No one does. We emerge into the Chicago night with a *whoosh* that the revolving door makes as it releases trapped air, and us, onto the sidewalk. As I glance over my shoulder, I can make out Graham Van Houten emerging from the elevator. Miraculously, the Jeep is sitting in front of us. I don't see the Guardian anywhere. His shift must have ended. Apparently, his replacement is more efficient—

either because the late hour means fewer cars to fetch or the night shift functions better without such strict adherence to rules. I prefer to believe the latter.

I open the door for Moira and she practically dives into the Jeep, like a soldier leaping face-first into a trench to avoid a spray of shrapnel. I circle to the other side. The attendant holds the door for me. I sit down, shutting the door hard behind me with my good right hand. There is a knock at the window and I prepare to surrender myself, but it is only the attendant dangling the keys in front of my questioning face. I put the window down, again with difficulty, since I must use my right hand, take the keys, and notice his open hand. I reach for my wallet just as Graham comes bursting through the revolving door. I can hear him yelling. "Stop! Stop those people!"

The attendant looks up. "Let's get the hell outta here," Moira yells.

It's then that I notice the squadcar behind us, its red lights whirling. I put the key in the ignition, rev the engine, and pull into the street, tires squealing. The squadcar doesn't follow. Evidently it's empty; all of the cops are inside. I turn at the first corner, then turn again at the second and third as I slowly make my way in a zigzagging pattern toward Michigan Avenue.

"I can't believe," Moira says, "that you were actually going to try to take the time to find a tip for that guy."

"Well, he did get the car in a hurry." We both laugh, as much in relief as for any appreciation of humor. "Do you see anyone behind us?"

"No."

"I'll bet the cops have other people looking for us by now. The attendant can give them a description of the Jeep, even the license number from our hotel registration, and I'm sure that Graham is giving them an earful."

"What about Kelly?"

"Dial 911 and give me your cell phone. I have an idea."

She does as I ask. "What're you doing?"

"You'll see."

A woman's voice, sounding rather sleepy says: "This is 911 dispatch. What is your emergency please?"

"There's a dead woman in Room 423 of the Courtyard Marriot Hotel downtown. Her killer is a guy named Graham Van Houten. He's in the Wyndham Hotel across the street. Police are talking to the guy right now, but they don't know he's the murderer. He's from Detroit. That's all I know. Thank you."

The dispatcher, now very much awake, tries to get more information from me, but I hang up the phone.

I look at Moira. She's smiling. "You really are a sleazy bastard."

"All's fair in love and war."

"Why did you tell them that?"

"It'll keep the attention of the police on him for the moment. We'll straighten it out later. I don't think they'll listen to a tirade about a runaway girlfriend when they have a murder suspect. Besides, I don't like the sonofabitch."

She nods her head in agreement. "I can see we're not going to sleep well tonight."

"It all has to end tonight, or we'll never sleep well again."

"The blue Ford Taurus, that's what the woman at the Loon Lake grocery said that Sweeney was in when he—"

"I know."

I finally turn onto Michigan Avenue. "Look for the church. It's right along here somewhere. If it's across from the Hancock Building like that waiter said, we oughta be able to spot it without...there. There it is."

I glance at my watch. It's almost midnight.

I pull to the curb across the street from the church. At this time of night, there are very few cars on Michigan Avenue. The building is imposing. It was built, I would learn later, long before all the shops and hotels and other businesses would sprout around it, creating the tourist Mecca called the Magnificent Mile. Other than the old water tower a block or two over, it's the oldest building on Michigan Avenue north of the Chicago River. Some guy named Ralph Adams Cram designed it, the same architect who was known for his work on the world's largest Gothic cathedral, the cathedral of St. John the Divine in New York. Fourth is supposed to combine the very best of English Gothic and French Gothic styles, with gargoyles, gremlins and goblins keeping sentry from its magnificent heights, despite the fact that it was paid for and is occupied by the descendants of those dour Puritans who scorned ornamentation. Facing us is the main building, housing the massive sanctuary, and slightly behind it, to the left, as you observe the structure from the street, is the octagonal steeple, whose surface is ornately-carved stone on all sides and seems to rise to the stars. All along the sidewalk on Michigan Avenue is a covered 'cloister' walkway supported by a series of Gothic arches creating a kind of open 'tunnel' which connects the front of the church with the manse a hundred feet or so away. With various other buildings established behind the manse and coming around to connect with the sanctuary wall again, (a parish house, a great hall, etc.), a kind of courtyard is created, in the center of which is 'The Children's Fountain', a gift from the architect, Howard Van Doren. One could walk off the street into the courtyard.

I hear a ripping sound and turn to see that Moira is shredding the pillowcase she took from our room. "Give me your hand," she says. I twist in my seat to extend my left hand. "God, Tin. It's bruising up badly." It's a chilling observation. She begins to wrap my hand in wide strips of soft muslin. I try to concentrate on other things.

"Who the hell do you suppose went through our room like that?"

She is squinting against the dim light from a street lamp that dimly illuminates her operating theater.

"I don't know," she says. "If it was the same guy who killed Kelly, he'd had to have done it before we saw him. He wouldn't have had time afterward, not with Graham showing up there when he did."

"Ow, God!" Despite the fact that the air conditioner is blowing in my face, I'm sweating profusely. The pain is excruciating. I sincerely hope that my nurse is not doing more damage than good.

"Sorry."

"Whoever he was, what do you think he was looking for?"

"Us, maybe?"

"When he's supposed to meet us later anyway? Why tear the room apart?"

"I don't know. There. Better?"

"Great." It's a lie. My hand, which was becoming accustomed to its newly ruined condition, now throbs dramatically.

She produces a handful of Tylenol from her small purse. "Take three or four."

I swallow them eagerly.

"What now?"

"Do you have the number for Buck's cell phone?"

"Yeah," she says, "I programmed it in. Do you want me to call them?"

"We need to find out where they are. I don't see the Cadillac or the pick-up—"

"Or the Ford Taurus," she reminds me.

"Call them."

She punches it in and hands me the phone. One ring, two, then a woman's voice answers. "Hello?"

"Sabina?"

"Yeah."

"It's Tin. Where the hell are you guys?"

"In the parking lot at the back of the church. Where are you?"

"We're in front, on Michigan Avenue. Where's my brother?"

"He's sitting in the back seat with Moon."

"Let me talk to him, will you?"

"Sure. Hang on."

I hear some shuffling, then my brother's voice. "Tin?"

"What's going on?"

"It took us a while to find this parking lot. When we pulled in, there was another car already here. It's a Ford Taurus. We didn't see anybody though. We got out and looked at it. Nothing really significant there. There's some kind of valise or briefcase in the front seat. That's all. Buck parked a little ways behind it and I pulled the pick-up next to him. Moon and I got in the Caddy and the four of us have been waiting here for you to show up. You want us to look around? There's this recreation hall or something right in front of us but it looks like it's locked. We could walk around to the front though and nose around that courtyard or whatever it—"

"No! Don't move, damn it!"

"Alright. Jesus, Tin, take it easy will ya?"

He doesn't know. I realize that he doesn't know. "Satch."

"Yeah."

"Remember the woman we were talking about, the woman in the hotel across the street who was watching us?"

"What about her?"

"We went over there. I tried to force my way in. Some guy was in her room. A big tall guy with reddish hair."

There is a long silence.

"Satch?"

"That's gotta be Connor."

"That's what we figured."

"Did you talk to him?"

"He punched me, knocked me out for a minute or two. He ran away."

"You okay?"

I look down at my throbbing hand. "Peachy."

"And Moira?"

"Yeah, she's fine." A car goes by us. It's full of late-night revelers hooting obscenities out the window. They pass quickly and it's quiet again. "Satch?"

"Yeah?"

"We went into the room. We found the woman. She'd been shot in the back of the head."

"Jesus!"

"It was Kelly, Satch. Wendy's sister, Kelly."

"That kid?"

"She was twenty-seven."

"Guess it's been a long time since I saw her last. God! The sono-fabitch really does mean business, doesn't he?" I hear him say, "just a minute." His voice sounds edgy, irritable. Apparently the other three occupants of the Caddy are assaulting him with questions. "What did Kelly have to do with all this?"

"I don't know. Where the hell is this parking lot where you guys are?"

"You're in front of the church?"

"Right."

"When you're looking straight at it, there's a side street to the left of all those arches by the sidewalk. You see it? It's kind of hidden by all the trees."

At first, I can't see anything but trees and arches and a few streetlights. Then I notice the gap between two large maples. "Got it."

"Come down that side street a little ways. There's a manse right on the corner, then some kind of parish house, a couple of other smaller buildings, then the driveway that'll lead you in here. It'll be on your right."

"Be there in a minute. Don't move 'til we get there."

"Okay."

Just as I flip the phone shut, a patrol car cruises by us on the opposite side of the street. I can see him slow down. It's clear the cop is scrutinizing us with more than casual interest. In the rearview mirror, I watch him make a U-turn and then slowly pull up behind us. His flashers go on. "We're screwed," I say, as I watch him get out of the car.

"Kiss me," Moira says.

"What?"

"Kiss me, dammit, and make it good."

Before I can question her any further, she grabs the back of my neck and pulls my face to hers. I want to ask her what the hell she's doing, but her tongue has taken care of any further attempts at oral communication—at least of the kind that involve one's voice. With her free hand, she's fumbling with the buttons on her blouse.

There's a knock at the glass behind my head. She suddenly lets go of me and issues a startled shriek of embarrassment. She reaches across my lap and lowers the window. She knows that my left hand is useless. She slaps me on the chest and urgently tries to rebutton the blouse she's just unbuttoned. "I told you we should have waited until we got back to the hotel, you idiot," she shouts at me. "I'm really sorry Officer," she coos. "I know we're parked illegally. I told my husband to keep driving but he's got this hormonal problem, you know? He can't keep his damn hands to himself."

The face at the window is tired and mildly amused. The cop is probably in his late twenties. He's watching Moira carefully as she puts her clothing back in order. "You folks from the city?" he says.

"Michigan," Moira responds before I can open my mouth. "We're down here on our honeymoon."

"Where're you staying?"

"The Drake," Moira says.

The officer laughs. "Why that's only a block away, just up the street."

"I know," Moira shrugs. "See what I mean?"

"Okay. Hate to ticket newlyweds, but you can't park here. Better get going."

"Yes sir," I say.

"Thank you soooo much," Moira gushes.

"Yes ma'am," the cop replies, tipping his hat and smiling pleasantly. "Have a nice night."

"We intend to," Moira whispers, winking at the flushed face of one of Chicago's Finest as he straightens up and returns to his car.

"I can't believe it. The guy didn't even try to i.d. us."

Moira giggles.

"How did you even know about the Drake Hotel?"

She points down the street. There's a large neon sign a few hundred feet away, far above the street. Its bright letters say 'The Drake', as do the letters far below it, emblazoned on a green canopy that stretches from the building to the curb.

"You'd better get moving," she says, barely disguising the wry smile on her wonderful face. I pull out and move slowly down the street. As I do, the cop makes another U-turn and heads back in the direction of his original destination.

"You need to change your major," I tell her.

"To what?"

"Espionage."

She laughs. "You should talk. The police back at the Wyndham must not have called in Graham's description of our Jeep, which he most surely gave to them. I think your phone call has them focusing on him. Eventually he'll show them our room and spill the whole story and then they're really going to want to talk to us, but for now your lie has bought us some time."

I drive up to the next side street beyond the Drake and turn right, then turn around in a driveway. I don't want to make a U-turn on Michigan and draw further attention from some other cop who may happen to be cruising by. As we drive by Fourth Presbyterian, I can see that beyond the Gothic-arched passageway from the manse to the sanctuary is a large courtyard. There's a fountain and trees in it. Anyone could walk in off the street and meditate there if they wished.

"Someone's in there," Moira whispers, her face pressed to the glass window on the passenger side.

"What?"

"There's someone in that courtyard."

"Maybe it was just the shadows from the trees or something."

"No. He moved, just as we were going by. God, Tin, I'm scared."

"Me too."

"He could just shoot us when we get close, then kill Sweeney."

"I don't think he'd kill his own brother-in-law and niece, would he?"

"I don't know. Besides, he hasn't been working alone, we know that. Kelly was part of it and God knows who else. When he went after Kelly, someone had to be watching Sweeney—"

"Here's the street."

A few hundred feet brings me to the driveway of the parking lot in back. As I pull in, I can see Buck's white Cadillac and Joolie Bullkiller's pick-up truck parked next to one another behind the Ford Taurus. We park on the open side of the Caddy and its four occupants emerge from it to greet us. We find ourselves standing in a circle in front of the Jeep. I feel very conspicuous. The yellow lights that normally illuminate the tarmac for exiting worshippers expose us, making us superb targets for anyone lying in wait in the darkness beyond.

"Jesus, Tin," Satch exclaims, "what happened to your hand?"

"I put it somewhere I shouldn't have."

I expect some tasteless joke from Buck, but he seems very self-absorbed. He doesn't smile and concentrates on the pavement.

"That Taurus was here when you guys arrived?" I say to Satch, pointing at the vehicle.

"Yup. We figured it belonged to someone who works here, but whoever owns it had gotten here just ahead of us."

"How do you know that?"

"When we went over to look inside, Sabina leaned against the hood. She pointed out that the engine was still warm. Smart lady."

Buck says nothing. I wonder why he's behaving so out of character.

I fill the rest of the group in on the story of the blue Ford Taurus that Nettie Hines saw at the Loon Lake Grocery.

"Then you think that the kidnapper is here, Tin?" my brother asks. "Is that what you're saying? Cian Connor is here?"

"I guess so," I respond. "Either that or we've got a hell of a coincidence. The thing that's got me confused is how Connor could be in Kelly's hotel room, punch me in the jaw, and then drive over here before you guys got here. What time *did* you get here?"

"Shit," Buck says, "we been sittin' here a long time." He seems to be studying me. "The woman in the hotel," he says, "she was shot?"

"Yeah. In the head."

He grimaces. "She was your sister-in-law, Satch says?"

"Yes."

I leave the group and walk over to examine the Taurus more closely. I take my lighter out, spin the wheel against the flint, and hold the flame close to the car's surface. The color is dark green—difficult to see in dimmer light, but undoubtedly a shade of green when viewed up close. I walk around to the rear of the car and look at the license plate. It says 'Land of Lincoln' on it—issued by the state of Illinois. "This isn't the car," I say, as the rest of the group gathers around me. "You didn't even check the plates to see where the car was from?" I look first to Buck, then to Satchel. They both shrug.

"They're not professionals," Moira says. "It's not easy, in this light, to tell what color that car is. Besides, my uncle lives in Chicago—has for about the last seven or eight years."

"Then where the hell is he?"

"After you guys saw him at the hotel, he may have just shucked the whole thing and decided to run," Satchel says.

"With Sweeney?"

"Or not."

"What does that mean?"

"I dunno. Do you think he'd kill his own relative? He murdered Kelly. He shot me. We know he's capable of some pretty bad shit."

"May I help you folks?"

We all turn in the direction of the summons to see a tall man, dressed entirely in black except for a white clerical collar. "Is there something wrong with my car?" he says as he approaches us. "I'm John McIntosh," he says, "like the apple. I'm one of the associate ministers here at Fourth Presbyterian. I was just leaving for the night."

"I'm sorry, Reverend," I say. "We're looking for a friend and he drives a car similar to this one. We were supposed to meet him here."

"At midnight?"

"We were going out to an all-night club," Satch says. "Take the girls dancing, you know?"

"Ahh," he says, in a way that indicates he doesn't believe a word we've said. "Well, what do you plan to do now? I mean now that your friend hasn't shown up."

"I guess we'll just wait here for a while to see if he does," Moira says, in that sweet voice that I've come to realize she uses very insincerely at times, "if that's okay with you, Father."

"I'm Protestant, my dear," he responds, turning his attention to her for the first time. He is, cleric or no, obviously charmed. "No need to address me as Father." He calls her 'my dear' as if she were his daughter or someone far younger than he, although he can't be more than twenty-five or six.

"Sorry," she says, shrugging cutely, "I come from a long line of Irish Catholics. It's certainly obvious that you're not old enough to have children."

He smiles warmly. "I have two, actually."

"No way," Moira coos.

"Yes, it's quite true. I'll be thirty next week." I know what he's thinking, and it has nothing to do with his wife. Moira does this so effortlessly that I begin to wonder how much of the charm that was directed at me was genuine.

"That *is* quite remarkable," I say. "How long have you and your wife been married?"

"Seven years," he answers, without turning away from Moira.

"Un-bee-leave-able," Moira says. "Your wife's a lucky woman."

Sabina rolls her eyes. Buck, uncharacteristically, remains silent. He seems very troubled for a man who, in my experience, has rarely taken the bull by the horns but, far more often, has generally ignored the animal altogether.

"What are your kids' names?" Satchel says.

"What? Oh. Evan is five and Margaret is three."

"Would you mind if we waited here for our friend?" Moira says. One of her hips is cocked to the left, allowing her blouse to slide more to the right, exposing the majority of her smooth waist. Her lower lip is projected in a suggestive pout that makes me want to jump her right here.

"As long as you'd like," the good reverend responds, obviously wrestling with similar demons. "Just remember the buildings, including the sanctuary, are locked. We used to leave them open so people could go in and pray when they wished to, but several cases of theft and one of vandalism have forced us to lock the doors after nine at night."

"Thank you soooo much. You're a sweetie."

"You're very welcome." The minister turns away, reluctantly it seems to me, and opens his car door.

"You don't live at the manse?" Moira asks.

"No, no, our senior minister lives there with his family—one day perhaps." He winks at Moira and she gives him a gushy smile. I suddenly have this epiphanic vision of the young Puritan returning to his home and masturbating in his study to the mental image of my girlfriend while his wife sleeps alone upstairs.

He fires up the Taurus and pulls away, grateful, I think, to escape any further temptation. We are again left alone.

"So whadda we do now?" Buck asks, finally shaking the cat from his tongue.

"Do you think Connor is actually here somewhere?" Satchel's question is directed at me.

"I don't know, but we should've known that he wouldn't park his car in plain sight if he is. We don't even know for certain if this is the place that's referred to in the note, or if Cian Connor even sent it. I don't know what to believe."

"I say if we run into the bastard that we let Moira handle him," Moon says. "She seems to have a way with the opposite sex."

The girls laugh in unison.

"I think we ought to walk around to the front of the church. If anyone's waiting for us, I think it would be in that courtyard behind the arches by the sidewalk. Anybody can go in there, any time of day or night, and there are plenty of places to hide. Moira and I thought we saw someone moving in there when we went by it a few minutes ago."

"Good thinking," Buck says, and he heads across the parking lot toward the sidewalk.

Chapter twenty-five

When we reach Michigan Avenue, I stop, and the rest stop with me. We are still hidden from the courtyard by the manse. To me, the courtyard is the only conceivable place where our quarry might be hiding. As the good pastor said, the church is locked, as are the other buildings.

"I go on alone from here," I say.

"No way," is Moira's swift reply.

"Strength in numbers," Satchel adds.

"Look, we know that Connor or whoever is doing this is armed. We also know he's capable of killing people. None of us have any weapons. A gun is a great leveler. It erases numerical superiority. He said in the note to come here alone. That's what I intend to do. It's me he's after."

"You sure of that, brother?" Satchel says.

"What do you mean?"

"How many opportunities do you think he's already had to pick you off?"

"I still don't see—"

"Shit, he could have gone to Loon Lake and plugged you there. He could have broken into your room at the Wyndham or just walked up and knocked on the door like I did, shot you, and left. He was at Navy Pier and undoubtedly knew you were there or he wouldn't have sent that note. He probably had a dozen opportunities there. If it was him who killed Kelly, why did he just punch you? Why didn't he just open the door, let you in, and leave two bodies in that hotel room?"

"What are you saying?"

"I'm saying that it doesn't make sense. I'm saying that I don't think you're the target, or at least not the only one. I'm pretty sure that Kelly's death wasn't an afterthought. He planned that and I think he wanted you to see it. I think that's at least part of the reason we're in Chicago. Don't forget Sweeney *told* me that you and Moira would be in Chicago, several days before you two got that coded message and came down here. He knew what hotel you'd be at and he knew the room number. You said the note was in his handwriting. Now what that means to me is that either he masterminded this whole damned thing or he's working with Connor." He hesitates a moment, looks at Moon. She smiles encouragingly at him. "There's something else too...something I haven't told you yet."

"Yeah?"

"Joolie Bullkiller, Moon's dad, had a strange experience last week. He was sitting at his desk, writing out checks, when the phone rang. He picked it up. The unidentified person on the other end asked for me by name—my real name, Satchel Balune. I had taken the earlier call from Sweeney, so Joolie was very suspicious since I hadn't used that name the whole time I'd lived at the Bullkiller ranch. Everyone there, including Moonie here," he smiled at the woman by his side, "knew me as Joe Reed. Joolie told the caller that no one who lived or worked there at the ranch went by that name, even though I had revealed my past and true identity to Joolie and his family some time before the call. Joolie knew I was a wanted man. He also knew of his daughter's belief in me and my love for her." Moon, her arm through

Satchel's, squeezes his. "I'd already made up my mind to come to
Chicago after I'd talked to Sweeney. I'd reasoned that Sweeney knew
where I was and that meant that it wouldn't be long before other
people did too. I wanted to get this whole god-awful mess straightened out so that Moonie and I could be married and start living a
relatively normal life—even at the risk of going to prison."

"So Sweeney was calling again? Why? To make sure you were
coming?"

"It wasn't Sweeney."

"How do you know that? You said the caller was 'unidentified'.
You talked to Sweeney the first time, but Joolie Bullkiller took this
call. How would Joolie know, just from listening to the voice, that
it wasn't Sweeney?"

"Because," Satch says, "the caller was a woman."

I am flabbergasted, dumbfounded. "Why didn't you mention
this before, for Christ's sake?"

"I wanted to see if you'd slip up and make some reference to
it. You didn't. Then again—"

"What?"

"I wanted to see what your reaction would be when I finally
did say something about it. I had to know, Tin, if you were a part of
all this—if this was just some kind of way for you to draw me into
the open so that you could get revenge. You'd sent Connor to find
me, after all. It was pretty apparent, just now, that you didn't have a
clue. You don't know who made the call, do you?"

"No. What did she want? What did she say?"

"She told Joolie that she knew he was lying to her—knew I
was there—and that he was to give me a message."

"Which was?"

"She knew that I didn't kill Wendy and she wanted to make
sure that I was coming to Chicago so that we could all find out who
did."

"Who do you think was calling? Did you ever find out?"

"I had no idea at first, but now I'm pretty sure it was Kelly."

"Why?"

"Well, from what we know now, and what I suspected then, it's pretty obvious that she was working with Connor, maybe Sweeney too. She had to get the phone number for the Bullkiller ranch from either Sweeney or Connor. Besides, that 'kidnapping note', the one that brought you here, how did you decipher that so easily?"

"Well, I knew that *Windy* was one of your favorite songs—that you always associated it with Wendy—in fact substituted her name in it. You had once even told me that Wendy was from the Windy City which I remember you referring to more than once as the 'Wendy city'. And she talked about it too, later on...after we were married. We came down here to visit Kelly and her parents and I remember her talking about it with Kelly late one night as we sat around the kitchen table at Kelly's apartment."

"Then Kelly had to give that information to Sweeney or Connor, if you didn't. She knew that you would recognize that song, that it would draw you here. She had to be a part of this...this—"

"Conspiracy, Satch? Because that's what you're suggesting here."

"Call it what you will. She had to be the one who posed as your agent and reserved the room at the Wyndham."

"That would make sense," Moira interjected. "The whole 'pigs fly' thing...and she lives here. She would have known about the Seurat exhibit."

Satch looks at us questioningly.

"Some of the other clues in the note had to do with the impressionists and pointillism."

"Oh." I can tell by my brother's confused expression that he's not up on his nineteenth century art. "Well," he continues, "we're fairly certain that Kelly's the one who was keeping an eye on you and Moira from the hotel across the street. She was probably convinced that she was helping us—or at least you. You said she waved to you, as if she knew who you were. I don't know why she didn't just come up and talk to you—or me, for that matter. I think what she told Joolie is what she expected—reconciliation between you and me and the discovery of who really killed her sister. Somebody was lying to her, made her think that all this secrecy was for a purpose. I think she got into some deeper shit than she'd ever imagined."

"But why bring us all to Chicago, Joe?" Moon says, apparently unable to get used to Satch's real name.

"I don't know for sure, of course, but my guess would be that since Connor lives here and Kelly does…did, too…whoever wrote the note didn't want Moira around…lots of reasons."

I shake my head. I still can't really believe that Kelly is dead. "So you think that this Connor guy, this private detective or uncle or whatever the hell he is, is a part of this—along with Kelly and possibly Sweeney? What about Buck and Sabina? You think they're supposed to be here too?"

Satchel opens his mouth to respond, but the answer comes from behind him.

"Yeah, we are Tin," Buck says.

I turn to Buck. He and Sabina have both taken a couple of steps back from the group to gain some space. Drop-jawed, I stand and stare at him. He's holding a gun and it's pointed directly at my sternum.

"Buck, what the hell—"

He motions with the weapon. "We're all gonna move into the courtyard now."

"You're a part of this!?" I say. It can't be happening. I look to Sabina.

"Just do what he tells you," she says.

"Buck," Moira says, "why would you do this? You're Tin's *friend.*" I can see that Buck is struggling with himself. This is something he was told to do, I'd wager. It clearly is not something that he is enjoying.

"You son of a bitch," Satchel says.

Satchel's expletive seems to rouse Buck from his uncertainty.

"There's all different kinds of sons," Buck says, "and all different kinds of bitches too. Now *move!*" I can see that his massive hand is trembling. I don't think he's accustomed to handling firearms, which probably increases the likelihood that he might pull the trigger.

No one takes a step. We're either frozen with fear or we're all too astounded by his betrayal. He turns the gun on Satchel.

"Move *now,*" he says, scowling at me. "Do it, or I'll drop your brother right here." Buck's voice, like his hand, is unsteady, but I'm not prepared to risk my brother's life to find out how committed he is.

"Buck, why—" Moira says.

"You want answers?" he responds, "they're waitin' for ya in there. That's the end of the fucking conversation. Next person to open their mouth gets a bullet. *Now move, goddamnit!*"

Buck is shaking, but whether with rage or shame or fear, I don't know. I grab Moira's hand and begin to pull her slowly down the sidewalk. Satch and Moon follow. On our left, the manse is dark. Apparently the senior pastor of Fourth Presbyterian is either gone or asleep. Once past the cleric's quarters, the Gothic arches begin. They separate the courtyard from the sidewalk. "Turn in," Buck says.

Lacking any alternative, we do as we're told. "What're we going to do?" Moira whispers.

"I don't know."

As we pass under the archway, we emerge into the courtyard. I can hear the water gurgling in the fountain just in front of us, but visibility is poor. I look up to see that the moon is half-obscured by a gray cloud. We must be virtually invisible from the street, only a few feet away. I hear a car move slowly by, but I don't turn around to look. Our footsteps echo on the stone floor. There are two large trees in this open area. They are in the corners, diagonally across from one another. Under the shadows of one, to our right, I can barely see the outline of a man standing watching, obviously expecting our arrival.

"There's someone over there," I whisper to Moira.

"More than one," she responds quietly, though I cannot see the second figure.

"Go to your right," Buck orders.

His betrayal and the realization that we have been manipulated like rats in a maze overwhelm my mind and heart. Our seemingly coincidental meeting at the Stoppe Inn the other night was arranged—had to be. So was running into Buck and Sabina at Navy Pier. I would never have thought that he could be conspiratorial, so convincingly deceitful. What is he getting out of this? Money? From all appearances, he doesn't need it, unless it was a life-changing fortune, and who has that kind of money to give?

"Stop!" This voice comes from in front of us, somewhere under the tree. I see a flash of moonlight reflected on metal and know that the figure ahead, like the one behind, is armed.

Moira was right. There are two men there, one much taller than the other.

Satch stops next to me. I can see that he's trying to keep Moon behind him, out of harm's way, and I want to tell him that death has us surrounded, but I say nothing.

"So," one of the shadows in front of us says, "we're finally all together." The voice has an accent—Irish.

"Uncle Keenan?" Moira says. Her voice echoes above the sound of falling water.

The voice softens for a moment. "You look so much like my sister, now that you're grown," the voice says, emanating from the wraith-like, taller figure. "Mary was a beauty too."

"Look," Satchel begins, "what the hell are you guys—"

"Shut your mouth you piece of shit." The words are not shouted. The voice is calm, cold, devoid of the emotion that such words should carry.

"You shouldn't have come, Moira," the other shadow says.

"Sweeney?" she says.

"We told you not to come."

"We?"

The two men step out from under the canopy of the tree. Simultaneously, the moon escapes its cloud cover and I can see, very clearly now, what they look like. Sweeney is the smaller one. He's not bound. He is, in point of fact, armed with a pistol like his much taller companion. "We didn't want to get you involved in this, honey," he says to Moira, "but I can't tell you what to do. I couldn't tell your mother either. I guess it's just the way of things."

"I...I don't understand," Moira says. She looks to me. I shrug helplessly.

"Of course you don't," Sweeney says. "I've tried to protect you, like I tried to protect your mother. Neither one of you would listen to me."

The taller man has to be Cian Connor. He has grayish-red hair that flops down over his low forehead like a discarded mop. He towers over everyone else. He's very powerful looking, in spite of the fact that he must be in his fifties or sixties. His lean face, with its high cheekbones, sunken jowls and dark, tiny eyes give him a predatory mien. The only features to disrupt this hateful appearance are his hair and his clownish teeth, which protrude from his upper lip, like Disney's Goofy. I notice a pen in his white shirt pocket. "How's your hand?" he says to me in his conspicuous brogue. It's a voice I recognize from many phone conversations, although I haven't heard it for years. The malicious grin that accompanies the question leaves no doubt in my mind as to who punched me in the jaw and broke my fingers in Kelly's hotel room door.

"I'll live."

His smile broadens. "That remains to be seen. And what about yours, asshole?" he continues, turning toward my brother.

"It's healed nicely, Connor," Satchel says. "Thanks for asking."

It's now clear that Moira's uncle and the private detective that I hired are the same person. It's also apparent that he's Kelly's murderer—a fact whose revelation he does not seem to mind. This doesn't bode well for anyone's safety.

"Sweeney," Moira says, "you're a part of all this? You wrote all the notes, set this up?"

He responds, but doesn't look at her when he speaks. He simply says: "Kelly helped me set it up, but she didn't know what Keenan...what we...were after. She thought...well, we've been waiting a long time."

"Too long," Cian Connor scoffs. "Now this shithead is fucking *your* daughter and his motherfucking brother almost managed to get away."

"Death isn't suffering, Keenan," Sweeney says impatiently. "I wanted Satchel to suffer, that's all." He looks down at the courtyard stones.

"Sure. But now they've lived long enough to return the favor."

I glance over my shoulder, looking for some opportunity to get out of this. Buck is right behind me and, judging from his position, his weapon is pointed right at the center of my back. I catch Sabina's eye. She quickly looks away.

"Sweeney," Moira says, her voice low and carrying a hint of desperation. "What are you doing? What the hell is going on here? What do you have against Tin?"

My father's old fishing partner studies his feet. "It's not about Tin," he mumbles. "Tin was the bait. Now, well—"

"Well *what* then?" I say.

"Ask big brother there," Cian Connor says, gesturing toward Satchel with his gun.

Moira and Moon and I all turn to Satchel inquiringly. He shrugs, but I detect a color in his cheeks that was not previously there.

"I told you to stay away," Sweeney moans, obviously talking to Moira. "I didn't want you to have to deal with all of this."

Something drives me to intervene. I don't know where it comes from. I think it's angry impotency or it may be that I'm only holding one decent card. "What makes you so paternal now, Sweeney? The girl can't even call you 'Dad' and you know why. You say you want to protect her? For what reason? So that you can sneak into her bedroom and try again? Is that it?"

"Tin," Moira says.

For the first time since we came into the courtyard, Sweeney looks someone directly in the eye, and it's not me, it's Moira. His expression is one of painful betrayal. His pale blue eyes glisten in the moonlight. She doesn't look away. He turns the gun and his attention, on me.

Connor for the first time seems unsure of himself, confused. "Hiram," he growls, "what the hell is he talking about?"

Sweeney ignores the giant. He's obviously shaken by what I've said. He simply says: "I suggest that you keep quiet."

"Why? Don't want anyone to know about it, Hi? Mr. Connor or O'Connor or whatever the hell his name is doesn't know that you tried to come on to his niece? He doesn't know that she spent her teen years sleeping with her bedroom door locked, afraid that her father would try to poke her?"

Sweeney's normally pleasant façade is twisted into a stygian grimace. The muscles of his jaw clench as he grinds his teeth. He wipes dripping sweat from a brow that is furrowed with anxiety.

I brace for an explosion. Sweeney's weapon can't stay quiet much longer in that tremulous hand.

"What's he saying?" Connor's voice has a censorious tone. "Did you—"

"He's lying," Sweeney answers before the terrible question can be completed. "He's trying to divide us."

"He's not lying," Moira says, "and you know it, Sweeney."

"I never did a thing to you."

"Only because I wouldn't let you."

I expect Sweeney to melt under this barrage. He doesn't. His face contorts in anguished memory. "You weren't my child. You were a teenager, a very mature one, always running around half-naked. Once…only once, in a moment of weakness…and nuthin' happened, you know that. You asked me to leave and I did." Connor is staring at him. Sweeney sees it and turns away, back to Moira. "You'd rather commit incest with your uncle, is that it?"

Moira looks as mystified as I must do. "What're you talking about? Uncle Keenan has never—"

"I don't mean your mother's brother. I'm referring to your *father's* brother."

"You are so full of shit, Sweeney," she says. "You've told me, more than once, that you don't know who my father is. Mom never told you. She never told me."

"I was trying to protect you. But now, well, it's too late now. I didn't have to be told. I knew who he was from the beginning. I caught them in the act." He slowly swivels his head to look at my brother. "He was just a kid, not more than sixteen or seventeen, son of my good friend. Can you imagine that? My Mary was the noble mother to motherless sons. She cared for those boys—cared too much. Satchel, why don't you tell Moira who her *real* father is?"

Everyone turns to look at him. "Satch?" It's all I can say. I squeeze Moira's hand, waiting for him to deny this obvious lie. His silence is worse than anything he could say. A terrible nausea rises in me. All that was good in the world goes away. I feel Moira's hand grip mine harder. She's trying to hang on…hang on.

"I was out fishin'," Sweeney continues, though no one wants him to. "It was the summer, July of '86. I come back early 'cause they weren't bitin' and the sun was gettin' too hot. 'Sides, I'd lost mosta my line. When I'd left, Mary was makin' breakfast for Satchel. Tin was at some kinda camp for baseball and the pastor, well he was sittin' on his porch readin' his Bible. He was still there when I come up from the lake. I remember I was gonna yell at him, to say hello, but he was so absorbed that I think I woulda scared him. Normally, I woulda come right through the front door of my place and put my gear in the corner by the fireplace, but I'd caught my line in a tree branch that was overhangin' the water when I was castin' and I'd had to cut it loose. So, I thought I'd get some new line outta the shed and re-string the reel. I walked to the west side of the cabin, the side away from yer boys's place, and got the line outta the shed. I was walkin' past the cabin wall, next to where my bedroom'd be, when I heard Mary moanin'. The curtains were parted a little ways from the breeze blowin' at 'em. I looked in. I thought maybe Mary'd hurt herself or somethin'. But that sure wasn't the case, was it Satchel?"

My brother is silent, looking at Moon.

"Mary and Satchel was naked on my bed…*my* bed. Yer brother was lyin' on top 'a her Tin, pumpin' away like a overgassed piston."

"Alright, Sweeney," Satchel says, "that's enough."

"Why's that son? You don't wanna tell yer girlfriend there how you humped my wife?"

Satchel turns to me. "I was seventeen, Tin. The only girl I ever dated in high school had just broken up with me that spring. I was still trying to get over Mom's death. I'd had a bad few months. I guess everything just built up. I was almost crazy, sobbing and carrying on. Mary put her arms around me, kissed me on my forehead, my cheek, then my mouth. I don't know how it happened, really, still don't to this day. I didn't know what the hell I was doing."

"Oh, God," Moira moans.

"After it was over, Hiram, your wife apologized to *me*. She told me that you had contracted diabetes a few years earlier and that you were...having difficulty. The diabetes, she said had caused impotence. She was lonely, she said...she missed that intimacy...it just happened."

Sweeney's face is twisted in embarrassment. There are tears in his eyes. His voice echoes in the courtyard. "Yeah," he says, "I lost my...ability, but you never lose your desire, did you know that?" He glances at Moira and when she catches his eye, he quickly looks away. "You never lose your love for someone when you really love them—even if they betray you."

"Look, it happened, Hiram. I'm sorry," Satchel says. "I was seventeen, for God's sake...and after, well, I thought you never knew about it. I thought if Mary wanted to tell you, she would, then you two would have to work it out. I...never went back. It never happened again, I can tell you that. I tried to put it away." My brother looks at me. "I tried to put it away, Tin, you know? Not long after, I was in the minors and away all the time. That was the end of it."

"Not for me," Sweeney says.

I'm too astounded by this revelation, and my brother's admission, to respond. All I can think about is Moira and the sinking, throbbing sensation in my chest that makes me forget all about my ruined hand. Mary Sweeney? She was such a sweet, kind, maternal presence in my life—and Satchel's. Now I learn that she and my brother.... It slowly dawns on me, why my heart is pounding against my sternum like a crazed stallion trying to kick down a stall door. Sweeney is not Moira's father, she told me. Satchel was seventeen when it happened, maybe eighteen when Moira was born. That was seventeen, eighteen years ago—Moira's age now. God!

I look at her and can tell immediately by her expression of dread that she is thinking similar thoughts, making similar, heinous calculations.

"So you just let it go, Sweeney?" my brother says. "You never confronted your wife with this?"

"Oh I tole 'er I knew. She never denied it."

"Then why didn't you come to me, to my father, get it in the open?

"Mary didn't want that. She begged me not to say anythin'. She didn't want to hurt you, hurt the pastor. Yer old man was still tryin' to get over his wife's death. He didn't need no more tragedy in his life. He was my friend." Sweeney's voice trailed off and, I think for a short moment, so did his mind—to another, a better, world. Then he was back. "So fer her sake, and the pastor's, I put on a smile and tried ta act like nuthin' ever happened."

I look at my brother. "Is Moira...Moira, then is...." I can't bring myself to say it.

"I don't know, Tin. Mary was pregnant shortly after, but I don't know for sure."

"Mary and me didn't have sex for a long time before that day in July of '86 and we never touched each other after it," Sweeney says. "Moira was born in April of '87. Figure it out fer yerself."

I place my arm around Moira's shoulder. Her body is shaking badly, like someone in the throes of epilepsy. She's staring at Satchel with incredulity. Her lovely mouth is hanging open. "Jesus," she whispers next to me, "what've we done?"

I know then that my own life is over—that it should have ended in that leaky boat on Loon Lake. Before I die, though, I want to know everything—the whole Balune tragedy. "Who killed Wendy?" The words drift around our stone surroundings like a caged bird.

"Mary kilt herself over guilt," Sweeney says, ignoring my question. "I told you she drowned, Moira, and it was true, but it wasn't no accident. She didn't get tied up in the weeds and panic. She hated the water anyway."

I do remember now, that Mary never went swimming in the lake that was fifty feet from her cabin door. She never went in the boat either. In fact, I don't ever remember her venturing onto the dock. She was the only person from the Sweeney and Balune clans, except me, who didn't know how to swim. Because of it, I remember feeling an even greater comraderie with her after our mother died.

"She walked into that water intentional. She couldn't live with herself. She kilt herself. You kilt her, Satchel. She died 'cause a you." Sweeney's voice breaks, his head bows. I can see tears falling to the stone floor in the moonlight. He lifts his head again and stares at Satchel as one might stare at a vampire, a werewolf, or some other supernatural monster that one can't quite believe exists but must face anyway.

"Tin asked you who killed Wendy, Hiram," Satch says. "You gonna blame me for that one too?"

"That was the main idea," Connor answers, his low, sinister voice issuing from the darkness like a disregarded viper.

"*What?*"

Connor lifts his face into a toothy, ridiculous expression that could be mistaken for a smile, though it has more of grimace in it. "When Mary died, nobody could just let that pass, boy. She was my sister. She lived through a hell of a lot of horror in her life, but she couldn't live with guilt. She was never the same after you ruined her. When Hiram showed me the note—"

"Wait a minute," I say, "what note? What the hell are you talking about?"

"Here," Sweeney says. He pulls a piece of yellowed paper from his pants pocket, moving the gun clumsily to his left hand. It's apparent to me that Sweeney has never handled a firearm before. He hands the paper to me as if it were a sacred icon, a wafer of communion blessed by a priest. I take it and read.

It's written in the carefully formed words of someone who values order. Its soft, small lettering make me guess that it is a feminine hand.

Dearest Hiram:

I'm so sorry for the pain I've caused you. I've been cruel to you. I can't continue to live this way. My dreams are full of nightmares. He's ruined me. I tried to love him. I see him every-where and live in fear of what he could reveal. Take care of my baby girl. Try to make her understand that I love her, in spite of what I do.

Mary.

I look up in total disbelief at my brother. "Did you threaten her somehow?"

His answer is swift and full of assurance. "No."

Moira grabs the note from me and reads. Her face is stoical, cold. She gives it back to me. She is biting her lip, trying, I think, to keep it from trembling. She looks at my brother. I give the note to Satchel.

"This is a lie," Satchel protests. "She isn't writing about me. She can't be." He looks at me. "Tin, you've got to believe me. She isn't talking about me—if she even wrote this. It's bullshit." He gives the note back to me as if he were handling a vial of ebola virus.

The note is old, worn, faded. It's been handled many times and could easily be fifteen years old. I look at Moira. She is staring at Sweeney and Connor as if they were strangers in her life. Worse, she turns that look on me.

"I found her body when I woke up that morning," Sweeney says, his voice coming apart in ragged gasps, "floating face-down off the end of the dock, just after I discovered the note on the kitchen table. It's in her writin'. It damned near kilt me." He looks sympathetically at Moira. "I never tole ya what really happened, Sweetheart, 'cause I didn't want ya ta think that yer mama didn't love ya. She did, she really did." He begins to cry, but he stiffens and struggles to hold back his emotions. Moira says nothing.

"You killed my sister," Connor says to Satchel.

"I didn't tell your uncle right away, how she died either, Moira,"

Sweeney says. "Suicide is a damning sin. The soul goes straight to hell. I couldn't add to his awful grief with that truth, let her be buried outside the grace of the church, in unhallowed ground. I didn't tell anyone, kept the note to myself."

"Until I moved here, to Chicago," Connor says.

"Yes," Sweeney concurs. "When you told me you were looking for a private detective, Tin, someone to find Satchel, I knew that Keenan could do it. Keenan had worked with the IRA, hunted down people before. He knew how to do it. I told him then about how Mary had had an affair with your brother and how she'd drowned herself over it. He swore he'd make you pay."

"And I have, haven't I, you son of a bitch."

"Then…then *you* killed Wendy," Satchel stutters, "to get back at me."

"I knew you were headed back to Michigan," he said, smiling. "Got there a few days ahead of you. I saw your brother and father leave. I assumed they were going to the family cabin on Loon Lake. Sweeney confirmed it a couple of hours later by phone." He casually lights a cigarette. "I didn't even have to break in. The front door was unlocked."

How many times had Wendy and I argued about locking the doors? I just couldn't get her to do it. *Smilin' at everybody she sees.*

"I walked in and waited for her," Connor continues. "Found the baseball bat inscribed, touchingly I thought, *from Satchel to Tin on your birthday.* Bad job of wood burning though." He looks up at the half-obscured moon. "It was just meant to be."

Satchel takes a step forward. Connor stiffens his arm and aims directly at my brother's chest. Moon grabs him and pulls back. "Don't, Joe, don't do it."

"Better listen to her, Mr. Balune. Good advice."

Sweeney looks over at Moira and me. "I didn't know Wendy was goin' suffer like that," he says, though I can't tell which of us he's addressing.

Moira shakes her head. "And you think that makes it okay?" is her choking response. "God, I've been raised by a monster!"

"She was *your* mother!" Sweeney pleads. "Her soul's in everlasting torment because of what *he* did!" Sweeney points at Satchel, who is still being barely restrained by his diminutive girlfriend.

"And now you want to send my father to hell."

She has said it. I feel very empty, as if everything inside my chest has come loose and fallen into the saddle of my hips.

"*I'm* yer father," Sweeney shouts. His voice echoes in the courtyard. "I'm the one fed ya and clothed ya and drove ya ta school ever day. It takes more'n one jump in the hay ta be a father."

"You're right about that, Pa." It is the voice of Buck Wolfram.

Chapter twenty-six

Sweeney looks up at Buck. "Stay out of it boy, ya don't know everything."

Satchel and I turn to look at our traitorous companion. Pa? Is that what he said? What the hell is happening?

"You told me no one'd get hurt. You said you were goin' lure Satchel in 'n turn him over to the cops, tole me that Satchel murdered Wendy. You never tole me that the girl, the sister, would get killed."

Sweeney lowers his head and his gun simultaneously. He looks accusingly at his brother-in-law. "I didn't know Kelly would be hurt neither. There're things you don't understand, son."

"I understand the difference between the truth and lies. I understand when I been played for a fool. I been with these boys, and I know *they* didn't kill Kelly. They didn't kill Wendy neither and you just *admitted* that Keenan did."

My head aches and feels like it's about to come apart. It's racing in reverse, searching for connections. I remember my father's words: "Sweeney has a friend who runs a ferry service from the mainland to

Mackinac Island, transporting tourists. If you want, his friend can give you a job this summer working on one of his boats. Since you decided you didn't want to play summer league ball this year, I think it'd be a good opportunity for you to make some college money. What do you think?" *Sweeney has a friend...*

Moira's voice: "Tin and I are going to stop and get something to eat.... It's called the Stoppe Inn I think, just south of Traverse City." She called Sweeney. She didn't want Sweeney to worry. *Sweeney.*

Sweeney sent us to Chicago. Sweeney wrote the notes. *Navy Pier. Eight o'clock. You shouldn't have brought her.* Buck shows up at Navy Pier. *Sweeney.*

"Buck," I say. "If I'm gonna die, I need to know why. What the hell is going on?"

The crude giant looks at me. "He got me into this, Tin," he says, gesturing toward Sweeney, "jest like you. The difference is I came along because he's...he's family, he's my pa, believe it or not. But he tole me there wasn't gonna be no violence. We were gonna get Satchel turned in and be done with it. But I keep finding out that I been fed a pack of lies."

"*Sweeney?* Sweeney is your *father?*"

"Yeah, he is."

"But Mary—" Satchel begins.

"No, she wasn't *my* ma."

I feel my knees beginning to give. The mind and body can tolerate just so much. I look over at Moira, beautiful Moira, staring in disbelief. She is Satchel's child? I have fallen in love with my niece? My life has become a maudlin soap opera with Tin Balune in the starring role. Moira! Oh God, how did I come to this?

"An eye for an eye, boys," Connor growls from the shadows. "I learned a long time ago, when I was a boy, that you can't let 'em get away with nuthin', or they'll keep on hurtin' you. You fuck with me and mine, you pay, and you ain't through payin' yet."

Behind us, I hear Sabina's voice. "Jesus, Buck, what have you gotten us into?"

"AHHHHHHHHHHI I!" Satchel howls his agony and rushes past me toward Connor. The suddenness and sheer ferocity of the attack startles Wendy's killer. He fires twice, rapidly, in our direction. The bullets whistle harmlessly above my brother's hunched and charging figure. My left shoulder explodes with pain. I feel warmth splatter up onto my neck and face. Satchel plows into the towering killer. Simultaneously, Sweeney turns his gun on me, but he hesitates. There is an opening. I rush forward too. Rage, rage, unstoppable and insane. Caution and death are no longer considerations. Fear is gone. Life is gone. Love must go. There is only wild, feral, bestial rage. Sweeney has his weapon pointed in my direction, but he does not pull the trigger before I collide with him and take him down. My shoulder explodes with pain. My injured hand erupts into a dreadful cacophony of protesting nerves. I ignore both. I raise my good fist to strike Sweeney, but he is motionless beneath me. His eyes are closed. The brute force of my attack and his subsequent collision with the stone floor has either killed him or driven him into that unthinking state that has so often become a part of my own life. I rise to my knees to see that Satchel and Connor are still struggling. Though older by twenty years or more, Connor is winning. He punches Satchel viciously in the throat. I hear Satchel gag and watch him grab at his neck as if he is being strangled. Connor struggles to his feet and delivers a malevolent kick to the abdomen of my genuflecting brother. Satchel crumples to the stone floor. I watch in horror as the murderer stoops to retrieve his gun, which had been knocked loose from his hand by the impact of Satchel's charge.

Behind me, Buck's plaintive cry rises above the echoes of our struggle. "No!" he wails. "God, Sabina no!" His cry is a piercing, screeching, bellow of agony, like the sound of a water buffalo being disemboweled by lions.

I turn to see the woman slumping in his arms, a dark red stain spreading in her platinum hair. He guides her tenderly to the stone floor, kneeling beside her. "Sabina, darlin'. Sabina!" She struggles to speak. I can see her lips move. There is no sound. Her head slumps to one side. She's still. He shakes her, tries to revive her, but she doesn't respond. There is nothing worse to watch than a strong man blubbering like an infant. I know. I know.

"All right, you prick," Connor growls, pointing his recovered weapon at Satchel. "Get to your fucking feet. I wanta see the expression on your pussy-face when I pull this fuckin' trigger."

Beneath me, Sweeney moans. I stand too. I don't want to die on my knees.

Satchel does as he's told. The rage is gone. There is only remorse, regret. He glances over at Moon and smiles. She smiles back, bravely, proudly. Moira turns to look at me. "Tin," she cries. "You're hurt. Oh my God!"

"Let the girls go," Satchel says. "They haven't done anything. Let them go."

"Moira, sure. She's my sister's kid, even if she is yours too. The other one though, your little Indian girlfriend there—that's a different story. When we started, we were only after you. Now, well, too many witnesses."

Buck's low voice, tinged with black edges of hate, comes forward like a vampire bat from its cave. It flies through the darkness, filled with bloodlust. "You've shot her!"

Everyone turns toward the sound. The big man is standing over Sabina's inert body. He's still holding the gun he used to usher us into this hellish place. It's aimed directly at Connor's chest. "There ain't gonna be no more killin'," he says. "No more death, not even yers, unless ya don't put that away."

"Buck—"

"Shut up. Ya goin' tell me ya didn't mean to shoot Sabina? All right. But them other two...and these...ain't gonna happen." He looks at me. "Tin, you and Satchel take the women and git." Tears are streaming down his jowls.

Sweeney has risen to one elbow. He is regaining his senses. The gun is still in his grip. My left arm and hand have gone cold. My shirt clings to me, wet and sticky. Connor turns his gun on me.

"Don't," Buck warns. "I'll kill ya right where ya stand."

"You couldn't kill me boy," Connor says calmly, "You ain't capable of it."

Buck looks down at his wife's twisted, prostrate form on the stone floor. "A life for a life," he says. "Satchel, Tin, you get Moira and Moon to the car."

"You're an accessory," Connor says. "They'll put you away for life. Put your weapon down and let's finish what we came here to do."

Satchel doesn't hesitate. He takes Moon's hand in one of his and Moira's in the other and turns toward the lights of the manse which have just flickered on.

"I can't leave you here alone," I say.

"I helped to get ya into this," Buck says. "I'll get you out. Go."

I back up, as Sweeney, apparently unharmed, climbs to his feet. "I'm sorry, Tin," he says. "I didn't mean for this to happen to you. I wanted Satchel, not you. Get Moira outta here." Connor takes a step toward me, but Buck moves into his sights to cover my retreat. Sweeney, too, aims his revolver at the killer. Moira's voice, behind me, calls my name. I turn and walk away. Somewhere in the dark void beyond is the banshee-like wailing of police sirens. I see a face appear at one of the windows of the manse, then shroud itself quickly with curtains. As I step under the Gothic arches and onto the sidewalk of Michigan Avenue, I look back at Buck. He's still standing there, Sabina at his feet. He is as motionless as she. I hear Sweeney say: "Put it down," although I don't know whether he's talking to his brother-in-law or his son. There is no response.

The street lamp on the corner reveals my scarlet shirt for the first time. I have lost a lot of blood. My shirt sticks to my skin. I can see the nasty hole in my upper shoulder and I question why I continue to live. My left arm dangles uselessly at my side. I wonder if I will ever be able to use it again, then realize that this is a moot point. Dead men don't care about such things. I continue to stumble along only because Moira calls me and Buck has ordered me to go. There is nothing of self-preservation in it.

I stagger along the sidewalk. I can see Satchel ahead. He's pulling Moira along, but her face is turned back toward me. Moon has her arm around Moira's waist, also trying to propel her forward. She breaks free, runs back to me. She puts her lovely arm around me. "You have to believe me," she says, "I didn't know. You have to believe that."

"I do."

A gunshot rings out behind us. "We have to move."

She pulls me along faster than I thought I was capable of moving. My head is swimming, and I'm fairly certain that it won't be long before the rest of me is too. Satch and Moon are waiting a hundred feet ahead, past the parish house, where the parking lot begins.

"Keys!" Satchel yells. "Do you have the keys to the Jeep?"

"My pocket."

We stop. A few minutes ago, Moira would have reached into my shorts to get them. Now, she waits for me to do it. This I notice, through the swiftly darkening whirlpool around me. She will never touch me in the same way again, and because of that, I welcome the sinking. She takes the keys from me and hands them to Moon who is, somehow, now beside us. "Hurry!" she says to Moira, and dashes off. I admire the way she runs. It is the effortless, smooth, almost joyful sprinting of a wild mare, her black mane flowing freely behind her. Satchel will find his happiness with her. He will live and prosper and I am glad for that.

We are at the Jeep. How did we get here? I don't remember the steps. I only know that Moira is pushing me into the back seat, among the discarded bottles and cans and cigarette packages. Satchel and Moon are in the front seat. He turns the key in the ignition. I think my eyes are open, but darkness is coming. I see nothing but shadows now.

"Tin?" I know this voice so well, though it comes from a niece I have just met. "Tin, can you hear me? Hang on, my darl…oh Tin, Tin," she cries. I feel her hands on my face. They're cold. She pulls them away. "Tin…oh Tin."

"Hang in there, Tin Man," my brother says. When did he last call me that?

"Did you really do it, Satch?" The voice is mine, though it sounds distant and very faint, like the whisperings of a small child. "Did you make love to Mary Sweeney?"

"Yes," is the singular, terrible, response—so brutal in its brevity and assurance.

I think I say good-bye, but I'm not sure. The dark whirlpool comes spinning down, pulling me under. Somewhere in the maelstrom is the soft touch of Moira's hand. I think I've closed my eyes, but it makes no difference. Darkness is all around me anyway. The sybaritic strains of "Cell Block Tango" capture my dying attention for a brief second. I believe I smile when I recall the lyrics. *"He had it comin'...He had it comin'..."*

Chapter twenty-seven

In spite of myself, I come back. I thought I might wake, if at all, in a hospital somewhere—that they would fix my damaged hand and shoulder, then release me to waiting police. Instead, I discover that I am still in the back of my Jeep, my head leaning against the soft bosom of my brother's child. I can see that Moon is still in the front seat, but Satchel is gone. With great effort, I sit upright and wait until the world explains itself.

I notice that something has been stuffed inside my shirt covering my wound and it seems to have stanched the flow of blood. My shirt is beginning to dry. My shoulder has become numb but my hand, still wrapped in its makeshift bandage, is throbbing mercilessly. Moira looks at me with such pain that I have no empathy with self. "Stay still," she commands. She turns the other way, intent on watching whatever is transpiring outside the Jeep.

"I need a smoke."

She helps me to withdraw a packet of Basics from my shirt pocket. She discards several of them before she finds one that isn't soaked with blood. She helps me with my lighter. She looks for a long time at the bulls-eye with its little heart in the center, then slips the Zippo back into my shirt pocket. I inhale deeply. Knowing I am doing myself some small kind of harm is comforting.

In the darkness outside, I can see Buck standing next to the window. He's holding Sabina. Her head is erect and her arms are clinging to his neck. "Sabina's alive? What's happened?"

"When we got in the car," Moira explains, "Buck called us on Sabina's cell phone. He'd thought she was dead, but the bullet apparently just scraped the side of her head. There's quite a bit of blood, but she's regained consciousness and she's alive. When she spoke to him, he was so startled that he knelt down to tend to her—and that's when Keenan disarmed him. Buck begged us not to leave or Connor would kill Sabina."

"There *was* a shot—"

Moira lowers her head.

"Sweeney's not here," Moon says.

I use my good arm to raise myself slightly in the seat so that I can see what's going on outside. Moira turns to help me, but says nothing. Satchel and Connor are standing near the hood of the car, facing each other. Connor has a gun in one hand, and another tucked into the front of his pants. Buck is standing next to our door, cradling Sabina in his arms. He's ignoring them. Buck's entire concentration seems to be on his stricken wife. The sirens are drawing closer.

Suddenly, everyone is moving. Satchel opens the door.

"What's up?" Moon says.

"We have to take another car," Satchel responds. "C'mon." He grabs my legs and swings them outward. "Welcome back, Tin Man," he says, "can you stand up?"

"I think so."

He helps me get my feet on the pavement. As I rise, my head spins and I falter. I feel my brother's strong arm under my good one. The pain in my hand is excruciating, worse than the bullet in my shoulder. I struggle to stay conscious. "We...we should try to stall...till the cops get here."

"Won't work," Satchel whispers back to me while looking over his shoulder and helping me to stagger over to Buck's rented Cadillac. "He says if we're not out of here by the time the cops get here, he's goin' start shootin' all of us. I believe him, Tin. He's crazier than a shithouse rat."

"Isn't that what he's going to do anyway?"

"No. Just me," Satchel says calmly, as he lowers me into the backseat of the Caddie and Moira climbs in next to me from the other side. Buck is already behind the wheel with Sabina ensconced between his own bulk and Connor's on the other side. Moon and Satch squeeze in next to us. My arm is shoved against the door and there is an explosion of pain. Buck starts up the car and heads down a side street, away from Michigan Avenue. I twist my head to look behind us, and I can see the whirling red and blue lights from cop cars flashing above the courtyard beyond the buildings that separate it from the parking lot.

"Why the Caddie?" I ask.

"The hotel people have seen Joolie's pick-up and your Jeep," Satch explains. "Buck's Caddie is rented. They won't be able to trace us to it."

"What about Sweeney?"

"Shut the fuck up," Connor growls without turning his head to look at me.

Buck drives slowly, silently, as he maneuvers along the back streets. I watch his silhouette as the occasional headlight or street lamp highlight his head and massive shoulders. He's said nothing since we began moving. The amiable giant has become a dark and brooding Grendel. He has tried to be loyal to an undeserving parent, and now that parent has been left behind, probably dead. No one speaks of Sweeney. No one speaks at all. Connor has silenced us with his anger and volatility and we have silenced each other with shame. Buck is ashamed to look at the people he helped to bring to this end. My brother is too ashamed to look at his daughter. I cannot bring myself to look at my niece. I don't think she is looking at me, but she knows my thoughts. A few minutes ago, we were lovers.

We were talking about marriage and a future together. Beyond her, Moon is crammed into the small space between Moira and Satchel. If Satchel lives, tiny Moon will be Moira's stepmother. Oh, Providence has a caustic sense of humor! Moira's father looks out the window at the dark houses we pass by. I think that to look anywhere else would be too difficult.

The throbbing in my hand is terrible, but I welcome it. It's like the custom of some Native Americans I read about once; they injure themselves when grieving for a loved one. Since pleasure is out of the question, physical pain gives one another focus. I think that I should have died before this. I should have never fallen asleep in that boat. But still I know that I wouldn't trade anything that has happened since that moment, in spite of the prohibitions of man or God. If it costs me my soul, my brief affair with Moira might just be worth a few millennia in the burning chambers of hell. I'll have the thought of loving her to sustain me. I don't know if I believe in hell, but if it's there, Mary Sweeney would not be bad company.

A new resolve overtakes me. It has nothing to do with any further hope for happiness. *My* former joy is unrecoverable, but I can help to save the future for others. Moira must survive. She's young enough to find happiness beyond me. Satchel and Moon have to live. I have cost my brother enough. His youthful indiscretion was only anticipatory vengeance for my betrayal. I have done much to ruin his life and it must be set right. Sacrifice. Atonement. I just have to find the right time, the right time…then act quickly. I find that it's liberating to set one's mind on a single purpose and to have nothing to lose.

"There," Connor says. "At the next corner. Turn left and go up to Michigan Avenue."

Buck's large head nods. He does as he's told. The gun that Connor is pressing against Sabina's muddled head turns Buck into an obedient automaton. The Caddie swerves left. After a couple of blocks, it stops under the bright lights of the Magnificent Mile. The car turns right, bringing my head back to Moira's shoulder. I force my face closer to her and whisper in her ear. "Do you still have your cell phone?" She nods very slowly, keeping a wary eye on the front of the car. "Give it to me." A police car rushes past us in the opposite lane, its lights and sirens going at full tilt.

Connor looks back at us. His buckteeth and large ears, normally objects of humor, give him the appearance of a thin John Wayne Gacy in clown make-up—ridiculously lethal. I close my eyes and feign unconsciousness. Moira, I think, looks straight ahead. When I feel her begin to fidget, I open my eyes again. Connor is facing forward. She has it. She puts it in my good hand, which is lying across her naked leg. I raise it slowly to my bloody shirt pocket and slip it in.

"Here," Connor says. "Turn right and just go to the entrance."

I force myself to sit up a little, but I don't really have to see in order to know where we are. I can smell the water and see the lights of the boats in the harbor. The boat show banner is flapping in the steady breeze that comes in across the open expanse of Lake Michigan and, off to the right, metal children are frolicking in the shadows of the moon.

Buck guides the Caddie to the front entrance of Navy Pier and parks. "Leave the keys in the ignition," Connor orders. "How far is it?"

"About a couple hunnerd yards on the north side," Buck responds.

"Everybody out."

It finally dawns on me that our destination is Buck's new boat. Of course. No one will be looking for a tour ferry—or a boat of any kind for that matter. It's the perfect vehicle for a getaway. Buck was made a part of this plot for a reason. The middle of Lake Michigan is also the ideal burial ground if you don't want a body to be found. The authorities will never look for us out there. I begin to think that the meeting at Navy Pier earlier this evening was when all this was supposed to happen, but Buck couldn't get us on the boat and Satch had separated from us. My heart is beating violently. I have to think of something. The phone! If I can be the last one out of the car, I can dial 911, leave it on the backseat and close the door so that no one hears the emergency operator's response. I remember watching some crime show in which they revealed that the authorities can't normally trace a cell phone call, but when there's a 911 call, they can. If I can do it without being discovered, at least the cops will come here, find the Caddie. I put my hand underneath my shirt and the padding over my gunshot wound. It comes away wet and sticky and scarlet. On the white leather surface of the back of the driver's seat in front of me I use my bloody finger to write: *Killer on boat to MI.* I'm assuming of course. I don't really know our destination, but I'm pretty sure we're taking Buck's new boat to get there. Moira watches me. She nods her approval. It's the first time I've seen her smile since she learned about....

Moon and Satchel are already out of the car. Connor is occupied with watching everyone outside. I manage to get the phone back in my gory hand. The 911 call will bring the police here, they should see my bloody message and maybe they'll alert the Coast Guard. It's all I can think of at the moment. Connor's ugly face appears where Satchel and Moon have just exited. Moira shifts herself to block his vision of me and begins to get out. She slams the door behind her. "I'll have to help Tin get out from the other side," she says for Connor's benefit. "He's pretty weak."

I watch them as they begin to circle the car. I have to wait until the last possible second to dial, otherwise the operator will respond too soon and Connor will hear the voice. I'm trying to flip the damned thing open with my blood-covered hand. My other is useless, yet my right is so slippery that to pop this phone open with it is an Augean labor. Still, it appears that I might be able to accomplish this by prying the top up with my thumbnail before Moira and Connor, who are now circling the car's trunk behind me, arrive at my door.

Suddenly the voluptuous strains of "Cell Block Tango" startle me so badly that the phone slips from my grasp and falls into my lap. Graham? What impeccable timing.

The tune is deafening to me. I'm certain that Connor must be able to hear it clearly as he comes around the rear fender toward my door. I'm sweating profusely. My glasses are streaked with salty stains and my eyes sting. My bladder feels distended to the point of explosion.

I'm relatively certain that if Connor opens the door and discovers the phone in my hand he will kill me without hesitation—but the anticipation of death is not what's causing my body to scream out its alarm. I just don't want to die *yet,* not now, not during this childish ignominy of hide-and-seek, losing the chance for redemption.

I finally grip the phone and slide my thumb up and down the side of it, hoping that the silencer button is located there, as it was on the one I used to have. My hand is shaking badly. Any moment they'll open the door...any moment.

Silence. I use my thumb to pry it open. I hit end, to cut off whoever is trying to call. Then I hit nine...one...one again. The door opens. Moira leans in, ostensibly to help me to climb out. She can see what I've done. I force the phone into the crevice of the seat.

"Move your ass, Balune," Connor growls from behind Moira.

His voice overpowers the muffled question from the phone. "What is your emergency please?"

I struggle to my feet as quickly as I can and step away from the Caddie. Moira slams the door shut with authority.

For the first time since he pulled a gun on us, I look Buck Wolfram directly in the eye. He's standing just a few feet in front of me, his arm around Sabina who is, apparently, now able to stand without assistance. Her face is still covered in dried blood and she looks a bit woozy, but other than that, she seems okay. Buck looks down at the pavement, obviously finding it difficult to face me. It's hard to believe that a few hours ago we were all laughing over dinner and Dom Perignon.

I stagger a bit, and Satchel comes to my aid, pulling my uninjured arm around his neck. With Connor in back of us, we all move toward the pier and the dark waters beyond.

I wonder about Sweeney again. Is he dead? Did his brother-in-law, his co-conspirator, shoot him? Did Sweeney turn on him? Was that Graham trying to call? Have the police cleared him and let him go?

I've lost a lot of blood, I think, if my shirt is any indication. How much blood can a person afford to lose before he collapses? I try not to worry about it. Besides, the pain in my broken hand is more than enough to focus on.

It seems like an eternity before Buck finally stops and looks at a huge ferry that's docked in front of us, rocking gently to the soft rhythm of the Lake Michigan deep. "This is it," Buck says. In a single, graceful leap he's on the boat and lowering the gangplank for the rest of us.

Connor immediately moves next to Sabina. It is through her that he controls the captain and the ship. "Get on board," he says to the rest of us, "and sit down."

There are two decks. The lower one has many pew-like seats running both starboard and port as well as down the center—all of them well protected from the elements with a number of wide windows for watching the progress of the ship and enjoying the view. Here we sit down, huddled together in the center rows. There is a metal stairway with grab rails amidships which must open onto the unsheltered deck above.

I had hoped that we might see someone along the pier. A few hours ago the place was overrun with tourists and although I knew Navy Pier had to be closed to the public at one in the morning, I'd thought we might encounter a clean-up crew, a late-working shop owner, the night-shift harbor master, anyone. But the place is completely dark and deserted. Luck is, for the moment at least, with the Irish.

Connor stands beside us, gun at the ready, while Buck goes about the business of casting off the bow and stern lines and sealing the gangway. Moira and Moon sit on either side of Sabina on one of the benches amidships, tending to her as she mumbles something unintelligible, at least to me. My left ear isn't what it used to be. Satch and I sit on either side of the women. As Buck returns, rather breathless from his efforts, Connor issues another command: "Get to the bridge and fire 'er up."

Within a few minutes, we hear the rumbling of the ship engines and the running lights flash on.

In a very short time, Navy Pier dwindles beyond the gunwale, and we are moving, windward, into the vast, rolling expanse of Lake Michigan.

Chapter twenty-eight

Every attempt at communication within our wounded and exhausted party is silenced immediately by Keenan O'Connor. Our first crisis on the ship arises when Buck comes below with a Red Cross first aid kit, intent on tending to his stricken wife. Connor angrily orders him back to the bridge. The helm, he shouts, can't be left unattended for long, and Buck's the only one who knows how to handle this gigantic craft. Buck doesn't move, staring down the muzzle of Connor's gun with utter disdain. I'm sure he would have taken a bullet just to comfort Sabina, but Moira and Moon promise Buck that they will take care of Sabina so, considering his wife's ultimate safety, he complies.

Long before we are out of sight of the lights of downtown Chicago, Connor binds Satchel's hands and feet and secures him to the deckbench on which we are seated. He does the same to me, with the exception of leaving my left arm free, rightfully convinced that it is entirely ineffectual. The women are moved to a bench on the port side, across the aisle, but they are allowed the use of their limbs in order to keep their word and wrap Sabina's head in gauze.

I keep looking out at the dark water, hoping that some kind of rescue or pursuit is underway, but the surface of the lake is as black as pitch and only the distant lights from nocturnal freighters keep me from believing that we are utterly alone.

An hour passes. Connor sits a few feet away. He hasn't moved since he tied us to the bench. He just sits and stares at us with his dark, psychopathic gaze. I am beginning to believe that he is, somehow, supernatural. While the rest of us doze or shift in our discomfort, he sits rigidly erect, his piercing black eyes studying us as if we were mice in a cage. He seems indefatigable. While I long for something to drink or smoke or eat, he sits there stoically, a slight grin on his goofy countenance, apparently enjoying the power he holds over us. It is enough, it seems, to overcome all corporal considerations.

I'm convinced that when Connor finds the right spot, Satchel will be killed and dumped overboard. It's clear from both his words and actions that this whole fiasco was perpetrated in order to get to Satchel. It's Satchel that he holds responsible for his sister's ruin. Why, I don't know. I can't believe that a teenager, especially one with as little experience as Satchel, would be held accountable for a liaison with a grown woman. He was a shy kid, almost afraid of the opposite sex. Besides, Mary lived on well after that traumatic event. Moira was what, three, when Mary died? They lived next door with that secret, went through the pregnancy and birth, stayed friends with my widowed father.

Satch admitted to the affair. There's little question that Moira is his child. Connor hates him because his sister killed herself over guilt? There's got to be more to it than that. What's happened to Sweeney? My thoughts fall upon each other like snow sliding off the cottage roof, until all are buried in an incomprehensible muddle.

The worst part of the journey is not the pain in my arm or hand, the insufferable weight of all that has pressed down on us this night, not even the threat of inevitable death (because I believe that when Satchel is murdered, I will be too), but rather it's the separation from Moira. She looks at me, but the flirtatious smile is gone. She can't see me that way anymore. Connor is not her uncle—I am. This proud, intelligent, beautiful woman can never be my lover again, but I can never look upon her as my niece.

Another slow ten minutes passes. It's after three. The sun will be rising in an hour or so and I find it hard to believe that Connor won't make some sort of move soon. Murder must be done under cover of night. Dark deeds must unwatched go. Macbeth? I can't remember anymore. If the authorities were going to trace the cell phone and find my message, they would have done so already. Something's gone wrong. No one is coming.

"I have to go to the bathroom," Sabina moans.

Connor turns his attention away from Satch and me for the first time. "No," he says flatly.

"But I'll piss myself."

"Then do it."

"I have to go too," Moira says. "I'll take her." She begins to get up.

Connor stands and aims point blank at my head. "Sit down or I'll kill them both."

Moira doesn't try to leave, but she doesn't sit either. Moon stands up as well. "I have to go too. You can escort the three of us and wait outside the door. We can't go anywhere. The men are tied up and can't do anything. Please! We can't possibly do you any harm."

He studies Satch and me. My brother appears to be sleeping and I must look too incapacitated to be of use in any kind of rebellion. He reluctantly nods his assent. My guess is that he must have to relieve himself and his agreement has more to do with his own needs than any merciful disposition. "All right. The head is just around that side, in the bow below the bridge. Move ahead of me, single file." Moira shimmies out from between the benches and heads down the aisle. She doesn't look at me. Sabina and Moon follow her. As Connor falls in, he gives us a parting warning: "Don't try anything, or you'll never see them again." Satchel's head is still down. His eyes are closed. I simply nod agreement for both of us.

As soon as they're gone, Satchel raises his head. His voice startles me. "Can you use that free arm?"

I try, but it's frozen. Besides, the fingers are tightly wrapped in linen. "No."

He struggles with his bonds, but it's obvious that Connor has done a thorough job.

"We're screwed," he says.

"I left Moira's cell phone in the car after dialing 911. If they can trace it, I also left a message on the back of one of the seats in the car, letting them know that we're headed for Michigan."

My brother looks at me with renewed admiration. "How the hell did you manage that?"

"Never mind. What happened to Sweeney?"

"I don't know. I assume Connor shot him."

"His own brother-in-law? His co-conspirator? Why would he do that?"

"Either that, or Buck shot his own father. Something happened to him. He's not here."

There is a long silence between us as Satchel continues to struggle with his bonds. "I have to know, Satchel, before we die."

"What?"

"What happened between you and Mary Sweeney?"

I hear Connor growling at the girls to hurry up. They can't be too far away. We haven't much time.

"You're not going to die."

"Listen, a couple of days ago I took the old rowboat out into the middle of Loon Lake to drown myself. I was in an alcoholic stupor, a state I've been in most of the time since Wendy was murdered and I thought you were her killer. Moira saved me. I found my life again with her. I got my brother back. You don't know what joy that gave me. I only had a few minutes to let it all sink in before I'm told that my life really is over. So, brother, I need to know why. Are you going to tell me?"

He raises his eyes from his lap and stares at me. "Okay. I was outside the cabin, sitting at the picnic table, listening to a ballgame.

Like Sweeney said, you were at baseball camp and Dad was occupied with reading the Bible. Mrs. Sweeney came over to me and asked me if I could help her get a box down from her attic. Naturally, I said yes. You know how much she'd done for us since Mom's death. It was a heavy box, full of letters and journals and stuff like that. When I finally wrestled it down the stepladder, she opened it and pulled out a photo album. She showed me some pictures of her when she was a lot younger. I remember telling her that she had been very pretty. She said, laughing, you mean I'm not now? I told her I didn't mean that. She laughed again and feigned a kind of girlish pout. I told her I had always liked her accent. She asked me if I had a girlfriend and I told her that girls kind of made me nervous. I didn't know what to say to them, but I had dreams about them all the time. She asked me what kind of dreams and I was too embarrassed to tell her. She kissed me then, like I told you—my forehead, my cheek, my mouth. She asked me if I wanted to see what a woman looked like without her clothes. I remember thinking that something was wrong, that I should leave, but the truth is I really did want to see that. I thought maybe she had some more pictures, from a magazine or something. I didn't move. I stared at the floor for a long time. She stood up. She told me to look at her. She had removed her blouse. I couldn't move. My limbs were frozen. She grabbed my hand and told me to get up. She turned around, lifted her hair off her shoulders, and asked me to unhook her bra. I fumbled with the little hooks. She finally had to do it. When she turned around, I couldn't stop staring at her breasts. She was still a very good-looking woman, even at her age. You remember."

"Yes."

"She asked me if I would like to touch her. One thing led to another. I wasn't responsible, Tin. She *wanted* me to do it. At the time, I thought it was one of the best things that ever happened to me. I think she felt that way too. I can't see her killing herself over it.

"When I got home, Dad didn't even know I'd been gone. You know how oblivious he could be."

I did indeed.

"After that day, I wanted to do it again, but Mary had changed. She never allowed it. She refused to even speak of it. I was lovesick for weeks, mooning about. After a while, I began to wonder if it had even happened at all."

"Did you know that Sweeney knew?"

"No. He never said anything to me about it—until tonight. That's the truth. She became pregnant after that. I kept my distance for the rest of the summer. The following year I graduated and went on to minor league ball. She had Moi…the baby. I stayed away. That's how it happened."

"Then you were seduced."

"I guess you could say that. I didn't fight it, that's for sure, but I really didn't know what I was doing. I was *seventeen,* Tin. She must've been close to forty. I was terrified that she'd tell Dad or Sweeney or someone, but nothing like that ever happened. When she died, I figured that our secret died with her. I met Wendy, and it all seemed to me like it never happened. I think I had pretty well convinced myself, in fact, that it had just been a teenager's wet dream."

"Sweeney really never said anything to you about it?"

"I told you, not until tonight, no. I wasn't around much after that. When I did see him, he seemed a little distant but, just to show you how my mind was working at the time, I thought maybe he'd found out about how we wrecked his trophy fish that he kept over the mantle. I was that sure he didn't know."

"What's happened to Sweeney?"

"Now, you mean? I don't know anymore about that than you do. I heard gunshots after we left the courtyard of the church. I just don't know." There are tears in his eyes. "I'm sorry, brother. I never meant for this to happen to you, but think about how I must feel too. I can't look my…Moira in the face. How will she be able to deal with all this? And Moonie…Moon…what she must think…." He shakes his head as his voice trails off and he looks to the heavens as if an answer might be there. "Tin."

"Yeah."

He's straining his neck to look behind him.

"What is it?"

"We've changed course."

"What?"

"The North Star, the bright one at the end of the Little Dipper, remember? Dad used to tell us that you could always see what direction north was if you could see the stars. Ever since we left the pier, it's been straight ahead of us."

"So?"

"Now it's behind."

"That can't be. I didn't *feel* us turn, did you?"

"No, but out in the middle of the lake, in the dark, if Buck turned in a very wide circle and took it slow—"

"But what's he trying to do then? Head back to Chicago? Why would he do that unless the authorities were alerted somehow? He'd have to know."

"Better be quiet. They're coming back."

I hear the sounds of feet on the metal floor, just before I see Moira appear along the portside rail. The girls move silently to their seats, trying to maintain their balance as the ferry rocks and sways against Lake Michigan's swells. Connor is just behind them, still brandishing the gun. Moira risks a quick glimpse in my direction. It's just momentary eye contact, but it comforts me.

Our captor settles onto the bench in front of them with a deep sigh and, with one long leg folded up under him, keeps himself facing the women. Satchel has gone back to his pretense of sleep. Five minutes pass. Ten. Connor gets up, comes over to us and checks our bonds again. Apparently satisfied, he returns to his seat. When I look at him, he glowers fiercely, then turns his attention to a darkness beyond us.

I'm feeling, deeply, the effects of my injuries, in addition to thirst, hunger, nicotine withdrawal and, not least among my afflictions, the return of a nagging despair about life in general. I try to keep my head clear and focus on what can be done to save my brother and his daughter. I don't see much of a chance. Even with Buck apparently trying some kind of maneuver to help us, the results are likely to be the same. Connor has every intention of killing Satch. I can see this by the way he sits and stares at my brother. There is such hatred in that clownish face. He believes, I think, that Satchel is responsible for his sister's suicide. Nothing else would logically cause such terrible, fixated, lengthy desire for vengeance. I understand that kind of hate. I carried it for so long myself. Now, even knowing that Connor was the murderer of my wife and her sister, I can only look at him with a benign kind of pity. Perhaps, it's not just love that has left me, but *all* passion. It's a good mindset to have when you're looking at death.

Suddenly, Connor's expression changes. He, too, has looked to the heavens and seen the yawing misdirection of our vessel. He leaps to his feet and leans over the guardrail to see whatever might be ahead of us. "Buck!" he screams. "You son of a bitch! Get your ass down here!" There is no response. He knows he can't leave us alone to check on the helm up on the bridge. "Buck!" he screams again. Silence.

He looks at us. His hateful black eyes lock first on the girls, then my brother and me. His buckteeth are protruding even more than normal as he grits his teeth and pulls his lower lip into a venomous grimace. "Fine, you motherfucker," he snarls under his breath. "I'll do it now."

He strides across the deck and gets behind Satchel and me. He fumbles with our ropes. I can feel them loosen. "Get up boys," he says, "it's time to pay for all the shit." Satchel rises and helps me to my feet. I wonder why he doesn't just shoot us here, while we're helpless and bound. But when he tells us to move to the guardrail farther aft, I realize it's because our bodies will be dumped in the lake, and he doesn't want to have to drag them half the length of the ship. He can't throw us overboard amidships because of the gunwale and the windows that don't open. He has to get us to the rear of the boat where a couple of good shoves with his foot will cast our bodies into the deep.

Satchel boosts my good arm over his shoulder and circles my waist with his left arm. I am dizzy, and stumble. "Hang on," he whispers to me.

I hear Moira's voice behind me. "You can't do this! My mother wouldn't want you to hurt anyone," she pleads. There's a terrible desperation in her voice.

"What would you know about it?" Connor growls. "Shut up and sit down."

"I knew my mother. She was a loving, gentle person. I loved her and she loved me. I know she wouldn't want you to do this...uncle."

"*I* loved her, loved your ma, Moira. Loved her more than anyone could. You don't know what we went through together, especially when we were kids. We kept each other alive. When she went with Sweeney, it almost killed me, but I knew she had to go, had to start her own life. Sweeney cared about, took care of her, but he couldn't make her happy, couldn't give her what she wanted most in the world...a baby." His voice trails off, becomes softer. Then, he comes back from his memories. His words regain their former animosity. "You don't know shit. This has to be done."

"Then you'll have to do it to me, too."

We stop. So does Connor. "Alright," he says. "You know I don't want to hurt you, darlin', but I can. I can overcome my personal attachments—ask Sweeney. And those two ladies standin' next to you, they're expendable as far as I'm concerned. You want to add them to the pot, it's okay with me. I can take care of what I came here to do and leave you gals ashore somewhere, or I can get rid of the whole lot of you, then walk away. It's up to you."

"Stay put." These words come from me, but they seem distant, detached. "Stay there. We'll be all right."

"Please, Moira," Satchel says.

Little Moon answers. "We'll stay." She pulls Moira back down to the bench. I look at my brother. He smiles at Moon and winks. She holds her head high. She smiles back. We resume our deathwalk.

I can hear Moira pleading as we reach the guardrail near the stem and turn around. Connor is standing five feet away, his gun pointed directly at Satchel's chest.

"Paybacks are hell, boys," he says and closes one eye, taking aim.

This is my moment. I rush at him with all the strength and resolve left in me. I see the surprised look on his face. I hear the gun discharge. I hear the women screaming. I feel another awful invasion of my chest, a terrible stinging sensation, as I grab Connor around the neck with my right arm and let the rest of my body go limp. He sinks his teeth into the meaty flesh just below my elbow. It doesn't matter. I don't hope to live. I'll just hang on...hang on for as long as I can. The gun explodes again. I will die this night. I will never know if what I did saved them or not. But it doesn't matter anymore. I have redemption. I will hang on. I will not let it go.

Chapter twenty-nine

I don't know how many resurrections an individual is allowed, but I know I've had more than my share when I surface once again and I can see Moira's beautiful face above me. She's softly calling my name, studying my eyes. When she sees recognition in them, she smiles. "He's alive," she says, and breaks into tears.

She's kneeling over me. Behind her, I can make out the fuzzy image of my brother.

"Where was he hit?"

"I don't know," she answers. I can see, muddle-headed as I am, that she's trying to regain control of her shattered emotions. "I don't see any fresh wounds, but I don't see how Connor could have missed him. He shot at him point blank." I feel her hands probing my chest and I am reminded of what I have lost in staying alive.

Moon's voice comes from somewhere beyond the tiny circle of my returning consciousness. "I've never seen anything quite so heroic," she says.

"No," Satchel says, "me either."

Moira leans down. I can feel her sweet breath on my face. She kisses my cheek and I feel her tears. She knows that valor had nothing to do with it. She knows. Sometimes what you want comes with a high price tag. Are you brave if you can afford to pay it?

"I want to get up," I say. Moira helps me to sit upright, then Satchel pulls me to my feet. He inspects me again, searching for injury. He can find none. I feel none. "It's nothing short of miraculous," he says, "although in the struggle I think his shoulder has started bleeding again. He's going to need medical attention soon."

"Where's Connor?"

"There."

The murderer is lying on the deck, not far away. Above him, Buck is sitting on the end of one of the benches, holding his gun. As far as I can tell, Connor is unconscious.

"What do we do now?"

"The police and coast guard are on their way." This is Buck's deep voice.

"How do they know where we are?"

"I gave them the coordinates."

I look over at Buck. He can see the puzzled look on my face. "You were able to use the radio? He didn't disarm it?"

Buck shakes his massive head. "Didn't have to. I told him I couldn't use it yet. The boat's too new. Didn't have my code registered yet with the FCC."

"You lied to him then?"

"Nope. It's true."

"Then how—?"

Buck reaches into his pocket and pulls out Sabina's cell phone. "He forgot about this."

Sabina is sitting behind him, her arms around his chest, as far as they can reach. Her head is resting on his back. "I'm really sorry fer all this, Tin. They tole me no one'd git hurt. I didn't know what that asshole was like," he says, gesturing with the gun toward Connor's prostrate form. "Sweeney said they jest wanted to bring Wendy's killer to justice. I trusted Sweeney. I was wrong."

"Buck saved your life," Satchel says.

"What?"

"When you were struggling with Connor, the sonofabitch got his gun free and pointed it right at your temple. He told me to back off. Buck came up from behind him and laid him out."

"What? How?"

"With that." Satchel points to a red cylinder lying near Connor's prostrate form. I can see, even from this distance, that it's a small fire extinguisher.

Moira helps me to limp over to one of the benches so that I can sit down. She sits next to me. Satchel has his arm around Moon. All of us look, almost unbelieving, at the still form lying on the deck. It's hard to imagine a monster so easily conquered.

"Look," Moira says, pointing in the direction of the bow. Far in the distance I can see the glow of lights. It's too early for dawn and the light is coming from the wrong direction to be the sun. "It's Chicago," she says. Below the skyline, the lights of several boats speeding toward us can be clearly identified against the dark water. "It's over," she says.

"Yes," I answer. "It's all over." She knows what I mean. "I've lost my smokes," I say, reaching into my bloody pocket. Satchel is quick to hand me one of his Marlboros. I manage to extract my lighter, but as soon as I feel it, I can tell it's misshapen somehow.

"Look," Moira says.

The mystery of my survival is solved. The Zippo is badly dented and bent. The insignia is shattered. Only a piece of it remains. There is a hole in my shirt pocket and, I discover, a terrible soreness in the flesh behind it, unnoticed until now because of the wound in my shoulder and my shattered hand, both terribly aggravated by my struggle with Connor. I'll have a bad bruise there, but it pales into insignificance when compared with the other injuries—at least physically. There's still something in my pocket. I reach in and pull out a stubby bullet. It struck the heart—the wrong heart—a perfect bulls-eye.

Chapter thirty

Just as the Coast Guard ship pulls alongside and someone's voice megaphones a warning that we're about to be boarded, Connor regains consciousness. Frankly, I'm surprised that he's alive. He has a terrible swelling on the back of his head and he's lost a lot of blood. He's disoriented and confused. Moira asks him what happened to Sweeney, but he only responds with a kind of feral grunting. I expect it'll be some time before he's able to be coherent. I wonder, in fact, if Buck's blow might not have done some permanent damage—or rather, added to the permanent damage that must have been done to that brain a long time ago.

Three uniformed cops board us by means of a rope ladder, weapons drawn. Buck quickly surrenders the only firearm among us and, after a few minutes of explanation, Connor is handcuffed and taken. Buck is congratulated on bringing the monster down. No one says anything about the big man's earlier alliance with our captors. Sabina and I are carefully moved to the medical boat. Moira and Buck insist on accompanying us. Satch and Moon are boarded onto one of the Coast Guard cruisers and several sailors, in white uniforms, are left on Buck's ferry to guide it back to port.

Ironically, I feel no safer now than I did a few minutes earlier when Connor was about to finish us. Death, I guess, is the only kind of finality that will solve my dilemma. Yet I know, somehow, that I will not die—at least not by Connor's hand or my own. I will have to see my existence through. I will have to bear the long, slow heaviness of living. I am meant, like the beaver Moira once told me about, to die an unnaturally natural death. I'm marked for it. I can't ignore the clear message still contained in my shirt pocket.

I don't remember the ride to the hospital or the operating room, and it's well into the afternoon when I return from the dreamy, anesthetic-induced state with which I have become all too familiar. Moira is there, waiting for me. I look over at her. She's hunched in a leather chair in the corner. She has showered and changed into more conservative clothes—white slacks and a tangerine blouse. Her long legs are drawn up under her; she appears to be folding herself into a bulwark against life's continual assaults. Her voice comes from a face cloaked by the shadows of the window blinds, half-obscured, like it was when I looked up at her a few nights ago from the leaky rowboat on Loon Lake. "Are you back?"

"I think so. As far as I want to come, anyway." My voice is dry and raspy, but I think a cigarette would taste better than any liquid they would allow me.

"Sweeney's dead."

"I'm sorry, Moira." These are not empty words. I was always fond of Sweeney.

"They found his body in the courtyard at the church. Apparently, Connor shot him—after we left."

"Why?"

"I don't know. Connor admitted killing him, but he won't tell the police anything else." She rises from her chair and her beautiful face comes into focus as she walks over to the bed and stands next to it. She doesn't touch me. "I think it's because Sweeney decided to back out of the whole deal. It's what I believe, anyway."

"How long have I been out?"

"A good twelve hours or so. They took the bullet out of your shoulder and put a cast on you. You have three broken fingers on your left hand and a nasty bite wound on your right arm. It needed several stitches."

"Good old Uncle Con…" I stop as I realize that he is not her only uncle. I look at my hand, enveloped in plaster. The fingertips look blue.

"The prognosis is good," she says. "The doctor expects a full recovery."

I laugh. It's a bitter, scornful sound that I didn't intend. "Moira, I…certain things are unrecoverable."

"Yes." She turns away from me and goes to the window. She opens the blinds and I can see the late afternoon sun lighting up the other buildings of the Chicago skyline. She folds her arms together as if she were cold. I see her back muscles tense beneath the tangerine blouse. Her dark hair contrasts so boldly with the color. I sense that this will be the parting memory of her that I will replay innumerable times until God or Nature is merciful and kills me. I will have to keep trying to erase her image so that I can go on. I must do this so that I don't hurt her any further. Five years from now, she will send me a nice letter, telling me that she has met someone and that she would like me to come to the wedding. I will go and pretend that it doesn't kill me because I will do what I can to make her happy. I will help her to build the distance. It's the only thing I have left to give. "Where's Satchel?"

She turns and looks at me. My resolve evaporates. I want, with all my being, to kiss her. She can see it. "The Chicago Police and the FBI talked to us most of the night. They had an outstanding warrant on your brother for Wendy's murder, of course. He's still in custody. We tried to cover for Buck, but he admitted his part, took full responsibility. They've kept him too. The authorities are waiting outside. They want to talk to you now." It isn't until then that I realize that there are people standing just on the other side of the curtain that conceals me from the doorway beyond. As they step forward into the light, I can see that one is a distinguished-looking black man in a dark suit, and the other is a white woman who looks far too young to be his colleague, although that is, I discover, exactly what she is.

"Mr. Balune," the man says, "I'm special agent Valentine of the FBI and this is special agent Troudeau. Your physician, Dr. Fedderman, will be here in a minute to examine you, and then, with his permission, we'd like to talk to you, if you feel up to it." I look at Moira. She tries to smile.

"Of course. Can Moi…can Ms. Sweeney stay?"

"I'm afraid not," Agent Troudeau says.

"Moon and Sabina and I have taken a room at the Holiday Inn just a couple of blocks away," Moira says. "Sabina had to get some stitches, but she's all right—worried about Buck of course. I'll be back tomorrow. You try to get some rest, huh?"

"Sure." I watch her walk past the agents until she disappears behind the curtain from which they emerged. She doesn't look back at me.

Dr. Fedderman is pleased with my progress and pronounces me able to tolerate the interrogation. After he leaves, a matronly nurse appears and pulls back the curtain, revealing nothing but an empty bed on the other side, along with a couple of chairs. She sits in one of them. Apparently she is the guardian of my health. In the next few minutes, we are joined by two policemen dressed in standard blue uniforms, as well as a detective from the homicide division of the Chicago Police Department.

I tell them everything I can remember, starting with the trip that Moira and I took to Traverse City to drop off the rental truck. I do omit any details of the relationship between Moira and me. They are particularly interested in my hiring of Connor to hunt down my brother. They tell me that Connor is not a private investigator, but a professional assassin who got his start with the IRA and has been linked, in one way or another, to at least ten murders in the United States and the United Kingdom and one in Brisbane, Australia. I tell them what I know.

I strongly insist that my brother is innocent of Wendy's murder. They don't comment. They ask me if those are my fingerprints all over the room where Kelly was murdered. I tell them yes. They ask me if my blood is there. I tell them. Special Agent Valentine holds an x-ray of a hand up to the dying light in the window. Special Agent Troudeau asks me if I liked Kelly. The Chicago detective asks me if I called 911 and if I wrote the message on the back of the Caddy front seat and so on and so on.

When they all leave, I lie in bed under the dim light above my head. I look at the ink on my fingertips where they lifted my prints. They took a blood sample too. The nurse has just given me another shot for the pain, for which I'm terribly grateful. It's grown dark outside. The skyline is beautiful. I reach for the remote, and I shut off the light. I don't hear ghosts anymore. Dad and Mom and Wendy are far away, gone to whatever place holds them now. This, I owe to Moira.

Chapter thirty-one

She comes back in the morning as she promised. I'm surprised that I slept. The drugs did it, I suspect. She comes alone. Moon is staying with Sabina at the hotel, to tend to her. She asks me how I am. I tell her I'm fine. This is just the idiocy of smalltalk, because our professions of love, the pondering of a future together—everything of significance that relates to a united life is no longer permitted.

"What's going to happen to you now?" It's a question I have no right to ask

"I'll go back to school, as I planned." I can see that she's prepared herself for this. She will be strong. There won't be any tears. She will do this...for me.

"I won't see you anymore?"

"No."

It's like asking God if you can come into heaven. He gives you a simple negative. There are no explanations, none necessary really. You know the reasons in your heart. He doesn't have to elaborate. But you find it difficult not to feel like you've been slighted, that it isn't entirely your fault. After all, we're made this way aren't we? We're designed to fail. Planned obsolescence.

I look at her. She turns her head, then looks back. Her black eyes are fierce with resistance. "You have to promise me something," she says.

"What?"

"You'll go on."

"Until my teeth grow long enough to kill me?"

"Yes."

"If that's all I can do for your happiness, I will."

"Happiness?" She smiles. Only a smile can look so sad. "Fortitude might be a better word. You promise?"

"Yes."

She studies me, scrutinizes me for any sign of falsity. Apparently satisfied, she breaks off and looks at the floor instead. "Have they told you how long you have to stay in here?"

"I talked to the nurse last night. She said it would be up to the doctor, but she thought it would be about a week."

"Then what?"

"I'm going to try to get Satchel freed, do what I can for Buck."

"We'll all have to testify at Connor's trial, I suppose."

"Probably."

"And then?" She wants to know what will become of me. How can I answer such a question? Every plan I ever made in my life has fallen apart.

"I suppose I'll go back to teaching in the fall. Do some writing. I don't know."

"Oh Tin…." The façade is crumbling. She clutches the rail at the end of my bed and puts her head down so that I can't see her face. "Living is going to be so difficult without you."

"If there were someplace in the world we could go and be free of this, I would take you there. I would do anything to keep you…anything. But we can't overcome what we are—who we are, can we?"

I want her to have a solution. I want her to tell me I'm wrong. She simply says "No."

She throws back her hair and lifts her face to look at me, wiping away the tears that she can't stop. "I have to go."

"Back to the hotel?"

"Back to Michigan. Moon and Sabina are going to stay here for a while until they find out what's going to happen to Buck and Satchel. I called the housing office at MSU this morning. They're going to let me move in a month early. I can't stay at the cabin and I don't have anyplace else to go. I'm going to stop at Loon Lake, get my things, and move to East Lansing."

"You'll need my car."

"The police impounded it—for evidence. They'll be done with it by the time you get out."

"Then how—"

"Graham's waiting downstairs."

"Oh."

"He's been very sweet, Tin, especially when you consider everything we've put him through. He offered. I didn't have much choice."

"Of course not."

She forces a smile. So do I.

She comes around to the side of the bed. She leans over me and kisses me on my forehead. I breathe deeply to take in the smell of her one last time. She pulls away, looks into my eyes. She wants to say something. I want to say something. Neither of us can. She puts one gentle hand on my cheek. I grab it, kiss the palm fiercely, then she pulls away and runs from the room.

All that day, I beg for pain relief, both from God and the nurse. The latter, at least, is merciful. She also changes the dressings on my wounded shoulder and arm. The doctor comes in later to examine my injuries. The FBI agents return for another chat. Otherwise, I am generally lost in a miserable semi-consciousness. I eat, mechanically.

They get me up to piss. I feel very, very old. I will have to keep my promise to stay alive.

On my third or fourth day in the hospital, Moon Bullkiller walks into my room. She embraces me as if I have known her forever. I feel as though I have.

"I have a surprise for you," she says. "Something to cheer you up."

She looks toward the door. Silhouetted in the doorway is my brother.

"Satchel!"

"Tin Man!" he shouts and rushes to my bed, embracing me carefully. He even kisses my unshaven cheek. "They've dropped the charges, Tin. Can you believe it? I been in jail for a couple of days and it's the first time in years I've felt *free!* Now I really am free. They've dropped the charges! Connor's confessed! I'm really, actually, free!"

He lets go of me, grabs Moon, and does a little two-step with her around the room. She stops him in the middle of his jubilation and whispers something in his ear. He immediately gains control of himself, hangs his head. "I'm sorry Tin," he says, "I know how you must be hurting. I just couldn't help myself."

"It's okay, brother. I'm happy for you. I really am."

He falls into a chair and takes a deep breath. He looks around him as if the world is entirely different. I guess, for him, it is. Moon goes to the window and opens the blinds, letting in the glare of the afternoon light.

"Connor confessed?"

"Yeah. To Wendy's murder, to trying to frame me for it, to Kelly's death, to Sweeney's, to attempted murder on the boat— all of it."

"Why? Did he tell them why?"

His smile disappears. He takes out a cigarette, holds it to his lips, realizes that smoking isn't allowed in the hospital and slips it back into the pack. "Vengeance seems to have been his primary motivation. He insists that I was responsible for Mary Sweeney's death. She committed suicide because she couldn't live with the guilt of our affair anymore. I'm still not buying that explanation though. I think he's holding something back. So do the cops, but they can't get him to say anything else." He looks at me with that hang-dog expression that I remember seeing after every defeat in his life. He looks a great deal older now—the head is lower, the defeats have been many. "I guess Connor really loved his sister, was obsessed with her in fact. They went through some tough times together in Ireland as kids. Their parents were killed. He said that for quite a while he and Mary lived by scavenging for rats in abandoned buildings. He took care of her as best he could until the authorities put them in an orphanage. Anyway, when Mary died, and Sweeney showed him the suicide note, Connor blamed me."

"What happened to Sweeney? Why would he kill Sweeney then?"

"I don't know for sure. From what I understand, Sweeney backed out of the whole thing. He said he was tired of the killing. You saw him hold the gun on Connor. Connor asked him if what you'd said was true, about Sweeney trying to molest Moira. He admitted it. Connor told the feds that, after that, without a word, he just walked over to Sweeney and put a bullet in his head. Sweeney never raised his gun to protect himself. Buck has the same version."

I'm trying to let it all sink in.

"And how did Buck and Kelly get involved?"

"From what I gather, Buck Wolfram really is Sweeney's kid. His mother was from somewhere around Mackinaw City. I think they said her name was Lula, or something like that."

"Beulah," Moon corrects.

"Yeah, Beulah Wolfram. Sweeney met her there when he was a young man. I guess he and another guy were in that area fishing when they stopped in this restaurant. Beulah was a waitress there. Apparently they developed a pretty close relationship before Sweeney left to go back downstate. She wound up pregnant. By the time the woman found out where he lived and could reach him to tell him that she'd had his child, several years had gone by and Sweeney was engaged to Mary. They got married shortly after. Buck says that his mother raised him by herself, but when she was dying, cancer I guess, she told Buck who his father was. He got in touch with Sweeney. Sweeney floated him a loan to buy his first boat. Got you the job working on it that summer you met Buck. Sweeney asked Buck to help him in this. Told him a story about wanting to draw me in, bring me to justice, and they needed you for the bait. Buck was supposed to be on the inside, let them know how you were reacting to the notes, that sort of thing. Probably the real reason for getting him involved though, was to have a boat for their escape. The way I figure it, Buck didn't have any idea, like he said at the church, that there would be killing. When he realized what was going on, he got out."

"And Kelly?"

"That was Connor's idea. They wanted to make sure that I came to see you, to 'reconcile'. He wanted to 'take me out', as he put it to the agents, in a big city, someplace where they would have access to Buck's boat to get away. Chicago, I guess, seemed like the natural place, since that's where Connor had been living ever since he came over from Ireland. He knew his way around here. He told the police that they thought I'd feel less threatened here too, in neutral territory, away from Michigan where so many people knew me. Of course Kelly lived here too and they chose this time because Buck was supposed to be down here for the boat show anyway. The birthday thing was incidental. When Sweeney told Connor that Wendy's sister lived in Chicago, Connor contacted her and duped her into thinking that he was with the FBI and they were trying to lure me in since they'd come to believe that I wasn't Wendy's murderer and they needed to find out who was—accounting for all this clandestine shit. They told her that they just wanted her to pose as your agent, book the room at the Wyndham and have her keep an eye on you from the hotel across the street. They said that you were helping them, but they were worried that you might unwittingly try to interfere. She agreed. She gave them the information about Joey Buono's and the song, "Windy"—even helped them compose the note over the phone—and talked to Joolie at the Bullkiller ranch. I guess, eventually, she became suspicious of what was really going down. She told

Connor that unless he told her the truth, that she was going to call you and Moira, let you know what was going on. She told him to drop the whole thing or she was going to contact the police. I don't think she had a clue as to who or what she was dealing with."

"Was it Connor who tore our room apart then?"

"Yeah. The police said he wanted to make sure that you guys hadn't talked with Kelly or written down anything that might be incriminating. Then, he went to see her."

I find myself sifting through all that's happened. They didn't count on Moira. That was what had changed it all for Sweeney. He had expected her to take the truck back by herself. He hadn't envisioned that we would fall in love. When Moira called him from the restaurant south of Traverse City to tell him we'd be late, Connor must've already joined him at the lake. Connor would have been the other person that Juna Hines saw with Sweeney at the Loon Lake Grocery and Bait Shop. Sweeney bought the cigarettes for him. It was Sweeney who must have called Buck and told him to go to the Stoppe Inn to keep an eye on us, let them know when we were leaving. They wrote the note. *Windy.* Moira had hummed the song. *"I've heard this before. I think Sweeney has the CD,"* she'd told me. The cryptic note was in Sweeney's handwriting. They left the note, got into Connor's car, and drove to Chicago, but not before stopping at Nettie's to buy some smokes.

"What kind of car does Connor have?" I ask my brother.

"What?"

"He had to get to Chicago. What did he drive? Sweeney's car was left at the lake."

His eyes open wide. He looks at Moon. "So that's the car they were talking about."

"What?"

"Yesterday. The cops asked me if I knew about the other car they'd found. I guess it was parked a block over from the church and had been sitting there for several days. The city cops had it hauled away. It had an Illinois plate on it. They asked me about it. I had the truck of course. You had your Jeep. The Caddy was Buck's."

"What kind of car was it?"

"A Taurus I think."

"Blue?"

"Yeah." I can see my brother's dawning awareness. "The Taurus, of course. We found the green one, the one that belonged to the minister. This one had to be Connor's."

"We should tell the authorities," Moon says.

"If they checked the registration, they probably already know. I would guess that it'd be listed under his alias, Cian Connor. I think they asked you that question to see how much you knew, not who it really belonged to."

We sit for a few minutes in silence, trying to understand all that's happened to us. The nurse comes in with lunch. It is the usual small portion of some indistinguishable meat, a variant of potato, a little corn, milk, coffee, bread, jello. Standard hospital fare. I sigh. "I'd give my left nut for a greasy cheeseburger, fries and a chocolate shake."

Moon rises. "I'll go get it," she quips, "but I'm going to hold you to your offer."

Before I can object, she's out the door.

"She didn't have to do that," I say.

Satch smiles. "She probably figured we needed some time alone."

"Do we?"

"Yeah." He rubs the palm of his hand, where the awful scar is. I think it's habit. I forget how much he's suffered on my account. Now, rightfully I suppose, I will spend the rest of my life atoning. "I just can't figure why Connor didn't kill me earlier. He had plenty of chances. Why shoot me in my hand and not my head?"

"I think, like Sweeney said, they wanted you to suffer—they wanted it to last. Once you'd found a new life on the Bullkiller ranch though, you'd found happiness, no longer running, free of drugs, well—"

"You saved me," he says.

"What?"

"On the boat. You saved us all."

"Least I could do."

"We've hurt each other a lot, Tin. And the sad thing is, I don't think either one of us wanted to." Tears form in his eyes. It's so unnatural to see him this way. As a kid, he never quit smiling.

"No, I don't think we did." Then, I bring it up, because otherwise it will always be between us and I don't want anything between us anymore. "Are you going to talk to her?"

"I have already, Tin. It didn't go very well. Too new to deal with, I think. We're going to give it a few months, then try again. She's my daughter. I want to stay in her life."

"I can't you know. I can't be her—"

"I know. It's okay. I'll let you know how she's doing."

"Thank you." I press the little button that makes the bed push me into a sitting position. "We've gotten so far away."

"From what?"

"From what we were as kids."

"Yes."

"We can't ever go back."

"What would be the use of it?"

"Taking away the pain."

"We had pain then, Tin. We wanted to stay up later and they wouldn't let us. We couldn't choose our own food. We got the flu and the chicken pox and measles. We had to sweat out report cards and the discovery of lies and long church services and cases of poison ivy. We had to deal with our mother's death and our father's perverse scrutiny. There was pain. You've just forgotten or minimized it. But it was real then. All of it went away. This will go away too."

"I don't think so."

"Do you love her as much as you loved Wendy?"

"Yes."

"Did you think that that would be possible on the night you came home and found your wife on your kitchen floor?"

"No."

"Well?"

317

"Moira was my second chance. Moon is yours. I don't believe there'll be a third."

"But you did believe in a second?"

"No."

"You'll hang in there though? You'll keep trying?"

"I told you about the boat and the drill."

"Yes. Moira did too, Tin. She wants you to survive. So do I."

He gets up from the chair and comes to my bed. When Moon walks in, we are once more caught in an unmanly embrace, weeping like little children. Together. Moon joins us. I have a family again.

Chapter thirty-two

I t is the first Saturday in October and I have come back to Loon Lake. I'm not sure why. The school year is underway and the cast is off my hand. My shoulder aches now and then, but nothing compared to what it was like. I will have some scars. We all have scars.

When I walked into the cabin this morning, for the first time since Moira was with me, I spotted an empty cigarette pack on the kitchen table. I almost threw it away before I noticed the piece of white paper stuck in the cellophane. It was my suicide note of course, given back to me by Moira for services rendered. She said I would look at it someday and laugh. I didn't today, but she could always argue that someday isn't necessarily today. I put it in the junk drawer. I stopped at Nettie's place on the way in and put in a supply of Jim Beam. She asked about Sweeney. I told her he had died. She seemed genuinely distressed. I haven't touched the whiskey.

Satchel and Moon came to visit me in Grand Rapids just before Labor Day. As I'd promised, I took Satch to see Wendy's grave, and that of our father. Neither of us said anything. At dinner, he told me that Buck had been released since none of us were willing to press charges and, with Sabina, went back to Mackinaw City. I have decided that I will go to visit them this winter. We have not talked, but I think it's because he feels too badly about his part in all this. I need to let him know it's okay.

Sweeney's body was shipped back to Michigan and, I was told by Satchel, Moira had him buried next to Mary. I arranged, in the absence of any close relatives, for Kelly to be interred next to her parents. I did not attend either funeral.

Keenan O'Connor goes on trial in two months. Sometime around Christmas I will have to go back to Chicago to testify. I will see Moira again then. I don't know if I'll be able to stand it, but I'll show her that I'm alive and keeping my promise.

Satchel and Moon seemed very happy and when they left they begged me to come out to the Bullkiller ranch for Christmas. I told them I would.

I sit down on the picnic table and look out at the lake. The colors are early this year. The far side is blazing with orange and red, which is doubly effective by being mirrored in the placid lake. The sun is actually hot, but I shiver in the shade. I've never been able to tell if I should wear a jacket or not in Michigan in October.

I walk down to the lake. The rowboat, still moored to the dock, is half-sunk in the shallows. I can see the drill on the floor of the boat, though it's partially obscured by sand and dead leaves. I decide to leave it where it is. I doubt if I will ever use it again—for anything.

I light a cigarette with my new butane lighter. The Zippo that saved my life is tucked safely in a drawer in the Grand Rapids house. I have looked at it twice since my return and will probably never look at it again.

I told myself on the drive up here that I wouldn't go anywhere near the Sweeney cabin, but it looks neglected and lonely, even if it can feel nothing. It is so much like me that I must get inside. I try the side door. It's locked. So is the one in back. I should just leave, but something makes me circle around to the door facing the lake. It's unlocked. I push it open.

The place is a mess. Moira apparently spent as little time as possible clearing out her things, and she left a great deal behind. It's apparent that the FBI have been here too. Sweeney's stuff has been ransacked and most of it removed. In Moira's bedroom I find that the beaver skull is still on the little table by her bed. In the living room, medals and other awards still adorn the mantle. Sweeney's trophy fish, sans one fin, still swims across the brick façade of the fireplace.

I'm about to leave when I hear the rummaging shuffle of some living thing in the ceiling above me, scrabbling about in reaction to my unwanted intrusion. Something has gotten into the attic. Whatever it is, it's directly above my head. I should just walk away and leave it to its newfound home, but I'm afraid that anything larger than a mouse—say a raccoon or squirrel—might do some serious damage to either whatever is stored up there, or the wiring, or both.

I go to the attic entrance, which is a piece of plywood painted to match the ceiling of the kitchen. I grab a broom and push the handle against the plywood, forcing it out of the way. I feel a *whoosh* of cold air, then a black squirrel leaps from the hole onto the top of the refrigerator, down to the floor, and out the door that I have left ajar. The damned thing scares the shit out of me, and I find myself panting. Another cigarette calms me. No matter how hard I try, of course, I cannot finagle the plywood cover back into place with the broom. I take one of Sweeney's kitchen chairs and place it underneath the opening. Even standing on the chair, I'm still not tall enough. I'm about to give up when I remember seeing a wooden stepladder leaning against the outer wall of the cabin inside the porch area. I fetch it, open it up in the kitchen, and climb up to the opening. At the top, I grab the plywood cover and am about to shimmy it into place when I touch something buried in the blown insulation near the opening. I should leave it alone, but it's the first time I've been curious about anything in quite a while. I grab it and bring it down. With my feet back on the linoleum, I blow the dust off the object. It's an old journal. I think either the authorities or Moira have taken the box full of pictures that Satchel told me about, but apparently they have overlooked this.

I wander over to the kitchen table and sit down. I open the journal and two pictures fall out onto the oilcloth. I pick up the first photo. It's old and becoming mildewy, but the images are still clear enough. There is a little girl, very young, standing next to some older people. I can only assume that this is Mary with her parents. Another shows her, a bit older now, standing by a tall, gawky-looking boy of fifteen or sixteen, his buck-teeth and shock of wiry hair identifying him as her brother. He has his long arm wrapped protectively around her shoulders. He's glaring at the camera. There are some others photos, but none of them have any meaning to me.

I pick up the leather-bound notebook. It's well-worn and filled with entries. I open it to the first page. The writing is small and neat and feminine. I have seen it before.

> *Arrived in Michigan today, a state in the United States of America. Keenan has arranged for me to live with the Sweeneys. They are friends of our parents. They moved to America just before mother and father died. I don't really remember them, but they have been very kind. My brother will join me when he is released, which he hopes will be soon. He says the royalist courts will have to let him go. They have no proof. My poor brother, I owe him so much.*

Another entry, dated six months later.

> *Keenan was sentenced today. He says there is no justice for true Irishmen. His lawyer is appealing, but he doesn't think it will work. I pray for him daily. The Sweeneys are so very good to me and have told me that I may stay with them as long as I'd like.*

Several pages later.

> *The Sweeney's oldest son, Hiram, is a good friend and sympathetic ear. Today, he told me he loves me. I didn't know what to answer.*

The next few pages are taken up with notes about her graduation from high school, her job as a clerk at a department store in Detroit, various comments about holidays, a terrible winter storm and other such minutia. Most interestingly, nothing more about Sweeney. Then:

> *Hiram and I were married today. I am determined to make him a good wife and become a mother.*

Another entry, dated over a year later:

> *I want very much to have a child, but Hiram is having difficulties which seem to intensify each day. The doctor has diagnosed him with diabetes and says that this could be the explanation for his inability to 'perform'. I so hope that this can be treated somehow, that the insulin will help. I want a baby. He loves me. There is no lack of desire, only this discouraging inadequacy. We still try. He does other things to satisfy me, but none of them will give me a child or give him release.*

I read for the better part of an hour. The journal is filled with many meaningless items—recipes, more notes about the weather, elections, baseball scores. But scattered throughout is the common thread of sexual discontent—Sweeney's record of continual failure. There is also the consistent written desire of Mary Sweeney to be a mother.

> *My good friend and neighbor, Katie Balune, has died in a terrible automobile accident. Her husband, Pastor Balune, is grief-stricken. Her boys, Satchel and Tin, (only sixteen and ten years old) seem lost without her. They spend much of their time at our cabin and I am trying to be a substitute mother to them. They are such sweet, manly boys.*

I rummage through several pages, looking for something, I don't know what—perhaps more answers. I come across a page that's dated, 'Summer, 1986'. I thumb through a few entries, then, the discovery of something that explains a great deal. I turn on the kitchen light against the falling shadows of the late October afternoon and read.

> *My brother, Keenan is coming today. He has finally been released. I am anxious, excited, scared. I have not seen him since Hiram and I were married— more than two decades. He writes frequently, but his letters frighten me. He speaks to me as if I was his wife instead of his sister. He professes his love, his devotion. He wants me to leave Hiram and come back with him to Ireland. He was very angry about our marriage. He has always been obsessive about our relationship. I suppose it comes from too much responsibility at an early age. Still, I am frightened.*

Then, on the next page, I find this:

> *Keenan got into it with Hiram. The two of them had been drinking through most of the evening. My brother demanded to know why Hiram had no children yet. Hiram told him it was none of his business and stormed out of the house. Humiliated, I went to my room, but Keenan followed me there. He told me that he could give me a child. He said that he loved me like no one else in the world could. I told him to get out, to go back to Ireland and stay away from us. I could see that something snapped inside him. He tore off my clothes, silenced me with his hand, had his way. Dear God, my own brother raped me! When he was through, he begged my forgiveness. He cried so pitifully. He was on his knees before me. He said no one had ever loved him but me. He has saved me so many times. I owe him my silence and will only write it here. Oh God, what a curse it is to be loved!*

My heart is pounding, my hands sweating. Connor. That sonofabitch!

I grab the journal and rush out of the cabin. I get back to my cabin just as Felix the Cat meows four times. I pace, up and down, back and forth. What can I do? What *should* I do? I read the entry again. I slam it on the table and go outside. I walk down to the lake and slump down in the sand by the dock. A loon cries somewhere across the water.

Mary Sweeney, raped by her own brother! She took her life because it was *Connor* that laid that fear and guilt on her. It was Connor she was referring to in her suicide note! My brother's seduction may have been her attempt to erase that ugly picture, to give her hope that if she became pregnant, the child she so longed for might not belong to her brother. I wonder if anyone but me has seen this journal. Does Moira know? Certainly not. She would have taken it with her. It's a sure bet that Sweeney knew nothing about his wife's secret narrative. The sky has grown very overcast. It looks like winter is coming. This season, more than any other, announces itself in the sky. I don't quite know how. It just does. One can, if one has the time or inclination to watch, see it coming.

Of course I realise that Moira may not be my brother's child, but the alternative is just as bad, maybe worse. I would like to go to the phone and tell her that I might not be her uncle, that there is still a chance for us, but what kind of happy revelation would that be for her? Would she be relieved to know that she is the product of the union of a brother and sister? That her brutal, murdering uncle was her real father? That she is the result of incestuous rape? Good news, Moira, your real uncle didn't fuck you, he fucked your mother.

I decide that I must read the rest of the journal. I trudge up the hill to the cabin, grabbing a couple of logs from the pile outside to start a fire and drive away the nocturnal chill. Inside, I pour a glass of Jim Beam to the same purpose, I tell myself—but certain kinds of cold cannot be driven away. No, this is not northern or southern—just comfort.

I sit down at the table and open the journal again.

Today I sent my brother away. He is going back to Ireland. He refused to leave at first, but I threatened to tell Hiram and the authorities, if necessary, about what he has done. My conscience is stricken. He seemed so forlorn and lost. He has given up so much in his life to keep me safe, but I can't do what he wants me to do. God help him. God help me. I am sick at heart. Hiram is continually asking me what's wrong and I can't tell him.

My heart goes out to Mary Sweeney. I can only imagine her suffering. What would these words do to Moira? Then:

> *I have done a great wickedness. God forgive me. I have slept with young Satchel, brought him to my bed. It has helped me somehow. There has been so little intimacy in my life. Hiram can't help it, but I have dreams all the time. Satchel is a sweet boy. He only did what I wanted him to do. He had no experience, I could see that. He is only a teenager. It was quiet and gentle and lovely. He told me he was sorry. Poor, manly young Satchel. He felt responsibility for his own seduction. I think I'm losing my mind. Too much. Too much. I have been a mother to him, now a lover. Hiram saw us through the bedroom window. He asked me why I did this and I can place blame wherever I wish, but I think I just wanted to erase the recollection of my brother's brutality. I wanted a better memory of what may be my last sexual experience. I don't tell him this, of course. He wants to blame the boy, but I think he knows better. He threatens to leave me. I don't know what he will do. He has always been so kind. He doesn't deserve this. What ruin my existence has brought on so many! I have dark thoughts.*

Mary Sweeney never told Hiram about how she was raped by her brother. He probably died without knowing.

I come to the last few entries. They are brief but, unlike all the others, carefully dated:

> *August 12, 1986   I am pregnant and my dark thoughts must be set aside. I will become a mother. Hiram agrees to help me raise the child, to try to forget. He believes the baby is Satchel's. He doesn't know what my brother has done. It could belong to either of them. I don't know. I hope he is right.*

April 6, 1987 Moira Marie Sweeney is here! She is adorable and I love her beyond comprehension.

May 15, 1988 Moira is walking. She is such a bright little thing. Satchel is becoming a famous baseball player. Young Tin spends a good deal of time over here. I think his father doesn't spend enough time with him. Who am I to judge? Hiram is remarkable. He loves Moira, I think, but he struggles. Who wouldn't?

October 20, 1989 Keenan keeps writing. Will he never leave me alone? It is a horrible thing, but I wish he would die. I need peace.

April 30, 1990 Hiram went into a rage today. I only mentioned Satchel's accomplishments in baseball. He screamed at me. He has been so good, continuing his friendship with Pastor Balune and his many kindnesses to Tinker. The awful anger he has toward Satchel frightens me, but he adores little Moira. Oh God, it all seems so pointless.

May 11, 1990 Keenan is coming. He says he is going to live in America, maybe Chicago. Hiram can't believe my objections. I can't face this anymore, not even for my darling girl. When I am finished here, I will hide this in the attic and go to sleep. Forgive me, my sweet Moira. All I ever wanted was you.

Mr. Beam and I finish each other. I sleep deep into Sunday. I'm not sure at what point I make the decision, but I wrap up Mary Sweeney's journal in brown paper and take it back to Grand Rapids with me. I put it in the drawer with my lighter.

On October 31st, I am handing out candy to the neighborhood children when the phone rings. I expect a parent of one of my students, since progress reports just went home a couple of days ago and it has not been a very productive semester for a number of my charges.

"Tin." It is *her* voice.

"Moira, it's so good—"

"I just want you to be quiet and listen."

"Okay."

"Something inexplicable has happened and I need to know what you and Satchel are keeping from me."

"What do you mean?"

"The police took blood samples from all of us. They said they were going to do DNA comparisons before anyone could be absolutely cleared of any involvement in the killings."

"I know. They called me and told me the readings matched our stories."

"Yes. They called me too—a second time."

"Why?"

"I'd asked them if there were comparisons they could make to tell if someone was related to someone else. They told me they could. I asked them to compare all the samples, that it might have some bearing. They agreed. They called me this morning."

"And?"

"There were three matches, Tin. Buck and Sweeney. You and Satchel. Me and Keenan O'Connor."

I want to shout my happiness, but I remember that it is not my happiness that I have pledged to defend.

"Buck and Sweeney," she says, "are father and son. You and Satchel are brothers. Keenan and I are uncle and niece. We're all supposed to share DNA, I guess. So, who the hell is my father?"

"Hold on." My heart is beating violently. I can't tell her. I can only read it. "I think there's something you need to hear." I retrieve the journal from the drawer and begin to unwrap it as I tell her what it is, how I got it.

"Read," she commands.

I do, but only the part about her mother's rape. She doesn't come apart. She doesn't cry. She just sighs very deeply. "Then I don't have Keenan O'Connor's DNA just because he's my uncle."

"No."

"My uncle is actually my father?" she whispers. "My mother and father were brother and sister."

"Moira—"

"How much depravity can there be in one family?"

"Moira."

She's silent for a few minutes. I don't press. I listen to the sounds of her breathing. It's labored, as if she has been running, accented by an occasional sigh. "Then my uncle was doing what, trying to cover his own guilt? Did he think we knew about it?"

"Possibly," I say, "or maybe he just got things twisted around in his own mind. Maybe he couldn't admit to himself what he'd done and shifted the blame to Satchel."

"Transference," she says, no doubt recalling another lesson from her psychology class.

"However it was, there's little doubt in my mind that the person your mother was talking about in her suicide note was Keenan O'Connor—not my brother."

"And Sweeney? Do you think he knew?"

"I don't think so. Maybe Connor feared that he'd find out. I don't know."

"Is that all there is in the journal?"

"No. There's a great deal more."

"Will you mail it to me?"

"Certainly."

She gives me her address at her dorm at Michigan State.

"I need to sort this out, Tin."

"Of course."

"I'll call you."

"Sure." The flat monotone of disconnection.

Chapter thirty-three

I saw her at her uncle/father's trial. She was very stoic and distant. She was polite, but very obviously avoided any private moment with me. Graham was at her side.

Keenan O'Connor was surprised when his sister's journal was introduced as evidence. He stared hard at Moira. She looked at him, but her face was a mask of apathy. He was sentenced to life in prison.

Satchel told me later that Moira was constantly glancing at me when I couldn't see her, but I think he was just trying to cheer me.

I spend Christmas at the Bullkiller ranch, partially to visit, partially to attend Satch and Moon's wedding. Joolie and Santy are wonderful people and the surrounding land is something I've never seen before. So vast and open and uncomplicated, like the people who live here.

My second semester of teaching goes okay except for a few too many sick days spent recovering from my old friend Jim Beam. On Memorial Day weekend, I make my second trip to Loon Lake since returning from Chicago. I haul a new fiberglass boat on a new trailer, purchased with my latest royalty check from my book, which has been doing well of late. It is my intent to spend the entire weekend fishing. I have left all paperwork at home. These are the kinds of things that people do when they are quietly desperate.

By mid-morning on Saturday, I have the boat safely in the water. The new oars feel good in my hands. I row to the little cove at the east end of the lake where, long ago, I caught the Monster. I have remarkable success fishing, but I let them all go. Perhaps I have learned that their lives are not dictated by my whims.

Back at the cabin, I read for a while. I have rediscovered the Victorians and am currently poring over *Tess of the d'Urbervilles*. At midnight, I open another bottle of Jim Beam to help me get through Hardy's rural hell imagery. I listen to the radio for awhile. The Association sings "Windy". For the first time since I was at the lake in October, it takes a whole bottle of Beam to get me to sleep. I awake an hour later, throw up in the toilet, smoke a cigarette. When I lie down again, God's voice says: "I'm still here."

In the early light of dawn, I hear the screen door open. If it is an intruder, they may take what they want. If it is a killer, I may be lucky tonight. Fear left me long ago.

"Tin!" It is *her*. I am dreaming. The door did not open. No one is here.

Then she is sitting next to me. I feel her breath, her lips. Her arms wrap around me. "Do you remember me?" she says. "I'm Moira Sweeney, Mary's kid." She crawls in with me, pulls my arms around her. There's no point to words. There is only an enormous relief—that lifting of the impossible weight of the sepulcher door.

I still wonder why people suffer—some more than others. But what is the world without pain? What is life without conflict? Nothing is learned. Nothing is appreciated. I don't know how long I'll live. I don't know how long she'll live. I hope that we can grow long in the tooth together. There are no more ghosts, no more demons. I have a boat that doesn't leak. For now, at least, I am happy—and that's enough.

About the Author

David Turrill

Davidavid Turrill is a teacher, theater director and writer who lives on a farm in Rockford, MI, near Grand Rapids. He is the author of three other books: *Michilimackinac: A Tale of the Straits, A Bridge to Eden,* and *An Apology for Autumn,* which was published by *The Toby Press* in 2004.

The fonts used in this book are from the Garamond family

Other works by David Turrill available from *The* Toby Press

An Apology for Autumn

The Toby Press publishes fine writing,
available at leading bookstores everywhere. For more
information, please visit www.tobypress.com